THE FORBIDDEN TERRITORY

DENNIS WHEATLEY

EDITED BY MIRANDA VAUGHAN JONES

BLOOMSBURY READER

LONDON · NEW DELHI · NEW YORK · SYDNEY

First published in Great Britain 1933
This paperback edition published 2013

Copyright © 1933 Dennis Wheatley

Bloomsbury Publishing Plc
50 Bedford Square
London
WC1B 3DP

www.bloomsbury.com

Bloomsbury Publishing, London, New Delhi, New York and Sydney

A CIP catalogue record for this book is available from the British Library

ISBN 978 1 4482 1306 1
10 9 8 7 6 5 4 3 2 1

Typeset by Hewer Text UK Ltd, Edinburgh
Printed in Great Britain by CPI Group UK Ltd, Croydon CR0 4YY

To
Joan

This souvenir of one of the most difficult years of my life, which by our united efforts has turned out to be one of the most successful, and, thanks to her, has certainly been one of the happiest.

CONTENTS

INTRODUCTION

Dennis Wheatley was my grandfather. He only had one child, my father Anthony, from his first marriage to Nancy Robinson. Nancy was the youngest in a large family of ten Robinson children and she had a wonderful zest for life and a gaiety about her that I much admired as a boy brought up in the dull Seventies. Thinking about it now, I suspect that I was drawn to a young Ginny Hewett, a similarly bubbly character, and now my wife of 27 years, because she resembled Nancy in many ways.

As grandparents, Dennis and Nancy were very different. Nancy's visits would fill the house with laughter and mischievous gossip, while Dennis and his second wife Joan would descend like minor royalty, all children expected to behave. Each held court in their own way but Dennis was the famous one with the famous friends and the famous stories.

There is something of the fantasist in every storyteller, and most novelists writing thrillers see themselves in their heroes. However, only a handful can claim to have been involved in actual daring-do. Dennis saw action both at the Front, in the First World War, and behind a desk in the Second. His involvement informed his writing and his stories, even those based on historical events, held a notable veracity that only the life-experienced novelist can obtain. I think it was this element that added the important plausibility to his writing. This appealed to his legions of readers who were in that middle ground of fiction, not looking for pure fantasy nor dry fact, but something exciting, extraordinary, possible and even probable.

There were three key characters that Dennis created over the years: The Duc de Richleau, Gregory Sallust and Roger Brook. The first de Richleau stories were set in the years between the wars, when Dennis had started writing. Many of the Sallust stories were written in the early days of the Second World War, shortly before Dennis joined the Joint Planning Staff in Whitehall, and Brook was cast in the time of the French Revolution, a period that particularly fascinated him.

He is probably always going to be associated with Black Magic first and foremost, and it's true that he plugged it hard because sales were always good for those books. However, it's important to remember that he only wrote eleven Black Magic novels out of more than sixty bestsellers, and readers were just as keen on his other stories. In fact, invariably when I meet people who ask if there is any connection, they tell me that they read 'all his books'.

Dennis had a full and eventful life, even by the standards of the era he grew up in. He was expelled from Dulwich College and sent to a floating navel run school, HMS Worcester. The conditions on this extraordinary ship were Dickensian. He survived it, and briefly enjoyed London at the pinnacle of the Empire before war was declared and the fun ended. That sort of fun would never be seen again.

He went into business after the First World War, succeeded and failed, and stumbled into writing. It proved to be his calling. Immediate success opened up the opportunity to read and travel, fueling yet more stories and thrilling his growing band of followers.

He had an extraordinary World War II, being one of the first people to be recruited into the select team which dreamed up the deception plans to cover some of the major events of the war such as Operation Torch, Operation Mincemeat and the D-Day landings. Here he became familiar with not only the people at the very top of the war effort, but also a young Commander Ian Fleming, who was later to write the James Bond novels. There are indeed those who have suggested that Gregory Sallust was one of James Bond's precursors.

The aftermath of the war saw Dennis grow in stature and fame. He settled in his beautiful Georgian house in Lymington surrounded by beautiful things. He knew how to live well, perhaps without regard for his health. He hated exercise, smoked, drank and wrote. Today he would have been bullied by wife and children and friends into giving up these habits and changing his lifestyle, but I'm not sure he would have given in. Maybe like me, he would simply find a quiet place.

Dominic Wheatley, 2013

Chapter I

A cry for help

The Duke de Richleau and Mr. Simon Aron had gone in to dinner at eight o' clock, but coffee was not served till after ten.

Aron had eaten sparingly of each well-chosen course, and to one who made a hobby of such things the wines had proved a special pleasure. Since their mutual friend Richard Eaton had brought them together, he had dined on many occasions with De Richleau at his flat.

A casual observer might have considered it a strange friendship, but despite the difference in age and race, appearance and tradition, the two had many tastes in common.

Both the young English Jew and the elderly French exile loved beauty in its many forms, and could linger happily over a jade carving or a page of prose. They had also developed a pleasant rivalry in producing for each other great wines, fine food, and well-matured cigars.

Aron accepted a long Hoyo de Monterrey from the cedar cabinet which the Duke's man presented to him, and his dark eyes flickered towards his host.

During dinner the impression had grown upon him that there was some special reason why the Duke had asked him to dine on this occasion. His intuition had not deceived him. De Richleau exhaled the first cloud of fragrant smoke from another of those long Hoyos, which were his especial pride, and drew from his pocket a dirty piece of paper, which he flicked across the table.

'My friend' he said, raising his grey eyebrows a little, a slightly cynical smile on his thin lips, 'I should be interested to have your opinion on this curious document.'

Simon Aron unfolded the piece of grimy paper. It had light blue rulings upon it, and was covered with a pencil scrawl; it might well have been a page torn from an exercise-book. Simon's full mouth broadened into a wide grin, and, with a sudden gesture peculiar to himself, he gave a little nervous laugh, stooping his bird-like head with its pronounced nose to the hand which held his long cigar.

'Well, I'll tell you, I'm no good at puzzles,' he grinned, 'never done a cross-word in my life – but I'll see what I can do.' As he spoke he took a pair of tortoiseshell spectacles from his pocket and began to study the crumpled paper, reading it out slowly as he did so.

Dear Comrade,

Since I left the New York centre I have been investigating the possibilities of mineral wealth in this country.

There is one mine containing valuable deposits which has been closed down for a number of years, and I had hoped to get it going. Unfortunately, before I could do so, I was sent to the place where Comrade Eatonov was for a short time.

Work at the London centre must be almost at a standstill with the present reactionary Government in power, and if my transfer from here could be arranged for, I should badly need skilled assistance at the mine, so if you could come over, your help would be most welcome.

I would like to have met you in Moscow, but that will be impossible now. You can get all the information regarding the mine at Jack Straw's. If little Simonoff is still with you, perhaps both of you could come.

I certainly need help pretty badly in my present position – it's too much for me alone.

Your old comrade and fellow-worker,

Tsarderynski

Simon Aron shook his head with a little wriggle of his narrow shoulders. 'How did it come to you?' he inquired.

The Duke passed over a flimsy envelope with which he had been toying. 'Just so, my friend,' he said, lightly, 'you will note that this bears a Finnish stamp, and was posted in Helsingfors.'

Simon examined the writing on the envelope. It was thin and angular – very different from the pencil scrawl of the letter – and bore the legend:

Monsieur Ricillou,
No. 1 Maison Arrol,
Londres,
Gde. Bretagne.

'I – er – suppose it's not a mistake?' ventured Simon, thoughtfully. 'I mean, it is meant for you?'

The Duke ran the tips of his fingers down his lean, handsome face. 'At first I was inclined to suppose that it had been sent here in error, but now I am convinced that it was intended for me.'

'Wonder it ever got here – addressed like this!'

'Yes, the name misspelt – also Errol House, no mention of Curzon Street, or Mayfair, or any district number. But tell me – who do you think it is from?'

'Tsarderynski,' Simon murmured, 'don't know – never heard of him; looks like a letter from one Bolshie agent to another, on the face of it.'

'May I suggest that you endeavour to translate the name?' The grey eyes of almost piercing brilliance, which gave character to De Richleau's face, lit up.

'"Tsar," that's Cassar – King,' Simon Aron began, '"*de*" of, or from – "*ryn*" – ah! now wait a minute – this is interesting, very interesting—' He sat forward suddenly and began nodding his narrow head up and down. 'Of course – this is from our old friend Rex Van Ryn!'

His host smiled encouragement.

Simon read the letter through again. 'And Rex is in a muddle – a really nasty muddle,' he added jerkily.

'Exactly the conclusion I had arrived at,' De Richleau agreed. 'Now what do you make of the rest of the letter?'

For some little time Simon did not reply. In his left hand he slowly revolved the bowl-shaped glass that held some of the Duke's wonderful old brandy, in his right he held the long evenly burning cigar. For the moment his thoughts had left the beautiful room with its lovely old panelling, its four famous pictures by great masters, and the heavy carpet which seemed to deaden every sound.

He was thinking of Rex Van Ryn – that great hulking American with the ugly face and the enormous sense of fun. He could see Rex now, in the little sitting-room of the house in Trevor Square which he always took when he came to London. He could hear him dilating on the question of drinks – 'Never give a guy a large cocktail, but plenty of 'em – make 'em dry and drink 'em quick – come on, boys – it takes a fourth to make an appetite – here's to crime!' – and now this strange letter out of Russia. What sort of wild escapade could have taken Rex to such a place? What kind of trouble was he up against? For Simon had not the least doubt that he *was* in trouble, and Simon was worried – he was very fond of Rex.

De Richleau meanwhile sat silent at the head of the table, a striking and unusual figure. He was a slim, delicate-looking man, somewhat above middle height, with slender, fragile hands and greying hair; but there was no trace of weakness in his fine distinguished face. His aquiline nose, broad forehead, and grey devil's eyebrows might well have replaced those of the cavalier in the Van Dyke that gazed down from the opposite wall. Instead of the conventional black, he wore a claret-coloured Vicuna smoking-suit, with silk lapels and braided fastenings; this touch of colour increased his likeness to the portrait. He watched Simon with a slight smile on his firm mouth. He knew the cautious, subtle brain that lay behind the sloping forehead of his guest too well to hurry his deliberations.

'Let's go through it carefully,' said Simon at last. 'What's all this business about a mine? I didn't know that Rex ever trained as a mining engineer.'

'Nor I,' agreed the Duke. 'What do you make of the passage about Eatonov?'

Simon's dark eyes flickered over his spectacles at the Duke.

'That's where the muddle comes in – Eatonov is Richard Eaton, of course – and poor Richard went to Brixton! Rex is in prison – that's what it seems to me.'

'Without a doubt,' De Richleau nodded, 'that reference to Eaton was a clever way of putting it – no ordinary person could understand it, but he would know that, to us, it would be abundantly clear. If one needs further confirmation, one has only to note the suggestion about his transfer being arranged for, and that "it will be impossible for him to come to Moscow *now* to meet us"; he is somewhere in Soviet Russia, but he is not a free man.'

'The letter was posted in Finland,' Simon remarked.

'Certainly.' The Duke pushed the old brandy across the table to his guest. 'It looks as if the letter was smuggled out of Russia, evidently Rex was afraid that his messenger might be searched at the frontier, and so made him commit the address to memory. From the envelope I doubt if the man could even speak English. The whole thing, with its talk of centres, comrades, and reactionary Governments, is obviously designed to throw dust in the eyes of any Soviet official.'

'Who is Jack Straw? I don't – er – understand that bit at all. The only Jack Straw's that I've ever heard of is the Castle on the Heath.'

'Jack Straw's Castle – what is that?' The Duke looked puzzled.

'An inn on Hampstead Heath – place where Dick Turpin, the highwayman, used to make his headquarters ...' Simon corrected himself, 'Though I'm not certain that wasn't The Spaniards.'

'What can an inn on Hampstead Heath have to do with a mine in Russia? There must be some other explanation.'

'Perhaps,' Simon hesitated, 'it is the meeting-place of some secret Bolshevik society.'

'But, my friend, if Rex has fallen foul of the Ogpu, surely they would be the last people to give us any information about him?'

'It might be a society of counter-revolutionaries, and Rex has been arrested for being in touch with them.'

'If you are right, Rex may have gone to Russia on behalf of these émigrés, and been arrested on that account – if so, the mine may be anything of value – perhaps even secret information.'

'Well – I'll tell you,' said Simon, 'I don't like it a little bit – look at the last sentence in that letter – *"I certainly need help pretty badly in my present position, it's too much for me alone!"'*

The Duke gently laid the long blue-grey ash of his cigar in the onyx ash-tray. 'There is not a doubt,' he said, slowly, 'our good friend Van Ryn is a prisoner in Soviet Russia – Rex is one of the bravest men I have ever known, he would never have written that last paragraph unless he were in dire distress. It is a cry for help. Where he may be in that vast territory which constitutes the Union of Soviet Peoples, it will be no easy task to discover. He has found somebody – a fellow prisoner, perhaps – who was about to leave the country, and persuaded him to take this letter in the hope that it would get through. The chances were all against it reaching it's destination, but as it has done so – the point is now – what are we to do?'

Simon Aron leant forward and laughed his short, jerky laugh into his hand. 'Well – er – I hate to say so,' he laughed again, 'but it seems to me that you and I have got to take a trip to Russia.'

Chapter II

A plan of campaign

'Now this,' said the Duke, 'is indeed a pleasant surprise. I thought you might bring fresh light to bear upon some aspect of this affair – but to have your actual help was more than I had dared to hope.'

'Very fond of Rex,' said Simon briefly.

'I know,' De Richleau nodded, 'but our situations are so different. My life is one of leisure – in fact, now that old age is creeping upon me, and more and more pursuits become barred to a man of my years – I find it increasingly difficult to pass my time in an interesting and agreeable manner. You, on the contrary, as a young partner in a great financial house, have always to be on the end of the eternal telephone. You even grudge a single afternoon spent away from your office in the City. I had imagined that it would be quite impossible for you to get away.'

'Well, to tell you the truth, I was – er – thinking of taking a holiday – going down to Monte for a few days – might just as well go to Russia!'

De Richleau smiled rather grimly. 'I fear that this will be a very different kind of holiday, my friend. However, we will not talk of that. It is some days since I received this letter, so I have already made certain inquiries and preparations.'

'Tell me,' said Simon, shortly.

'First I cabled to my old friend, the President of the Chesapeake Banking and Trust Corporation – Van Ryn the elder – for news of Rex. Let us go into the other room, and I will show you his reply.' As he spoke the Duke left the table and threw open the door for his guest.

'Yes, I'd like to see that – I'll take my brandy with me, if you don't mind.' Carrying his glass, Simon Aron led the way into the big library.

It was not so much the size or decoration which made this room in the Curzon Street flat so memorable for those who had been privileged to visit it, but the unique collection of rare and beautiful objects which it contained. A Tibetan Buddha seated upon the Lotus; bronze figurines from Ancient Greece. Beautifully chased rapiers of Toledo steel and Moorish pistols inlaid with turquoise and gold, ikons from Holy Russia, set with semi-precious stones, and curiously carved ivories from the East.

The walls were lined shoulder-high with books, but above them hung lovely old colour-prints, and a number of priceless historical documents and maps.

De Richleau went over to his desk and, taking a few flimsy sheets from a drawer, handed them silently to Aron.

Simon read out the contents of the cable:

Rex very unsettled since return from Europe last summer – went lone hunting expedition in Rockies August September – went South America October – stayed West Indies on return trip – went Russia late November against my wish ostensibly investigate commercial conditions properly accredited by me – letter received dated December fourth stating safe arrival no news since – became worried end December put inquiry through Embassy – Rex left Moscow December eleventh destination unknown – all efforts to trace movements so far unavailing – spare no expense cable any news immediately now very anxious Channock Van Ryn.

Simon nodded. 'Expensive cable that!'

The Duke crossed his slender legs, as he settled himself comfortably in an armchair. 'That I think would hardly matter to Channock Van Ryn, and Rex, you will remember, is his only son. I am not surprised that he is anxious, but if there was ever any doubt about the message having come from our young friend, I think this cable places the matter beyond dispute.'

'Umm,' Simon nodded. 'Now let's see – today's the 24th of January, isn't it? At any rate, it's nearly seven weeks since he disappeared from Moscow.'

'Exactly, but there is one comfort: we know at least that he has not been knocked on the head in some low quarter of the town and his body flung into the river – or pushed under the ice, rather – for, of course, the Moskawa river will be frozen over now. He must have fallen foul of the secret police in some way – our young friend is nothing if not inquisitive – and I believe there are very definite restrictions as to what visitors to the Soviet may, or may not, see during their stay.'

'Wait a moment!' Simon slowly revolved his brandy-glass, holding it in the palm of his hand to warm the spirit through the thin transparent glass – 'Wait a minute,' he repeated, 'that cable said "left Moscow FOR an unknown destination"!'

'Yes,' agreed the Duke, 'and during the last few days I have been gathering information regarding other places to which he may have gone. I think you would be surprised at the knowledge which I now possess of the towns and railways of the Soviet Republic.'

'How – er – did you set about it?' Simon asked curiously.

'The obvious way, my friend.' De Richleau's clever face broke into a sudden smile. 'I paid a visit to the London office of the "Intourist", which, as you may know, is the official travel bureau of the Soviet. For some time now, Stalin and the present group of Kommissars have thought it desirable that people of the anti-Bolshevik states should be encouraged to visit Russia. For one thing they spend money which the Soviet badly needs – for another, they are shown certain aspects of the Bolshevik State, such as the great metalurgical works, and scientifically run agricultural centres, of which the Kommissars are justly proud. It is hoped that they will return to their own countries with a glowing picture of the benefits of Communism for the masses.'

'But you can't just take a ticket and go to Russia, can you?' Simon spoke doubtfully.

'Almost – but not quite, they have been very clever.' The Duke spread out his slim hands. 'You wish to go to Russia? Good! To what part would you like to go – Leningrad, Moscow, Kieff, Odessa, the Crimea, the Caucassus? Would you like to stay four days – or four weeks? To start in the north, or in the south? All you have to do is to tell – us – the Intourist'. We will be your servants in a country where there are servants no longer. Here are all sorts of itineraries, all ready planned. They can be varied to suit your purpose. Is it the treasures of the old world, that we have so carefully preserved, which you wish to see – or the marvellous industrial developments, by which Russia will lead the world in a few years' time? Let us plan your journey for you. We will take your railway tickets in advance, and provide you with hotel accommodation during your stay. Of both there are four grades; and which you choose depends only upon what you wish to pay. Good meals will be provided for you, and the prices of the tours include not only entrance to all museums and sights of interest, but to the theatres and places of amusement as well. What is that? You fear you may have difficulty with the language? But not at all! An interpreter will be placed at your disposal – You do not wish to go with a crowd of people like a tourist? Certainly not! You shall have an interpreter entirely to yourself – there is no extra charge. You see, my friend – ' Once more the Duke spread out his elegant hands as he finished his word-picture of the persuasive advertising agent of the Bolsheviks.

'Clever,' Simon said softly. 'Oh, very clever!'

'Exactly.' De Richleau smiled again. 'And that little Bolshevik interpreter will be your guide, philosopher, and friend, from the time you arrive until the time you leave this very interesting country. You can secure neither railway tickets nor hotel accommodation without consulting him, and although this excellent "Intourist" will cheerfully get your passport *visa* for you to *enter* the Soviet – should you by chance desire to change your plans, and forget to inform the little interpreter – you will find it quite impossible to secure the necessary *visa* to get *out.*'

'I see,' Simon laughed his little nervous laugh. 'And that's where the fun begins. Supposing we wanted to get off the beaten track – to some place that the itineraries don't mention – what happens then?'

'That,' said the Duke, slowly, 'is a different matter. I talked vaguely to the polite young man at the bureau of visiting Archangel. He pointed out that the port would be frozen over at this time of year; an uninteresting place to visit, he seemed to think. I spoke of other towns not mentioned in the official guide – and the winter scenery in the Urals. He said that there would be no suitable accommodation. In fact, he was not helpful in any way.'

'Have you any idea what conditions are like out there now?'

De Richleau shrugged. 'It is difficult to say – the reports of people to whom I have spoken vary so greatly. There is little doubt that the towns are overcrowded and food scarce. Everyone has to surrender thirty-five per cent of their wages to assist in the accomplishment of the Five Year Plan. The whole population is pauperised to this one end.'

'That's more or less what I've heard.' Simon solemnly nodded his head up and down.

'Every day thousands of young people are graduating from the enlarged universities under high pressure, and every one of them is a Communist. That is one great factor in their favour; they control the intelligent youth of Russia; the other is their fanaticism. With them the Communist ideal is a religion. Ambition, comfort, leisure, personal relations, everything *must* give way to that. That is why I believe in the long run they are bound to triumph.'

Simon's eyes narrowed. 'Perhaps – I don't know,' he said slowly. 'Christianity hasn't triumphed, or Islam – and they were fanatical enough. Still it won't be yet awhile, and anyhow it's not our business. When do you think of starting?'

'I am leaving tomorrow,' the Duke replied, somewhat to Simon's surprise. 'You will understand, I had not counted upon your company, and I felt that every day was of importance. Traces that our friend may have left in his passage will tend more and more to become obliterated; and I do not care to contemplate what Rex may be suffering in a Bolshevik prison. It was for that reason that I made all speed – even to securing a special diplomatic pass through a certain Embassy, where I have particularly obliging friends.'

'All right,' Simon agreed. 'I shan't be able to get away for a few days, but I'll follow you as soon as I can.'

'Do not follow me, my friend, but join me in Moscow. I have elected to go by sea to Gothenburg, and hence by rail *via* Stockholm and St Petersburg – or rather Leningrad as they call it now. It will take some days longer, but you will remember that the messenger posted Rex's letter in Helsingfors. It is my intention to break my journey there for forty-eight hours; I shall advertise in the Finnish papers for news of Rex, and offer a substantial reward. If fortune is with us, the messenger may still be in the town, and able to inform us more exactly regarding our poor friend's misfortune and his present whereabouts.'

'Yes – that's sound. Thanks.' Simon helped himself to another cigar. 'We shall miss our Hoyos – he laughed suddenly.

'Not altogether, I trust,' De Richleau smiled. 'I have dispatched two hundred in an airtight case to await our arrival.'

'Won't they be opened at the frontier? Customs people pretty troublesome about anything like that, I should think.'

'Not these, my friend – I sent them in the Embassy bag – and that, at least, is one privilege that we, who used to rule the world, retain – as long as we have friends in the diplomatic service there is always that wonderful elastic Embassy bag – passing the Customs without examination, and giving immunity to correspondence.'

Simon's dark eyes flickered at the Duke with an amused smile. 'That's wonderful,' he agreed, 'and if the food's going to be bad we shall enjoy the Hoyos all the more. I'll tell you one thing I'm worried about, though. I can't speak a word of Russian! How are we going to make our inquiries?'

'Fortunately I can,' De Richleau replied. 'You probably do not know it but my mother was a Plakoff – her mother again was a Bourbon-Condé, so I am only one-quarter Russian – but before the War I spent much time in Russia. Prince Plakoff possessed immense estates in the foothills of the Carpathians. A part of that territory is now in the enlarged Roumania, the other portion remains in the new Soviet of the Ukraine. I stayed there, sometimes for months at a time, when I was young. I also know many of the Russian cities well.'

'That's lucky,' said Simon. 'Now what exactly would you like me to do?'

'Go to the "Intourist" and arrange for a stay of perhaps a fortnight in Moscow; let them obtain your passport *visa* in the ordinary way – that will take some little time. Book by the direct route to Moscow, *via* Berlin and Warsaw – you will cross the frontier at Negoreloye; I will meet you in Moscow after making my inquiries in Helsingfors, and combing the Consulates in Leningrad for any information which they may have.'

Simon nodded. 'What about the Embassies here? I suppose you've done what you can?'

'Yes, but quite uselessly. The American Embassy had already been questioned by Washington on behalf of Channock Van Ryn, but they could add nothing to Moscow's report that "Rex left on December 11th for an unknown destination".'

'How about mun?'

'Who?' asked the Duke, vaguely.

'Money – I mean,' Simon corrected with a grin.

'I would suggest a good supply. It is permissible to carry any currency into Russia, only the amount must be declared, in order that no question can be raised as to taking it out again.'

'Won't they be suspicious if I – er – bring in more than I should need in the ordinary way?'

'Yes, perhaps. Therefore it would be best if you declare only one third of what you bring; conceal the rest about you – in your boots or the lining of your waistcoat. I am sending a reserve for myself by way of that excellent Embassy bag. It is quite possible that we may need a considerable sum for bribes, and, if we can find Rex, for arranging a method by which he can be smuggled out of the country. If we declare all that we have when we go in – it might be difficult to explain upon what it has been expended, when we go out. You must remember that all travels, hotels, food – practically everything is supposed to be paid for before we start.'

'Jack Straw?' queried Simon, suddenly 'I can't help wondering what he meant by that. Do you think there's anything to be done there?'

De Richleau ran his hand lightly over his forehead. 'What do you suggest?'

'Well, I'll tell you. I don't think it would do any harm if I went up to Hampstead one evening – had a look at the people that go there these days – we might get a line.'

'An excellent plan; you will have ample time.'

'Do you happen to have an atlas?' Simon asked with a little laugh. 'I've almost forgotten what Russia looks like!'

'But certainly, my friend.' De Richleau produced a heavy volume. For a long time the handsome grey head of the Duke remained in close proximity to the dark profile of Mr Simon Aron, while the two talked together in low voices.

Some two hours later, De Richleau saw his guest down the broad stair-way of Errol House to the main hall, and out into the silent deserted streets of Mayfair.

'You will not forget Jack Straw?' he said as they shook hands. 'And twelve o' clock at the Ilyinka Gate a fortnight hence – it is best that we should seem to meet by chance.'

'I'll be there,' said Simon, adjusting his top-hat upon his narrow head. 'The Ilyinka Gate, Moscow, at twelve o' clock, fourteen days from now.'

Chapter III

Valeria Petrovna

Simon Aron stepped out of a taxi in front of his cousin's house in Hampstead one night, a little more than a week after his dinner with the Duke.

Simon was a very rich young man, but it was an interesting point in his psychology that he lived in one small room at his club, and did not own a car. The taxi-driver, however, had no reason to be dissatisfied with his tip, although he had had a long and chilly wait outside Jack Straw's Castle.

His cousin Miriam's house was one of those long, low, modern mansions standing back from the road in its own grounds. The short gravel drive and the roadway on each side were lined with private cars of all makes and sizes; the windows of the house were a blaze of light; it was evident that a party was in progress.

Having greeted the maid at the door as an old friend, and divested himself of his silk scarf, white kid gloves, stick, and shining topper – Simon was soon in conversation with his hostess.

'Good party tonight, Miriam?' he asked her in his jerky way, with a wide smile.

'I hope so, Simon dear,' she replied a little nervously. 'I've taken an awful lot of trouble – but you never know what people will like – do you?'

'Of course it will be a good party, Miriam,' he encouraged her, 'Your parties always are good parties! Anyone special coming?'

'We've got Gian Capello – he's promised to play, and Madame Maliperi is going to sing; it's a great help having Alec Wolff too, he's really very clever at the piano; Jacob says he'll go a long way – and knowing him so well I can get him to play at any time.'

'Of course you can – Alec's a nice boy.'

'I tell you who I have got here – ' she went on hurriedly. 'Madame Karkoff – you know, Valeria Petrovna Karkoff – from the Moscow Arts Theatre; she's over here on a visit with Kommissar Leshkin. Jacob met them at the film studios at Elstree last week.'

Simon's quick eyes flickered about the wide hall; with sudden interest he asked: 'Does she – er – speak English?'

'Oh yes. Simon dear, I do wish you'd look after her, will you? They don't know anybody here. It would be an awful weight off my mind. Look! There she is – the dark-haired woman, in the yellow dress. She's awfully good-looking I think – will you?'

'Well – er—' He appeared to hesitate. 'Taking on a bit of a handful, isn't it?'

'Oh, no, Simon. You get on so well with everybody. Of course,' she went on a little wistfully, 'I do love giving parties, but you know what Jacob is – he just asks everybody that he can think of – and I have to do all the work. Do be a dear!'

Simon allowed himself to be led over. 'Oh, Madame Karkoff, I want you to meet my cousin, Mr Aron.' Simon's hostess smiled a little unhappily. 'He's awfully interested in the theatre.'

' 'Ow do you do, Mistaire Aron?' said Madame Karkoff, in a rich, deep, almost husky voice, as she lifted her fine chin and held out a long slender hand. 'Come – sit 'ere by me.' With a quick gesture she made a pretence of drawing aside her dress.

Simon accepted the invitation, and produced his cigarette-case. She took one with a giggle.

'I 'ave been dying for a cigarette,' she confessed. 'Ah, sank you.' Almost before the cigarette had reached her scarlet lips Simon's other hand had left his pocket, and the patent lighter in it flickered into flame. It was a much-practised little trick of his.

'So you are interested in the theatre, eh?' She regarded him curiously. 'Tell me about the theatre, Mistaire Aron!'

Simon leant forward and laughed his little nervous laugh into the palm of his hand. ' 'Fraid I can't,' he chuckled. 'Mind you, I'd love to be able to, but we haven't got a theatre in England!'

'Ah! So you know that, do you?' A gleam of appreciation showed in her large dark eyes.

'Of course,' he nodded vigorously. 'There is no theatre here in the sense that you know it; there are some people who try pretty hard, but they don't get much encouragement – and they've got a lot to learn.'

He studied her thoughtfully, marvelling at her dark beauty. The dead-white skin, the narrow arched eyebrows; the rather flat face with high cheek-bones, relieved by the sensual scarlet mouth and slumbrous dark eyes. No one would have thought of her as other than a woman, although she was actually little more than a girl. He put her down as about twenty-five.

'You are Jewish – are you not?' she asked suddenly. He laughed jerkily again, as he ran his finger down his prominent nose. 'Of course. I couldn't hide this, could I? And as a matter of fact I've no wish to try.'

She laughed delightedly, showing two rows of strong, white, even teeth. 'I 'ave of the Jewish blood myself,' she said then, serious again in a moment. 'My grandmother – she was Jewish. It is good; there is no art where there is not Jewish blood.'

Simon looked round the big lounge-hall. 'Well then we're in good company tonight,' he said. He smiled and waved a greeting as he caught sight of his friend, Richard Eaton, who was one of the Christian minority.

'I would like champagne,' declared Madame Karkoff, suddenly – throwing back her dark head, and exhaling a cloud of cigarette-smoke. 'Lots and lots of champagne!'

'All right.' Simon stood up. 'It'll be in the billiard-room, I expect.'

She made no attempt to rise. 'Bring it to me 'ere,' she said with a little shrug of the shoulders.

'Ner.' He shook his head rapidly as he uttered the curious negative which he often used. It came of his saying 'no' without troubling to close the lips of his full mouth. 'Ner – you come with me, it's so crowded here.'

For a moment her mouth went sullen as she looked at the slim figure, with its narrow stooping shoulders, that stood before her, then she rose languidly.

He piloted her through the crush to the buffer in the billiards-room. An obsequious waiter proffered two glasses; they might have held a fair-sized cocktail, but they were not Simon's idea of glasses for champagne. He waved them aside quickly with one word – 'tumblers!'

Two small tumblers were produced and filled by the waiter. As Simon handed one to Madame Valeria Petrovna Karkoff she smiled approval.

'They are meeserable – those little glasses for champagne, no good at all – all the same, chin-chin!'

Simon laughed, they finished another tumbler apiece before they left the billiards-room. 'Come on,' he said. 'I think Maliperi is going to sing.'

'Maliperi?' she exclaimed, opening wide her eyes. 'Come then, why do we stay 'ere?' and gripping him impulsively by the hand she ran him down the long passage to the music-room at the back of the house.

They stood together in a corner while Maliperi sang, and marvelled at her art, although the magnificent voice that had filled so many opera houses was too great for the moderate-sized room, and a certain portion of its beauty lost.

'Let us 'ave more champagne,' said Valeria Petrovna, when it was over. 'I feel I will enjoy myself tonight.'

Simon led the way back to the buffet, and very shortly two more tumblers stood before them. As they were about to drink, a big red-headed man put his hand familiarly on her shoulder, and spoke thickly, in what Simon could only imagine to be Russian.

She shook his hand off with an impatient gesture, and answered him sharply in the same tongue.

He brought his rather flabby, white face, with its short, flat nose, and small, hot eyes, down to the level of hers for a moment with a wicked look, and spoke again.

Her eyes lit with a sudden fire, and she almost spat the words back at him – so that her melodious, husky voice became quite harsh for a moment. He turned, and stared angrily in Simon's face. With his great, broad shoulders, powerful jaw, and receding forehead, he reminded Simon of a gorilla; then with a sudden scowl he swung upon his heel and turned away.

'Who – er – is that?' Simon asked, curiously, although he knew already who the man must be.

She shrugged – smiling again in a moment. 'Oh, that – that ees Nicolai Alexis – Kommissar Leshkin. We travel together, you know – 'e is a little drunk tonight, I think.'

After that they heard Capello play; the Maestro was in form and drew marvellous music from his cherished violin.

'Oh, it 'ees tears 'e makes me cry,' Valeria Petrovna exclaimed passionately after he had played one aria, and the gallant Simon found it difficult not to cry out with pain, as she unconsciously dug her sharp nails into his hand which she held between her own.

They returned to the buffet and drank more tumblers of champagne, then Simon suggested that she might like to powder her nose. She seemed surprised at the suggestion, but accepted it; actually it was Simon's way of saying that he wanted to use the telephone, he also wanted a word with Richard Eaton.

He found his friend without difficulty – and led the way to a quiet corner. Richard Eaton was a young man of medium height. His dark hair was brushed straight back from a widow's peak, grey eyes twinkled out of a tanned, clean-shaven, oval face; he had a most attractive smile. He smiled now at Simon. 'You are hitting it up, my boy – who's the lovely lady?'

Simon looked a trifle sheepish – 'Madame Karkoff,' he mumbled. 'She's a Russian – Moscow Arts Theatre – nice, isn't she? But, look here, where have you been all the week? I've been trying to get hold of you for days.'

'I've been staying with the Terences, down near Reading – he's great fun – commanded a battalion of the Coldstream in the Chinese shemozzle. I've got my new plane down there – been trying it out.'

'I see,' Simon nodded. 'Well – I wanted to see you, because – er – I'm off to Russia in a few days' time.'

'My dear old boy, you have got it badly!'

'Don't be an ass.' Simon wriggled his neck and grinned. 'No, honestly, there is a muddle on.'

'What sort of a muddle?' Richard Eaton asked, serious at once.

'It's Rex. He's in Russia – spot of trouble with the authorities. He's in prison somewhere – we don't quite know where.'

'Phew!' Eaton let out a long whistle. 'That's a nasty one – poor old Rex – and you're going over to try and get him out, is that the idea?'

Simon nodded. 'That's about it.'

'Well,' said Richard Eaton, slowly, 'you can't go off on a job like that alone – I'd better come, too. I owe Rex a turn over that mess of mine.'

'Ner – awfully nice of you, Richard, but De Richleau's coming, in fact he's already gone – probably there by now, but I'll tell you what I *do* want you to do.'

'Go right ahead, Simon.' Eaton took his friend by the arm. 'Just say how I can help. I was going to take the new bus down to Cannes for a week or two, but I can easily scrap that.'

'That's splendid of you, Richard, but don't alter anything,' Simon begged. 'As long as you don't kill yourself in your plane. I'm always terrified that you'll do that!'

Eaton laughed. 'Not likely; she's fast and foolproof – a kid of twelve could fly her – but what's the drill?'

'I shall arrive in Moscow next Tuesday. I've got a permit for three weeks; now if you don't hear from the Duke or myself that we are safely back out of Russia by then, I want you to stir things up. Get busy with the Foreign Office, and pull every wire you know to get us out of it. Of course I shall leave instructions with the firm as well – but I want someone like you, who'll not stop kicking people until they get us out.'

Richard Eaton nodded slowly. 'Right you are, old boy, leave it to me – but I'll see you before you go?'

'Um, rather – what about lunch tomorrow?'

'Splendid, where shall we say? Let's go and see Vecchi at the Hungaria. One o' clock suit you?'

'Yes. Look!' Simon had just caught sight of Valeria Petrovna again. 'There's Madame Karkoff – come over and let me introduce you.'

Richard shook his head in mock fright. 'No, thanks, Simon. I like 'em small and cuddlesome. I should be scared that Russian girl would eat me!'

'Don't be an idiot. I want to telephone – come and talk to her. I shan't be a minute.'

'Oh, if it's only a matter of holding the fort while you're busy, that's another thing.' Richard was duly presented, and Simon slipped away.

Eaton found her easier to talk to than he had expected, but she did not attract him in the least. He was glad when Simon came back, and took the opportunity to leave them when they suggested returning to the music-room.

Simon and Valeria Petrovna heard Alec Wolff play, which was a pleasant interlude – and a bald man sing, which, after what had gone before, was an impertinence.

Later, at the buffet, Madame Karkoff consumed two large plates of some incredible confection, the principal ingredient of which seemed to be cream, with the gusto of a wicked child, and Simon ate some *foie gras* sandwiches. They both drank more champagne, she lashing hers with Benedictine, because she considered it 'dry-thin' and much inferior to the sweet, sparkling Caucasian wine to which she was accustomed; but the amount which she drank seemed in no way to affect her.

At length Simon suggested that he might see her home. She looked round the crowded room with half-closed eyes, then she shrugged eloquently, and smiled. 'Why not? Nicolai Alexis will be furious, but what does it matter? – 'E is drunk – let us go!'

With a magnificent gesture she seemed to sweep her garments about her, and the crowd gave passage as she sailed towards the door, the narrow-shouldered Simon following.

They both assured the tired and still anxious Miriam that it had been a 'marvellous party', and reached the hall.

'Mr Aron's car? Yes, sir.' The hired butler nodded. 'One moment, sir.'

He gave a shout and beckoned, and a moment later a great silver Rolls was standing before the door; Simon had not telephoned in vain. He had a garage with whom he had an understanding that, at any hour of the day or night, a luxury car was always at Mr Aron's disposal, and he paid handsomely.

'Where – er – shall I tell him?' Simon asked.

'Ze Berkeley,' she said, quickly. 'Come, get in.'

Simon gave instructions and did as he was bid. Almost immediately they were speeding down the gradients towards the West End.

She talked quickly and vividly of the party and the people whom they had just left. The car had reached Baker Street before Simon had a chance to get in the question which he'd been meaning to ask; he said quickly: 'What about a little lunch one day?'

Her shoulders moved slightly under her ermine cloak. 'My frien', it would be nice – but it is impossible. Tomorrow I ave a 'undred things to do, an' the next day I go back to Russia.'

The car slid through Grosvenor Square, and into Carlos Place. Simon considered for a moment, then he said, seriously: 'Are you doing anything for lunch today week?'

She put her head back, and her magnificent laughter filled the car. 'Foolish one, I shall be in Moskawa – you are an absurd.'

'Ner,' Simon shook his head quickly. 'Tell me – are you booked for lunch next Thursday?'

The car sped through the eastern side of Berkeley Square, and up Berkeley Street. She pressed his hand. 'Silly boy – of course not, but I 'ave told you – I shall be in Moskawa once more!'

'All right,' said Simon, decisively. 'Then you will meet me for lunch at one o' clock at the Hotel Metropole in Moscow – Thursday, a week today.'

The car had stopped before the entrance to the hotel, the commission-aire stepped forward and opened the door.

'You make a joke! You do not mean this?' she asked, in her melodious, husky voice, leaning forward to peer into his face.

'I do,' nodded Simon, earnestly.

She laughed suddenly, and drew her hand quickly down his cheek with a caressing gesture. 'All right – I will be there!'

Chapter IV

Cigars and Pistols for Two –

At twelve o' clock precisely on the 7th of February, a very cold and miserable little figure stood ostensibly admiring the ancient Ilyinka Gate in Moscow.

It was Mr Simon Aron, clad in his ordinary London clothes. A smart blue overcoat buttoned tightly across his narrow chest, black shoes, gloves and stick, a soft hat pulled well down over his arc of nose.

Somehow, Mr Aron, for all his foresightedness in the realms of commerce and finance, had failed to bargain for the rigours of a Russian winter. The cold wind cut through his cloth coat, his feet were wet through with the slush of the streets, and the glare of the snow upon the open 'prospekts' was already beginning to hurt his eyes – never too strong at the best of times.

It was with more than ordinary relief that he saw a trim, soldierly form come through the gate; it was easily discernible among the crowd of town moujiks and porters. He recognised the Duke immediately, but how changed – in all but the clever, handsome face.

De Richleau was dressed in the manner of a Russian nobleman before the Revolution, or a high official under the Soviet Government. He wore a heavy coat, belted at the waist and with a vast fur collar, shining black Hessian boots, and on his head at a rakish angle – making him look much taller than usual – a big fur 'papenka'.

As the crowd instinctively made way for him, he looked sharply from side to side, evidently catching sight of Simon at the first glance – but taking no apparent notice. Turning to speak to a little man beside him, who wore a shabby coat and peaked cap which suggested some sort of uniform, he started to cross the street diagonally.

Simon knew the shabby individual to be a guide; he had just such another standing at his elbow, dilating to him on the history of the Ilyinka Gate. He turned to his man quickly. 'Let's go on,' he said. 'I'm cold,' and he began to walk down the pavement to the point at which the Duke would arrive.

De Richleau looked round suddenly when he was nearly across the road, and seemed to see Simon for the first time. He waved a greeting.

'Hello *mon cher*! And what are you doing in Moscow?'

Simon pretended equal surprise as they shook hands. 'Over here on a holiday – thought I'd like to see some of the wonderful improvements they're said to be making.'

'Indeed, yes,' the Duke agreed heartily. 'All educated people should know of the great progress which is being made for civilisation. I find it most interesting. Have you seen the Mogess power station and the Michelson Works?'

'Ner.' Simon shook his head. 'I only arrived last night.'

'I see, and where are you staying?'

'The Metropole.'

'Really! But that is excellent; I am there, too.' De Richleau took Simon's arm and led him down the street – their respective guides, who had been interested listeners, followed side by side. 'Are you alone?'

'Yes – friend who was coming with me let me down at the last minute – he couldn't help it, poor chap – lost his father suddenly.'

'Dear me. However, we shall now be able to see something of this fine town together.' The Duke spoke in loud tones, determined that the guides should not lose one syllable of the conversation. 'Some of the historical sights are of the greatest interest – and the museums, what treasures they have got! All the beautiful things that were formerly locked up in the houses of the nobles.'

'I saw the Kremlin this morning,' Simon volunteered. 'But I was a bit disappointed really – I mean with the old part – Lenin's tomb is worth seeing, though!'

'A marvellous sight, is it not, with all those precious metals sent from every part of Russia? The tombs of the Tsars are nothing to it. But you look cold, my friend!'

'I am,' Simon declared feelingly, and in truth his thin face was almost blue.

'But what clothes!' exclaimed the Duke, surveying him. 'You must get furs if you are to stay here any length of time, or else you will be miserable!'

'I shall be here about a fortnight,' said Simon doubtfully.

'In that case – most certainly. We will go to the trading rows in Red Square at once.' He turned, and spoke rapidly in Russian to the guides; they nodded, and looked sympathetically at Simon. The whole party then retraced their footsteps.

'It will not cost you a great deal,' De Richleau added. 'You see, if we buy well, you will be able to sell the furs again at a good figure before you go home. The comfort to you will most certainly be worth the difference.'

Before long they arrived at the trading rows, and after some sharp bargaining, which the Duke carried out with the assistance of the two guides, Simon found himself equipped in a fashion not unlike that of the traditional Cossack. In addition to furs, De Richleau insisted that he should have a pair of galoshes; for without these, no boots, however tough, could long withstand the continual wetness of the Moscow streets in winter; and as Simon looked about him he saw that everyone was wearing them.

'Let us lunch, my friend,' said the Duke, once more taking him by the arm when their purchases were completed. 'The Hotel Metropole is not the Ritz in Paris, or our old friend the Berkeley in London, but I am hungry – so it will serve!'

Arrived at the hotel, the guides wished to know 'the plans of gentlemen for afternoon'.

'Have you seen the Park of Culture and Leisure?' the Duke asked Simon.

'Ner, what's that?'

'It is in the Zamoskvarechye – the river district; a great park where there is every variety of amusement for the people – volley-ball, tennis, fencing, a circus and a children's town, a hundred things – it would be interesting – let us go there.'

'Um,' Simon nodded, 'yes, let's.'

'If situation is such, gentlemen will not need us?' proffered one of the guides. 'Gentlemen can find their way?'

'Thank you – yes,' De Richleau answered. 'I have the little map which you gave me.'

'What for evening-time?' asked the other guide.

'A theatre,' the Duke suggested. 'I have been to the Arts Theatre already – what of Meyerhold's Theatre? That is where they have all the radical new plays – mechanical scenery, a complete break with all the old stage traditions – shall we go there?'

'Yes – I'd like to see that,' Simon nodded vigorously.

'Certainly,' the guides agreed; again they would not be needed; they would procure seats, and leave the tickets in the bureau of the hotel; was there any other way in which they could be of service? They were polite and anxious to oblige. 'No?' Very well, they would call tomorrow morning.

The Duke and Simon were soon seated at a small table in the restaurant.

'Well – er – any news?' Simon asked at once, but the only reply he received was a by no means gentle kick, from the Duke's big Hessian boot under the table. Then that amazingly interesting and erudite man launched forth into a long dissertation upon the marvels of Moscow – its wonderful historical associations lying side by side with all these modern developments, which, in another two generations, might make it the capital of the civilised world.

It was well that De Richleau talked fluently, and enjoyed talking, since the service of the restaurant was quite appalling. They had to wait twenty-five minutes before a waiter condescended to take their order – and another twenty minutes before the first course arrived.

Despite his anxiety to hear if any news of Rex had been secured by the Duke in Helsingfors or Leningrad, Simon remained patient through the long wait and the plain but satisfying meal that followed. He never tired of listening to the Duke, and the dullness of the fare was relieved by a large helping of caviare. Simon, who was patient by nature, could be especially patient if the caviare was good and plentiful!

Directly they had finished they donned their furs, and left the hotel, but De Richleau did not take the road to the river district. Instead he turned up the Petrowka Boulevarde, saying to Simon as he did so: 'I feel that now is the time to ascertain about our Hoyo de Monterreys.'

'Mmm,' Simon agreed, 'hope they came through all right?'

'Yes, but I did not wish to collect them until you had joined me.'

They walked on for some twenty minutes, turning occasionally to right or left; meanwhile De Richleau still avoided the subject of Rex, and continued his dissertation upon Moscow.

Simon looked about him with interest. Moscow was quite unlike any large city he had seen – the great majority of the buildings were in a shocking state of repair, the paint peeling from shop-fronts and door-ways. The windows broken, boarded over, or covered with grime. Nine out of ten shops were empty and deserted; those that were still occupied had little in their windows other than a bust of Lenin and a Soviet flag, except here and there, where long queues of people waited outside one of the state co-operative stores. In contrast to this atmosphere of poverty and desolation, a great deal of demolition was going on, and in nearly every street new buildings were springing up – great structures of steel, concrete, and glass.

The side streets showed ruts and ditches guaranteed to ruin the springs of any car, but all the main roads had been newly paved with asphalt. Traffic was practically non-existent, which gave the streets a strange appearance.

The only regular means of transport seemed to be the trams – and at each stopping place the waiting crowds swarmed upon these like a flight of locusts; there seemed no limit to the number they were allowed to carry, and people who could not force their way inside hung from the rails and platforms at the back and front. One thing that astonished Simon was the extraordinary number of people in the streets – they all seemed to be hurrying somewhere, and he thought that some sort of national holiday must be in progress, but when he suggested this to the Duke, De Richleau shook his head.

'No, my friend – it is only the effect of the five-day week! There are no more Sundays in Russia, or Saturday half-holidays. Everybody works at something, in a series of perpetual shifts, so that from year's end to year's end there is no cessation of industry. The factories are never idle, but each individual has every fifth day free – therefore, one-fifth of the entire population of this city is on holiday each day.'

'So that is why there are so many people about – I'm surprised at the queues, though; I thought all that was done away with.'

'While there is no system of delivery there must be queues.' De Richleau shrugged his shoulders. 'A great part of everybody's free time is spent in queueing up for necessities; besides, there is never enough of anything; if you apply for a hat or a pair of new boots, your co-operative society notifies you when they receive a consignment. If you need your boots badly, you must run to be early in the queue, or else there will be none left to fit you, or perhaps no more at all. If you live in Russia now, you must even go out to fetch the milk in the morning – that is, provided you are entitled to a milk ration. Nine-tenths of the milk supply is turned into butter in order that it may be dumped in England, and more machinery bought for the new factories with the money. That's all part of the Five Year Plan!'

'God-forsaken place! Glad I'm not a Russian,' said Simon, feelingly; 'but what about the private shops? Why do the people go to the co-ops and queue up, when they can buy the stuff elsewhere?'

'It is a question of money; everything in the private shops costs from four to five times as much as in the state stores. The great majority of the people cannot possibly afford to buy from them.'

For some time they had been walking through less crowded streets, and at last they arrived in a small square of what must have been, at one time, respectable private houses. Most of them were now in a sad state of dilapidation.

De Richleau stopped outside one of the least disreputable, which bore the arms, painted in colour on a metal shield above the front door, of one of the lesser South American republics. The word 'Legation' was also written up, both in Russian and Roman capitals. He gave a quick glance round

– the little square was practically deserted – then he stepped up, not to the front door but to a smaller entrance a few paces farther on, and rang the bell sharply, twice.

The door was opened almost immediately, and the Duke pushed Simon inside, slipping in himself directly after.

'Is Señor Rosas in?' he asked. 'I come from Señor Zavala.'

'Yes, señor, this way – please to follow me.' The little man led them down a long passage to a room at the back of the house.

A swarthy individual rose to greet them with a charming smile. The Duke introduced himself.

'But, yes, Excellency – my good friend Zavala wrote to me from London of your coming. Your case has safe arrival in the diplomatic bag – it is here beneath the table.' Rosas indicated a small, stout packing case 'You would like it opened? But certainly!' He rang the bell, and asked for a chisel and hammer; very soon the wooden case had been prized open, and an inner one of shining tin, about two feet long by a foot wide and eighteen inches deep, placed upon the table. 'You would like the privacy to assure yourself of the right contents of the case, Excellency, is it not?' smiled Señor Rosas. 'Please to make use of my room – no, no, it is no trouble – only ring when you have finished, that is all!' He slipped softly out of the room, closing the door behind him.

'Now let us look at our famous Hoyos.' De Richleau seized the ring that was embedded in the soft lead strip that ran round the top of the case, and pulled it sharply. A wire to which the ring was attached cut easily through the soft lead, and a moment later he had lifted out the two cedar cabinets of cigars.

Simon opened one with care, and ran his fingers lovingly down the fine, dark oily surface of the cigars. 'Perfect,' he murmured; 'travelled wonderfully!'

'But that is not all, my friend!' The Duke had opened the other box. The cigars were not packed in two bundles of fifty each, but in four flat layers of twenty-five to the row, and each layer was separated from the other by a thin sheet of cedar wood. Very carefully De Richleau lifted out the top layer on its cedar sheet, and then the next. Simon looked over his shoulder and saw that, neatly packed in the place where the two bottom layers of cigars should have been, there reposed a full-sized, ugly-looking automatic.

The Duke removed it, together with two small boxes of ammunition and the packing. 'You will find a similar trifle in the other box,' he remarked, as he gently lowered the two trays of cigars into the place where the pistol had lately been.

Simon unpacked the second box with equal care, the Duke taking the two layers of cigars from it, and placing them in the box before him. When all was done, there remained one box full of cigars, the other – empty.

'What – er – shall I do with this?' said Simon, a little doubtfully, as he gingerly picked up the other deadly-looking weapon, with its short blue steel barrel.

'Inside your left breast pocket, my son. It is far too large to carry upon your hip – the bulge would show.'

Simon did as he was bid. They rang the bell, and Señor Rosas rejoined them.

De Richleau thanked him courteously. 'There is only one thing more,' he added, 'if we may trespass upon your good nature?'

'Excellency, please to command, I beg!'

'I should be grateful if you would be good enough to send this full box of cigars, in a plain parcel, addressed to me at the Hotel Metropole. The other – it contained some papers which I wished to receive undisturbed – I should be glad if you would burn that.'

'It shall be done!' The Spaniard's quick smile flashed out again. 'A thousand pleasures to be of assistance to you, Excellency.'

When they were once more out in the square De Richleau tapped his pocket with a grim little smile. 'We are short of a hundred cigars,' he said, 'but we may be infinitely more thankful to have these before we are out of Russia.'

Chapter V

The Tavern of the Howling Wolf

After walking for some half an hour they came at last to the Park of Culture and Leisure.

'Now,' said De Richleau, with a sigh of relief, 'we can talk freely.'

'Well, I'll tell you,' Simon laughed into the palm of his heavily gloved hand, 'I'm glad about that!'

'My friend,' said the Duke, seriously, 'before – it was impossible; there are eyes and ears everywhere. Have you noticed those little ventilators in your bedroom at the hotel? They are microphones, so that all you say may be overheard. In the restaurant, along the walls, there are microphones also; Russia is pleased to welcome the tourist or harmless business man, but always the Kommissars are terrified of counter revolution. It is not easy for the small Communist party to keep an entire population in subjection on short rations; and how can they tell who is the tourist, and who the secret enemy of the Soviet, only by watching? You may be certain that the parcel containing our Hoyos will be opened and examined before it is delivered to me – yes,' he smiled, 'and they will look below the two top layers; that was why I did not dare have the case delivered to me just as it arrived. Even the streets are not safe, a passer-by may overhear some chance word, and immediately one is suspect – that is why I brought you here. In these open spaces we are safe – we can speak our thoughts aloud – but only here, remember that!'

'I will,' said Simon, briefly. 'Now – any news of Rex?'

'No,' the Duke shook his head. 'My advertisements in the Finnish papers at Helsingfors brought no response. The messenger is, perhaps, by this time in Paris or New York, or more probably he is an illiterate who can hardly read. I had to word the advertisements with care, of course, and I did not dare to use my own name – the Russian authorities might have seen them, and refused to allow me to pass the frontier. I worded them as far as possible as if they had been inserted by the American Legation, or a relative who was seeking news of Rex. In any case they have proved useless.'

Simon nodded. 'Bad luck that; I didn't have much fun either. I went up to Jack Straw's Castle three times; got to know the barman and the manager quite well, but there wasn't a Russian near the place. Just the usual quiet, old-fashioned pub; no trace of any special club using it as a meeting place either, and very little business doing at this time of year.'

'That is bad – one moment!' The Duke swung on his heel, to confront a seedy-looking man who, although apparently uninterested in them, had approached silently from behind.

The man lurched up as De Richleau turned, and asked in Russian for a light; the Duke gave him one without comment, and they moved on until he was out of earshot.

'Do you think that chap was listening?' Simon asked, nervously.

'I shouldn't think so – just a lounger. Now tell me, have you had any ideas on the subject of Rex's mine?'

'Ner. I've been puzzling quite a lot about that. Have you?'

'No; it completely defeats me. I did not have any good fortune in Leningrad either, although I questioned everyone that I knew in the Consulates.'

'What's Leningrad like?' Simon inquired. 'As dreary as this place?'

'Worse, my friend; it is a dying city. These Kommissars are no fools; they know that all the wealth and fertility of Russia lies in the South, and it is here that they are making their great efforts for the future.'

'I suppose you've been to the American Embassy?'

'Yes, but they can tell us nothing that we do not already know. Rex arrived here on the 4th of December, did the usual round of sight-seeing, and left again on the 11th.'

'What do we do now?' Simon asked, thoughtfully.

'There is one possible line of inquiry which a friend of mine in the Italian Embassy suggested to me. It seems that there is a small "stoloveya", that is, a restaurant of sorts, in the lower quarters of the town, where certain discontented elements in the population meet. There is nothing at all against them, you understand, or they would be arrested at once by the Ogpu, but it is thought that many of the *habitués* have counter-revolutionary sympathies.

'My friend was told that Rex was seen there one night during his stay; I thought that we also might pay a visit to this place. It is called the Tavern of the Howling Wolf. He may have gone there only out of curiosity, but, on the other hand, it is just possible that we might learn something.'

'Going to be a bit difficult, isn't it?' Simon laughed. 'I mean with these wretched guides about.'

The Duke smiled. 'If it is agreeable to you, I thought that, for once, we might play truant this evening.'

'What – cut the theatre?'

'Yes, it is possible that they may not even know that we absented ourselves; but even if they do find out, I do not think that anything very serious can happen to us. We shall be duly apologetic, and say that, at the last moment, we decided on a change of plan for our evening's entertainment.'

'Splendid!' said Simon. 'Let's. I tell you one curious thing that happened to me before I left London.'

'What was that?'

Simon told De Richleau of his meeting with Valeria Petrovna Karkoff, and her appointment to lunch with him the following day.

The Duke was pleased and interested. 'That friendship can most certainly do us no harm,' he said; 'the famous artistes are as powerful here now as they ever were – more so, perhaps. It is always so after a revolution; the one thing which the people will not allow the dictators to interfere with is their amusements. The most powerful Kommissar would hesitate before offending a prima donna or a ballerina.'

The early twilight was already falling, and in the clear air a myriad lights began to twinkle from the houses and factories across the river. They made their way back across the crisp snow of the Park, and through the slush of the streets, to the hotel.

Dinner was a long, uninteresting meal, with many tiresome delays in service, and, since they could not talk freely together, they were glad when it was over.

After, they sat for a little time in the lounge, where dancing was in progress; it was a strange assembly. Most of the men wore the Tolstoyian blouse of the proletariat, or some kind of threadbare uniform; one or two were in evening dress; most of the better clad were Germans or Jewish. The women, for the most part, seemed blowzy and ill-cared-for, only a few were dressed in the special costume created by the revolution, most of them had shoddy copies of the fashions prevailing in London and Paris a year before. Here and there, and not necessarily with the best-dressed men, were women with expensive clothes, who would have passed muster in the smartest restaurants of the European capitals. Everybody seemed to be drinking freely, although the prices were prohibitive; the band was shocking, and the waiters surly. Simon and the Duke did not stay long, and were relieved when the time came at which they should have gone to the theatre. One of the limited number of hired cars that are to be had in Moscow had been ordered by the Duke; they climbed in and settled themselves upon its hard seats. De Richleau gave the address in a low voice to the driver, and the car started off, nosing its way through the crowded streets.

On each street corner, attached to the electric light standards, were affixed a cluster of loud-speaker megaphones – they blared continuously, not music, but a harsh voice, dinning short sentences into the ears of the moving multitude.

'What's it all about?' asked Simon. 'Loud speakers never seem to stop here! I noticed them this morning, and again this afternoon – can't be news all the time, can it?'

'It is the Five Year Plan, my friend,' the Duke shrugged. 'Never for one second are the masses allowed to forget it. Those megaphones relate what is being done all the time – how many tractors have been turned out at Stalingrad today – how many new teachers graduated with honours from the University of Karkov last week – how many tons of ore have been taken from the great Kuznetsky basin, which they are now beginning to exploit – how the branch of the young Communist Party in Niji-Novgorod has passed a resolution giving up their fifth day holiday, for a year, in order that The Plan may be completed the quicker – and every five minutes the announcer says: "You who hear this – what are you doing for the Five Year Plan? What are you doing that the Five Year Plan shall be completed in Four?"' He shuddered. 'There is something terrible about it, my son. These fanatics will yet eat us all alive.'

They fell silent, each pondering on the threat to the old civilisation of Western Europe, that was gaining force in this blind, monstrous power, growing beneath their eyes.

The car left the smooth asphalt of the more frequented streets, jolting and bumping its way down narrow turnings into the suburbs of the city. Eventually they stopped before a house in a mean street. Faint sounds of music came from within, and these, together with the chinks of light that shone through the heavily curtained windows, were the only signs of life.

They got out, and their driver knocked loudly upon the door; after a little it was opened, and they went in, bidding the driver to return in an hour. It was snowing heavily in the street, and as they began to remove their wraps they were astonished at the quantity of snow that had gathered upon them during the short wait on the threshold. They took a small table near the great china stove, blowing into their hands to warm their chilled fingers. A slatternly woman shuffled up to them, and after a short conversation with the Duke, set two small glasses of spirit before them; it proved to be some kind of plum brandy, similar to Sleigowitz.

In the low room were about twenty tables, some dozen of which were occupied. Men of all classes were present – several low-browed, stupid, or sullen-looking workers, in the usual Kaftan, here and there a better type, who from his dress seemed to be some minor official; one or two faces suggested the cultured European who has 'gone native', and known much suffering – one elderly man, with a fine domed head, sat staring with wide blue eyes into vacancy. The only woman there had a hard unpleasant face with the pink eyes of an albino, and patchy hair, alternate tufts of white and yellow.

There was little talking, and few groups of any size; most of the denizens of this dubious haunt seemed tired and listless, content to sit idle, listening to a monotonous repetition of gipsy music from the travesty of a Tzigane band.

The Duke and Simon sat for a long time studying the people, bored, but anxious not to miss any movement or word which might give them the opportunity to get in touch with the frequenters of this poor hostelry; but nothing changed, nor did anyone molest them. Even so, Simon was happy to be able to press the hard bulk of the big automatic between his upper arm and his ribs. He was aware that they were being covertly watched from a number of tables, and if many of the faces were tired, some of them were far from being free of evil.

Now and again a newcomer entered, heralded by a gust of icy wind and snow – occasionally a man pulled his extra long layers of frowzy clothing about him, and went out into the night. Beneath the low rafters the room grew thick with the haze of cheap tobacco smoke, the monotonous band droned on.

After a long time, as it seemed, three workmen arrived, bringing with them quite a drift of falling snow; they were a little drunk, and two of them began to clap, and call for '*Jakko*'. The face of the third seemed vaguely familiar to Simon, who caught him slyly glancing in the direction of their table. He noticed, with a feeling of aversion, that the man had a cast in one eye, and quietly, almost unconsciously, forked his fingers under the table.

The cry of '*Jakko*' was taken up by several others; the band of three struck up a livelier tune, and through a door at the back of the room appeared a dancer.

He was clad in a fantastic costume of ribbons and dried grasses, not unlike the traditional Hawaiian dress. As he pirouetted, his skirts flared out about him; he carried an enormous tambourine, and upon his head he wore a conical hat of reeds, reminiscent of Robinson Crusoe in the pantomime. Leaping into the clear space in the centre of the room, he began a wild and noisy *czardas,* in time to the steady clapping of the audience.

De Richleau looked at him for a moment, and then away with a slight shrug. 'This fellow will keep going for hours,' he said, impatiently. 'He is, or would pretend to be, a Shamman from the Alti – that is, a sort of witch-doctor from the desolate Russian lands north of Mongolia, where the Tartar tribes still worship the spirits of their ancestors. I think we had better go – there is nothing for us here.'

But Simon was not listening; his shrewd eyes were riveted on the gyrating dancer. He was careful not to look at the Duke, not even to appear to speak to him, but he nudged him slightly, and, placing his hand casually before his mouth, whispered:

'Don't you see? This is Jack Straw!'

Chapter VI

The Secret of the Mine

'You are right, my friend, you are right!' the Duke breathed back. 'I am thankful you are with me; I should have missed this altogether!'

For a long time they sat in silence while the dancer leaped and spun, crashing his tambourine, and making his grass skirts swirl around him. They could not see his features, since he wore a hideous mask. He was a big, powerful man, but even so the terrific exertion caused little rivulets of perspiration to run down his neck and arms, and such parts of his body as were naked soon glistened with sweat.

Meanwhile the stale smoke collected and hung in stratus clouds beneath the rough-hewn beams of the low ceiling. No breath of air was allowed to penetrate from outside, and the atmosphere of the overheated room became almost unbearable.

At last, with a final leap and a crash of the tambourine, the dance was over; De Richleau threw some kopecks on the floor and, catching the fellow's eye, beckoned. The dancer picked up the money and came over to the table. The Duke said five words only, in Russian: 'You will drink – sit down.'

It was not only the words he chose, but the accent which he put upon them, which made the man regard him with a sudden narrowing of the eyes; but De Richleau knew what he was about. He had purposely chosen the words and tone which a Russian aristocrat would have used in addressing an artiste who had pleased him in the days before the Revolution; not the cordial invitation from one worker to another, in a state where all men are equal.

The grotesque figure, still wearing the mask of a Shamman, pulled out a chair and plumped down on it. Without speaking he crossed his muscular legs and, producing a tobacco pouch and papers, began to roll himself a cigarette.

De Richleau called the slatternly woman, and a fresh round of the spirit resembling Sleigowitz was put before them.

With his brilliant grey eyes the Duke studied the dancer. He felt certain now that they were on the right track; had the fellow churlishly refused, or been abusive of that invitation issued almost in the form of a command, he would have felt that probably they were mistaken, and that the man was no more than an ordinary moujik. Since the man accepted in seeming serenity, the inference was that he realised their visit to be no casual one, and was himself no casual peasant dancer.

'We are visitors here in Moscow for a few days,' the Duke began, in a low voice. 'Americans. Do you get many Americans here?'

'*Könen sie Deutsch sprechen?*' the dancer inquired, softly.

'*Jawohl,*' De Richleau answered under his breath.

Simon pricked up his ears, for he had a fair knowledge of German.

'That is good,' the peasant went on in the same language, still looking the other way; the hideous mask hid the movement of his lips. 'I also am American, so also are all the people in this room – every one, just as much American as yourself, old one. Now tell me the truth.'

A glint of humour showed in De Richleau's piercing eyes. 'I ask your pardon,' he said briefly, 'but it is an American that I seek, and I thought that Jack Straw might give me news of him!'

'So?' The dancer seemed to consider. 'How do I know that you are not the police?'

'That you must judge for yourself,' the Duke replied, lightly. 'If I showed you my passport, you would say that it is forged, perhaps.'

'You are not of the police,' said the other, decisively. 'No spy of the Ogpu could call an artiste to his table as you called me. Yet it was a risk you ran – such is no longer the manner used in Moscow!'

De Richleau smiled, pleased that his subtlety had been appreciated. 'I must run risks if I wish to find my friend,' he said, simply. 'A tall, young American – he came here one night early in December – Tsarderynski, or Rex Van Ryn, which you choose, that is his name.'

'I know him,' the other nodded laconically, and spat on the floor.

'Did you know that he was in prison?' the Duke inquired, guardedly.

'No, but I suspected that, else he would have returned by now; but it is better not to talk of this here!'

'Where can we meet?' De Richleau asked at once.

'Where is your guide?' the dancer countered, quickly.

'We are supposed to be at Meyerhold's Theatre tonight, but we came here instead.'

'Good. It must be some place where he will not accompany you.'

'The Zoological Gardens?' suggested the Duke.

'That will do. In the Krassnaja Pressnja, inside the eagles' house,' he laughed softly; 'that is appropriate, eh? Eleven o' clock tomorrow, then.'

'Eleven o' clock,' De Richleau repeated.

The dancer pressed his mask more closely against his face, and swallowed his drink through the slit of the mouth, then he stood up quickly and, without another word, he left the table.

He had hardly disappeared through the back of the restaurant when the street door was flung violently open, five men pushed in – three appeared to be ordinary working men, the other two were the guides.

'Now we're in a muddle!' Simon laughed, but the Duke was equal to the situation, and even before the guides had had time to look round the dimly lit room, he had called a boisterous greeting to them. The three workmen sat down near the door, while the guides came over to the table near the stove at once.

'Hello, my friends, come and sit down, come and drink with us!' The Duke thumped the table, and called loudly for the woman who served the drinks, seeming suddenly to have become a little drunk himself.

Simon took up the cue immediately, and tipped his chair back from the table at an almost dangerous angle, while he allowed a fatuous smile to spread over his face.

'We believe gentlemen were at Meyerhold Theatre – ' began one of the guides, seriously.

'The theatre! Bah!' De Richleau shrugged. 'I lost the tickets, so we came here instead – it is better!'

'But, if gentlemen had asked for us we would have got other tickets,' the man persisted.

'What does it matter?' laughed the apparently tipsy Duke. 'Come, let us drink!'

'But please to understand, the situation is such – it is not good that gentlemen come to such a place alone, it is not of good reputation. The police do what they can, but there is bad quarter in every city, it is not safe for gentlemen.'

'We have come to no harm.' De Richleau lifted his glass, as the woman set more drinks upon the table. '*Good harvests – and prosperity to all!*' he cried loudly in Russian.

The guides bowed solemnly, and drank. It is a toast that no Russian ever refuses; the great mass of the people – whether under Tsar or Soviet – are too near the eternal struggle with the soil.

'We are only anxious for safety of gentlemen,' the guide who acted as spokesman protested. 'When we learn that gentlemen were not at theatre, we worry much; the situation is such because we are responsible.'

'Good feller!' Simon let his chair come forward with a crash, and patted the man on the back affectionately. 'Let's have another drink; you shall see us all safe-home!'

The two guides exchanged a swift glance – they seemed relieved. It was evident that their charges were harmless people, out on the spree and mildly drunk; they accepted a further ration of the fiery spirit.

After that things became easier – they drank: To the Russian People – To the British Socialist Party – To each other – and, finally, for no shadow of reason – To the ex-Emperor of Germany!

By that time the two guides were singing sadly together, and Simon and the Duke had had as much as they could comfortably carry, yet both had still their wits very much about them.

At last one of the guides rose unsteadily to his feet. He made his way to the street door and had to cling on for support as he opened it. The wind had risen, and after he had ascertained that the hired car was outside, assistance had to be given him before he could close the door again. At his suggestion the whole party left the Tavern of the Howling Wolf. The driver was fast asleep in the body of the car under a pile of rugs; they roused him up, and soon the party were bumping their way back through the white and silent streets to the hotel.

In the lounge dancing was still in progress; they had a final drink together, and parted for the night with many expressions of mutual esteem and goodwill.

The following morning neither De Richleau nor Aron felt inclined for breakfast, but neither of them had forgotten the importance of their appointment, and as soon as they were out in the fresh, crisp air, their spirits revived.

They had had no difficulty in dispensing with the attendance of the guides when they had declared their intention of visiting the Zoo; but they waited till they actually arrived in the Krassnaja Pressnja before they opened serious conversation.

'I'm worried,' said Simon, looking round to make certain that no one was within earshot.

'Why should you be?' asked the Duke, blandly. 'I thought our little adventure of last night passed off most fortunately. We have run Jack Straw to earth, and are, I trust, about to hear his story. I think, too, that our excellent guides are entirely without suspicion; it might have been a very different matter if they had arrived on the scene earlier, when we were talking to Jack Straw!'

'It's not that,' Simon shook his head quickly. 'Did you – er – notice the three workmen who came in before the dance?'

'Yes; what of them?'

'Well, I don't know, of course, but I'll tell you – I believe one of them was the chap who asked you for a light in the park yesterday.'

'Indeed!' De Richleau raised his slanting eyebrows. 'What makes you think that, my friend?'

'He had a cast in one eye; nasty-looking little chap. Mind you, I may be mistaken.'

'Would you know him again?'

'Um,' Simon nodded, 'I think so.'

'In that case we must keep a sharp look-out. It is by no means unusual, in countries where there is a large organisation of secret police, for one agent to be set to watch another. This man may be acting quite independently of our official guides, and unknown to them. We must be careful!'

They had entered the Zoo while they were talking, and found the eagles' house without difficulty, but they looked in vain for Jack Straw. A keeper stood near the door at one end; the only other occupant of the big aviary was an elderly gentleman with fine, flowing white moustaches. He looked as if he had seen better days.

As they walked slowly along the cages they drew near to the old man, who was advancing in the opposite direction. Pausing now and again to admire the birds, they came together before a cage of vultures near the centre of the house.

'Filthy brutes!' said the old man, suddenly, in a surprisingly youthful voice, as he pointed with his stick.

'They are as Soviet Kommissars to the Royal Eagles who are Tsars,' the Duke answered, softly.

'You fooled your guides well last night,' the other went on, in perfect English, 'but you must be careful – there are certain to be others watching you.'

'Thank you. Can you give us news of Van Ryn?'

'No, don't know what's happened to him, but I know why he came to Russia!'

'Good, that may be helpful.'

'He was after the Shulimoff treasure; the old Prince buried it himself before he cleared out in 'seventeen; there's said to be millions of roubles' worth of gold and jewels – God knows where it is, the Bolshies have been hunting for it for years – but that's what Rex is after.'

The effect of hearing this youthful English voice proceeding from the grey-moustached lips of the elderly Russian was so unusual that Simon had difficulty in restraining his mirth. They walked slowly down the line of cages towards the door at the opposite end from that at which the keeper stood.

'Stout feller, Rex,' their elderly companion went on. 'Knew him when he came over to play polo for the Yanks in nineteen twenty-nine. I hope he's all right.'

'I received a letter asking for assistance a fortnight ago,' said the Duke. 'It was posted in Helsingfors. He was in prison somewhere – but where, I have no idea, unfortunately; he must have run up against the authorities in some way.'

'Probably found wandering in forbidden territory; they're pretty strict about that. Large areas are closed altogether to foreigners.'

'Where – er – was Prince Shulimoff's estate?' inquired Simon. 'That might give us a line.'

'That's just the trouble; the old boy was fabulously rich. He had a dozen places; one outside Moscow, another near Leningrad; a villa at Yalta – that's the Russian Riviera, you know. Then he had an enormous territory near Tobolsk, in Siberia, and places in Pskov, and Yaroslavl, and the Caucasus as well; and being such a wily old bird, he may not have buried the treasure in any of them; the old scout may have thought it safer to stow the goods in one of the monasteries, or the cellars of a friend!'

'Looks as if we'd have to make a tour of Russia!' remarked Simon, with a chuckle.

'I say,' said the young-old man, suddenly, 'you might do a job of work for me, will you? When you get back to London – that is, if you do,' he added, smiling under his moustache – 'just drop into the Thatched House Club and ask for Colonel Marsden; give him this message from Jack Straw: "Stravinsky's got twelve, and six, and four". Will you? He'll know what that means – think you can remember?'

'Colonel Marsden – Stravinsky's got twelve, and six, and four,' repeated the Duke. 'Yes, I shall remember.'

'Splendid. I'll probably get that bit through another way as well, but one can't have too many lines. I'll tell you another thing. If you do make a round trip of the Shulimoff estates, and get anywhere near Tobolsk, keep your eyes skinned – there's a great deal of activity going on up there just now, and we'd like to know what it's all about, if it's just another commercial stunt connected with the Five Year Plan, or something military. Give Marsden anything you pick up; it's all the odd bits of information pieced together that make a whole, you know.'

De Richleau smiled. 'I trust that we shall not be called upon to visit Siberia, but you may be certain that we shall keep our eyes open if we do!'

'That's the spirit. Sorry I can't ask you fellows back to the Club for a drink, but my position is hardly – er – official, you know – Look out!'

They had almost reached the farther door of the aviary. Turning quickly, they saw a seedy-looking individual, dressed like a clerk, who had entered without their having heard him. He was apparently studying a hawk. After a second he glanced slyly in their direction, and both Simon and the Duke were quick to notice that he had a cast in one eye.

Both made a movement to leave the vicinity of their elderly friend, but as they turned again they found that Jack Straw had vanished – silently and completely away.

Chapter VII

Simon 'almost' falls in love

Later that morning, as Simon waited in the lounge of the Hotel Metropole, he wondered if Valeria Petrovna had remembered her promise to lunch with him. It was already a quarter past one, and she had not yet put in an appearance. He thought it more than probable that she had never taken his invitation seriously, and to guard against this possibility, on his return from the Zoo, he had caused the hall porter to ring up and leave a message at her apartment.

The clock marked two minutes after the half-hour when she arrived, looking radiantly beautiful, enveloped in magnificent furs, both hands outstretched as she hurried across the hall.

'Oh, Mistaire Aron, what a surprise to see you 'ere!'

'Well,' he smiled his little amused smile as he offered her his open ciga-rette-case, 'it's Thursday, isn't it?'

'Of course it ees Thursday, but nevaire did I think to see you, all the same; it was late at night when you ask me, after the party – I thought the champagne 'ad gone to your 'ead!'

'Ner – not the champagne!' said Simon, with a quick look.

She laughed delightedly. 'Silly boy! Next you will be telling me that you 'ave fallen in love with me!'

'Well,' said the cautious Simon, 'I don't mind telling you – I almost think I have!'

'You *almost* think, eh? That is rich; nevaire in all my life 'ave I met a man who only *thinks* 'e ees in love with me!'

Simon drank in her superb dark loveliness. What a woman! he thought, and then said aloud: 'Good thing I'm not given to falling in love, or I should be making a fool of myself! What about a spot of lunch?' he said, getting up from his chair and smiling blandly into her eyes.

'Lunch – yes, but a spot – what ees that?' she asked, turning and lead-ing the way to the restaurant.

'Just – er – an expression,' he laughed, in his nervous way as he followed her. 'I wish we were in London – then I *would* give you a lunch!'

' 'Ow! You do not like Moskawa?' she asked, with a quick frown, as he held a chair for her at a small table near the window.

He saw at once that he was on delicate ground. 'Oh, yes,' he prevaricated, hastily; 'wonderful city!'

'Ah, wonderful indeed,' she cried, earnestly, and he saw a gleam of fanaticism leap into her dark eyes. 'It ees marvellous what 'as been done in Russia these last years; you must see Stalingrad, and the Dnieprestroy; work created for thousands of people, electric light . . .'

'I'd like to see the Dnieprestroy,' he agreed; 'after Niagara it will be the biggest electric plant in the world, I believe.'

'*The* biggest!' she said, proudly.'

Simon knew quite well that Niagara was the bigger hydro-electric station, but tact was more essential than truth at the moment, so he nodded solemnly. 'Marvellous!' he agreed, looking at her sparkling eyes and flushed cheeks. 'I must see that.'

'And the great factory of tractors at Stalingrad,' she continued, enthusiastically; 'you must see that also, and the great palace of industry at Karkov – all these things you must see to understand our new Russia!'

'Well – I'll tell you – it's really your acting I want to see!' Simon smiled at her over the plate of excellent Boeuf Strogonoff he was eating.

'Ah, that ees nothing,' she shrugged; 'my art ees good, in that it gives pleasure to many, but it ees a thing which passes; these others, they will remain; they are the steps by which Russia will rise to dominate the world!'

'You really believe that?' he asked, curiously.

'But yes,' she answered, with wide-eyed fervour; ' 'ave you not seen in Moskawa alone the 'ouses 'ow they 'ave come down, and the factories 'ow they 'ave gone up? The Russian people no longer toil in slavery, it ees their turn to be the masters!'

For some time she talked on fervently and happily about the Five Year Plan – the tremendous difficulties with which Russia was faced through the bitter opposition of the capitalist countries, and the hopelessly inadequate supply of technical experts, but she assured him that they were making steady progress and would overcome every obstacle in time.

He was content to put in a word here and there, quietly enjoying the animation of his lovely guest, and gradually he found himself caught up by her faith and enthusiasm. It was true – all that she said. The capital, as a whole, presented an extraordinary spectacle of decrepitude and decay, rows of empty shops and houses that had not known paint and repair for almost a generation, yet, out of this apparent death fine buildings of steel and glass were everywhere springing up, and although the people in general seemed ill-clothed and underfed, the majority appeared busy and contented.

'What 'ave you come to do in Russia?' she asked, suddenly; 'do not say that you 'ave come all the way just to give me the luncheon – but you would not, I know you are not the liar – that, I think, is why I like you.'

It was a difficult question to answer. Simon had not forgotten the Duke's warning – that the walls of the Hotel Metropole have many ears, so he said discreetly: 'Well, it's a long story, but as a matter of fact, I've been meaning to come to Russia for a long time now, wanted to see all these wonderful new factories. I'm interested in that sort of thing, you know!'

As he spoke he regarded her steadily with his sharp expressive eyes, and evidently she understood, for she smiled slightly.

'You must come and visit my apartment, it is quiet there. You can tell me all about yourself; I am interested in you, Mistaire Aron, you do not make stupid love, like all the other young men; yet you like me, do you not?' Her smile became bewitching.

'I'd love to come,' said Simon, simply, and the world of meaning in his voice was a sufficient answer to her question.

'Let us see, then,' her eyes sparkled; 'it must be at a time when Leshkin ees not there. Oh, 'e ees so jealous, that one, you 'ave no idea! The scene 'e make me when I go off to lunch with you. I 'ad not thought for a little minute that you would be 'ere, and when your message come and I telephone 'im to say I cannot meet 'im – Ho! what a temper! It all comes, I think, because 'e 'as red 'air!' and she went off into peals of delighted laughter.

'What about the afternoon?' Simon suggested.

'Why not?' she smiled; 'you shall come back with me, and we will make what you call *Whoopee!*'

She was as infectious in her child-like gaiety as in her fierce enthusiasms, and Simon felt the spirit of adventure stirring in him.

'I'd love to come,' he said, again.

'Let us go, then – now, this moment!' She set down her coffee cup and rose impulsively.

He followed her out of the restaurant, and they secured their furs. Madame Karkoff's limousine was waiting at the hotel entrance; it was one of the few private cars that Simon had seen during his two days' stay in Moscow. The fact that the traffic was almost entirely composed of horses and occasional carts, and that their car was not once blocked en route, made Simon revise his lunch-time reflections as to the true prosperity of Soviet Russia; the traffic of a city is a very good index to its wealth and commercial activities. Making a mental note to consider the business aspect of the position later, Simon devoted himself to the lovely creature at his side.

Madame Karkoff's apartment was on the first floor of an old-fashioned block. She explained to him that all the new domestic buildings were composed of large numbers of small flats, modern in every way, with communal kitchens and wash-houses, and crèches for the workers' children, but that none of these flats were of any size. If one wanted spacious rooms, there was nothing to be had other than the mansions and apartments of the old *bourgeoisie*.

The outside of the building was depressing, with its peeling paint and rain-streaked walls, but the inside was a revelation.

The great rooms were almost barbaric in their splendour, with no trace of modern decoration. Magnificent tapestries hung from the walls and beautiful lamps in Russian silver filigree from the ceiling; the polished floor was strewn with furs and Persian carpets in glowing reds and purples.

A maid in a neat dark dress put a tray with tea in glasses, and sugar and lemon, on a low stool beside her mistress, and Valeria Petrovna drew Simon down on to the divan beside her.

'Now tell me,' she commanded, 'why, Mistaire Aron, you – come to Russia?'

'Simon,' he corrected, gently.

'Simon!' She went off into fits of laughter. 'Simon – that ees good – you know why I laugh?'

'Ner – ' he confessed, puzzled.

'It ees the childhood rhyme I learn when I have an English nurse: "*Simple Simon met a pieman, going to a fair; said Simple Simon to the pieman, what 'ave you got there?*"' and once more she dissolved into tears of childish laughter.

'Now look here,' Simon protested, 'that's quite enough of that!' but he smiled his kind, indulgent smile at her teasing.

'What ees a pieman?' she inquired, seriously.

'Chap who makes pies,' Simon grinned from ear to ear; 'you know – cakes, puddings, and all that.'

'Ah, well, I am glad I am not a pieman! Tell me, little Simon, what are you?'

'Well,' Simon hesitated, 'I'm a banker, in a way – but I'll tell you, I do all sorts of other things as well. I'm interested in chemicals and metals and phosphorus.'

'And what do you make 'ere in Moscow?'

'To tell you the truth, I'm not here on business exactly,' Simon continued, cautiously; 'I'm looking for a friend of mine; he got into some trouble with the police, I believe.'

She looked suddenly grave. 'That ees bad; they are powerful, the Ogpu – was it for politics that 'e got into trouble?'

Simon was in a quandary; he wanted to discover the whereabouts of Rex, but he could not tolerate the idea of lying to this beautiful and charming woman, who seemed to have taken such a liking to him, and in whom his own interest was growing deeper every minute. Honesty, with Simon, was not only policy, but a principle from which he never deviated – it had brought him the confidence and respect of business acquaintances and friends alike.

'Ner,' he answered, 'not as far as I know. Perhaps he may have gone somewhere he should not have gone, or got tight or something, but I don't think he got into a muddle with politics. The only thing I know is that he is in prison, poor devil.'

'But what could you do? Even if you know where 'e was, they would not let 'im out – '

'We'd get him out,' said Simon, promptly. 'If we knew where he was, we'd apply for his release through his Embassy; he's an American. But we can't, you see, if we don't know! That's the trouble.'

'I will see what I can do,' she said suddenly. 'Kommissar Leshkin 'as a great deal to do with the prisons. What ees the name of your frien'?'

'Rex Van Ryn.' Simon spoke the syllables carefully. 'Here,' he produced a gold pencil from his waistcoat pocket, 'I'll write it down for you – no, better write it yourself – you'll understand your own writing better.' He gave her the pencil, and she wrote the name in a large round childish hand as he spelt it out for her.

She pushed the piece of paper into the top drawer of a small desk that stood near her.

'You won't forget?' Simon asked, anxiously.

'No,' she shook her dark head; 'eet may take a little time, but an occasion will come when I can ask Leshkin – 'e may not know 'imself, but 'e will tell me if 'e does.'

'I – er – suppose Kommissar Leshkin is a great friend of yours?' hazarded Simon.

She made a little grimace. 'What would you – 'ow old are you? Twenty-eight; thirty, perhaps; three, four years older than myself – it does not matter. You are a man of the world; you know it, then. All artistes must have a protector; eef I'ad lived twenty years ago it would 'ave been a Grand Duke; now eet is a Kommissar. What does eet matter; eet is life!'

Simon nodded with much understanding, but he went on quietly probing. 'Of course, I realise that, but – er – I mean, is it just a political alliance, or are you really friendly?'

'I 'ate 'im,' she said, suddenly, with a flash of her magnificent eyes; ' 'e is stupid, a bore, 'e 'as no delicacy of feeling, no finesse. In the revolution 'e did terrible things. Sometimes it makes me shudder to think 'ow 'is 'ands they are cover with blood – 'e was what you call "terrorist" then. It was 'im they send to crush the revolt in the Ukraine; eet was 'orrible that, the people that 'e kill, 'ole batches at a time. Most of those terrorist they are finish now, but not 'im; 'e is cunning, you understand, and strong, that is 'ow 'e keeps 'is place among the others; if 'e 'as any attraction for me, it is 'is strength, I think – but let us not talk of 'im.'

Unfortunately they were not destined to talk of anything else, for raised voices sounded at that moment in the hall outside, the door was thrust violently open, and the big, red-headed Kommissar strode in with a scowl on his face.

Simon got slowly to his feet, and Valeria Petrovna introduced them, recalling to Leshkin their former brief meeting in London.

'How do you do?' said Simon, in his most polite manner.

'Thank you – and yourself?' said Leshkin, without any trace of cordiality in his manner; 'do you stay long in Moskawa?'

'Don't know,' Simon replied, airily. 'I rather like Moscow, I may stay for a month.' He was well aware that he had done nothing so far to which the authorities could object, and behind his passport lay all the power and prestige that gives every British subject such a sense of security in any part of the world. Moreover, passport or no passport, Mr Simon Aron was not accustomed to being browbeaten. Between his rather narrow shoulders there lay a quiet but very determined courage, so, ignoring Leshkin, he turned with a smile to Valeria Petrovna and asked her to dine with him that night.

'But 'ow can I? You forget the theatre; but you shall call for me, and we will 'ave supper after. Leshkin,' she turned imperiously to the Kommissar, 'do not be a bear; Mistaire Aron is the guest of Russia – 'elp 'im with 'is furs, and show 'im out.'

Leshkin's small eyes narrowed beneath his beetling brows, his great jaw came forward with an ugly curve – for the fraction of a second it looked as though he were going to seize the frail Simon in his big powerful hands.

Valeria Petrovna stood between them, her eyes never left Leshkin's face. With a sharp movement she flicked the butt of her cigarette from the long slender holder. Suddenly the Kommissar relaxed, and with a little shrug of his giant shoulders, obeyed.

Chapter VIII

The Price of Information

When Simon got back to the Metropole he asked his guide to get seats for that evening's performance at the Moscow Arts Theatre, and on this occasion he and the Duke really made use of the tickets.

Both were lovers of the theatre, and enjoyed the finish and technique of the production; De Richleau was enraptured with Valeria Petrovna and her performance. In the first interval he turned to Simon with a sigh.

'Ah, my friend, why am I not twenty years younger? I envy you the friendship of this lovely lady.'

Simon laughed a little self-consciously. 'Well, I shouldn't care to have you as a rival, as it is!'

'You have no cause to fear on that score.' De Richleau laid his hand gently on Simon's arm. 'The *chère amie* of a friend is always to me in the same category as an aged aunt, and in any case I think it best that you should not present me; develop this friendship with Valeria Petrovna on your own; it will give more time for me to work on other lines.'

When the play was over the Duke made his way back to the hotel alone, and Simon waited at the stage door, as he had been instructed. Valeria Petrovna appeared in a remarkably short time, and whisked him back in her big car to her luxurious apartment and a charming *petit souper à deux*.

She was in marvellous spirits, the room rang with her laughter as she told him of the scene she had had after his departure that afternoon with Leshkin.

'You should 'ave seen 'im,' she declared. ''Ow 'e rage and stamp 'is big feet, but I tell 'im 'e is a great fool. I am no little chorus girl to be told 'oo I entertain; a few years ago, that was different; but now, I will 'ave 'oo I choose to be my frien'! Come, fill up your glass, little Simon, that red-'ed can go to 'ell!'

Simon filled up his glass, also Valeria Petrovna's. He was just a trifle anxious that, instead of going to hell, the large and brutal Kommissar might wait outside for him on the pavement, but he put such unpleasant thoughts quickly from him; fate had sent him this delightful companion, who glowed with life and beauty, the heavy curtains shut out the falling snow, the subdued lights lent an added richness to the warm luxury of the room. With all the hesitant, tactful charm with which he was so well endowed, Simon set himself to captivate the lovely Russian.

Even if Leshkin had meant to waylay his rival that night, the long wait in the bitter cold must have quenched his furious jealousy, for it was some hours before Simon left the apartment, and even then Valeria Petrovna was reluctant to let him go.

The next few days were crowded with incident for Simon. In the mornings with De Richleau he visited the places of interest in the city. It was necessary – indeed, vital – to sustain their character of intelligent and interested tourists. They visited the cathedrals and palaces – the latter now turned into museums – the Lenin Institute, and the Museum of the Revolution, formerly the English Club.

They kept a sharp look-out for the man with a cast in his eye on these expeditions, and caught a quick glimpse of him now and then, so they did not dare venture near the Tavern of the Howling Wolf, or communicate with Jack Straw in any way. They felt that he would manage to let them know if he received any news of Rex.

The Duke's shrewd, observant eyes missed nothing of Simon's restlessness and preoccupation during these days; it was he who planned a different excursion for each morning, and exerted himself to interest and amuse his friend, recreating for him in vivid pictures the changes that had taken place in Moscow since he had first visited it in the early 'eighties, as a small boy of nine.

At lunch-time they parted, for Simon and Valeria Petrovna lunched together every day and spent the afternoon sleigh-riding, driving in her big car out into the country, or skating on the frozen ponds. Simon was a most graceful skater, and the swift motion in perfect unison was a delight to both of them.

The guides did not bother Simon, as long as he was with the famous actress. Valeria Petrovna was the idol of the Russian public, and Simon shone with her reflected glory in the eyes of the two interpreters.

He dined each evening with the Duke, and they went alternately to a theatre or the opera, the latter being one of Simon's greatest interests in life. Afterwards he would call for his beautiful lady at the Arts Theatre, and have supper with her in her apartment, only to leave her in the small hours of the morning.

Six days went by in this manner, but they had failed to secure any further information regarding Rex. De Richleau persisted in his inquiries through the Embassies and Legations, and also through various American and English trading houses to which he obtained introductions; but without result. Rex might have been spirited away by a djinn for all the traces he had left behind him. Simon raised the question tentatively with Valeria Petrovna several times, but she always brushed it aside quickly.

'I 'ave told you – it is not a thing which can be done at once. Leshkin must be in a good 'umour. What do you say – "wheedled", is it not? For this information which you want, at present it is 'opeless – 'e is so jealous, 'e is like a bear.' Then, suspiciously: 'Why are you in such a 'urry – are you not 'appy with me?'

Simon hastened to assure her. They had grown very intimate these two – a strong mutual attraction and many hours spent alone together for a number of days in succession is the soil on which intimacy thrives. Never before had Simon met a woman who had, at the same time, her beauty, her intellect, and her vitality.

Constantly he put away from him the thought that in a week or so at most he would have to leave Moscow. He grudged every moment of time not spent in her company, and bitterly resented the fact that they were in Moscow and not in London, Berlin, or Paris. In any of the latter cities he could have heaped flowers and gifts upon her – it would then have been *his* car in which they were driven about, *his* wines that they would have drunk together, but the limitations of life in Moscow taxed to the utmost his ability to display one-tenth of his innate generosity.

She was appreciative of the ingenuity that he showed to give her pleasure, but her generosity matched his own and she delighted to entertain him as her favoured guest. His subtle brain and mental gymnastics delighted her intellect, his charming humour and diffident, thoughtful kindness made irresistible appeal to her heart.

Kommissar Leshkin hovered in the background of the affair, arriving sometimes unexpectedly at Valeria Petrovna's flat, or glaring at them from a distance with his red-rimmed eyes when they were lunching at the hotel. Simon disliked the man intensely, and Leshkin displayed an equal hate, but Valeria Petrovna seemed unperturbed. She mocked the Kommissar in her soft Russian tongue when he came on his blustering visits; and Simon smiled his little amused smile as he watched her handling of this undoubtedly clever and powerful man.

It was the seventh evening that Simon and Valeria Petrovna had spent thus delightfully together; he thought that she seemed worried and depressed when he fetched her after the theatre, and taking both her hands in his he asked her gently what it was that troubled her.

'Alas, *mon ami*,' she said Sadly. 'I fear that I must love you very much.'

'Darling,' Simon murmured, clasping her hands more tightly, and gently kissing their rosy palms.

'Yes, I am sad – for I know now where is your frien'.'

Simon's eyes lifted quickly. 'He – he's not dead, is he?' he asked with a sudden fear,

'No, it was as you suppose, 'e is in a prison of the State.'

'But that's splendid – do tell me where!'

'I will tell you later,' she said with a sigh. 'The night is yet young – you shall know all before you go.'

'*But,* darling, why are you so sad about it? I mean, we'll get Rex out, that is, if we can – and even if I have to go back to London I'll come back here later – next month. After all, Moscow's only two days' journey from London by 'plane.'

'Ah, that is what makes me so sad, my Simon. I 'ave 'ad to pay a price for this knowledge about your frien'.'

'How – what exactly do you mean?' he asked anxiously.

She shrugged her beautiful shoulders. 'It was Leshkin 'oo tell me what I want to know. I 'ave been at 'im for the last two days.'

'I didn't know you had spoken to him yet.'

'How should you, little one? But I have promise you that I will 'elp you find your frien', and I ave succeeded!'

'But – er – what did Leshkin want?'

She smiled, though tears were brightening her eyes. 'That I promise 'im that you leave Moskawa tomorrow, and not return.'

For a time they sat silent; both had known that in any case Simon's stay in Moscow must be limited, but each had put that thought firmly at the back of their minds. And now the moment had come it found them utterly unprepared in the first mad rush of their passion for each other.

'You can come to London,' he said at last, suddenly brightening.

'Not for a long time, *Galoubchick,* it is so recent since I 'ave been there – the Soviet do not like their artistes to go to other countries. Besides, I 'ave my duty to the Russian people. My art is not of myself – it belongs to them!'

'I could meet you in Berlin.'

'Perhaps – we will see, but tell me, what will you do about your frien'?'

'Apply for his release or public trial, through his Embassy,' Simon suggested, but he had little faith in the idea.

'That will be of no use; officially the Kommissars will deny all knowledge of 'is existence. 'E was found wandering in forbidden territory. That is the bad trouble. 'E may know things that the Kommissars do not wish the world to know.'

'You – er – haven't promised that I shall leave Russia, have you? Only Moscow – '

She smiled. 'No, it is Moskawa only that you must leave, but I can guess, I think, what you will do – you will go searching for your frien' in the forbidden territory, like the balalaika player of the old days who search for your King Richard the Lion-'earted. Oh, my little Simon, it is you 'oo are Lion-'earted, but I am frightened for you!'

Simon laughed, a little bashfully. 'Doesn't seem much else to do, does there?'

She left the divan, and went over to an Empire escritoire in which she unlocked a drawer, taking from it a small, square ikon set with pearls. She looked at it carefully for a moment, studying the delicate oval miniature of the Madonna and Child which it contained – then she brought it over to him. 'Take this, *Batushka,* and carry it always with you. It will be of great protection to you.'

'Thank you, my sweet – why are you so good to me?' Simon took the sacred picture. 'I – er – didn't know that you were religious – I didn't think that Russia was religious any more.'

'You are wrong,' she said, quietly. 'Many of the popes have been done away with – they were evil, drunken men, unfitted for the service of God. That ees a good thing, but there is freedom of thought in Russia now. One can follow a religion if one will, and Russia – *Holy Russia* – is unchanging beneath the surface. With a few exceptions, all Russians carry God in their 'eart!'

Simon nodded. 'I think I understand – anyhow, I shall always keep this with me.'

'Eef it ees that you are in what you call a "muddle", send the little ikon back to me. Look!' She took it again, quickly, and pressed a hidden spring. 'In 'ere you can send a little letter – nobody will find it – all Russia knows Valeria Petrovna. It will come to me surely, wherever I am.'

'Mightn't it be stolen?' asked Simon, doubtfully. 'I mean these pearls – they're real.'

'They are small, and only of little value – also you will say to 'im 'oo brings it: "Valeria Petrovna will give you a thousand roubles if you bring this safe to 'er."'

'You've been wonderful to me,' said Simon, drawing her towards him. 'How can I ever tell you what I feel?'

The late dawn of the winter's morning was already rising over the snow-white streets, and the ice-floes of the Moskawa river, when Simon

Aron slipped quietly out of the block of flats which contained Valeria Petrovna's apartment; but he left with the knowledge that Rex was held prisoner amid the desolate wastes of the Siberian snows, in the city of Tobolsk.

Chapter IX

Beyond the Pale

The Duke and Simon were walking in the great open courtyards that lie between the many buildings within the Kremlin walls.

It was the Duke's quizzical sense of humour that had prompted him to choose this particular spot – the very heart and brain of Soviet Russia – in which to hold a conference, having for its end a conspiracy against the Soviet State.

When a tired but cheerful Simon had pushed a slip of paper across the breakfast table that morning, bearing the one word 'Tobolsk', he had only nodded and said: 'Let us go and see the Kremlin this morning.'

'Tobolsk,' said the Duke as they strolled through the first courtyard, 'is on the other side of the Ural mountains.'

'Yes,' Simon agreed, dismally. 'Sounds an awfully long way away.'

'It is about thirteen hundred miles, that is to say, a little less than the distance from here to London.'

Simon groaned. 'Somewhere in Siberia, isn't it?'

'It is, my friend.' De Richleau smiled. 'But Siberia is a large place – let us be thankful that poor Rex is not imprisoned at Tomsk, which is two thousand – or Yakutsk, which is four thousand miles away!'

'Well yes, I am glad of that, but how do we get there?'

De Richleau looked round carefully, to make sure that they could not be overheard. 'I spent some little time,' he said, slowly, 'before we left the hotel, examining the maps and time-tables that are provided. Tobolsk is unfortunately not on the main Trans-Siberian line – it lies about a hundred and twenty miles to the north of the railway; there is, I find, a local line from the little town of Tyumen, which is just on the border of Siberia and Russia proper, but the main-line trains do not halt there. There is another local line running back north-westward from Omsk, but that would mean going a further four hundred miles into Siberia to get to Omsk, and the loss of at least a day.'

'Seems a difficult place to get at!' Simon interjected.

'It is. I think that the best way would be by the Trans-Siberian to Sverdlovsk. That is the last town of any importance in European Russia, and all the main-line trains stop there. From there we could take the Trans-Siberian branch-line which heads direct for Tobolsk, but which is not yet quite completed. It comes to an end at the west bank of the Tavda river, *but,* there is only a hundred miles between the Tavda and Tobolsk, and it is almost certain that there will be a service of sleighs between the dead end of the railway and the town.'

'You – er – couldn't find out definitely?'

'No, nothing at all about the unfinished branch from Sverdlovsk or the branch-line from Tyumen, and furthermore we must be very careful in our inquiries not to arouse suspicions that we have any idea of venturing outside the prescribed limits for tourists.'

'I – er – suppose – ' Simon hesitated, 'the American Embassy couldn't do anything?'

The Duke laughed. 'How can they, my dear fellow; their position today is the same as yesterday. If we had actual proof that Rex was at Tobolsk it would be a different matter, but to charge the Soviet with holding him there on the information given you by Valeria Petrovna would only provoke another denial. They would move him at once to another prison. The only way is to go there and find out the truth – the problem is how to get there. Personally I favour the plan of going to Sverdlovsk and then trusting to chance.'

'Wonder if they'll let us?' said Simon, doubtfully. 'I haven't seen anything about it in the booklets that they issue.'

'That we must find out, but, in any case, they will not prevent me taking a ticket through to Vladivostock, and as all the trains stop at Sverdlovsk, I can drop off there. I think I should tell you, my friend, that it is not my intention that you should accompany me on this journey.'

'Oh! Why?' Simon's eyes flickered towards his friend.

'There are a variety of reasons,' said De Richleau, quietly. 'You are, I think, very happily engaged here, in Moscow – it would be a pity to curtail your visit. It was by your quick wit that we discovered Jack Straw, which, in turn, supplied us with the reason for Rex's visit to Russia. It is you, again, who have discovered his whereabouts – whereas, so far, I have done nothing. It is my turn now. When I step off the train at Sverdlovsk, I shall, I think, be outside the law; it would be a great comfort to me to have you here in Moscow, safe and free, and able, if I do not return in a short time, to stir up the Embassies on my behalf. It would be sheer foolishness for both of us to run our heads into the noose.'

'Um – I agree,' said Simon quickly, 'very silly. It's a good thing that you know the people at the Embassies, too – you'll have much more pull than I should. Obviously, you stay here, and I go to Tobolsk!'

'But, my friend – do not be foolish!' De Richleau frowned.

'I'm not.' Simon gave his jerky little laugh. 'Now I'll tell you. I didn't get that information about Rex for nothing. Valeria Petrovna got it from Leshkin, but he made her promise that I should be out of Moscow by tonight, so that settles it!'

'Indeed!' said the Duke, with surprise. 'But, even so, I fear it does not solve our problem. How will you manage in Tobolsk? You can speak no Russian!'

'Um!' Simon was a little dashed. 'That's a bit awkward!'

'We will both go,' said the Duke, with decision, 'and I will confess that I shall be more glad to have you with me.'

'Well, to tell you the truth, I should simply hate to go alone.'

'That is settled then! Let us go to the head office of the Intourist. We will talk about a change of plans, and that we should like to go into Siberia. We will not talk of Tobolsk, but of Irkutsk – that is some fifteen hundred miles farther on; it is quite natural that we should wish to see it, as it is a wonderful city in the very heart of Siberia, near Lake Baikal, just north of the Mongolian Plain. It is there that all the political exiles used to make their homes before the Revolution. It was a centre of enlightenment and culture.'

'I thought they were sent to the North,' said Simon. 'To the salt mines and all sorts of terrible things.'

De Richleau shook his head. 'Dear me, no, that is quite a mistaken idea; certain of the convicts – real felons and dangerous criminals – were, it is true, sent to the mines, but the politicals were only banished to the other side of the Urals, where they were free to trade and carry on their professions, moving from town to town, or settling in communities with similar aspirations to their own.'

When they arrived at the bureau of the Intourist the Duke announced their plans. The lean, shrewd-eyed man who interviewed them was not particularly helpful. 'Irkutsk? Yes, it was possible to go there – but there were many more interesting towns in Russia itself – Leningrad, now?'

'No,' the Duke truthfully replied. He had just come from Leningrad.

'Well then, Kiev, Odessa, Karkoff, Stalingrad?'

No, De Richleau and his friend thought of seeing all those wonderful places on their return – they had ample time – but above all things at present they desired to see Irkutsk!

Well, since they wished it, it could be done. The lean man proceeded to make out the tickets. Did they wish to leave tonight, Thursday, or on Sunday – or would they wait till Tuesday? The service ran thrice weekly.

Tonight? Just as they wished. The train left the Smolenski Station at fifteen hours thirty, and the Saverinii at seventeen fifty-five. They would motor to the Saverinii? True it was a big difference; there was over an hour's wait there, to take on mails, but they were advised to be there at least three-quarters of an hour before the time of departure – passports would have to be examined and luggage registered. He would have the tickets endorsed by the authorities and sent to their hotel.

'Do there happen to be any places of interest that we can see upon our way?' the Duke inquired in seeming innocence. 'Do we go through Niji-Novgorod?'

The man shook his head. 'No, you pass far to the north of Niji, going via Danilov, Bui, Viatka, Perm, Sverdlovsk, Omsk, Krasnoyarsk and Kansk.'

'What of Perm – that is a fine town, is it not?'

'Yes, you could break your journey there if you wish.'

'And Omsk – that again is a great town?'

'Yes, there also you could stop – but there is not much to see in these places.'

'And Tobolsk – do we stop at Tobolsk?'

'No, that is not on the Trans-Siberian line.'

'Ah, what a pity.' De Richleau's face took on a rueful look. 'Always, since I was a little boy, I have wanted to go to Tobolsk – it is, I think, the romance of the name. Is there no place at which we can change trains to go there? I should so greatly like to spend just one day in Tobolsk!'

The man looked away, impatiently. 'It is impossible – a long, uncomfortable journey. Besides, it is a wild place – not fit for foreigners, and the Soviet Government considers itself responsible for all travellers who are its guests.'

'Dear me, how sad,' said the Duke, politely. 'We will then go to Irkutsk and perhaps break our journey at Omsk and Perm on our way back.'

After they had left the Intourist bureau, Simon asked, softly: 'Why didn't you take tickets to Sverlovsk or Ekaterinburg, or whatever it's called – that's really as far as we want to go!'

'Because, my friend, there would most certainly have been one of these eternal guides to meet us there if we had. Even if we had managed to evade his attentions the alarm would have been given at once. We arrive at Sverdlovsk at 7.43 on Saturday morning. That is roughly a day-and-a-half's journey – the train does not get to Irkutsk till midday on Tuesday – that is more than three days later. If we are fortunate the hue and cry will not begin until the guide who is detailed to meet us at Irkutsk finds that we are not on the train.'

'What about the officials on the train?' demanded Simon.

'True – that is a difficulty to be faced, but if we can overcome it we should gain three days' grace, and much can be done in three days. But let us not talk here, we will go down to the bank of the river where there are fewer people.'

They walked for some time in silence, and when they reached the unfrequented embankment under the walls of the Kremlin, the Duke continued: 'Now, we must make plans seriously. You realise of course that we shall have to leave the bulk of our baggage behind?'

Simon thought ruefully of his beautifully fitted dressing-case. 'I suppose they'll pinch that when they find out?'

'No.' The Duke's eyes twinkled. 'We can defeat them there. We shall take one suitcase each, and that only for show. The rest of our luggage we will deposit this afternoon at the Legation that you know of, then, if we get out of this wretched country, it can be returned to us through the diplomatic bag.'

'Well,' Simon grinned, much relieved, 'I'm glad about that. I should have hated to see Leshkin with my dressing-case!'

'We shall have to get knapsacks,' the Duke continued, 'to hold all that is essential, and abandon our suitcases when we leave the train.'

'Where do we *get* the knapsacks from?'

'There are several places in the Kitaigorod where we can get them – that is the old town, where the narrow streets are.'

'And then?'

'The next thing is supplies. Luckily I brought certain things in case of such an emergency. We will buy some chocolate here, also some smoked ham and biscuits. Are you having a farewell luncheon with your lovely lady?'

'No, got all that over last night – thought it best.'

'And you were right,' the Duke agreed. Then, suddenly, but very low: 'Hush! I think our wall-eyed friend is behind us again.'

Simon allowed a minute to elapse and then glanced round casually; sure enough, it was the same wizened little man. Today he was dressed in the slovenly uniform of a Red Guard, but they knew his face too well to mistake him. They quickened their pace, and in the turning and twisting of the narrow streets, succeeded in shaking him off before they reached the Kitaigorod.

By the time that they got back to the hotel they found that the tickets had been delivered, duly endorsed for Irkutsk. In the afternoon they packed and deposited their luggage with the ever-obliging Señor Rosas. Five o' clock found them standing on the Saverinii Station platform, two suitcases beside them – the principal contents of which were food and the knapsacks into which it was to be transferred at Sverdlovsk.

They found their compartment on the train without difficulty. Being of the 'Direct Communication, 1st Category', it contained two berths only and a private toilette, and, owing to the wide gauge of the Russian railways, when the berths were stowed away it made a large, comfortable coupé.

Punctually, at seventeen hours fifty-five, the long train with its powerful engine began, almost imperceptibly, to move and, gradually gathering speed, started on its eleven-day journey to Vladivostock at the other end of Asia.

They settled themselves comfortably on the wide seats, and the Duke took out Norman Douglas's *South Wind,* which he was reading for the fourth time. Simon gazed out into the swiftly moving darkness and thought a little wistfully of these last unforgettable days in Moscow, and the loveliness of the smiling eyes of Valeria Petrovna. He found difficulty in realising that it was really Simon Aron who was even now speeding towards unknown adventures. His heart gave a little bump as he thought of what might lie before them – rescue, hardship by cold and hunger, flight for life, perhaps, and a little smile curved his lips as he found himself humming a tune. It was: '*Malbrouck s'en vat en guerre!*'

They dined better in the restaurant car than they had in the hotel, and Simon, at least, was grateful for an early bed.

When they awoke next day they had left Bui far behind and were crossing a seemingly interminable plain. Simon started to get up, but the Duke forbade him.

'You are ill, my friend,' he said, quickly.

'Ner,' said Simon.

'But yes,' said the Duke. 'You are feverish!'

'Never felt better in my life,' said Simon.

'That is a pity, since I'm afraid you've got to pass the day in bed!'

Simon grinned understandingly. He knew De Richleau to be a wily man, and felt certain that this was a part of some scheme which the Duke had hatched in the night to get them safely off the train at Sverlovsk.

When the train steward arrived with the news that breakfast was ready, De Richleau held a long conversation with him in Russian. He was a fat, jolly man, and seemed much concerned. Simon groaned and made himself look as ill as possible, but later he supplemented the weak tea and toast which the sympathetic steward brought him, with several rolls that the Duke had smuggled out of the restaurant car.

All that morning they rolled through the unending plain, until at a little after half past one they came to a halt at Viatka, where the Duke got out to stretch his legs. Simon, of course, had to remain in bed, and his luncheon was, perforce, meagre.

The scenery in the afternoon was more varied; they ran for many miles through the valley of the Chepsa river, but the early winter's dusk had blotted out the landscape by four in the afternoon. It was quite late at night when the train snorted into Perm, but another consultation had been held by De Richleau and the jolly steward earlier in the evening, and certain drugs were procured during the halt, so the drowsy Simon found himself compelled to sit up and pretend to swallow capsules as the train steamed out. The Duke also took his temperature with great gravity in front of the now solemn and anxious steward.

This second night the train laboured and puffed its way through the Urals, but in the black darkness they could see nothing of the scenery. At a little after six the Duke woke Simon and said, with his grey eyes twinkling: 'My poor friend – you are very, very ill I fear – dying almost, I think.'

Simon groaned, in truth this time, but De Richleau put on his dressing-gown and fetched the steward. 'My friend,' he cried in Russian. 'He will die – he is almost already dead!'

'What can we do?' said the fat steward, sympathetically shrugging his broad shoulders.

'We must get off at Sverdlovsk,' said the Duke.

'You cannot,' said the man. 'Your tickets are marked for Irkutsk!'

'What does that matter?' protested the Duke. 'The only hope for him is hospital.'

The man shook his head. 'The station authorities – they will not permit.'

'It is three more days to Irkutsk,' said De Richleau, almost weeping. 'You cannot let him die on the train!'

'No, no, he cannot die on the train!' agreed the steward, obviously frightened and superstitious. 'It might mean an accident!'

'Then we must get off at Sverdlovsk!'

'You must see the officials, then – it is the only way.'

'Bah! the *Tchinovinks!*' De Richleau cried. 'The officials, what use are they? All your life you have lived under the *Tchinovinks,* and what have they done for you? Tsarist or Bolshevist – they are all the same – delay, delay, delay, and in the meantime my poor friend dies. It must not be!'

'No, it must not be – ' echoed the steward, fired by the Duke's harangue. 'The *Tchinovinks* are either rogues or fools. I have it! Always before we arrive at Sverdlovsk we draw into the goods-yard. You shall descend there!'

'Is it possible?' exclaimed the Duke.

'But yes, it shall be done!'

'My brother!' cried De Richleau, flinging his arms round the fat man's neck!

'Little father!' exclaimed the steward, using in his emotion an expression that must have been foreign to his lips for many years.

'Come, let us dress him,' said the Duke, and without warning Simon found himself seized; he played up gallantly, letting his head loll helplessly from side to side, and groaning a little. It was a longish job, but at last they had him dressed and propped up in a corner.

De Richleau packed for both of them – gathering their few belongings together in the two suitcases the steward had left them.

They jogged on for a while through the grey light of the coming dawn, and at last, after a series of shrill whistles, the train came to a standstill; the steward returned, and with breathless mutterings in Russian, helped the Duke to get the apparently comatose Simon out of the compartment and along the corridor, then down the steps at the end of the carriage. He pushed their bags out after them, and, recognising in the half light the high value of the banknote which De Richleau thrust into his hand, broke into voluble protestations of gratitude.

The Duke looked quickly about him; the dark masses of buildings seen indistinctly, and the glimmer of lights a few hundred yards ahead, was evidently the main station. They stood in the snow. About them were timber stacks, coal dumps, and immediately in their rear some rough sheds. With a heave the train moved slowly on – the steward still leaning from the window. As it gathered speed and disappeared into the gloom, De Richleau ceased to pretend that he was supporting Simon.

'Come,' he said. 'This way – quickly!' and seizing one of the bags he headed for the cover of the sheds. Simon gripped the other and followed. They were not more than half way across the yard when Simon's quick ear caught a crunching sound, as of someone stumbling suddenly over cinders. He whipped round, just in time to see in the semi-darkness a figure that had evidently leapt off the last coach of the train, scuttle behind one of the stacks of timber.

'We're spotted,' he gasped.

'No matter. Leave this to me,' said the Duke, as he darted behind the shed. 'Here, take this,' and he thrust the other suitcase into Simon's free hand.

Simon stood, helpless and gaping, the two heavy bags, one in each hand, weighing him down. De Richleau flattened himself against the side of the shed – they waited breathlessly.

A soft, padding sound came to their ears, as of someone running on the thick carpet of snow; a second later a small man came round the corner full upon them. He made a rapid motion of recoil, but it was too late, the Duke's left hand shot out and caught him by the throat. The small man did not utter a sound – he stared with terrified, bulging eyes over De Richleau's shoulder, full at Simon, who saw at once that in his left eye there was a cast!

Then there happened a thing which shocked and horrified the mild, peace-loving soul of Simon Aron, for he had never witnessed such a thing before. With almost incredible swiftness the Duke's right hand left the pocket of his greatcoat – it flew back to the utmost stretch of his shoulder, holding a long, thin, glittering blade – and then, with a dull thud, it hit the little man in the side, just under the heart. His eyes seemed for a second to start out of their sockets at Simon – then his head fell forward, and he dropped limp and soundless at De Richleau's feet.

'Good God!' said Simon, in a breathless whisper, utterly aghast. 'You've killed him.'

The Duke gave a grim laugh as he spurned the body with his foot. 'What else was there to do, my friend – it was either him or us. We are in Soviet Russia, and when we stepped off that train, we placed ourselves beyond the pale.'

Chapter X

'Where the Railway Ends'

Simon felt his knees grow weak beneath him – he was almost overcome with nausea; he was not frightened for himself, only appalled at this sudden slaying of a fellow human without warning. 'It's – it's awful,' he stammered.

'There, there, my son,' said De Richleau, soothingly. 'Do not waste your great heart on this scum. You would not pity him if you had seen all that I have – a thousand horrors committed at the instigation of your friend Leshkin and his kind. It is a nightmare that I would forget.'

Simon put down the suitcases and drew a breath. He was a natural philosopher, and once recovered from the shock, accepted the awful thing as part and parcel of this astounding adventure into which he had been drawn.

The door of the shed was fastened only by a piece of rope, and they found it to be filled with old farm implements.

Quickly, and as noiselessly as possible, they moved a stack of bent and broken shovels – carried in the body of the wall-eyed man, and piled the shovels over him until he was completely hidden; they secured the door more firmly, and, having obliterated the blood marks in the snow, hurried through the maze of wood stacks towards another group of sheds, the roofs of which were rapidly becoming plainer in the growing light.

The goods-yard seemed deserted, and they were fortunate in finding an empty shed. Once inside it De Richleau flung his suitcase on the ground, and, kneeling down, commenced to unpack. Simon followed his example. In a few minutes they had stuffed the rucksacks with the supplies of food and their most necessary belongings. Next they defaced the labels on their bags and stowed them in an opening between two sheds, heaping stones and rubble on top to hide them from view.

Wherever they moved they left large footprints in the snow, and Simon, greatly perturbed, pointed out their tracks to the Duke, but De Richleau did not seem unduly worried.

'Look at the snow,' he waved his hand about him. 'They will be covered in an hour.' And, with the coming of day, the snow had begun to fall again, softly, silently, in great white, drifting petals that settled as they fell, increasing the heavy band of white on every roof and ledge.

'Well, I never thought I should be glad to see snow,' said Simon, with his little nervous laugh. 'What do we do now?'

De Richleau adjusted his rucksack on his shoulders; he frowned.

'We have a difficult task before us – while attracting as little attention as possible, we must find out how the trains run on the branch line to the Tavda river, and then secure seats.'

'How far is it – I mean to Tobolsk?' Simon inquired.

'Two hundred miles to the dead end of the railway, and a further hundred across country – but we have at least one piece of good fortune.'

'What's that?'

'That we should have arrived here early in the morning; if there is a train today we cannot have missed it!'

'Today?' echoed Simon, aghast. 'Aren't there trains every day?'

De Richleau laughed. 'My dear fellow, it is not Brighton that we are going to. In such a place as this, trains run only twice weekly, or at best every other day!'

Simon grunted. 'Thank God we didn't arrive in the middle of the night, then.'

'Yes, we should have been frozen before the morning.'

While they were talking they had left the goods-yard and turned down a road leading away from the station. There were no houses, only timber-yards and back lots.

After they had walked about half a mile De Richleau spoke again. 'I think we might now turn back. Our train should have halted here for about twenty minutes, and it must be forty at least since our good friend the steward set us down.'

'Poor chap, I hope he doesn't get it in the neck over this job.'

'Let us hope not. If he has any sense he will say that we left the train without his knowledge. They are certain to question him at Irkutsk, but if he says that he did not see us after dinner last night, they cannot put the blame on him.'

Simon began sawing his arms across his narrow chest. 'My God, it's cold,' he said suddenly. 'I could do with some breakfast!'

De Richleau laughed. 'About that we shall see. We are coming to a cluster of houses, and that building on the left looks like the station. I should think there is certain to be some sort of inn near it.'

He was right; they found a small third-rate hostelry, of which the only occupant was a solemn peasant seated near the great china stove, sipping his tea and staring into vacancy.

The Duke clapped his hands loudly, and the landlord appeared, a clean, honest-looking fellow in a starched white blouse. After some questioning he disappeared, presently to return with two plates of eggs; true, they were fried in lard, but the two travellers were so hungry and cold that almost any food would have been welcome, even the black rye bread and bitter tea which accompanied the eggs.

When they had finished De Richleau drew the landlord into conversation. They were Germans, the Duke said; fur buyers, seeking new sources of supply. How were the markets in Sverdlovsk for such commodities?

'Bad,' said the landlord. 'Bad; the trappers will not go out any more. Why should they?' he shrugged; 'the Government will not pay them for their skins, and there are no longer the rich who will buy. They go out for a few weeks every season that they may catch enough to keep their families from starving by exchanging the skins for corn and oil. For the rest – they sleep!'

The Duke nodded. 'You speak truly. Why should a man work more than he need if there is no prospect of his becoming rich? What of the north? Think you our chances would be better there?'

'I do not think so. Not if what one hears is true. Things may be better in the towns that lie to the east, perhaps, but I do not know.'

'To the eastward?' said the Duke softly. 'You mean in Omsk?'

The landlord shrugged. 'There, and at other places in Siberia, there are not so many *Tchinovinks* as here, trading is more free.'

'What of Tobolsk?'

'That would perhaps be the best place of all if you could get there, but Tobolsk is in the forbidden territory.'

'The forbidden territory? What is that?' asked the Duke with a frown.

The man shrugged again. 'It is some madness of the *Tchinovinks*; a great area, where, without special papers, no man may go – but they are the lords, and it is useless to protest.'

'If we could get within reasonable distance of Tobolsk we could send messengers,' the Duke suggested, 'and the traders could bring their furs for us to see.'

'That should be possible. There is a train which goes to Turinsk; farther than that you may not go; the railway to Tobolsk is finished, but it is for the officials and the military only.'

'And how often do the trains run?'

'It used to be only once weekly, but since the line is finished it is every other day. Many military and *Tchinovinks* go through.'

'Is there a train today?'

'What is today?' the man asked vaguely.

'It is Saturday.'

'Yes, there is a train – it leaves at midday.'

'Do you know how long it takes?'

'To Tobolsk, about eight hours – to Turinsk, some five hours, perhaps.'

'And are permissions necessary?' De Richleau asked casually.

'It depends,' said the landlord; 'for Turinsk no special permission is necessary, but in the case of foreigners I should think your tickets would require endorsement; however, it is of no great moment; the *Tchinovinks* hate to be bothered. They sleep all day; if there is trouble, give a few roubles and all will be well.'

'Thank you, my friend. In that case I think we will go to Turinsk on the midday train, and, if we may, we will remain under your hospitable roof until then. We shall require another meal before we go.'

'Welcome, and again welcome,' said the landlord, with all the inherent politeness of the peasant.

'All is well.' The Duke turned to Simon as he spoke, for the latter had not understood one word of this conversation. 'There is a train at midday which will take us as far as Turinsk; after that the forbidden territory begins, and we shall have to use our wits.'

'How about tickets?' asked Simon, doubtfully.

'Bluff, my friend. I gather that the officials here are lazy and careless, and open to bribes, very different to those in Moscow.'

'Better say we left the other tickets in the train!'

'Yes, that is an excellent idea.'

'I've been wondering about that Shulimoff treasure,' said Simon, in a low voice. 'Do you think Rex got it before they got him?'

'How can we say?' De Richleau raised his slanting eyebrows. 'We know that Shulimoff had estates near Tobolsk. Evidently the treasure must be buried there, or Rex would never have ventured into this dangerous area.'

'Fun if we could take a few souvenirs out of this rotten country!' Simon chuckled into his hand.

'Let us not think of that. We shall have our work cut out to get Rex out of the clutch of these devils!'

At eleven o' clock the landlord produced two wooden bowls containing a kind of stew, mainly composed of skinny mutton and barley. With it was the inevitable rye bread and bitter tea.

In spite of the unappetising nature of the fare they both ate heartily, since they realised that it might well be the last food they would touch for many hours.

When they had finished they paid the landlord handsomely, and crossed the road to the station. At the booking office there were difficulties. The Duke explained that through some misunderstanding their baggage, and with it their tickets, had been carried on that morning by the main-line train, and that they were merchants from the great fur market of Lemberg, anxious to trade. There was much argument, but De Richleau had been clever in that he had not allowed much time before the train was due to depart. It was too late for them to return into the town for an examination by senior officials – their passports were in order – only the tickets were missing.

At the sight of the Duke's wallet stuffed with money, the man gave way. 'It could be managed, perhaps,' he said. 'It was irregular, of course – also the tickets were expensive! The fares, in fact, had more than doubled since the tickets were printed. They were old stock.'

So the affair was settled, and the Duke and Simon took their seats in the train for Turinsk. In this branch-line train there was none of the comfort they had found on the Trans-Continental. Hard seats, and a foul wash-place – a crowded compartment where the mingled odours of unwashed humanity fought with that of the smaller birds and beasts, which seemed to be the principal impedimenta of their travelling companions.

'Well, this is another stage on our journey as good as accomplished,' said De Richleau, as the train drew out of Sverdlovsk, only twenty minutes late in starting.

'Um,' said Simon. 'But we're going to be in a muddle when we get to Turinsk!'

'On the contrary – ' De Richleau disagreed. 'There we shall be able to show our tickets and get accommodation, which we could not do here.'

'You've forgotten one thing.'

'And what is that?'

'We were counting on a sleigh service to get us where we want to go, weren't we?'

'Yes.'

'Well – if you're right about the railway line being finished, there won't be any sleigh service – and it's quite certain that the people at Turinsk won't let us go on in the train.'

'That's true,' said the Duke, thoughtfully. '*Mon Dieu*, how these people stink!'

'Pretty awful,' Simon agreed, and then both he and the Duke lapsed into a thoughtful silence.

The scenery was completely different from that which they had seen the day before; the train puffed and snorted excitedly as it wound its way, at a fair speed, in and out along the snow-covered valleys; they had passed the tops of the Urals during the night, and were now descending through the foothills on the eastern side.

The snow had ceased falling, and the sun came out at midday, but now, in the early afternoon, it was sinking rapidly, and dusk was upon them when they reached Turinsk just before five.

Turinsk seemed little more than a long, straggling village. The train actually ran through the high street, in the most populous part of which it came to a jerky halt.

Nobody asked for or examined their tickets, but Simon noticed that several men with lanterns went carefully along the train, searching each compartment to see that it was empty, and the soldiers and officials, who remained seated in the coach nearest to the engine, had their papers inspected before the train moved on.

The two fur traders from Lemberg made their way to the hotel, a rambling, wooden building, and ordered the best meal that the place could provide. They had decided, at all costs, to get hold of a sleigh that night and continue their journey. All too soon Soviet officials would be on their track; every moment of their precious start must be utilised. De Richleau asked the landlord if it were possible to obtain a sleigh.

'At this hour?' He seemed amazed and hurt. Where did they wish to go? Was not his hotel good enough?

The Duke, on this occasion, told a completely different story. He said that he had just come in on the train from Sverdlovsk, and that on his arrival he had been handed a telegram to say that his wife had had a serious accident. He must return at once.

'You can get the train back at three o' clock tomorrow – ' the landlord suggested. 'It leaves Tobolsk at an hour before midday, and arrives in Sverdlovsk at eight o' clock.'

'I must go tonight!' The Duke seemed distraught with anxiety. 'Please help me, and get a sleigh – then tomorrow I can be beside my poor wife.'

'I cannot.' The man shook his head. 'Tomorrow – yes, you shall have my cousin's *troika* – a fine affair. He will drive you himself, but he lives six versts from here. I cannot send for him tonight.'

'In that case I might as well wait for the train,' the Duke protested. 'It would be quicker in the end!'

'You speak truly,' the landlord nodded. 'It is sad about your wife, but there is nothing I can do.'

At that they had to leave it. 'Come,' said the Duke to Simon. 'Let's walk down the village street. It is possible that there may be another inn at which we may have better luck.'

They shouldered their knapsacks, and left the hotel under the land-lord's disapproving eye. He looked as though he guessed their purpose.

Outside the darkness of the long Siberian night had already fallen, lights glimmered from the narrow windows of the houses casting a beam here and there on the crisp, frozen snow. The air was cold, but invigorating like wine, the night fine, cloudless and starlit.

Not many people were about, and to their disappointment they failed to find an inn of any size. As they were walking back to the hotel, a fine sleigh passed them at a trot, and pulled up in front of a small brick building, which had an official air.

De Richleau hurried forward, and was in time to intercept the driver before he entered the building. The man, a tall fellow with high Mongolian cheekbones, was tying his reins to a wooden post.

'Will you hire me your *troika*?' the Duke asked at once.

The man looked up in surprise. 'But no,' he said. 'This *troika* is not for hire.'

The Duke launched into the same story again, of his sick wife and the urgent necessity of his immediate return to Sverdlovsk.

The tall man was not impressed. He shrugged his shoulders and entered the little brick building.

It was a fine *troika*, with three well-fed horses, the arch above the centre horse brightly painted and with little hanging bells; fur rugs were scattered over the interior.

De Richleau made up his mind instantly. 'Jump in,' he cried, giving Simon a little push. 'He may be back in a minute.'

Even as he spoke he was untying the reins, and scrambling into the driver's seat; with one crack of the whip they were careering down the street, the sleigh bells jingling loudly.

The owner came running out of the building, shouting and gesticulating as he ran, but there was nothing to bar their progress, and they very soon had left the town behind.

The whole thing had been so sudden that Simon had hardly time to realise what had happened until they were out in the open country, then he leant forward and shouted in De Richleau's ear:

'The way – will you be able to find it?'

The Duke's only answer was to point with his whip to the stars. High above them, and a little to the left, Simon made out the 'Great Bear', with its pointers to the North Star. They were the only stars he knew, but it was enough. He realised that they must be going in the right direction.

The three horses carried them forward at a fast trot, but De Richleau was too old a soldier not to know the necessity of economising their staying-power. Once he felt that they were safe from immediate pursuit he reduced the pace. At the end of each hour he halted for ten minutes, carefully rugging up the horses against a chill.

Mile after mile was eaten up as the night wore on; the road twisted and turned a little here and there, but in the main it led them through vast stretches of glistening, snow-covered forest, ever to the eastward, towards the heart of Siberia.

At one o' clock in the morning they reached the Tavda river. There was no bridge and only a primitive wooden ferry.

They knocked up the ferryman, but he refused to turn out and take them over at that hour. De Richleau did not press the point or attempt to bribe the man; the horses badly needed rest if they were to be fit to travel next day. Simon and he had been up since six that morning, and both of them were worn out.

They found stabling for the horses in the ferryman's barn, and rolled themselves up in their furs on the floor of his living-room – in spite of its hardness they were soon asleep.

Next morning they were up early and soon away, the horses – hardy beasts – seemed as fresh as ever. All through that long monotonous day they drove onwards, halting with military regularity, but never exceeding their allotted time of rest, except once, at midday, when they made a hurried meal at a wayside farmhouse.

Such farms were few and far between – during the whole of the long journey they scarcely saw a human being. Wide, desolate wastes of snow alternated with long vistas of silent mysterious forest. The whole land was so deeply in the grip of winter that it was almost impossible to imagine it otherwise, and to picture the fields bright with the thousand flowers of the short Siberian summer.

As the sun was sinking, a dull red globe, into the forests from which they had come, they passed first one farmstead and then another; they topped a hill, and there, in the gathering darkness spread below them, lay a town. They knew that they had reached their journey's end, and that this must be the city of Tobolsk.

Chapter XI

Which Shows That a Little Yiddish Can Be Useful

They halted at the side of the road and held a short consultation. The first question was what to do with the stolen sledge – no doubt its owner had notified the police in all the neighbouring towns.

'I think it would be best to abandon it in that small wood to the left there,' said De Richleau, climbing stiffly from his seat. 'We can turn the horses loose, they will find shelter somewhere.'

'Ner,' Simon protested. 'If we can find a stable for them they may be useful later on.'

'As you will,' agreed the Duke, wearily. He was over sixty, and the long drive had been a great strain upon him. 'But where do you suggest?'

'Farm,' said Simon. 'Lots of farms round here.'

'Don't you think they will be suspicious – surely they will wonder why we do not drive on and stable our horses in the town?'

'Lame one of them,' suggested Simon, quickly.

'Lame a horse! What are you saying?' De Richleau was nearly as shocked at the idea as Simon had been, thirty-six hours earlier, when the Duke had killed a man.

'Say one of them is lame,' amended Simon.

'That is different – they will take them in I do not doubt. One thing is certain – we dare not drive into the town; we could not abandon the *troika* in the streets, and to attempt to stop at an hotel would be almost as good as walking into the bureau of the police.'

Simon nodded vigorously. 'Better try a farm. If there's a real muddle and the police are after us the farm people may refuse to let us have them again, but if we do as you say, we'll never see them again anyhow!'

De Richleau roused himself and climbed once more into the driver's seat. 'Ah, what would I not give to be once more in the Hispano,' he said, with a little groan. 'Heading for Curzon Street, my evening clothes and dinner. May the curse of God be upon the Soviet and all its works!'

Simon chuckled. 'Wouldn't mind Ferraro showing me to a table at the Berkeley myself, just at the moment!'

De Richleau whipped up the tired horses, and they proceeded a quarter of a mile down the road, then Simon tapped the Duke on the back. 'What about that?' he suggested, indicating a low house to the right that had several large barns and outhouses clustered round it.

'Ah!' exclaimed the Duke, starting – he had almost fallen asleep over his reins. 'Yes, why not?' He turned the horses into the side-track that led up to the farm. 'Why is it, Simon, my friend,' he added, sadly, as they pulled up and he climbed down once more, 'that you have never learnt either to drive a pair of horses or to speak Russian?'

'Never mind – we're nearly through, now,' Simon encouraged him. Simon had not only slept soundly from one o' clock the previous morning till six in the ferryman's hut, but, while the Duke was driving the solid twelve hours after they crossed the Tavda river, he had been able to doze a good deal of the time. He was therefore feeling full of vigour and enthusiasm now that they were so near their journey's end.

'Nearly through!' the Duke echoed. 'You have taken leave of your senses, my son – we have hardly started on this mad journey of ours.'

The farmhouse door had opened, and a dark-skinned woman, enveloped in so many layers of clothing that all semblance of waistline had vanished, stood looking at them with round, dark eyes.

Immediately De Richleau's ill humour and fatigue vanished. He went up to her, breaking into voluble Russian. It was evident, however, that she had some difficulty in understanding him – and he her. Even Simon could appreciate that her harsh patois had little resemblance to Valeria Petrovna's sibilant tongue.

A lad of about seventeen was fetched, also a little girl and an aged crone. The latter regarded them with bleary eyes, and for some mysterious reason shook her stick threateningly at Simon.

De Richleau produced his well-filled wallet once again, and it was obvious that whatever might be the ideas and wishes of the Kommissars, hard cash still had a certain value in the eyes of the thrifty Russian peasants.

The young boy unharnessed and led away the horses, the Duke gave liberal payment for their keep in advance, and soon the two friends were trudging down the track to the highway.

'Have you considered what we should do now?' Contrary to custom, it was the tired Duke who asked the question.

'How far to the town?'

'Three miles,' said De Richleau, bitterly.

'Come on, old chap.' Simon thrust his arm through that of the older man. 'It'll be all right – don't you worry.'

They trudged on through the darkening evening; somehow, since they had left Moscow, it had always seemed to be night, the short, sunny days of these high latitudes were gone so quickly.

De Richleau walked in a stupor of fatigue. Simon was racking his able brain for some idea as to where they could spend the night; some shelter must be found, that was certain – they could not sleep in the snow. The hotels in Tobolsk were barred to them in this forbidden territory.

Simon almost wished that they had begged a night's lodging at the farmhouse, in spite of the threatening ancient and her stick.

As they trudged on the houses became more frequent, until the road developed into a mean and straggling street. It seemed endless, but it gradually grew narrower, and the buildings of more importance. At last they entered a large square.

On the corner they halted. How much Simon wished that this was some provincial town in England. He looked about him anxiously; few people were passing, and these few seemed to be scurrying from one glowing stove, with its attendant pile of logs, to another. Then, suddenly, Simon stepped forward, drawing De Richleau after him.

He had seen a strange figure shamble by – a man, whose dark curls were discernible even in the faint glow from the irregular lamps; a man who wore a strange, brimless high hat, puffed out at the top, not unlike a chef's cap, only that this was made of black velvet instead of white linen.

Simon laughed into his free hand. 'Now,' he said. 'If only I haven't forgotten all my Yiddish!'

He addressed the figure, hesitantly, in a strange tongue. The man halted, and peered at him suspiciously, but Simon was persistent. Forgotten words and phrases learnt in his childhood came back to him, and he stumbled on.

That the man understood was evident. He answered in a similar language, asking some questions and nodding at the Duke.

'He is Jewish,' Simon explained to the Duke.

'It is well – come with me,' said the stranger, who was a rabbi of the Jewish faith.

They followed him down many narrow turnings, until he stopped at last before what seemed, in the dark, to be a large, old-fashioned house. The rabbi pushed upon the great nail-studded door, and it swung open upon its leather hinges.

Simon kept on his fur papenka, for he knew at once by the Shield of David on the windows, and the perpetual light burning before the ark, that this was a synagogue; although in every way different from the smart

Liberal Synagogue in London, of which he was a recognised, but non-attendant, member.

This synagogue in Tobolsk was not used for fashionable ceremonies, but as a meeting-place – a club almost – frequented daily by the more prominent members of the Jewish community.

The Rabbi led them through the place of worship to the school. A number of persons were present – no women, but about twenty or thirty men in various costumes. They sat round a long table, reading and discussing the Torah, and the endless commentaries upon it; just as their progenitors had, in this or similar synagogues, for upwards of three thousand years.

Their guide took them to an elderly man, evidently the chief rabbi, whose white curls fell beneath his high velvet hat on to his shoulders.

Soft words were spoken in the guttural Yiddish tongue. 'It is the house of God,' said the old rabbi. 'Peace be upon you.'

Simon and the Duke found a warm corner near the stove, and a young man brought them a large platter each of smoked salmon – that age-old Jewish dish. They both agreed that it could not have been better cured if it had been served at Claridge's or the Ritz. With it were wheaten cakes and tea.

After, they sat talking a little in low tones, but De Richleau's answers became shorter and more infrequent, until Simon saw that he had dropped asleep.

The evening's debate upon the eternal 'Law' seemed to have come to an end, and the members of the synagogue left in twos and threes. At last only Simon, the sleeping Duke, and two or three students remained.

The Rabbi they had first met came up to Simon. 'You will stay here?' he suggested. 'We shall meet in the morning.'

Simon rose and bowed. 'So be it,' he said in Yiddish.

The Rabbi bowed in return, his hands folded before him, and covered by the sleeves of his long gown. Simon settled himself beside De Richleau, and wrapping his furs around him, was soon asleep.

In the morning the rabbi who had befriended them came to them again. Simon had been awake for quite a time before he arrived, and had been trying to translate what he wished to say into simple Yiddish phrases. He told the rabbi the plain truth, without either elaborating or concealing anything.

The rabbi looked grave. It was his duty to avoid bringing trouble or discredit upon his community, yet he wished, if he could, to aid this brother in the faith from a far country.

'I can take you to the prison,' he said at length. 'There are Jewish prisoners whom it is my duty to visit from time to time. It may chance that you shall see the brother whom you seek, but more than this I cannot do. I think it wise, also, that you do not stay here longer than another night, else it may be that you will bring trouble upon us, who have ever many troubles.'

Simon inclined his head gravely, more than happy to have secured so much assistance. 'When can we go?' he asked.

'I must speak to the chief rabbi. If he consents we may leave here at once.'

When he had gone Simon translated the conversation to De Richleau, who had woken stiff, but much refreshed.

'I fear we have undertaken a difficult task,' De Richleau shook his head, despondently. 'How are we to plot an escape for a prisoner, which may take days of careful organisation, when we are suspects ourselves? However, we can only trust our luck will hold, we've been very fortunate so far.'

After a little while the rabbi returned. 'It is well,' he said. 'The rabbi consents. Let us go.'

Simon pulled on his furs, and followed the rabbi through the great wooden door into the narrow street.

They walked quickly and silently – the cold was piercing. Their way lay through the twisting streets of the old town, and at last they came to a high wall surrounding a number of bleak, two-storeyed stone buildings. The great gates in the wall stood wide open. One heavily bearded man, wrapped in a great top coat, sat in a little watch-house, warming his feet at an open brazier. He nodded to the rabbi, and they walked through into the courtyard. A very different business, Simon thought, to the regulations which he had encountered when he had had occasion to enter Brixton Prison on account of Richard Eaton.

Several men were playing a game of volley-ball in the courtyard, but Simon saw that Rex was not among them. They entered a long, low room in one of the buildings. Most of the occupants seemed to be asleep.

The place was furnished only with trestle tables, hard benches, and the usual big porcelain stove. The floor looked as though it had not been swept for weeks.

Simon's sharp eyes travelled backwards and forwards, while the rabbi spoke to one or two of the prisoners, evidently men of the Jewish race, but there was no sign of the big American.

They left the building, and entered a hall in the second block; it was furnished in the same way, and was identical in size with the first. No warders were in evidence, and it seemed that the prisoners were allowed to move freely in and out just as they liked. Here also the majority of the occupants were sleeping or talking quietly together – still no sign of Rex.

In the common-room of the third block, a similar scene met Simon's eyes; filth, discomfort, lassitude, but no attempt at any ordered control. It was in the third building that he noticed a curious thing – none of the men wore boots! Instead, they had list slippers. He was just pondering over this when his attention was attracted by a small group squatting on the floor in the corner. Two little Yakuts, with merry faces and long Mongolian eyes, sat with their backs to the wall; before them, facing away from Simon, was a fat, bald-headed man, and a broad, strapping fellow, of unusual height, with powerful shoulders.

The bald man shook a small box that rattled, and it was evident that the four were engaged in a primitive form of dice.

Simon looked again at the colossal back of the young giant. 'Could it be? If it was – gone were the dark, wavy curls – this man's head was close cropped. Suddenly, in a loud voice, he spoke: 'Come on, digger – spill the beans!'

Then Simon knew that the first part of their mission was accomplished. In this sordid Siberian prison, he had run to earth that most popular figure among the younger generation of society from Long Island to Juan les Pins – Mr Rex Mackintosh Van Ryn.

Chapter XII

Escape

Simon was in a quandary – he could not see any guards, but did not know if it was better to go up and speak to Rex, or wait till the latter saw him; either way there seemed to be the risk that Rex might give the show away in his surprise. The problem was solved by the American turning round, and Simon saw that he had been recognised. Rex kept his head – he did not stand up at once, he played two more rounds of dice, and then, getting lazily to his feet, strolled out of the room.

Simon followed him slowly – he found Van Ryn eagerly waiting for him round the corner of the building, none of the other prisoners was in sight.

'Say, boy!' Rex exclaimed, seizing his shoulders in an almost painful grip. 'If this isn't just marvellous. I'll tell the world, I never thought to see you in this Godforsaken quarter of the globe.'

Simon grinned, delighted. 'See too much of me if you're not careful – I'll be in there playing dice with you.'

'How in heck d'you make this place?'

'Two trains and a stolen sleigh,' Simon chuckled.

'Good for you! The Duke'll have got my chit, I guess.'

'Yes, he's here, too – in the local synagogue!'

'Holy smoke!' Rex shook with silent laughter. 'What perfect hide-out. No one will go looking for the big thief there!'

'Oh, he's all right for the moment – but how are we going to get you out, now that we are here?'

Van Ryn laughed, showing his white, even teeth. 'That's easy,' he said casually. 'I'll walk!'

'Aren't there guards and warders?'

'Not so 's you'd notice them. They've got peculiar ideas about prisons in this city. It's got Sing-Sing beat to a frazzle! No one tries escaping, 'cause they can't get anywhere – no money, and no boots, that's the bars they use in this burg; that, and one spy in each block to let them have the low-down about any little plans to frame a get-away.'

'But lots of the prisoners must have friends in the town – surely they could get out first and get help later?'

'That's where you're all wrong. Not a man in this prison was raised in Tobolsk. The local crooks get put on rail for a lock-up a thousand miles away – so what could a fella do, anyway, with no friends, no boots, no money, and a couple of hundred miles of snow between him and the next town?'

'You can get out, then, if we can get you away afterwards?'

'I certainly can! About five o' clock'll be the best time.'

'How – er – will you manage?' Simon asked, a little doubtfully.

'Get a pal to have a yarn with the man on the gate – it'll be near dusk – I'll be able to slip through all right – the rest of the guard sleep most of the day. They start in rounding us up for the night about six, locking us in our own blocks and doing a sort of inspection round.'

'They will miss you at once then? That's a pity.'

'We'll be unlucky if they do. The inspection they have in this place would give the Governor of Dartmoor fits. I'll leave a bundle of stuff in my bunk. Ten to one they'll never realise it isn't me!'

'Where will you go when you get outside?'

'Down to the north-west corner of the prison wall. That's to the right going out of the gate, get me? And for the Lord's sake don't forget to bring me boots – if you do my toes'll drop off under the hour in this cold. Say, Simon, you haven't by chance got any food on you, have you? I'm that hungry I'd pinch peanuts off a blind man's monkey.'

Simon searched his pockets and found a decrepit bar of chocolate. He proffered it dubiously.

'Thanks!' Rex seized and bit into it ravenously. 'My, that's good and no mistake. I guess I'd eat ten dollars' worth if you'd got it. Now tell me about the Duke.'

'He drove the sleigh for seventeen hours yesterday. He was about all in last night.'

'Did he, though? At his age! I'll say he's the greatest man in Europe, is our Duke, and you're a close second, Simon!'

'Don't be silly – I've done nothing.'

'Honest, I mean it.' Rex patted Simon's arm affectionately. 'I don't know two other guys who'd risk getting into this place to get another fella out. I was never so glad of anything in my life as when I saw your ugly mug just now,' Rex grimaced. 'Another month or so of this and I'd have had to wring the neck of one of these fool guards, just to make life more interesting.'

Simon chuckled. 'Wouldn't have been much good our coming if you had!'

'No. I reckon it would have been a free ad in the wrong end of the hatched, matched, and dispatched column of the *New York Times* for this child. Still, praises be you've come. I guess we'd better separate now.'

'Yes. I'll get back. We'll be waiting for you at five.'

'Sure – ' Van Ryn moved away with a last grin. 'See-yer-later, Simon – round about cocktail time!'

Simon rejoined the Rabbi. They visited three more of the barracks and then left the prison. Simon's heart was high with the good news that he was bringing to the Duke. True, Rex was lean and cadaverous now, but well and cheerful.

The Duke, meanwhile, had been exercising his stiff limbs. The long drive from Turinsk had been a great strain on him. He thought, ruefully, of his marble bathroom at Curzon Street, and the gentle ministrations of the excellent Max, but not for long. If it had been his habit in recent years to spend much of his time idling in the pleasant places of the earth, he had, during his earlier life, been soldier, hunter, and explorer, and the experiences of those strenuous days stood him in good stead now. At one period he had had a Japanese manservant, from whom he had learnt many things about the human body. Among them was the secret of certain exercises, which relaxed the muscles and relieved their strain. He ceased therefore to think of Lubin's bath essence, and applied himself to these continual and gentle revolutions, much to the astonishment of the morning gathering of students in the school of the synagogue.

On Simon's return the two retired to a quiet corner, and began to make their plans.

The sleigh seemed to be their only means of escape, and very glad they were that they had not abandoned it the previous night.

The man who owned it would have notified the police at Turinsk of the theft, but, fortunately, the story which the Duke had told of his dying wife in Sverdlovsk, had also been told to the innkeeper at Turinsk, therefore it was to be hoped that the main hunt would take that direction. In any case, even if the police in Tobolsk were on the look-out, it seemed hardly likely that the people at the farm would have been questioned, for the farm was three miles from the centre of the town. With any luck they might secure possession of it again without difficulty.

The next question was – should they attempt to get hold of it before or after Rex had made his escape? If there was going to be trouble with the farm people, it would be a help to have him with them – on the other hand it meant delay. It was an hour's trudge from the prison to the farm, and if Rex's disappearance was discovered at the six o' clock inspection, the alarm would be raised before they could get a decent start, and mounted patrols scouring the country in all directions.

If the farm people were questioned afterwards, and Rex had been with them, the police would immediately connect the escaped prisoner with the stolen sleigh. It was far better that these events should remain unconnected in their minds. Simon and the Duke decided to attempt to retrieve the sleigh early that afternoon.

Then the problem arose – which road should they take? They would have liked to have gone to the west, back into Russia, but to do that was to run right into the centre of the hue and cry for the stolen sleigh at Turinsk. The route to the east led farther into unknown Siberia. They would be placing an even greater distance between themselves and the Embassies, which were their only hope of protection. The choice, then, lay between the north and the south. The former, with its vast impenetrable forests, was uninviting in the extreme; whereas to the south, some hundred and fifty miles away, was the Trans-Siberian Railway – their only link with civilisation. But, they agreed, that was the direction in which the escaped American would be most keenly sought. The authorities would reason that he would try and reach the line and jump a goods train. Finally they agreed that they would make due north. In that direction, at least, there was good cover. If they could get a start it should not be difficult to evade their pursuers in the depths of those trackless woods. Later, if they were successful in throwing off the pursuit, they would veer west, and try to recross the Urals into Russia.

Having come to these important decisions, they discussed the question of boots with the friendly Rabbi. To procure these seemed a difficulty – boots had been scarce in Tobolsk for years – new ones were an impossibility. These could only be obtained from the state co-operative, if in stock, but, in any case, a permit was necessary. Possibly a second-hand pair could be bought in the market – that seemed to be the only chance. The rabbi agreed to go out for them, and see what he could do. Simon explained to him that the boots must be of the largest size if they were to be of any use at all.

After half an hour he returned. No boots were to be had, but he brought a pair of peasant's sandals – great weighty things, with wooden soles an inch and a half thick, and strong leather thongs.

He explained that if plenty of bandages were wrapped round the feet and legs of the wearer, they would prove serviceable and not too uncomfortable, so with these they had to be content.

At a little after three they left the synagogue with many expressions of gratitude to the kind rabbi who had proved such a friend in need. There could be no question of payment for food and shelter, but Simon pressed a liberal donation on him for his poor.

Following the Rabbi's instructions, they avoided the centre of the town, and were soon in the suburbs. Fortunately their road lay within a quarter of a mile of the prison, and they could see its high walls in the distance, so they would have no difficulty in finding it on their return. The cold was intense, and a bitter wind blew across the open spaces. It seemed more like six miles than three, but they trudged on in silence, their heads well down.

At last they reached the farmhouse – it looked dreary and deserted under its mantle of snow – no other buildings or trees were near it, so they had no reason to fear an ambush of red guards or police, unless they were concealed in the house or barns.

At the door the fat woman met them once more. She was wreathed in smiles – evidently the lavish payment for the stabling of the horses had won her heart. She was ignorant and avaricious, close to the soil – a peasant yet a landowner; bourgeois in sympathy, yet hating the people of the towns except for what could be got out of them. The youth was summoned and De Richleau asked for the horses and *troika* as soon as they could be harnessed. The lad ran willingly to obey. His quick eyes travelled over Simon and the Duke, as he brought the horses from the stable.

'You are not of the Party?' he questioned, with a flash of his uneven teeth.

'No, we are not of the Party,' De Richleau answered, slowly.

'I knew that – else why should you pay?' the youth looked up quickly. 'They never pay – those devils, they eat the lands.'

The Duke regarded him with interest. 'Why should they pay? They are the lords now!'

The young peasant spat. As he lifted his face again there was a sudden fire in his eyes. 'We killed three last winter, my friends and I – they are as a blight on the land. The land is mine,' he went on fiercely, 'why should I give them the Kleb, for which I work? What are their beastly cities to me? I am a *kulak* – independent. My father was head man in the local council, till they killed him!'

'So they killed your father?' said the Duke softly. 'What year was that?'

'The year of the great famine,' answered the lad. 'Little men, who could not have ploughed half a hectare, or they would have died – but they were many, and they hung him in the great barn – he who could plough a hundred furrows in the time that big Andrew could plough only eighty-nine.'

'And you have had blood for blood,' De Richleau nodded.

'Blood for blood – that is a good law,' said the youth with a twisted smile. 'They worry us no more; unless they come in batches they are afraid. At first we had a half thought that you were one of them when you came last night; the old one, who is the mother of my mother, was for fetching the neighbours to make an end of you, but I knew by the way you spoke that you were not of them, even if your companion is much as they!'

The Duke looked at Simon, and laughed suddenly, 'It is well, my friend, that you did not come to this part of the world alone. These good people take you for a Communist, and would have thrown you head first in the manure pit!'

The boy was buckling the horses into the *troika*; he did not under-stand a word of what De Richleau said, but he grinned quickly. 'You should have been here to see the one we cooked in the stove last winter – a silly man who wanted to teach his silliness to the children in the school. We put him feet first into the stove. How we laughed while we held him there, and the mother of my mother beat him; each time he howled she struck him in the mouth with her big stick, crying: "Shout-ing does not feed the children, oh, man who reads letters – give us back our corn"; and the more he howled the more she struck him, till all his teeth were gone.'

It was as well that Simon understood nothing of all this. The Duke – who did – climbed into the *troika* and took the reins; for him it was only a nightmare echo of those years when he had fought with the White Army; it interested him to know that outside the towns, where the Communist Party held undisputed sway, this internecine war was still going on. Not a good omen for the completion of the Five Year Plan!

He gave the youngster a hundred-rouble note, and told him to say no word of them should the Reds come from the town to make inquiries. The lad promised willingly enough, and ran beside their horses down the cart track until they reached the main road, shouting and cheering lustily.

They drove slowly, saving the horses, for they had ample time. As it was, they had to wait on the corner opposite the prison. It was an anxious quarter of an hour; twilight fell, and the shadow of the arch above the central horse of the *troika* grew longer and longer. At last, in the gathering dusk, a tall figure came towards them at a quick run. Both knew instinc-tively that it was Rex.

He halted beside the sleigh, panting and a little breathless.

'Say, it's real good to see you boys again. All afternoon I've been think-ing that I'd gone crazy and just dreamt it!'

De Richleau laughed. 'I wish that we were all dreaming and safe in our beds at home – but anyhow, we are together again – jump in, Rex – quick, man!'

As he spoke a Red Guard came suddenly round the corner of the wall full upon them. With one look he recognised Rex as a prisoner, and raised his rifle to fire.

Chapter XIII

Stranded in Siberia

For a moment the group remained immovable; De Richleau with the reins in one hand and his whip in the other; Simon leaning back in the sleigh; Rex standing in the snow beside the horses; and the soldier halted, his rifle raised, only a few feet away.

The Duke gave a sharp, rasping command in Russian. It was so sudden, so unexpected, that the man was taken off his guard. Before he had realised what he was doing he had jerked back his shoulders and raised his rifle preparatory to 'grounding arms'; the next second he had checked his automatic impulse, but it was too late. The instant his eyes left the American's face and his rifle tilted Rex sprang upon him, and they crashed to the ground together.

By the mercy of Heaven the rifle did not go off. Simon and the Duke leapt from the sleigh. Rex and the Red Guard were rolling in the snow; first one on top, then the other.

'Don't shoot,' cried the Duke anxiously, as he saw Simon whip out his big automatic.

The struggle was brief; the soldier was a big fellow, but not big enough to put up a serious fight once Rex had him in his powerful grip. In less than a minute he was on his back with Van Ryn's hands tight about his throat.

Simon did not hesitate – the lesson of Sverdlovsk had not been lost upon him. The man must be silenced somehow, or De Richleau's long knife would be between his ribs. He stooped and hit the man a stunning blow on the head with the butt end of his pistol.

The Red Guard lay still, a grey heap on the whiteness of the snow.

'What'll we do with this bird?' asked Rex.

'Can't leave him here,' said Simon. 'He'll raise the alarm when he comes to.'

'Throw him in the bottom of the sleigh,' De Richleau suggested. 'We will deal with him later.'

'Sure,' Rex agreed, with a laugh. 'Come on, big boy,' he addressed the unconscious soldier, as he picked him up by an arm and a leg, 'we're going to take you for a ride. Reckon your boots'll just about do for me!' He heaved the man into the sleigh and climbed in beside Simon.

De Richleau was already on the box again. He put the horses into motion; the sleigh slithered round the corner, and they took the road for the north. The lights began to twinkle from the wooden houses, and the stars came out one by one.

As they left the town behind, Simon and the Duke were conscious of one thought. They had succeeded in one half of their enterprise; now they were faced with the second and more difficult half, to get both Rex and themselves safely out of Soviet Russia.

It was Rex who broke their sombre train of thought. 'Say, boys,' he cried, with his ringing laugh, 'who'd want to be on a mucky little street like Broadway, when they could see stars like this!'

De Richleau let the horses have their heads. They were fine beasts, well fed and full of spirit. An hour's hard driving would not harm them for further service, and it was vital to get well away from the town as quickly as possible.

The three friends wasted no time in discussion. Rex asked which way they were heading. Simon told him they were making for the forests of the north, and he seemed satisfied.

The road lay chiefly along the west bank of the frozen Irtysh river; in places it left the course of the stream, and ran for long straight stretches beside the local railway, which linked up Tobolsk with the small towns of the north. The road was wide, and in far better repair than that on which they had travelled from Turinsk; since it must be the less important of the two, this struck the Duke as curious, but he did not puzzle himself to find an explanation. He was only thankful that this enabled them to make far better progress than he had hoped.

After an hour they pulled up to rest the horses. The place was wild and desolate. Sombre forests stretched away on either hand, an almost uncanny silence brooded over the shadowy darkness, broken only by the faint soughing of innumerable boughs as the night breeze rustled the pine tops. The moon was not yet up, and the starlight barely lit the narrow ribbon of road.

They had been fortunate in meeting no one since they had left Tobolsk. The one straggling village through which they had passed had been destitute of life, its roofless houses and charred remains among the many grim monuments that mark the years of bitter conflict throughout the length and breadth of Russia.

It was decided that they should press on all through the night, but at an easier pace to save the horses. Their prisoner started groaning, and showed signs of returning life. They tied his hands and feet securely, and put him in the bottom of the sleigh. Rex, having purloined his boots, took over the reins from De Richleau. Simon and the Duke curled up under the rugs to get what sleep they could.

The going for the next hour was difficult; heavy forests came up to the road on either hand, and the feeble starlight barely penetrated to the tunnel of darkness through which they drove. Later, when the forests fell away from the roadside, and the moon got up, its reflection on the snow made the whole landscape as bright as day. Rex was able to increase the pace considerably without straining the horses. In spite of the ever-increasing distance from Tobolsk, the road remained surprisingly even and well kept.

At a little before dawn they passed through the town of Uvatsk. It was shrouded in darkness, and fortunately the population still slept. De Richleau had stripped the sleigh bells from the harness on their previous journey, and except for the hoof-beats of the horses on the hardened snow, their passage was almost noiseless.

A few miles on the farther side of Uvatsk, Van Ryn drove the sleigh some way up a track at the side of the road. The place was thickly wooded, and when he was assured that they were well hidden from any chance passer-by, he stopped the sleigh and woke his companions.

The three set about preparing a meal. Simon and De Richleau had never allowed the rucksacks to leave their possession, and on inspection they found that they had enough food to last them for four or five days if they were careful; by that time they might hope to put a considerable distance between themselves and Tobolsk. After that they must trust to securing supplies from isolated farmhouses. The horses were a more difficult matter. The Duke had seen to it that the nose-bags were well filled the previous afternoon, but they would need to buy or steal fodder by the following day. If possible they must secure relays by exchanging their horses for others at some farm; if they could not arrange something of the kind their pace would be bound to suffer.

Their principal embarrassment was their prisoner. If they kept him they must feed him, and he would be a further drain on their supplies. He would have to be constantly watched or he might find some way of giving the alarm.

For the present they untied him; he was too stiff from his bonds to run away, and Rex had already secured his boots. They were careful also to remove his rifle from the sleigh.

The camping ground they had chosen for their meal was some twenty yards off the track, under the shelter of some bushes; the horses were unharnessed and hobbled.

De Richleau had a fair supply of 'Meta' fuel in his pack, so they boiled water for tea. While they were waiting, the Duke spread out a map and pointed to their approximate position.

'Here we are, my friends,' he said, 'half-way betweer Uvatsk and Romanovsk. We have covered something over a hundred miles since we set out fourteen hours ago. That is good going, particularly as we have reason to suppose that our pursuers will not look for us in this direction. But what now? It is over a thousand miles to the frontier. How shall we make that, with stolen horses, an escaped prisoner, and a Red Guard whom we must carry with us?'

Simon laughed his little nervous laugh into the palm of his hand. 'We're in a real muddle this time,' he said.

'Well, I'll say we've taken the right road,' Rex laughed. 'Romanovsk is just the one place in all the Russias I've been wanting to see for a long, long time.'

'Let us be serious, Rex,' De Richleau protested. 'We shall need all our wits if we are ever to get out of Russia alive.'

Van Ryn shook his head. 'I'm on the level. You boys wouldn't know the fool reason that brought me to this goddamn country.'

'Oh, yes, we do,' said Simon promptly. 'You're after the Shulimoff treasure – Jack Straw told us!'

'Did he, though! He's a great guy. Well, the goods are under fifteen miles from where we're sitting now, in the old man's place at Romanovsk; it'd be a real shame to go back home without those little souvenirs – we'll split up on the deal!'

'I should be interested to hear how you learnt about this treasure, Rex,' said the Duke; 'also how you were caught. Tell us about it now. We must give the horses at least an hour, they're looking pretty done.'

'It happened this way.' Rex pushed the last piece of a ham and rye bread sandwich into his mouth, and leant back against the trunk of a near-by tree.

'Last fall I went to take a look at some of those one-eyed South American States – tho', come to that, they're not so one-eyed after all. Of course, as kids in the States, we're always taught to look on them as pothole places – just crying out for real intelligent civilisation as handed out by Uncle Sam – but that's another story. On the way home I stopped off for a spell in the West Indies.'

'Cuba?' suggested De Richleau.

'Yes, Havana.'

'A lovely city. I was last there in 1926.'

'Sure, it would be a great town if there weren't so many of our folk there – it was like Coney Island on a Sunday!'

'You were there when? November, I suppose?'

'That's so. The American people treat Havana like Europe does Monte Carlo. Every little hick from the middle-west has to go to that place once, or he cuts no social ice in his home town at all. The bars are open night and day, and drinks about a tenth of the price they'd pay in a speakeasy back home, which isn't calculated to make 'em behave as tho' they were at the King's garden party. I should have cleared out on the next boat if it hadn't been for a Dago with a Ford!'

Simon smiled. 'You don't look as if you'd been run over!'

'Oh, it wasn't *this* child,' Van Ryn laughed. 'I was in my own automobile behind; I toured the Sports Bentley to South America with me. Anyhow, I was taking a spin out to the tennis-courts at the Jockey Club the second afternoon I was there, and just outside the town there was only this bird in the flivver in front of me. I was waiting to pass, when he swerves to avoid an oncoming car, and in swerving he knocked down a poor old man. Did he stop? Did he hell! He gave one look, saw the old bird lying in the ditch, and put his foot on the gas!'

'Brute,' Simon murmured.

'Brute's the word,' Rex nodded. 'Well, I don't stand for that sort of thing, and I'll not say Ford isn't a big man, but he hasn't turned out a car yet that can give the dust to a Bentley. I was after that guy as though I'd been a speed cop looking for promotion. In half a mile he'd got to take the sidewalk and the nearest light standard, or stop and have a word with me. He stopped all right, and started to jabber in Spanish, but that cut no ice with me at all! I just happen to have been born a foot too tall for most people to try any monkeying, so I didn't have much trouble with this little rat. When we got back they were picking up the old man.'

'Was he badly hurt?' the Duke inquired.

'Nothing serious; more shock and bruises than broken bones, but he was considerably upset, so we propped him up in the Bentley and I ran him down to the hospital. The driver I passed over to a real speed cop.'

De Richleau had been burrowing in his rucksack, and now produced a flat tin box, in which were packed a couple of layers of his famous cigars.

'Hoyo de Monterrey's, by all that's marvellous!' exclaimed Rex. 'Well, I'll say I never expected to smoke one of those sitting in the snow!'

'Unfortunately I had to leave most of them in Moscow,' said the Duke, 'but I thought we would bring a few, and this – if ever – is an occasion!'

Simon chuckled as he carefully pinched the end of the long cigar which the Duke held out to him. 'Thanks – d'you know, I believe if I meet you in the other world you'll still have a box of Hoyos!'

'If I have not,' said De Richleau, puffing contentedly, 'I shall send for my bill and move elsewhere!'

'Well, the whole party would have ended there,' Rex went on, 'if it hadn't been that I was bored fit to bust myself. So next afternoon, just to get away from all the sugar babies and card sharps in the hotel, I thought I'd go take a look at the old man.

'There he was, propped up in bed in the hospital, as wicked-looking an old sinner as ever you set eyes on; he spoke English better than I do, but he was a foreigner, of course; and, without being smarmy about it, he was grateful for what I'd done. You'll have guessed, maybe, that he was the old Prince Shulimoff.'

Simon nodded. 'I thought as much.'

'Yes, that's who he was, tho' he didn't let on about it that first meeting. Just said he was a Russian émigré, down and out. We talked a bit, mainly as to what sort of damages he'd get out of our Dago friend. He was a gentleman all right – got all het up 'cause he couldn't offer me any hospitality when I called. Well, then, you know how it is when you've done a chap a sort of kindness; you feel he's your baby, in a way, and you've got to go on. So I saw the American representative about getting his case pushed on, and of course I had to call again to tell him what I'd done.'

'Was the Dago worth going for?' inquired the cautious Simon.

Rex shrugged his broad shoulders. 'He wasn't what you'd call a fat wad, but he was agent for some fruit firm. I thought we might sting him for a thousand bucks. Anyhow, in the meantime, I became great friends with old wicked face – used to go to the hospital every afternoon for a yarn with the old man. Not that I really cottoned to him, but I was fascinated in a kind of way. He was as evil as they make 'em, and a lecherous old brute, but I'll say he had charm all right.'

'Surely,' remarked the Duke, 'Shulimoff must have had investments outside Russia before the Revolution. How did he come to be in such a state?'

'He'd blown every cent; got no sense of money. If he'd got a grand out of the fruit merchant he'd have spent it next day. But money or no money, he'd got personality all right; that hospital was just run for him while he was there. He tipped me off he was pretending to be a Catholic; all those places are run by nuns, and he knew enough about the drill to spoof them all; they fairly ran round the old crook! After I'd been there a few times he told me his real name, and *then* the fun started. He wouldn't open his mouth if anyone who could speak a word of English was within fifty yards; but, bit by bit, he told me how he'd cheated the Bolshies.'

'Are you sure he was not amusing himself at your expense?' asked the Duke. 'He seems just the sort of man who would.'

'Not on your life. He was in deadly earnest, and he'd only tell a bit at a time, then he'd get kind of nervous, and dry up – say he'd thought better of it – if the goods stayed where they were the Bolshies would never find them till the crack of doom; but if he told me, maybe I'd get done in after I'd got 'em, and then the Bolsheviks would get them after all.'

'And where had he hidden this famous hoard?' De Richleau asked with a smile.

'You've hit it.' Rex threw up his hands with a sudden shout of mirth. '*Where?* I'm damned if I know myself!'

'But, Rex – I mean,' Simon protested. 'You – er – wouldn't risk getting into all this trouble without knowing where they were?'

'I've got a pretty shrewd idea,' Rex admitted. 'They're at Romanovsk all right, and I was getting right down to the details with the old prince, when –'

'What happened? Did he refuse at last to tell you?' The Duke's shrewd grey eyes were fixed intently on Rex's face.

'No, the old tough just died on me! Rotten luck, wasn't it? He seemed all right, getting better every day; but you know what old men are like. I blew in one morning and they told me he was dead. That's all there was to it!'

'Surely, my friend,' De Richleau raised his slanting eyebrows, 'you hardly expected to find the jewels at Romanovsk on so little information. Remember, many people have been seeking this treasure on all the Shulimoff estates for years.'

'No, it's not all that bad,' Rex shook his head 'When things blew up in Leningrad in 1917, Shulimoff didn't wait to see the fun; he cleared out to this place here, bringing the goods with him. He thought he'd be safe this side of the Urals till things quietened down, or if they got real bad, he meant to go farther east. What he forgot was that he was the most hated man in Russia. The Reds sent a special mission to hang him to the nearest tree, and they did – as near as dammit! Took the old fox entirely by surprise. He'd have been a dead man then if some bright boy hadn't cut him down for the fun of hanging him again the next day! It was the old man's cellar that saved him. The bunch got tight that night, and they'd locked him in the foundry without any guards outside.'

'The foundry? In the village was this?' asked the Duke.

'Lord, no, in his own house. He seems to have been a bit of a metallurgist – made locks, like Louis XVI, in his spare time, when he wasn't out beating peasants or hitting it up with chorus girls from the *Folies Bergère*.

'This foundry was a kind of laboratory and study all in one. I reckon they chose it as his prison because it was one of the only rooms that had strong iron bars to the windows. That let them all out for the drunk! All being equal in the Red Army, no one wanted to miss a party to do sentry-go.'

'How did he get out, then,' Simon asked, 'if the windows were barred?'

'Easy; he had all his gear in the foundry, so he cut those bars like bits of cheese with an oxy-acetylene lamp. But the old man kept his head – as luck would have it, the jewels were in the foundry. He wouldn't risk taking them with him, in case he was caught, so he occupied the time while the Reds were getting tight in making something at his forge to hide 'em in.'

'What was it?' came Simon's eager question.

'Now you've got me,' Rex shook his head. 'That's just what I never squeezed out of the old fox before he went and died on me.

'It was some sort of metal container, and he put the stones inside. It was something that'd look like part of the fittings of the foundry, and something that nobody would trouble to take away. He soldered it in, too, I gathered, so that nobody could shift it without breaking the plant. You should have heard that wicked old devil chuckle when he thought how clever he'd been!'

'I can hardly imagine that it can still be there,' said De Richleau, thoughtfully; 'the place must have been ransacked a dozen times. They would not have overlooked the plant in the foundry, especially a portion which had been newly forged!'

'Old Shulimoff was an artist. I'll bet it's there to this day among a mass of rusty machinery. He realised they'd spot the new bit, so he had to make it all look alike. What d'you think he did?'

'Don't know,' said Simon.

'Set fire to the house, and then legged it through the snow. That foundry can't have been much to look at, even if there were any Reds left to look at it next day. He reckoned that he'd get back there when things were quieter, but he never did. He was lucky in falling in with a party of "White" officers, and later they all got over the Persian frontier together. I'll bet – '

But they were never to know what Van Ryn meant to bet. The crack of a whip brought them scrambling to their feet. Twenty yards away the sleigh had leapt into motion. They had all been so interested in listening to Rex that they had forgotten to keep an eye on their prisoner. He had stealthily harnessed the horses while their backs were turned. The Duke drew his automatic and fired over Simon's shoulder; the bullet hit an intervening tree and ricocheted with a loud whine. He ran forward, firing again and again, but the sleigh was rounding the bend of the track at full gallop on the road to Tobolsk. Rex snatched up the prisoner's rifle, but he threw it down again in disgust. Nobody could hit a moving target through those trees.

They looked at each other in real dismay. They were now utterly help-less in the depths of the Siberian forests, an easy prey to the hunters who would soon be on their tracks. It could only be a matter of hours until they were captured, or dead of cold and exhaustion in the wastes of these eternal snows.

Chapter XIV

The Secret of the Forbidden Territory

It was Rex who broke the unhappy silence. 'If we're not the world's prize suckers,' he declared bitterly, 'I'd like to know who are!' And he began to roar with such hearty laughter that the Duke and Simon could not forbear joining in.

'This is no laughing matter.' De Richleau shook his head. 'What the devil are we to do now?'

'Walk,' said Simon, the ever practical, and in truth it was the only thing they could do.

'Good for you,' Van Ryn exclaimed, patting him on the shoulder with one large hand while with the other he picked up the rifle and the strap of Simon's rucksack. His cheerful face showed no hint of his quick realisation that the pace of the party must be that of the slowest member, or his anxiety as to how many hours it would be before Simon's frail physique gave out under the strain. He only added: 'Come on, let's beat it.'

De Richleau collected his things more slowly. 'Yes,' he agreed, 'we must walk – at least, until we can buy or steal horses. But which way?'

'To Romanovsk,' said Rex. 'That way's as easy as any other, and I'd sure like to have a cut at those jewels before I go back home.'

'As you wish.' The Duke gently removed the ash from his cigar. 'We have had no time to tell you our own adventures, Rex, but there is one little episode which makes me particularly anxious to avoid capture.'

'Give me that sack and let's hear the worst,' Rex remarked casually, as he slung the Duke's rucksack over his shoulder next to Simon's.

'My dear fellow, you can't carry two!' De Richleau protested, 'particularly after having driven all night.'

'I certainly can,' Rex assured him. 'I'd carry a grand piano if I felt that way, but I'll give 'em back quick enough if I get tired, don't you worry. Let's hear just how you blotted your copybook!'

'An agent of the Ogpu followed us as far as Sverdlovsk. If his body should chance to be discovered, and we are captured, it might prove a little difficult to explain,' said the Duke mildly.

Rex whistled. 'You gave him the works, eh? Great stuff; but if that's so, they'll not be content to put us behind bars this time; it'll be we three for the high jump!'

'We – er – hid the body,' Simon remarked; 'if we're lucky they won't find it till the spring.'

Side by side they walked down the cart-track, and turning into the road set their faces to the north. 'I'll say we're lucky today anyhow,' Van Ryn threw out; 'if it had snowed last night we'd not make a mile an hour without snowshoes, as it is the going won't be too bad on the frozen crust.'

They trudged on for a long time in silence; there was no traffic on the long, empty road, and the intense stillness was only broken by a hissing thud, as a load of snow slid from the weighted branches of the firs, and the steady drip, drip, as the hot sun melted the icicles hanging from the trees.

It must have been about half past nine when Rex suddenly stopped in his tracks – he gripped the others tightly, each by an arm, as he exclaimed: 'Listen – what's that?'

A faint hum came to their ears from the westward. ''Plane,' said Simon, quickly. Even as he spoke Rex had run them both into the cover of the trees at the roadside.

'It's a 'plane all right,' he agreed, 'but that engine's like no other that I've ever heard – and I know quite a considerable piece about aeroplane engines.'

All three craned their necks to the sky from the cover of the larches – the deep, booming note grew louder, and a moment later the 'plane came in sight. It was a small, beetle-shaped affair, flying low and at very high speed; it turned north when it was over the road, and passed over their heads with a great roar of engines. In a few seconds it was out of sight, and in a few minutes out of hearing.

'The hunt is up, my friends,' laughed the Duke, a little grimly. 'These will be more difficult to throw off the trail than bloodhounds.'

'Somehow, I never thought of being chased with 'planes,' Rex admitted. 'That certainly puts us in some predicament!'

'We must stick to the forest,' Simon answered. 'Follow the road as long as there are trees, and leave it when there aren't.'

As they journeyed on other 'planes came over; that it was not the same one going backwards and forwards was certain – since the numbers on each were different. Each time one came over Rex strained to catch a glimpse of the design, so different to anything he had seen before. The others cursed the necessity of stopping every twenty minutes, and often having to make long detours to keep under cover when the trees left the road.

Simon talked little. He was not used to exercise, and knew that if he were to come through he must husband all his energy. De Richleau, in spite of the fact that he was far older than either of the others, walked briskly. It seemed that in this new adventure he had regained something of the vitality of his earlier years; even if he was a little out of training, his body was free of any superfluous flesh, and his tough sinews were rapidly regaining their elasticity.

It was Van Ryn who kept up the spirits of the party. Two months in prison – far from quelling his natural exuberance – seemed to have made him relish his freedom all the more. He told them of his capture when hidden in a coal truck on the military train from Turinsk to Tobolsk – of how he had used the lumps of coal for missiles when they had tried to arrest him. There must have been quite a number of sore heads and aching limbs among that detachment of Red Guards on the following morning, but in the end he'd had to throw in his hand; being sniped from four different angles with the snipers a hundred yards away was no fun for a man armed only with lumps of coal – however big that man happened to be.

Then De Richleau gave an account of his and Simon's activities since their arrival in Russia.

Simon was thinking of Valeria Petrovna – would he ever again, he wondered, behold her wonderful exotic beauty – touch the warm, golden softness of her skin, or feel her faintly perfumed breath on his cheek? Never would he forget those marvellous nights in Moscow, with a million stars shining in the frosty darkness from her window that overlooked the Moskawa river. It seemed absurd to think that he had only spent a week in Moscow. His well-ordered office in London, with its quiet, efficient routine, its telephones and typists – all seemed incredibly remote, like people and things in some former life. What would his able, unimaginative partners think if they could see him now? An accessory to a murder – on a forced march to escape capture by the police – and going where? After some absurd treasure buried by some mad prince. He gave one of his quick, sideways glances at his two companions. Surely the whole thing was a dream – a nightmare – and he would wake up in his comfortable bedroom at his club! Even as he turned his head the slight pressure of Valeria Petrovna's ikon against his chest assured him that it was all very real indeed.

They had halted in sight of the first houses of a small village. De Richleau and Van Ryn began to discuss the advisability of raiding some lonely farmhouse for horses and a sleigh; the Duke was for an immediate attempt to obtain them at all costs – by purchase, if possible, and if not, by force.

Van Ryn was against this – he argued that if they were to get a sleigh now, in the early afternoon, they would almost certainly be spotted by the aeroplanes, since they would be forced to remain on the road. By comparing a big sweep in the river with their map, he pointed out that it could not be more than five miles to Romanovsk, so he proposed that they should stick to the woods and walk the remaining distance. By nightfall they would be safe from aeroplane observation. He was willing enough to beat up any farm if need be – but let it be after dark!

Simon sided with Rex, and so it was settled; they made a wide detour, leaving the village on their right. The forest was of larch and pine, with little undergrowth, and in its shelter they found walking easier, for the heat of the sun had started to thaw the frozen crust of the road, and progress on it had become increasingly difficult.

It was during this detour that they saw the first flight of big 'planes. They were crossing a wide clearing at the time, and dodged hastily back among the trees. Six giant 'planes, flying in perfect formation, and at less than a thousand feet, roared over their heads – they were followed by six more, and yet another six, in quick succession.

De Richleau looked at the other two. 'This is very strange; the small 'planes which we saw all the morning may have been searching for us, but we can hardly suppose that they would turn out flights of bombers on our account!'

'Must be an air-park somewhere around,' suggested Rex.

'Jack Straw told us to keep our eyes open for anything military up this way,' nodded Simon.

'If it is,' drawled Rex, 'it'd sure interest the secret service folks in Washington.'

'An air-park,' murmured the Duke. 'And you say, Rex, that these 'planes are of a completely different type to those generally used in Europe and America?'

'Sure, the wings are set at a different angle, and they're shorter – you can see how much more like dicky-birds they look than ours.'

They continued their way through the forest, but after they saw the first squadron of big bombers, the hum of innumerable aeroplanes was always in the background, loud or faint, breaking the silence of the afternoon.

In threes or in sixes, or singly, the sky was rarely free of them as they swooped or hovered, practising their revolutions.

They had just breasted a slight rise when they first saw the fence; it stretched away on either hand, some fifty yards in front of them, the height of a man, and formed of six strands of copper wire, which shone brightly in the sunlight – the wires stretched taut throughout steel uprights. It looked innocent enough, but De Richleau, at least, had seen fences of that type before – on the enemy frontiers during the War.

As they walked up to it, he laid his hand on Simon's arm: 'Be careful, it is almost certain to be electrified – it would be instant death to touch it!'

Rex pointed to a dead ermine that lay a few feet away. 'Sure thing, that poor feller crashed it. I guess he never knew what hit him. I'll say they're mighty keen to keep people out of their backyard in these parts.'

For some time they walked parallel to the fence, which ran roughly north and south. After they had covered nearly half a mile Rex halted suddenly; Simon stopped too, having, at the same moment, caught sight of a grey figure among the trees. De Richleau instinctively followed their movement as they flung themselves on the ground. He looked at them questioningly.

'Sentry,' whispered Simon, pointing. And there, between the trees, on the other side of the wire, they could make out the form of a Red Guard. He was standing quite still, with his back to them, as he leant on his rifle. He was a little man, and his overcoat was too big for him; his hat was thrust on the back of his head, and his attitude bespoke dejection. He was a pitiful, rather than a frightening, figure – nevertheless they had no desire to be seen, and crept stealthily back until they were well out of view.

'God-forsaken job,' said Simon, as they proceeded on their way again. 'Standing in the snow all day – guarding an air-park a thousand miles from anywhere, that no one knows exists!'

'That's just why it's so important,' remarked the Duke. 'Nobody knows it exists!' Even as he spoke they came out of the belt of trees, the ground sloped sharply away to their left front – a wonderful panorama was spread in front of them.

The electric fence came out of the wood and ran down the hill a quarter of a mile to their left; beyond it stretched a great open amphitheatre of at least three miles across in each direction, the whole surrounded by the dark ring of forest.

Line upon line of aeroplane hangars lay spread below them – squadron after squadron of 'planes: bombers, fighters, scouts, looking like toys in the distance, their wings flashing silver in the afternoon sun. Row upon row of hutments and barracks, offices, and repair sheds. All the time little flights of 'planes rose and descended with perfect precision on the numerous landing grounds. In every part of the park some sort of activity was going forward – tractors were pulling 'planes in and out of hangars, little groups of soldiers were drilling or being marched from place to place; for many minutes the friends stood silent, watching this amazing spectacle.

'The forbidden territory.' Simon laughed, suddenly.

De Richleau nodded. 'Yes, this is the secret they are so anxious to preserve – it must have been in order to create this gigantic air-camp that they finished the railway to Tobolsk, and put the road we came on last night in such good repair.'

'I reckon Jack Straw would like to give this place the once-over,' said Rex.

'He's given us the name of Colonel Marsden, at the Thatched House Club, in London. If we get through we must let him know of this,' De Richleau replied, thoughtfully. 'How many 'planes do you think there are, Rex?'

'All of a hundred and fifty squadrons – two hundred, maybe, just take a look at those hangars – it's impossible to count.'

'Well, now, I'll tell you,' said Simon, quietly. 'I never did believe what they say in Moscow about being frightened of a combined attack by the capitalist countries – they're out to conquer us – that's a certainty; I wonder how they feed this lot – the road was empty, and we've never been more than a mile from the local railway – yet we haven't heard a single train go by!'

'Can't you see?' Rex extended a long arm. 'On the far side there, they've rail-trucks and engines – that little one-eyed decavil that runs by the river couldn't supply five per cent of this outfit – they've scrapped it, and built a new one direct from Tobolsk through the forest. I'll say it – '

They were so interested that they had not noticed the approach of soft footsteps, deadened by the snow. Suddenly a voice behind them said, quietly:

'A dangerous secret for foreigners to know.'

Chapter XV

Enter the Princess Marie Lou

The three men swung round; the challenge was so unexpected that De Richleau's hand jumped to the butt of his automatic – in spite of the fact that the voice was that of a woman; when he saw that she was alone, he relaxed his hold.

She was laughing quietly at their comical air of consternation. Eyes of the deepest blue, an adorable retroussé nose, and a red mouth, which curved deliciously in laughter. Under a sheepskin hat, set at a rakish angle, peeped tight little curls of chestnut-brown. She wore a short coat of squirrel, now almost hairless in places, but in spite of her worn clothes she had a chic and neatness altogether astonishing. She stood no higher than the Duke's shoulder, but her tiny figure was perfectly proportioned.

Her blue eyes suddenly became grave. 'It is not a good place for Englishmen, this,' she said.

De Richleau removed his papenka and bowed with a gesture which would not have ill become him had it been made to a lady of his acquaintance at Ascot or Auteuil. 'We are fortunate,' he said, 'in being discovered by Mademoiselle – that we should have seen this' – he motioned, with a smile, towards the giant air-park. 'It is, by the way, our one wish to be back in England as soon as possible.'

'England, eh! That is a long way,' she said, seriously.

'Unfortunately,' the Duke added, quietly, 'we have had some slight difference of opinion with the authorities, therefore we may not take the train; also our horses and sleigh were stolen from us by a rascally driver this morning. All today we have been wandering in the woods, hoping to find a farm where we may hire a conveyance.'

'Monsieur is very trusting to tell me this!'

De Richleau bowed again. 'No one with the eyes of Mademoiselle could be unkind or indiscreet,' he smiled.

'You know that I am not a Russian, eh?'

'Mademoiselle at this moment should be taking her tea at the "Marquis de Sévigné".'

'"The Marquis de Sévigné"?' She frowned, puzzled. 'What is that?'

'Surely, I cannot be mistaken? Mademoiselle is French, and "Sévigné" the most fashionable tea-shop in Paris. It is there that you belong.'

She smiled a little sadly. 'I do not remember Paris, but I am French. How did you know?'

The Duke spread out his elegant hands. 'The carriage of Mademoiselle proclaims it from the house-tops – the way Mademoiselle wears that little hat is in the manner born of the Parisienne.'

'My mother was French,' she admitted.

De Richleau spoke earnestly. 'Mademoiselle, as a foreigner here you are no doubt regarded with some suspicion, the last thing that we wish is that you should incur danger on our behalf, but, if without doing so you could inform us where we should be likely to obtain horses, we shall owe you a great debt of gratitude.'

'Come with me.' She turned abruptly on her heel. 'For the present you shall remain in my cottage, later – we will see.'

'That's real kind,' said Rex, smiling. 'But I'm afraid we can't accept your hospitality. It would mean big trouble for you if we were found in your place.'

She shrugged, impatiently. 'I am the teacher of languages there, in the school. I am not a foreigner to them – they have known me since I was a child – come, then!'

They followed her through the darkening woods – the shadows of the trees grew rapidly longer, and it was almost dark when they reached a small cottage, carefully fenced about. No other houses were in sight.

The interior of the tiny place was like the girl herself, neat and cheerful; the furniture was clumsy and old-fashioned, but the covers and curtains were of bright woven stuffs. A long shelf of well-thumbed books had been carefully recovered in sprigged linen that suggested a bygone bedspread; each bore a little hand-printed label.

The Duke and Simon had not been inside a comfortable room since they had left Moscow; Van Ryn had known the rigours of a Bolshevik prison for the last two months. They all sank into Mademoiselle's comfortable chairs with relief, and praised Heaven that she had found them.

'Permit us, Mademoiselle, to introduce ourselves. My friends are Mr Rex Van Ryn of New York, and Mr Simon Aron of London. I am the Duke de Richleau.'

She smiled at each in turn and to the Duke she said: 'So you also are a Frenchman?'

'Yes,' he said, 'but unfortunately, like yourself, I am an exile.'

'Ah, that is sad.' The smile died from her face. 'Myself, I left France when I was five. I do not remember it, but always I long to return. But what am I thinking of – you must be hungry after your long journey!'

They hardly had the courage to protest; only Simon, thinking of the difficulties which he knew existed about rationing, began half-heartedly to unpack the cold food from the rucksacks.

She waved it impatiently aside. 'I leave you for quarter of an hour, perhaps,' she shrugged, with a typically French gesture, as she resumed her worn furs. 'No one will come here – you will be as safe as can be.' Before they could protest she was gone with a smile and a wave of the hand, closing the door softly behind her.

De Richleau stretched his tired legs. 'We are in luck,' he said to Simon. 'It is certain that we have one guardian angel left between us.'

A slight snore drew their attention. Rex was sound asleep on the sofa. It was the first sleep he had had since he had risen from his bunk in the prison at Tobolsk, little knowing that his friends were near, thirty-six hours before.

'Hope she doesn't get in a muddle through helping us,' said Simon, thoughtfully.

The Duke took out his automatic, and removing the magazine, began to clean it carefully from the fouling of the morning.

In a very short time the girl returned, bringing with her a basket of eggs. She took down her largest frying-pan, and started to break the eggs into a basin.

Simon questioned her, while Rex snored loudly in the corner. How had she managed to evade the rationing laws?

She threw back her head, and gave a delicious ripple of laughter. That rationing – what nonsense! It was gone long ago, in the country towns at least. It had failed miserably; the greedy peasants lied and cheated, always withholding secret stores. In the end it had been thought better to let them do as they would, although there were still heavy penalties in force against anyone who was discovered hoarding. The only redress that the Communists had was to charge them higher prices for the goods, which they could obtain only from the co-operative stores. For her it was simple – her little pupils liked her – the peasants, their parents, were her friends – she had but to ask and for her there was always plenty and to spare.

As she talked she was frying a great yellow omelette. Rex was roused from his short slumber, and soon they were all seated round the table enjoying this unexpected treat. De Richleau declared that it could not have been better cooked by Mère Poulard of the Mont St Michel herself.

'Ah, Monsieur,' she answered, 'the making of an omelette is one of the many things that I learnt from my poor mother.'

'Your mother is dead then, Mademoiselle?'

'Alas, yes – in the year of the great famine. It was terrible, that. I do not know how any of us survived.'

'May one ask why your mother came to settle in this wild place, so far from home?'

'It was le Prince Shulimoff, Monsieur. My mother had known him many years – before even I was born. She was of gentle people but very poor, you understand. When I was five he offered her a position as companion to his niece. Never would he permit this niece to live in St Petersburg or Moscow – here only, in the solitude of the great Château among the woods, and so we came to live in the Château, also. That was a year or so before the War.'

De Richleau nodded. 'It is remarkable that you should have escaped in the years of revolution, Mademoiselle.'

She shrugged. 'My mother was much respected in the town; all her interests were with the poor and sick. She was the Châtelaine – none but her and the little Princess Sophie and myself lived in the Château. And Monsieur le Prince, he was a strange man. On his occasional visits to us he would sneer at her charities one day, and give her great sums of what he called 'sin money' the next, to spend as she would. When the troubles came there were many to protect my mother. She had, too, the great courage, she feared to go nowhere, and she organised the hospital – nursing Reds and Whites alike.'

'Would the Château be any great way from here?' asked Rex, who had been listening intently.

'No, Monsieur, not more than half a verst on the far side of the highway. One could walk there in fifteen minutes.'

'Would there be any folk living there now?'

'Ah, no. A great part of it was burnt. It is said that Monsieur le Prince himself set it on fire when the Bolsheviks came. I remember it well, that night; it was the day after my tenth birthday. I cried and cried because all my presents were destroyed. I was not old enough to be frightened for my mother or Monsieur le Prince. I thought nothing about all the beautiful and valuable things which were burning up in great columns of red flame. We stood there, on the lawn, watching the peasants throw the furniture out of the windows, saving what they could. That was until they thought of the cellars. Then, when they began to loot the sweet wine and brandy, we had to go away.'

'So what was left of it has stood empty ever since?' said Simon.

'In the bad times the brigands used it as a headquarters; they terrorised the countryside. Sometimes there were as many as two hundred there at one time, but in the end they were massacred by the Whites. After that it was empty for a long time until the Stiekomens came to live there.'

'The Stiekomens?' Simon looked puzzled.

'A religious man, and his disciples. He was a leader of one of the mystic religious brotherhoods which are always springing up in Russia. They were a harmless people, wanderers in the forest before they settled here. They lived a simple, communistic life in the great ruin for perhaps a year, then, one day, a detachment of real Communists – the Red Guards – marched through the village. For a reason that no one knew they butchered the poor Stiekomens against the Château wall. Since then there has been no one.'

'They are evil times that you have lived in, Mademoiselle – it is marvellous that you should have come through unscathed,' said De Richleau, regarding her thoughtfully. With her pointed chin, incredibly blue eyes, well-marked eyebrows and close-cropped curls, she reminded him of a prize Persian kitten as she sat, curled up, with her legs tucked under her on a corner of the divan, but his shrewd glance showed him that the blue eyes were very direct, the pointed chin very firm, and the red mouth could take on a determined curve as well as the slight wistful smile which was habitual to it.

She smiled. 'There is one good thing about Communism, Monsieur. If you give your labour to the State no one can harm you or compel you in marriage. I earn my living by teaching in the school. I am free to come and go. That is better, surely, than to be married off as a young girl to some man whom you have hardly seen, as in the old days. That must have been horrible!'

'Perhaps,' the Duke agreed. 'But I imagine that for a long time there was no safety for anyone.'

'There were difficulties,' she said, simply. 'Much of the time my mother kept me hidden in the roof – often for days together. Once I was caught by some soldiers in the woods, but I shot the ear from one with the little pistol that I carry. See, here it is.' As she spoke she produced a tiny, old-fashioned revolver with an inlaid mother-of-pearl handle. 'The others thought it so funny to see their comrade running up and down, howling with pain, that they stood in a ring and jeered at him, while I ran away. It was lucky for him that I did not fire quite straight!'

'Good for you!' laughed Rex. 'What a poor boob that bird must have felt, getting his ear shot off by a girl!'

'Mademoiselle,' said the Duke, seriously. 'If we were to be found here, I fear it would mean trouble for you. Will you add to your great kindness by telling me if there is any chance of our procuring horses, in order to proceed on our way?'

She frowned. 'But I do not want you to go – this is, what you say, a red letter day for me – to talk with people who are of my mother's world. I have a thousand things I want to ask; tell me about Paris – I can remember nothing but the busy streets, and the caraway seeds on the little rolls of white bread, of which I was so fond. Stay here for tonight, and I will see if I can arrange for horses tomorrow.'

All three shook their heads, and Rex put their thoughts into words. 'It's this way,' he said, slowly. 'It's just great of you to offer, but I've just broken prison, and there's other matters too. We couldn't have them find us here, with you, so if there's no chance of horses we'll just have to walk.'

She jumped to her feet with a little grimace. 'Oh, you are pig-headed. It is sad that you should go so soon, but if it must be, I know a *kulak* who has horses. His daughters are friends of mine, they are to be trusted – but have you money? If you are fugitives he takes the risk of an inquiry afterwards. His price will be high!'

De Richleau took out his pocket-book and handed a roll of notes to the girl as he asked: 'Do you wish us to accompany you, Mademoiselle, or shall we remain here?'

'It is best that I should go alone, Monsieur.'

'What about the Château?' Simon suggested. 'Think that it is – er – worth having a look at while Mademoiselle is gone?'

'Why not?' agreed De Richleau. 'We have our torches, if Mademoiselle would be so kind as to guide us there.'

Rex stretched his arms and yawned. His half-hour's nap before their meal had only served to make him more drowsy. 'Not for this child,' he declared, wearily. 'I guess I'll wait till we've got horses – it'll not run away, and I've just got to have another shut-eye before we start.'

'All right, Simon and I will go,' said the Duke. 'We can spare an hour for our inspection while you sleep, and perhaps save another visit.'

'You wish to go to the Château?' said the girl, with a puzzled look. 'But why?'

'If it is not troubling you too much, Mademoiselle. I have heard so much of the Prince Shulimoff that I would like to see his Château even in a state of ruin. We could find our own way back.'

'It was a lovely place,' she admitted. 'Even now it is imposing in the moonlight – but the moon will not be up for some time.'

'No matter,' said the Duke. 'I would like to see it if we may trespass on your kindness so far.'

'Come then.' She turned to Rex. 'And you, Monsieur – you will stay here?'

'Sure thing,' he laughed. 'How long do you reckon you'll be?'

'An hour – an hour and a half perhaps.'

'Then I'll be sleeping like a log. If I don't wake, bang me on the head with the frying-pan!'

'No,' she laughed back, as he settled himself on the divan. 'I will fill your big mouth with a handful of snow. *Au revoir, Monsieur.*'

He waved one large hand, but he was already half asleep. De Richleau and Simon had put on their furs and left the cottage with the girl.

She led them along a narrow path through the woods and across the high-road, then by a cart-track through thicker woods to a place where two great stone pillars showed faintly in the starlight. To one a big wrought-iron gate still clung, rusted and broken, half overgrown with brambles. Here she paused.

'This is the entrance to the grounds,' she said, in a low voice. 'It is too dark to see from here, but the house is straight ahead from where we stand. Are you certain that you can find your way back to the cottage?'

'Certain, Mademoiselle,' De Richleau replied, softly.

The night was utterly still and they were quite alone, but instinctively they spoke with lowered voices. 'We shall hope to return within an hour, but this is a strange country – may we know your name? We have to thank you for such very great kindness.'

'My name is Marie Louise, but my mother's name for me when we were alone was the Princess Marie Lou. It is pretty, that, do you not think?'

'Enchanting.' The Duke raised her little hand to his lips: 'Princess, I am the very humblest of your servants.'

With Simon she shook hands, as he murmured his gratitude.

'*Au revoir, Messieurs, et bonne fortune,*' she laughed, gaily. 'I will take care of your big friend!' A moment later her little figure disappeared in the shadows.

The garden had become a wilderness. The Duke and Simon followed the path as well as they could through a tangle of briars until they came at last to a big open space which must once have been one of the lawns.

It was freezing hard, and so still that the only sound was that of their own footsteps on the crisp snow. They mounted one terrace and then another. Suddenly the great, black bulk of the house loomed up before them in the faint starlight. As they came nearer they could see its gaunt outlines; through the blank upper windows patches of sky showed, where the roof should have been. The great façade was reminiscent of a miniature Versailles – the pile was splendid, even its in decay.

They mounted to the last terrace, with its broken stone balustrade, and flashed their torches on the walls. A long line of French windows, opening on to the terrace, stretched on either hand. De Richleau tried the nearest, but it was securely locked. The glass was gone, but it had been stoutly boarded over. They walked along to the left, inspecting each window as they went. All were the same, and each had loop-holes bored in the planking shoulder-high.

'Evidently the bandits Marie Lou spoke of fortified the place,' said the Duke, impatiently. 'Let us try the other end.'

They turned, and in the other direction, at a short distance from where they had started, found a window that actually stood a few inches open. The silence was eerie, and Simon started nervously as the Duke swore softly. 'What's up,' he asked.

'I forgot to put my pistol back in my pocket after I'd cleaned it. It must be still in the cottage.'

'I lent mine to Rex,' whispered Simon. 'In case anyone turned up while we were away!'

'No matter,' whispered back the Duke. 'There is nothing to be frightened of here; that is,' he added, with a laugh under his breath, 'unless the ghost of Prince Shulimoff has come back to do us the honours of his house.'

He pulled the window open as he spoke, and it yielded with a loud creak.

Simon had never felt such a strong desire to run away from something unseen and menacing; his ears felt as if they would burst with the intensity of listening; the house seemed to him an evil place, full of danger; he told himself that he was a fool. The Duke seemed quite unaffected, so he summoned up all his courage and followed him through the window.

It was utterly dark inside; not a vestige of light penetrated the inky blackness. De Richleau's torch shot out a beam of light, it rested for a moment on the ceiling and travelled quickly along the cornice. The room was long and lofty – traces of a handsome moulding still remained, but the plaster hung in strips, and in places had altogether disappeared.

With a jerk the Duke lowered the beam to the skirting, and ran it round the edge of the wall. It had not moved more than two yards when it disclosed a large pair of field boots – instantly the light went out.

Simon felt the Duke push him violently in the direction of the window, but it was too late – a dozen torches flashed into their dazzled eyes – they were surrounded.

A group of silent men, each holding an automatic, stood before them.

'Good evening, Mr Aron,' said a quiet, sneering voice. 'Welcome to Romanovsk. We have been expecting you and your friend for some little time!'

In the glare of the torches Simon saw the big red head and white, evil face of Kommissar Leshkin.

Chapter XVI

The Dark Château

Leshkin rapped out an order in Russian; Simon and the Duke were gripped by the arms and led out of the room, across the echoing flag-stones of a great central hall – roofless and open to the night sky. In the faint starlight they could see the broken balustrade of the grand staircase leading up to – nothing. At the far side of the hall they were led into the pitch darkness of a narrow passage and into a small room at the end.

Two lanterns were lit, and they saw it was furnished only with a trestle table and a few soap-boxes. Leshkin sat down heavily at the far side of the table and gave another brief order. The guards ran their hands over the prisoners, but the only weapon they found was the long, slender stiletto with which De Richleau had killed the spy at Sverdlovsk.

Leshkin motioned to the guards and they left the room, with the exception of one huge Mongolian, who leant against the wall behind the prisoners. Simon caught a glimpse of his face in the lamplight, – a hare-lip showed his broken, yellow teeth.

The Kommissar placed his automatic on the table before him, his little, red-rimmed eyes screwed up into a malicious smile as he looked from one to the other of his prisoners; he addressed Simon.

'We have met in London – we have met in Moskawa – and now we meet in Romanovsk – is it not, Mr Aron?'

Simon nodded.

'I am very happy to see you in Romanovsk, Mr Aron – it gives me opportunity to entertain you in my own fashion. I have been wanting to do that for a long time.' There was a world of unpleasant meaning in Leshkin's voice.

'That's very nice of you,' said Simon, suspiciously.

Leshkin ran his finger-nails with a rasping sound through his short, stubbly red beard. 'Do not mention it,' he said, with mock politeness. 'I owe you a very special debt for the way in which you have entertained Valeria Petrovna when you were in Moskawa. That debt shall be paid in the true Russian manner.'

'Thought Russia gave up paying her debts at the time of the Revolution,' murmured Simon.

'Silence,' snapped the Kommissar, with a sudden change of manner. 'Now, you,' he addressed the Duke. 'You call yourself Richwater?'

'That is so,' replied De Richleau. 'You will see that from my passport.'

'The passport lies; it is not so that you are known in London – in Curzon Street, or at the Mausoleum Club, for instance?'

The Duke smiled. 'You are well informed. I do not always use my title, and if I choose to translate my name at times, it is my own affair. Doubtless if you knew so much you would be aware that I am the Duke de Richleau.'

'A bourgeois,' Leshkin sneered.

De Richleau raised his grey eyebrows, and his smile deepened. 'A bourgeois? Indeed you are enchanting, Monsieur le Kommissar. My friends and my enemies have called me many things, but never before have I been called a bourgeois!'

'You are an hereditary enemy of the workers – it is enough.' Leshkin lit a cigarette and leaned back, regarding them in silence for a few moments. Suddenly he said:

'What have you done with your friend – the American, why is he not with you?'

Simon and the Duke both looked blank.

'*Come*, do not pretend that you do not know who I mean.' The Russian's voice was quiet and cold. 'You made inquiries about this man in Moskawa. I, myself, supplied the information to you through Valeria Petrovna that he was in prison in Tobolsk. He escaped only yesterday – and with you, in a sleigh. Where is he?'

'Well, I'll tell you,' said Simon, slowly. He realised that if the Kommissar knew so much of their movements it would do none of them any good to deny all knowledge of Rex. 'Van Ryn wanted to strike back to the railway, and we were for going farther north, so we separated – that's why he's not here.'

'When was this?'

'Early this morning, after we – er – lost our sleigh, you know!'

'Lost!' Leshkin sneered. 'That is good – and you say that your friend, the American, after coming six thousand miles to spend one hour in Romanovsk, decided to run away when he was only a little twelve miles from his destination?'

'Well, if he hadn't he'd be here with us,' Simon parried.

'So – then he has passed the secret on to you – is it not?'

'Secret? What secret?' said Simon, vaguely.

'Mr Aron, you make me laugh.' Leshkin sat back and slapped his stomach with his fat hands. His laughter was not good to hear. 'What do you take me for – a fool?'

'Oh, no,' Simon assured him, earnestly. 'I wouldn't do that!'

'Does it not occur to you as strange that I should be waiting for you here?'

'I was never so surprised in my life.'

Leshkin nodded heavily. 'I have followed your movements since you left Moskawa with great interest, Mr Aron. Last night I was informed that Van Ryn had escaped from Tobolsk. Of your stealing the sleigh in Turinsk I already knew; it was not unreasonable to suppose that by this evening you would be here. I left Moskawa by aeroplane in time to meet you – that is all! Come now – you have the secret, let us not waste time.'

'I don't know what you're talking about.' Simon shook his head.

'Listen.' The Kommissar leant forward and tapped the table with a fat white forefinger. 'The American comes to Moskawa, two – three months ago, is it not? He disappears – all right, we find him again – on our train, attempting to enter the forbidden territory. Is he a fool – is he a spy? We do not know, all right – put him in prison – that is that. Then you come to Moskawa. All night – all day, you inquire for the American. One day our agent hears you talk with a man in the Zoo – the name "Shulimoff" is spoken. All Russia knows of the buried treasure of the Shulimoffs. We know now that Romanovsk was the American's destination. It was for these jewels he came to Russia. I have only to supply to you, through Valeria Petrovna, the information that he is in prison at Tobolsk; you will go there to procure his release – then you, or he, or all of you, will come on here to find the treasure. All I have to do is to make my plans to meet you here. Where are the jewels? Let us waste no more time!'

'Elementary, my dear Watson,' murmured the Duke into Simon's ear.

Simon chuckled suddenly into his hand.

'What you say?' snapped Leshkin.

De Richleau bowed. 'Merely a little joke we have in England about people with red hair!'

As Leshkin glowered at the Duke, Simon added: 'Sorry we can't help you.'

An unpleasant light came into the Kommissar's small, red-rimmed eyes. 'You do not think so now, perhaps, but I shall find ways to persuade you.'

De Richleau intervened. 'You will excuse me,' he said, politely. 'Aron has already told you that we have parted from the American. Both of us have heard about the jewels, but neither of us know where they are.'

The Russian gave him a shrewd look. 'There may be something in what you say. Fortunately the American cannot get away – we shall catch him by tomorrow night. However, if you know nothing, you are of no use to me – again, why should we waste time? I will have you shot!'

'And why should you do that?' asked De Richleau, quietly.

'You have helped a prisoner to escape – you are in the forbidden territory where, perhaps, you have seen too much. In any case, you are an hereditary oppressor of the workers, and therefore an enemy of the Party – it is enough – be thankful that I have you shot! For Aron I have a very different programme.'

The Duke smiled. He appeared to be perfectly calm as he said, slowly: 'You have asked Aron if he takes you for a fool! I most certainly do not, but you will be, if you have me shot.'

'Why so?' asked Leshkin, quickly.

'Because dead, I may be very dangerous to you – alive, I may be of some service.'

'So!' Leshkin shrugged. 'This is but talk, you can serve me not at all.'

De Richleau leaned over the table and fixed his grey eyes with their strange, piercing brilliance on the Kommissar. 'If you are so sure,' he said, softly, 'tell me the name of the third man who sat with Aron and me in the Tavern of the Howling Wolf on our second night in Moscow.'

'I do not know – also I do not care.'

The Duke nodded, then he smiled slowly and turned away.

'No,' he said, lightly. 'Stalin does not tell everybody everything – why should he?'

At the name of Stalin – the Iron Man – Kommissar of Kommissars, who rules Russia more autocratically than any Tsar, Leshkin stiffened where he sat. There was a brief, pregnant silence in the little room, nothing stirred – save the faint flicker of shadows on the ceiling.

'Stalin?' echoed Leshkin very softly; there was a note of reverence in his voice – a shade too of fear.

De Richleau followed up his advantage. 'Have me shot then. I am an old man. I have faced death many times. I am not afraid, but remember that you shall answer for it to . . . Stalin.'

'If this is true, you have papers.' Leshkin held out his hand. 'Show me the passes of the Ogpu.'

'I have no papers.' De Richleau made a disdainful gesture. 'There are forces outside the Ogpu – forces outside the Soviet Union; Stalin uses many strange weapons for the good of the Party.'

'I do not believe this,' Leshkin murmured, sullenly.

'Do you know anything of my history?' De Richleau went on. 'If you do, you know that I am a political exile from my own country; driven out as a young man, nearly forty years ago, by a capitalist government. Do you know why Aron was received by Madame Karkoff immediately on his arrival in Moscow? On instructions. Between them there was no thought but of the secret work that must be done for the Party. We made pretence of seeking information in order that even the Ogpu should not suspect our true intentions. Do you know who the American is? He is the son of Channock Van Ryn, one of the richest men in America. It was for us to gain his confidence – far greater issues hang upon this American than a simple attempt to recover these jewels – they are an old-wives' tale. I doubt if they are here at all!' He paused impressively, holding the Russian with his eyes.

Leshkin sat silent for a little – again he clawed his sparse red beard. He knew that Stalin employed secret spies outside the Ogpu – was it possible that these were members of the inner circle? Then his eyes took on a cunning look, and he said, sullenly:

'Why, then, did you let the American go south alone? No – ' he hit the table with his big, white fist. 'I do not believe it – you are intriguing foreigners – I will have you shot.'

'So be it.' De Richleau gave the suggestion of a bow. 'The choice is yours. I have only one regret – I shall be unable to be present when you are called upon to face our master. That will be a bad half-hour for you, Comrade.'

The Kommissar stood up. At his call the guards came back into the room. He gave short instructions and the Duke and Simon were led out. They were taken down the passage again, across the great, echoing hall, and through a second passage, into another wing. Here a door was opened and they were thrust into the darkness. The door slammed behind them and they heard a heavy bold shot home.

'Phew!' Simon let out a short whistle as he drew his hand across his forehead. 'I don't like that man.'

De Richleau placed a steadying hand on his shoulder in the dark. 'Neither do I, my friend, but you were magnificent, so calm – you showed a splendid courage.'

'Well, I'll tell you,' Simon confessed, 'I didn't feel it. Do you think he'll have us shot?' They both spoke in whispers.

'Not for the present – he half believes my little story about Stalin; none of these people trust each other. It is quite likely that we might be Stalin's secret agents; he will do nothing till he has communicated with Moscow.'

'Um. I thought it was wonderful, the way you put that over. Of course he'll send a wireless from the air-park. When the reply comes we shall be in a real muddle!' As Simon used his favourite expression for any sort of trouble, instinctively he laughed his nervous little laugh.

'That's better,' said the Duke. 'To hear you laugh so is good. Much may happen before they receive that reply. I'm angry with myself, though, that I should have brought you into such danger. I wish now that I had never shown you the letter from Rex.'

Simon laughed again. 'I'd never have forgiven you if you hadn't – but, talking of Rex, I suppose there's just a chance that he may get us out of this?'

In the dark De Richleau shook his head. 'I fear he cannot help us – there must be at least a dozen secret police with Leshkin. Rex does not even know of our plight. I only trust he does not come to look for us and blunder into their clutches.'

Simon produced his torch, covering the bulb with his fingers, so that the light should not shine under the door. He pressed the button. 'Might as well see where we are,' he suggested. 'Try and help ourselves if there's no one else to help us!'

The faint glow, coming pink through his fingers, was insufficient to light the room; only the Duke's face showed faintly, heavy with shadows. Simon turned his back to the door and took his fingers off the bulb.

A quick glance showed them that the room was empty. It seemed to be some portion of the servants' quarters – stone-flagged, and with a big, round copper built into the wall at one corner. Simon turned the light up to the roof. It was lath and plaster, supported by small beams at intervals. In one corner there was a rent, only about six inches wide – but enough, when they stood directly below it, to see three or four stars shining brightly.

'If we could widen that!' Simon suggested.

'Ah, if we could,' the Duke agreed. 'But it is too high for us, my friend.'

As he spoke a single shot broke the silence of the night. It was followed by a burst of firing.

'Rex!' exclaimed Simon. 'Hope they haven't got him.' He clicked out his torch as the door of their prison swung open. Outside, with a lamp in one hand, stood the big Mongolian with the hare-lip. In the other hand he held a deadly-looking automatic, which he levelled at them.

The Duke and Simon were at least ten feet away. There was no possible chance that they might rush the man. It was evident that he meant to shoot on sight if they made the least move. Wisely they put their hands above their heads.

Then came the sound of another single shot – then another burst of firing from the other end of the Château. The Mongolian looked quickly down the passage in that direction, but only for a second; his dark eyes returned to them almost immediately, and he held them covered all the time.

The sound of shouting came to them from the garden – there were running footsteps which seemed to be crossing the big hall – a perfect fusillade of shots, and the whine of a ricochet. A man screamed – there were three more single shots, a murmur of angry voices – then silence once more.

The Mongolian swung the door shut, and shot the bolt. They were alone again in the darkness.

Both had been holding their breath while they listened to the fight outside; sharply now they released it. Was Rex dead, or had he escaped? Someone had been hit – that was certain, but there had been shots after that – the Bolsheviks, perhaps, taking a last shot as Rex ran off into the night, or finishing him off as he lay, wounded, on the ground. Which? Such were the thoughts teeming through their minds.

'Do not fear,' said De Richleau, trying to comfort both himself and Simon. 'He will have got away, he is a splendid shot, and he would have the advantage of the darkness – the others would be in the light.'

'Unless they surprised him in the house,' Simon argued, pessimistically, 'then they'd use their torches on him and he'd be dazzled by the light, just as we were.'

'We must hope for the best, but let us look again at the hole in the roof.'

Simon flashed his torch on it. 'I think I could reach it if you could bear my weight.'

'Let us try.' De Richleau stooped, and Simon put his legs round the Duke's neck, sitting on his shoulders. It was a difficult and unsteady proceeding in the dark, but once Simon managed to catch hold of a beam it was easier. He inspected the hole from a closer range with his torch.

'There is nothing above us,' he said in a whisper; 'this must have been a sort of outbuilding – fire couldn't have reached this wing either – the roof's tarred felt.' He shifted the torch to the hand with which he was steadying himself, and began to work swiftly.

It was a slow process. He dared not make the least sound or the Mongolian would come in at once to see what was happening. He pulled away little bits of plaster and pushed them out through the hole, leaving for the moment the broken framework of the lath. That part was comparatively easy, but tearing away pieces of the thick tarred felt was another matter. They had to take frequent rests, for De Richleau could not bear his weight for very long at a time. When he had worked for an hour the hole was no more than a foot in diameter.

'We shall never do it,' said Simon, despondently; 'it will have to be three times that size for us to get through.'

'Not a bit,' the Duke encouraged him in a quick whisper. 'Where a man's shoulders can pass, there his body can pass too; we shall be a little scratched, but what matter? Make your hole broader at each side now; another three inches will do it.'

Simon grunted; it did not look to him as if a cat could get through in comfort. He had torn his nails, and his finger-tips ached excruciatingly, but he continued to work away.

When they next rested De Richleau encouraged him again. 'It is early yet, it cannot be more than ten o' clock; another hour and we shall be out of this. Listen! What was that?'

With straining ears they stood in the darkness; the noise did not come from the passage, but from above. Something heavy was moving on the roof. As they watched, a black form blotted out the stars that had, a moment before, been shining through Simon's hole; something moved in the opening, and suddenly a bright light blinded them. It went out instantly, and they heard the welcome sound of Rex's voice:

'Holy smoke! I'm glad it's you!'

'Thank the Lord you're safe,' whispered Simon; 'there's a guard outside the door, but if you can make the hole a bit bigger we'll soon be out.' He mounted on the Duke's shoulders again, and in feverish haste they worked away at the roofing.

'Did you hear the dust-up?' Rex whispered. 'Two of those birds'll never see Manhattan Island any more. I ran right in on 'em – thought they were you!'

'How did you find us?' Simon whispered back.

'The Snow Queen kid got rattled when you didn't get back in the hour, so I came up to have a look-see. Ever since the dust-up I've been snooping round, mostly on the roof – or what's left of it. Good thing I had that practice in the Rockies last fall. Then I spotted your light, and a hand throwing bits of roof out. Reckon you can get through now?'

Simon slid to the ground and they surveyed the hole with their torches. Rex's big hands had made a lot of difference; De Richleau nodded. 'That will do; up you go, Simon.'

'No, go on,' said Simon, 'you first.'

The Duke's answer was to pick his young friend up by the knees and hold him aloft. 'You waste time,' he said, tersely.

Simon wasted no more, but thrust up his hands. 'Don't grip the roof, it may give,' whispered Rex. He gripped Simon's wrists and hauled him up. There was a slithering noise, a slight scrape, and he was through.

The Duke looked apprehensively towards the door – surely the guard had heard. Two laths had cracked with a dry snap. He lost no time, but mounted the stone copper – Rex could not have reached him on the floor; by leaning forward his hands would be within a few inches of the hole.

'Make it snappy,' whispered Rex, thrusting his arms down from above. The Duke leaned forward and grasped them firmly, then he swung off the copper. As he did so there was a crash of falling masonry – the cement that held the top row of bricks round the copper had long perished – De Richleau's boot had brought them rumbling to the floor.

Instantly the door swung open. Lantern in one hand, pistol in the other, the Mongolian rushed in. The Duke found himself hanging, suspended, looking right into that cruel, hare-lipped face. The man dived for him. The Duke kicked out, his boot took the soldier on the upper part of his right arm; the man staggered back, dropping his gun.

'Pull, Rex, pull!' shouted the Duke, but to his horror he found that Rex had let go one of his hands. He dangled by one arm, revolving slowly.

The Mongolian did not stop to find his pistol; he flung himself on the Duke. De Richleau found himself being dragged down; the bestial face was within an inch of his own.

Suddenly there was a blinding flash, and a terrific report within an inch of his ear that almost shattered the drum; the man sagged and slipped backwards with a horrible choking sound. Rex had shot him at close range through the upper mouth.

The next thing the Duke knew was that he was out in the cold air of the roof; Rex and Simon were on each side of him, dragging him from one level to another. There was the sound of running feet, and lanterns could be seen below. A sudden shout – a shot, a bullet whistled past his head, and then the shooting began in earnest.

Chapter XVII

The Fight on the Roof-tops

A hail of bullets spattered the brickwork against which they had been standing a moment before.

'Don't shoot,' whispered Rex hoarsely, as they moved crouching along the gutter under the protection of a low wall. 'The flash will show them where we are.'

'I have nothing to shoot with,' said the Duke, bitterly. 'I deserve to be shot myself, at my age, for leaving my weapon behind.'

'Good Lord, I forgot.' Rex thrust the other pistol into his hand. 'I found it after you'd gone. Look out!'

They had come to the end of the low wall on the front of the house. A series of roofs at different levels lay before them. They were those of the outhouses that had survived the fire.

'What do we do now?' asked Simon in a whisper.

'Back the way we came,' Rex answered promptly. 'More cover in the ruin, and they'll be round here directly.'

Even as he spoke they could hear voices below them; quick jerky questions and answers. A light flashed on to the roof of one of the outhouses. They crept stealthily back to the far end of their cover, Simon leading.

As he rounded the corner he ran full tilt into a crouching form. Luckily the man had no time to use his gun. Simon felt a hand clutch at his throat; they crashed to the roof together.

Simon kicked and struggled; each moment he thought they would roll over the edge and break their necks in the garden, twenty feet below. He struck blindly at the man's face, but the fellow dodged his blows. The grip on his throat tightened, the darkness seemed to grow blacker before his eyes, there was a buzzing in his ears. Through it Rex's voice came faintly to him. 'Stick it, Simon, good boy; give him top place, and I'll crack his skull!'

With a last effort Simon flopped forward and rolled over; the Russian, thinking he had overcome his adversary, gave a guttural laugh and sprang on his chest – the laugh ended in a moan as Rex smashed his head in with a blow from the butt end of his pistol. The awful grip on Simon's throat relaxed, and he crawled out from beneath the body.

The men below had lost no time in hurrying back when they heard the sounds of the struggle. De Richleau stood calmly above the prostrate Simon; he fired four times rapidly into their midst. There was a sharp cry; at least one of his shots had found a mark. The group scattered quickly; the Duke ducked down behind the wall as the return fire spattered about them.

'Give me a hand,' muttered Rex, and Simon helped to prop his late enemy in position against the wall. The appearance of the Russian's head and shoulders drew a further volley from the bushes below; a bullet thudded into the man's chest.

'Get his gun, Simon.' The Duke kicked the pistol that lay at the man's feet. Simon picked it up quickly.

'See that window?' Rex whispered, pointing to the main block. 'It's level with these leads. Think we can make it?'

'Ner,' said Simon briefly, 'it's twenty yards away.'

'This cursed snow,' the Duke agreed; 'they'll see our every movement once we leave this wall.'

'Got to take a chance,' protested Rex. 'If they storm the roof both ends of the wall we're done. Once in that room we'll hold 'em till daylight – or, better still, maybe we'll be able to make a break from the window round the corner, across the garden.'

'Yes, I agree, we cannot stay here.' De Richleau peered round the wall. 'I can see one fellow from here; I'll kill him in a minute.'

Rex tapped him on the arm. 'Wait – I'll creep to the other end – see if I can spot another. When you hear me fire, give your bird the works and beat it. You, too, Simon, don't wait for the Duke; go like smoke. Good luck, both of you!'

Before they could answer he had moved off down the gutter.

'No time to argue, Simon,' said the Duke, in a low tone, as he covered his man from where he crouched. 'Don't lose a second when I fire. If you're not through that window when I get there, it may cost me my life.'

It seemed an eternity, waiting there in the intense cold; it numbed their fingers round the butts of the automatics. There was a sudden crash of shots from the garden, all directed to Rex's end of the wall. Simon, whose nerves were at the highest pitch, leapt forward into the open. De Richleau's pistol cracked behind him; in a second almost he was clambering through the empty window frame, the Duke hard behind him. A single bullet hissed through the snow on to the leads; another moment and De Richleau stood panting at his side.

'The fool!' he gasped; 'did you see?'

'Ner – what happened?'

'He deliberately stood up to draw their fire.'

'Hope they didn't get him.'

De Richleau put his head out of the window. A vicious '*phut*' sounded in the woodwork near his head. He drew it in again sharply; Simon flashed his torch quickly round the empty room.

In addition to the window through which they had come there was another overlooking the terraces and gardens at the back of the house. 'Lucky that wasn't under the window.' As he spoke Simon shone his torch on a great jagged rent in the floor several feet in width.

'Put out that light!' whispered the Duke angrily.

Simon obeyed; carefully avoiding the hole, he made his way round to the doorway. There was no door, it had been wrenched off.

'Think they'll come this way?' he asked.

'Too dangerous!' said the Duke, who was still peering out of the window as far as he dared. 'They know we are armed – who would be brave enough to be first man round that doorway ?'

A single shot rang out; a volley came from the bushes below in answer. De Richleau gave a sudden laugh. 'Rex is all right,' he said; 'at least, not dead; he may be wounded. How many shots have you in that pistol?'

Simon unclipped the magazine. 'Five,' he said, after some hesitation.

'Good,' the Duke's voice came back. 'It is our turn to make a demonstration now. Stay where you are.'

Simon heard him shuffling round the room. Next moment De Richleau's hand was on his arm.

'Is there a staircase leading below?' he asked. 'One flash of your torch – no more; and hold it sideways, at arm's length from your body.'

The little ray of light pierced the thick darkness, showing a landing outside the doorway and a narrow wooden staircase. Simon switched out the light and edged out of the room. For another brief moment he flashed it on; nothing was stirring.

'Let us go down.' said the Duke. 'Keep as quiet as possible.'

Simon followed him; the wooden stairs creaked abominably. On the floor below, the faint light from a broken window made the landing just perceptible.

'We are in luck,' De Richleau murmured. In the dark, Simon could sense from his tone that he was smiling. It came to him suddenly that the Duke was actually enjoying this nightmare. Once free, and with a weapon in his hands, it seemed that he had none of Simon's desire to slip away, to run, to be safe again; to do anything, short of deserting his friends, in order to get out of range of these smashing, tearing bullets, that made men gulp, or scream with pain.

'See,' the Duke went on, 'this window will serve us admirably; from here we can survey the front. I shall fire one shot into those bushes there. You take the right-hand flash as they reply; aim for it and fire three rounds, then duck. I shall fire as I choose, but the right-hand flash is yours; you understand? And no more than three shots. Are you ready?'

'Um,' said Simon, nodding in the dark. 'Go ahead.'

De Richleau fired; a burst of shooting answered him at once; eight men at least must have been lurking in the shadows below. One was almost directly beneath the window, less than ten feet away. Simon let fly at him, leaning out to do so. There was a scream of pain at his second shot – then the Duke wrenched him back by the neck, so that his third shot went into the air.

'Are you mad,' De Richleau shouted, 'to lean out so?'

'Sorry,' said Simon humbly; 'I got him, though!'

'You did,' said the Duke dryly; 'it is only by the providence of Heaven that he did not get you. Have you never been in a fight before?'

'Ner,' said Simon nervously. 'Ner – never.'

A sudden thud sounded in the room above, accompanied by a fresh burst of firing from the garden. 'Rex,' said De Richleau quickly; 'let us go up.'

The stairs creaked and groaned as they reascended; the Duke paused on the upper landing.

'You all right, Rex?' asked Simon, stepping forward.

The Duke jerked him back.

'I'm fine,' came a reassuring voice from the lesser darkness by the window. 'Thank God,' said the Duke, releasing his grip on Simon's arm. 'For a moment I feared it might be one of them. Mind that infernal hole.'

'Great stuff you gave 'em just now,' Rex went on. 'I got across without so much as a farewell wave.'

'Listen,' said the Duke. 'I propose that we should try the garden at the back – the stairs are free.'

'That's O.K. But where'll we make for when we get there?'

'To Marie Lou. Did she get horses? Are they at her cottage?'

'She did not. Her hick farmer friends had been given the wire about us; they wouldn't sell.'

A sudden spurt of bullets on the ceiling made Rex duck his head.

'No matter,' De Richleau went on quickly, 'we can only go one at a time, and her cottage is the only place that we all know; it is the only place to rendezvous.'

'Can't we all beat it together?' Rex suggested.

'You know we cannot,' said the Duke sharply, 'they would follow us. One of us must run while the others cover his retreat from the window. Simon is to go first.'

'Why me?' said Simon. 'You want to get rid of me!'

'Don't be a fool – you waste time talking. In any case, you have only two shots left in that pistol. Rex, watch that side window while I speak to Simon.'

'Listen.' De Richleau's voice dropped to a lower, more persuasive tone. 'It is a big risk you run; there may be men already at the back of the house. There soon will be. Marie Lou has failed to get horses. Well, then, some-one must go to her – at once, she is our only hope – and she is a brave child. I take responsibility for this. Ask her to show you somewhere where we can hide. We will give you half an hour's start; but when we arrive, be ready. Go now, every moment counts.'

A shattering crash came as Rex fired into the darkness at a moving shape on the roof.

'All right; that's different,' said Simon.

'That's better. Good-bye, my son.'

'Missed him,' said Rex from the window, 'but I guess he won't try that cat burglar stuff again for a bit!'

'Lord be praised that we've got that boy out of this,' sighed the Duke, as Simon could be heard making his way down the stairs.

'Think he'll make it?' said Rex.

'Why not? There has been no sign of movement in the garden up to now. Fire again from your window to show that we are still here.' As he spoke De Richleau watched the terrace and lawns below him. He tapped his foot impatiently. 'They will be round here in a moment. They must know that this room looks out on the back!'

Simon came out on the terrace. He looked quickly to right and left, then darted down the stone steps. The Duke watched anxiously as he ran across the first lawn. 'Fire again, Rex,' he said nervously, 'fire again; don't let them suppose that we're not here.'

Simon took the second terrace at a jump. To De Richleau he was now only a faint blur against the whiteness of the snow. The Duke breathed more freely. There had been no sign of the enemy, and the darkness swal-lowed Simon up.

A bullet sang through Rex's window, and thumped into the wall. Some-one was firing from a new angle, but De Richleau did not heed it; he was watching the distance into which Simon had disappeared. Suddenly there was a spurt of flame somewhere in the bushes by the lower lawn, and then a sharp cry.

'Good God,' the Duke groaned, 'they've got him.'

Another flash, some way to the left, speared the darkness for a second. De Richleau leaned out of the window in his excitement and anxiety.

'Don't shoot,' he yelled at the top of his voice, 'he can see you by the flash.' But even as he called his warning there came two more spurts of flame from opposite directions, about fifteen feet apart, and another cry. The Duke gripped the window-sill in his agony. He feared that Simon, already wounded, had used his last shot. At the bottom of the garden all was silence once more.

'Did they get him?' Rex asked in a strained voice.

'God knows – I fear so; they had a man in the bushes by the gate. Never shall I forgive myself if I have sent that boy to his death. I will go down.'

'You'll stay right where you are,' Rex replied promptly, 'and for the land's sake come away from that window – they'll pot you where you stand.'

The Duke drew in his head, but he remained staring gloomily into the darkness.

'You couldn't help it,' Rex tried to hearten him; 'you just thought it would be an easy get-away for him; 'sides, I'll bet little Simon's all right. Almighty difficult to hit a running man in the dark; he can take care of himself better than you think. I'd back Simon against any Bolshie that ever lived.'

'You mean it kindly, but you're talking nonsense, Rex. Simon would be as helpless as a child against one of these men, and he's gone to his death through my foolishness.'

A pistol cracked from the terrace below – De Richleau staggered back, dropping his gun with a clatter on the floor as Rex caught him.

'Steady,' said Rex in a whisper, 'steady – tell me you're all right?'

'Don't worry,' he managed to gasp, 'they got me in the shoulder.'

'Hell's luck. I was just beginning to think that we might get out of here. Is it bleeding much?'

'No, don't worry – watch the roof.' De Richleau leant against the wall. After a moment he spoke again. 'Bone's scraped, not broken, I think – bullet's in the ceiling.'

'Can you use your gun?' Rex asked anxiously.

'Yes. Mustn't use right arm; bleed too much. I can fire left-handed.'

Rex groped for the pistol on the floor. 'I'll reload it for you,' he said quickly, slipping out the magazine.

'Thanks. A bit quieter, isn't it? I don't like it,' said De Richleau suddenly. 'They're up to some mischief.'

'I should worry,' Rex laughed. 'Keep clear of that garden window and we'll be O.K.; they can't rush us except from the roof or the stairs – and they'd just hate to try either.'

'Yes, we're safe for the time being, I suppose – if only poor Simon were still with us,' the Duke groaned.

'Maybe he's only been winged, like you. Anyhow, we've knocked the guts out of this racket already, or I'm mistaken. How many do you reckon there were to start with?'

'Twelve, perhaps.'

'Right. Well, there was the big boob who tried to stop you coming through the roof – that's one. The two bums I outed on my first visit makes three; then the chap with a head like an egg-shell who found the butt of my automatic – that's four.'

'Simon shot one from the landing window.'

'Yep, that's five.'

'There was the man I shot from the corner of the wall – I saw him drop,' added De Richleau.

'That's six, anyhow, and we've had quite a few additional hits, according to the shouting,' Rex grinned. 'I'll say there's not many of the bunch haven't got sore spots some place.'

'The advantage of fighting upon interior lines,' De Richleau smiled in spite of his pain. 'Or shall we say "a demonstration of the superiority of the defensive when using modern weapons".'

'That's the idea. It's good to hear you talking again like that.' Rex peered from the window. 'I'd like to know what these birds are up to, all the same.'

After the almost continuous firing the silence was uncanny. 'Perhaps,' De Richleau suggested, 'they have gone for reinforcements; the air-park can't be more than a mile away. They will return with machine-guns and a searchlight!'

'It'll be the end of the party if they do. I guess we'd better get out of this while the going's good.'

'Yes, no good waiting to be shot like rats in a trap. Let's try our luck!'

They moved towards the door. No sound came from below. De Richleau swore softly. 'How these stairs creak.'

'Which way?' said Rex, when they reached the bottom. 'Better go by the garden and see if we can't pick Simon up.'

'No,' said the Duke miserably; 'it's useless. If he's not dead or captured, he'll have reached the cottage by now. There is more cover in front; we can work our way round by the outhouses.'

With the greatest precautions they stole along the passage to the big roofless hall, pausing a full minute before they crossed it. Not a sound met their ears; the great entrance door stood wide open.

'If we have to run for it, do you think you'll faint?' whispered Rex. 'Just put me wise if you think it's likely. I could carry two like you; but don't do it on me without warning.'

'I shall not faint,' the Duke assured him, 'I've lost very little blood. If we're separated we rendezvous on Marie Lou's cottage, remember – but in no circumstances until we've thrown off the pursuit.'

'We shan't be separated,' said Rex briefly. 'All set?'

For answer De Richleau left the porch, and began to creep along in the deep shadow of the outside wall. On their other side they were protected by thick shrubberies; but for the stars above it was black as pitch. The bushes were a splendid screen, but had the disadvantage that they rustled at every movement.

The Duke suppressed an oath as he stumbled over the body of the man that Simon had shot from the landing window. He was quite dead. They passed the low brew-house where they had been held prisoner, and beneath the higher level of the wall behind which they had sheltered. With the wall the shrubbery ended.

They peered out from the last bushes, straining their eyes and ears for the least movement. If Leshkin had gone for reinforcements it seemed impossible that he had not left the rest of his men posted about the grounds to keep watch. Yet there was no sign of them.

Rex crept forward into the open, his automatic held ready for instant action. De Richleau followed, peering into the shadows on the right. The snow silenced their footfalls. They rounded the corner of the first outhouse.

Almost simultaneously Rex and the black shadow fired at point-blank range. The Russian pitched forward with a sharp cry. Rex crashed backwards, carrying De Richleau with him as he fell.

The Duke's pistol went off with the impact, the bullet hissing through the trees. He rolled from under Rex, and covered the Russian from his position on the ground. It was unnecessary. The man lay, face downward, a pool of blood running from his head, staining the snow.

Rex lay where he had fallen. His groans were terrible. He writhed in agony on the ground. De Richleau asked no questions. He staggered to his feet, changed his pistol to his right hand, and, seizing Rex by the collar, dragged him back into the shelter of the bushes.

It took all his strength and, with the effort, his wounded shoulder began to lose blood again. It was some thirty feet, and he accomplished it with only a few seconds to spare.

Shouts and running footsteps came from three directions. Leshkin's voice could be heard yelling commands; a group of men gathered round the dead soldier. One switched on a torch. For a second De Richleau was tempted to fire into their midst. He lowered his weapon – it would have been madness – there were four of them beside the Kommissar. An angry order, and the torch went out; but there was time for the Duke to see that they were looking at the roof.

A sudden volley of shots in that direction confirmed his idea that they believed their comrade to have been shot from Rex's old position at the window. There was a whispered consultation, and then Leshkin and his men withdrew.

What a golden opportunity to escape now, thought the Duke, if only it were not for Rex. He sighed. Rex had ceased groaning, and lay quite still. The Duke feared that he was dead. 'Rex,' he whispered softly.

'Yes,' to his surprise came the reply.

'Thank God,' breathed De Richleau. 'I thought they had finished you. Are you badly hurt?'

'It was a darned near thing,' Rex said, as he sat up slowly. 'Another inch either way, and it would have been me for the golden shore.'

'Are you all right? Aren't you wounded?'

'No, not a scratch. The bullet hit the steel buckle of my belt. Gosh, it was agony – like the kick of a mule, and every ounce of breath knocked out of my body. I'll bet my tummy's black and blue.'

'Can you walk – or run if need be? They believe us to be still upstairs.'

Rex got painfully to his feet. 'O.K. Let's quit this party. I guess we've had enough for one night.'

'We will break right away from the house, then, this time,' whispered the Duke. 'If we make a big circle to the left we should strike the road.'

As he spoke they left the cover of the bushes once more, creeping forward among the trees that bordered the drive.

They heard footfalls to their left, and stood stock-still; Leshkin had evidently posted a man there to watch the window. The steps moved away, and they proceeded stealthily. Another five minutes and they were able to break into a quick walk.

Guided by the stars, they made in the direction in which they believed the road to run, and a quarter of an hour later they came to it. Turning left again they walked quickly on, keeping a sharp look-out for the track that led to Marie Lou's cottage.

They passed three other cottages on the way, but these were dark and silent. At last they found the path and struck off to the right along it.

'If only Simon's there,' said Rex, breaking the long silence.

'If he's not, it's a thousand to one against our ever seeing him again.' The Duke seemed suddenly to have grown very old and tired.

The windows of Marie Lou's cottage were shuttered, and only a crack of light showed through. With a sigh of thankfulness at finding their one refuge again, De Richleau thrust open the door.

Mademoiselle Marie Lou stood upon the threshold, clasping her little mother-of-pearl revolver, her big eyes wide with fear; but of Simon Aron there was no sign.

Chapter XVIII

Simple Simon Met a Gunman

'God be praised that you are safe returned, Messieurs,' she said, with a little gesture of relief, lowering the toy weapon to her side.

'Our friend?' asked the Duke anxiously. 'Have you seen him?'

'What, the little one? Is he not with you?'

'We sent him on ahead nearly an hour ago. It is as I feared. He has been shot.' De Richleau sank heavily into a chair.

'Monsieur le Duc is wounded,' she exclaimed, as she saw the blood oozing from his shoulder.

'It is nothing, Mademoiselle; a flesh wound only.'

'Wait but one minute, and I will wash the wound.' She set water to boil, and took some strips of linen from a cupboard.

Rex was still standing at the door. 'Guess I'll go back and look for Simon,' he said simply.

'Let Mademoiselle dress my hurt, and I will come with you.' The Duke grimaced with pain as he struggled out of his greatcoat.

Rex helped him with his jacket, and the girl cut away his shirt. The place was laid bare – a gash about three inches long. The bullet had ploughed its way up the shoulder-blade and out at the top.

'You stay put,' said Rex. 'I'll go after Simon.'

'One moment.' The Duke detained him with his free hand. 'First let us hear from Mademoiselle if it is quite impossible to obtain horses.'

'Absolutely impossible, Monsieur. The peasants had been warned. I tried four farms, and at each it was the same. They dared not sell their horses. There is danger even now that one of them may have spoken to the police about my visit.'

'I thought, Mademoiselle, that these people were your friends. It is as I feared. We shall bring trouble upon you – ah, gently with my shoulder, please.'

'The water is a little hot. There is one peasant only who I do not trust – the man Rakov. I would not have tried there but that I know him to be always greedy. I thought he would be tempted to take a risk for the high price which you would pay.'

'In that case we must leave at once – we must not be found here.'

'That I will not allow.' Marie Lou's little pointed chin stuck out firmly. 'Where would you go, at night, and in the snow? Monsieur le Duc is of my own people; we are in a strange land together; I will hide you if they come.'

'You stay here,' said Rex. 'I'll go and see if I can't find any trace of Simon.'

De Richleau made an effort to rise; the girl pushed him back. 'Monsieur the American is right,' she said. Let him look for your little friend; you will stay here that I may bandage this poor shoulder. Afterwards I will hide you in the loft.'

'As you will, then; only promise me this, Rex – if Simon has been captured you will return for me before you attempt anything.' The Duke smiled at Marie Lou. 'Mademoiselle, you are a woman of great courage. To allow you to take such a risk for us is against every principle of my life, but we are in desperate straits. I accept the shelter that you offer with the deepest gratitude.'

'There, now you talk sense at last. Rakov may say nothing after all; he will think, perhaps, that it is only another of my madnesses. Because I live differently to them, the people here think that I am strange – if it were not that the children like me, and for the memory of my mother – I think that fifty years ago the peasants would have burnt me for a witch.'

For the first time in hours Rex laughed, his ugly-attractive face lit with its old merry smile. 'I'll say you're a witch all right,' he murmured. 'I've half a mind to go get wounded myself if you'd promise to take a hand healing it!'

'Monsieur is pleased to be gallant,' she said demurely. 'He would be wiser to seek tidings of his friend and return unwounded.'

'Take care, Rex,' begged the Duke, 'and don't be longer than you can help.'

'I'll be right back, and I'll give three knocks on the door, so you'll know it's me. See-yer-later.' With a cheerful smile Rex went out into the night.

When De Richleau's wound was cleaned and dressed, Marie Lou barred the cottage door, and showed him a cupboard hidden behind a curtain. It contained a collection of old clothes, but behind these was concealed a series of stout shelves, up which it was easy to climb to the loft. She told him that she had hidden there many times during the evil times, when Reds, Whites and Greens had ravaged the country indiscriminately.

The rifle was taken up to the loft, also the knapsacks and De Richleau's furs. All other traces of the travellers were disposed of in anticipation of a surprise visit; then they put out the light, that the occupant of the cottage might be presumed to be sleeping, and sat together in the darkness near the stove.

'When I heard all the shooting,' she said in a low voice, 'I thought that I should never see any of you any more.'

'Surely you could not hear the fight at this distance?' he asked, surprised.

'Ah, no – but when I was unable to get the horses I woke Monsieur the American, and he begged that I would conduct him to the Château. I should also have been in the trouble if he had not persuaded me to turn back at the gate where I left you. He had a feeling, I think, that all was not well. I like your big friend; he is so gentle.'

De Richleau nodded sadly. 'He's a fine fellow, but it is the little one I am troubled for. He was more gentle still.'

'You were very fond of him?'

'He had become almost like a son to me in my old age.'

'Monsieur Van Ryn will rescue him, perhaps – he is so strong. He could make mincemeat of half a dozen of these little Red soldiers.'

'Perhaps – he has rescued us once already this evening – but I fear poor Simon is lying dead in the snow among the bushes at the bottom of the garden. Tell me more about yourself, Mademoiselle, to take my thoughts off this terrible business.'

'What shall I say?' She shrugged her shoulders. 'Life here has been supportable – the people are not unkind. They do not understand me one little bit; that I choose to live alone and will not marry or seek a man – that is strange to them. But in a way it is part of my protection. Many husbands look at me, but I always turn away my head, therefore the wives have nothing to fear from my good looks.'

'Have you never thought of going back to France?'

'Often, Monsieur, I have thought of it, that beautiful France that I know so well from books, and from my mother's stories. But how? I have no money even if the authorities would let me make the journey.'

'Have you no relatives to whom you could have written?'

'None, Monsieur. As I have told you, my mother knew Prince Shulimoff since many years – long before I was born. She was cut off by her own people for that, you will understand?'

'I think so,' said the Duke, gently. 'You are the Prince's daughter.'

'Yes, Monsieur, I am his daughter, and legally so, for my mother was his wife, but he would never acknowledge that. It was a secret marriage made in Paris. I did not know of it myself until my mother told me when she lay dying. It seems that afterwards he made a great marriage here, in Russia, but later, when his wife died, he returned to my mother. She was in great poverty at that time, and he persuaded her to come and live at Romanovsk, but only as the companion of his niece. That proved to be our good fortune afterwards; they would surely have murdered us if they had known the truth.'

'You are, then, the Princess Shulimoff?'

She laughed gaily in the darkness. 'Yes, Monsieur, a poor princess who teaches in a school. It is like a fairy story, is it not, but where is the pumpkin that turned into a coach, and the little silver slippers, and the handsome prince? One day I think I must write that story. We will call it *The Fairy Story of the Princess Marie Lou.*'

'What became of your cousin – the Princess Sophie?'

'Ah, that was terrible – ' she broke off suddenly as three loud raps sounded on the cottage door.

Marie Lou unbarred it at once, and Rex staggered in, bearing Simon slung like a sheep across his broad shoulders.

The Duke gave a cry of delight, then asked anxiously in the next breath: 'Is he badly wounded?'

'Don't know – pretty bad, I guess.' Rex gently lowered his burden to the floor. He waved back the girl. 'Have a care, he's bleeding as if he'd been hit in twenty places.'

The Duke was already kneeling at Simon's side. 'Where did you find him?' he murmured, as he helped Rex to pull off Simon's blood-soaked clothes.

'Way outside the garden gate. I allow he crawled that far after he'd been shot.'

'He fainted, I expect, from loss of blood,' De Richleau replied, as with his long, slender fingers he carefully drew the shirt away from the wound. 'It is this one place only, I think,' he added.

'Well, that doesn't look any too good.' Rex bent over, and examined the ugly hole in Simon's thigh, from which blood was welling.

Marie Lou joined them with a bowl of water. 'Poor boy,' she sighed. 'He is so white and still – almost one would think him dead.'

'I fear he will be very much alive in a moment,' said the Duke, taking out his penknife, and holding it in the flame of the lamp.

'What are you about to do?' asked Marie Lou, who had started to bathe the wound gently.

'Probe for the bullet – remove it if I can. The pain will bring him round, I'm afraid, but it must be done. He will thank me for it if we ever get out of this country alive. Rex, take this cloth – hold it over his mouth to stifle his cries. Mademoiselle, perhaps you would prefer to turn your back on this rough surgery?'

She shrugged. 'It is not pleasant, but it is necessary. What can I do to help?'

'My rucksack is in the loft – in it there is a little bottle of iodine – if you could fetch me that.' The Duke knelt down again as he spoke.

Rex leant on Simon's chest, and pressed the cloth over his mouth. 'You fit?' he asked.

'Yes.' De Richleau straddled Simon's legs. 'Now,' he said. 'Hold him tight.'

For a moment nothing happened, then Simon gave a sudden squeal – his eyes opened, and he wriggled his head wildly as he glared at Rex.

'Take a pull, Simon – all over in a minute,' Rex tried to soothe him.

'I've got it,' gasped the Duke, in triumph. 'You can let him go.' Rex released his grasp on the unfortunate Simon.

'There,' said De Richleau, holding out the round lead bullet, much as a dentist might a first tooth that he had removed from a frightened child. 'Look, you would have had all sorts of trouble from that later!'

Simon looked – and then looked away, groaning, the wound had begun to well blood rapidly again.

Marie Lou began to try and staunch it. 'What have you done?' she cried, angrily. 'The poor little one – see how you have made him bleed!'

'No matter, it will heal all the better now we have the bullet,' smiled the Duke, taking the iodine from her.

'Now, Simon, my son, this is going to hurt.'

'Like hell it is,' agreed Rex, feelingly.

'Listen,' the Duke went on. 'The soldiers are perhaps searching for us in the woods at this very moment. If you cry out you may bring them upon us. Can you bear it, do you think, or shall Rex gag you again?'

Simon groaned, and looked from side to side. 'Give me the cloth,' he said, in a faint whisper.

They passed it to him, and he took it between his teeth, then nodded feebly. Marie Lou held one of his hands tightly in hers.

De Richleau applied the antiseptic – Simon gave a shudder and lay still.

'He's done another faint,' said Rex.

'All the better,' murmured the Duke. 'I can make a more thorough job of it.'

When Simon came to again his thigh was neatly bandaged.

'You'll feel fine now.' Rex patted him on the shoulder. 'We are going to pop you right between the blankets.'

Simon nodded, feebly.

'I killed him,' he said. 'That's two I killed, isn't it?'

'Sure,' Rex laughed. 'Al Capone won't have anything on you when you come to see me in the States next fall!'

'We must get him up to the loft – can you manage, Rex?' De Richleau asked. 'I'm almost useless with this shoulder of mine. It has begun to bleed again already.'

'I'll make it – don't worry,' Rex assured him. 'I'll go up backwards. You steady his game leg.' Very gently he took Simon under the armpits, and lifted him off the ground. He held him dangling in front of him as though he were a little child.

To negotiate the ladder of shelves was no easy task, but it was accomplished, and above Marie Lou had prepared a bed of rugs and skins. De Richleau delved in to his knapsack again and produced a bottle of morphine tablets.

'It is fortunate,' he said, 'that this is not my first campaign – I never travel without iodine and morphia.'

Simon was made as comfortable as possible, and given a couple of the tablets. The others went below to clear up the mess.

'How long do you figure it'll be before he can be moved?' Rex asked.

'If he were in London I should say a fortnight at least,' the Duke replied. 'Although it is only a flesh wound; here we must move when and how we can. After tonight's affair the chances are, I suppose, about a thousand to one against our getting away from here alive.'

'I wish to God I'd never met old Shulimoff,' sighed Rex.

De Richleau smiled. 'I fear we shall never see those famous jewels.'

'No, we'll never sit round fingering those pretties now!'

Marie Lou had just finished ramming the last of the bloodstained cloths into the stove. 'Did you say, Monsieur, that you had met Prince Shulimoff?' she asked.

At that moment there came a heavy knocking on the door.

Chapter XIX

Hidden Corn

De Richleau signalled Rex towards the cupboard with a wave of his hand. The American, with a lightness surprising in so large a man, tiptoed across the room.

The knocking came again, more persistently this time

'What is it?' called Marie Lou, in an angry voice.

'Open!' cried a voice, in Russian. 'Open in the name of the Soviets!'

De Richleau saw the iodine bottle, with its London label. He snatched it up quickly, and thrust it in his pocket.

'I am coming,' cried Marie Lou. 'One moment, I must get some clothes. She began to undo the scarf at her neck, and at the same time held out her booted foot to the Duke. He understood, and quickly pulled off first one boot then the other.

'Open!' cried the voice again. 'Do not delay.'

The Duke smiled at Marie Lou reassuringly, and held up his big automatic for her to see, then, like a shadow, he disappeared into the cupboard.

She arranged the curtain carefully, took a last look round, and ran to the door.

Two police officers, a civilian, and the *kulak*, Rakov, stood on the threshold. 'What do you want?' she asked, angrily.

The civilian pushed her aside and walked into the cottage. One of the policemen answered her.

'We search, Comrade, for three politicals – foreigners. It is believed that you gave them shelter here, in your cottage.'

'Here?' she exclaimed, her blue eyes wide with astonishment. 'I have seen no one.'

The civilian had been examining the inner room, which was her bedroom. He turned to her. 'I am of the Ogpu, Comrade, what is your work?'

'She is a teacher in the school,' the policeman answered for her – he was a local man and knew her well.

'How long have you been in bed?' asked the member of the Ogpu.

'I have not been to bed,' she replied, promptly.

'You keep late hours,' he said, suspiciously, 'here in the country – later than we do in Moscow.'

'If I am to teach, I must learn,' said Marie Lou. 'I read late if I cannot sleep.'

'Till one o' clock in the morning?' said the man. He was tall and thin and menacing. 'Come, these men were with you earlier tonight?'

She shook her head.

'You,' said the man, sharply, to Rakov. 'This woman wished to buy horses of you tonight – is that not so?'

Rakov bowed obsequiously – his straggly beard almost touched the level of his hands, which were hidden, Chinese-fashion, in the sleeves of his Kaftan. 'Yes, master, horses and a sleigh.'

'There are no masters now,' snapped the thin man, irritably. He turned on the girl. 'What have you to say, Comrade?'

'He lies, the greedy *kulak* – he lies in hope of reward. He would kill his mother for an egg,' Marie Lou said hotly.

'Oh – ou – ou.' Rakov laughed a greasy laugh, his thin lips drew back and his long narrow nose almost met his chin. 'To say that I lie – Rakov lies! It is well known that I give all that I have to the Soviets. I am an upright man!'

'You are a thief, and a hider of corn,' Marie Lou went on, accusingly. De Richleau, with his ear to a crack in the floor overhead, smiled as he heard her attack.

'Let us not trouble about that now,' said the civilian. 'It is known that these politicals seek horses to escape – it is strange that Rakov should report you as having tried to buy them. Explain that, please.'

'Rakov has heard the rumour that these people seek horses. Rakov smells money like a ferret blood!'

The peasant stepped forward, angrily – an ugly look on his mean face. He raised his fist to strike her.

'Enough,' cried the man from the Ogpu, thrusting him back. 'I am not satisfied.' He turned again to Marie Lou.

'Where were you when we came here earlier – two hours ago?'

'In the village,' she lied, glibly.

'What – at eleven at night?'

'It could not have been so late.'

'After ten, at least. Where did you go?'

'I was with friends.'

'She went to these others for horses,' sneered Rakov, 'before she came to me.'

'I know nothing of horses or politicals,' she protested. 'Go away – I wish to sleep.'

'Not yet,' said the agent of the Ogpu. 'First we will search for traces of the men.' He jerked his head in the direction of the bedroom and looked at the two local men. They disappeared into the inner room. He himself began to pull out drawers and open cupboards, while Rakov remained, a malicious grin on his face, by the door.

The policemen reappeared. '*Nitchivo,*' the elder reported. 'Nothing at all – the bed has not been slept in.'

The agent indicated the ceiling with his thumb. 'What is above, Comrade?'

'Nothing,' she said, firmly. 'The roof only.'

'Let us see it then.'

'There is no way up – if it leaks we patch it from the outside.'

'Where do you hang your onions in the autumn?'

'I grow no onions – when I need them I buy them from Rakov – he is cheaper than the co-op.'

'Good little Marie Lou,' whispered the Duke, who lay beside Rex on the floor above.

'She's a kid in a million,' Rex breathed back. He had picked up just enough Russian in prison to grasp the gist of the conversation.

The long-nosed peasant suddenly went pale – it was a terrible accusation to make in front of a member of the Ogpu. 'It is not true,' he protested, fearfully. 'I buy myself from the co-op.'

The tall man regarded him coldly. 'You shall have an opportunity of answering this charge at another time. It is sabotage to sell below the prices of the co-op.'

'It is not true,' the peasant wailed; he rubbed his hands together, nervously. 'My family eat a great deal – they are always eating – but all that they do not eat I give to the Soviet.'

'I am not satisfied about this roof, Comrade.' The agent regarded Marie Lou with his hard grey eyes. 'I will see it even if I have to pierce the ceiling. These men may have rested there.'

'Search then,' she cried loudly, in French, so that those above might be prepared, and reverting quickly to Russian she went on passionately: 'Do what you will – pull the house down if you wish – I do not care. I shall go to bed.' With a shrug she moved towards the inner room.

The agent caught her by the arm. 'Not so fast, Comrade.' He signed to the police. 'Search that room again, there must be some way we can reach the rafters.'

They obeyed, but returned as before. '*Nitchivo,* Comrade,' they said.

'Look behind the stove. There is a way and I will find it. What is hidden by that hanging curtain there?'

The younger policeman moved the curtain and disclosed the cupboard door.

'Ha, let us see,' exclaimed the agent, picking up the lamp, as he moved forward. He rummaged in the cupboard behind the clothes, found the shelves, and gave a cry of triumph. 'Here is fresh candle-grease, and a trapdoor above – had we broken in two hours ago we should have caught them while they rested.' He set down the lamp and began to climb. His shoulders disappeared from view, then his body, and finally his legs.

No sound came from above. Marie Lou stood tense and silent – every moment she expected to hear the crash of shots. The elder policeman stood in the bottom of the cupboard, peering up. 'Are you all right, Comrade?' he called out at length.

'Come up,' said a muffled voice, in Russian. 'Come up.'

The policeman followed his superior – again there was silence.

'I confess,' suddenly wailed Marie Lou. 'I confess! It is my hidden store of grain that he has found – I meant no harm. Now they will send me to prison.'

'Little fool,' said the younger policeman. 'I also will see this secret store.' He, in his turn, disappeared into the cupboard. The trapdoor slammed behind him and once more there was silence.

Marie Lou looked thoughtfully at the ceiling – nothing stirred. She looked at Rakov – he also was staring thoughtfully at the beams above his head.

'Rakov,' she said, sweetly. 'Would you not also like to see my secret store of grain?'

Rakov shifted his gaze to Marie Lou. His close-set, cunning eyes, divided only by the knife-like bridge of his nose, had suddenly become full of fear. He shook his head, quickly, and backed towards the door.

'I meant no harm,' he protested, 'and even if it is true about the onions, neighbours should not tell upon neighbours. About the horses – I was questioned – what could I say?'

Not the faintest sound came from overhead. Rakov looked up again, apprehensively. Secret stores of grain were not the only things that could be hidden in an attic – Rakov knew that! White officers, Red soldiers, politicals of all sorts had hidden in the roofs of cottages before now. Rakov felt that this was no place for an honest man who tried to wrest a living from the soil. His hand was on the latch, but as he lowered his eyes he found himself looking into the barrel of Marie Lou's little toy revolver – above it were her very steady blue eyes.

'No, Rakov, you filthy swine,' she spat at him, suddenly. 'Not so fast – away from that door, please, and into the bedroom – quickly!'

He backed before her, waving her feebly from him with ineffectual motions of his thin, knotted hands.

'Be careful, I beg, *Barina*, be careful, pray – it might go off, the little gun – I have a use for both my ears, point it the other way.'

'It *will* go off, Rakov – if you do not do just what I say.' She stood in the doorway of the inner room – he upon the far side by the wall. 'Hands above your head, Rakov, and turn your face to the wall.' She nodded approval as he obeyed her order. 'Listen now – if you so much as move your head the bullets will come crashing into that ugly curved back of yours. This door remains open, and I will shoot you for the dog you are.'

A movement at her side made her turn quickly – it was Rex, appearing from the cupboard.

'Great stuff,' he said, with his jolly laugh. 'Netted the whole party. I'll attend to this bum'; he walked over to Rakov.

The peasant swung round, his small eyes lit with the terror of death, he wrung his knobbly hands. 'Mercy, master, mercy,' he pleaded. 'I have a family, little ones – they will starve. I am an old man.'

'What about the horses?' asked Rex, in halting Russian.

'Yes, master, the best – and I should only ask a little price – less, much less than before; also you shall have my sleigh.' He trembled as he eagerly spread out his greedy hands.

'No,' said Marie Lou, decisively. 'He would play us some trick. Deal with him as with the others.'

'What you say goes,' Rex agreed, with a smile. 'Come here, you.' He seized the whining Rakov by the collar, and threw him face down on the bed. Kneeling on the peasant's back, he tied his hands behind him with a scarf, and gagged him with a towel. His feet he secured with the man's own belt. Then, picking him up bodily, he thrust him under the bed.

'What of the others?' asked Marie Lou, anxiously.

'Easy money. While they were giving you the once over down here, we made a sand-bag out of some sacking and your box of nails. De Richleau coshed 'em as they put their heads through the trap, and I drew 'em in. They're trussed up now all swell and dandy.'

'Mademoiselle, my congratulations.' It was the Duke who had joined them. 'As I speak Russian I was able to appreciate every word of that exciting conversation; your presence of mind was beyond all praise.'

The dimple on Marie Lou's little chin deepened as she smiled. 'It was a difficult moment, Monsieur, when the man of the Ogpu decided to go up. I feared that you would shoot. He was a brave one, that – or foolish!'

'Guess he thought he'd found our hide-out, but reckoned the birds had flown,' Rex laughed.

'Our danger is not over, Monsieur,' said Marie Lou, seriously. 'If Rakov has spoken of me at the police office, others will follow when these do not return.'

De Richleau nodded. 'Mademoiselle is right, we must leave immediately.'

'What of your wounded friend?' she asked.

'We must take him with us,' the Duke replied. 'Poor Simon, it will cause him much pain, but it is the only thing to do. I dread to wake him – he has slept soundly through all this.'

Marie Lou shivered slightly. 'It is terrible – two wounded men, and no shelter but the woods.'

'Let's think a bit,' said Rex. 'The Duke and I can manage someway. It's Simon who's the jamb. Can't you think of some folks who'd take him in – a lonely farm, maybe. We'd cash up handsome if they'd do it. Then we'd come back and pick him up when he's able to move round a bit again.'

'I would do it gladly, Monsieur, if it were possible – but it is not. No one would take that risk – it is too dangerous, and I, myself, shall soon be sought for by the police.'

'It is as I feared, Mademoiselle,' De Richleau said, sadly. 'We have brought misfortune upon you. After what has happened tonight you are forced to leave your home because of us.'

She shook her head. 'No, you are not to blame. I knew quite well the risk I ran – but ever since I can remember I have had a feeling of waiting – waiting for something to happen. I knew that I should not grow to be an old woman among these forests here. It may be that we shall die – it may be the beginning of a new life for me, who can tell – but I am not sorry, I am glad. It is, I think,' she smiled, 'the second chapter in the fairy story of the Princess Marie Lou.'

'I think you're just marvellous,' Rex grinned. 'Things aren't so almighty wonderful with us at the moment – but they might be a darn sight worse. We'll get out of this jamb yet – someway!'

De Richleau unthinkingly shrugged his shoulders; the sudden pain made him grimace. 'I wish I was so optimistic as you, my friend. Living in the woods in the depths of winter will play the devil with my old bones. How we shall keep from freezing to death, I cannot think.'

'We'll take every covering we can lay our hands on,' said Rex. 'We'll be all right if only we can throw the cops off our trail.' He yawned, loudly. 'Lord, I guess I never knew what it was to be so tired.'

'Which direction do you suggest?' asked the Duke.

'North – just as far as we can hike it. It's ten grand to a single greenback that they'll figure we're beating it back to Tobolsk and the steam-wagons!'

'That was our argument before,' said De Richleau, slowly. 'We might have been successful had it not been that Leshkin knew you were after the jewels. Now we have no sleigh, and Simon cannot be moved more than a few miles in any direction. I am for doing the unexpected; let us stay in the heart of danger, while they are beating the country on every side. Mademoiselle, do you not know a cave, or some place in the forest near here where we could hide. We can take food for several days.'

'No, Monsieur, there are no caves, and the forest, as you know, has little undergrowth.'

'Wait!' exclaimed the Duke. 'I have it, the Château! They will never dream that we shall return there, where we faced so much danger – there must be a hundred places in the ruins where we can hide.'

'That's a great idea,' Rex nodded. 'Leshkin and the boys'll be back in the town or the air-park long ago. That is, what's left of them.'

'You agree, Mademoiselle?' De Richleau asked, eagerly. 'I value your advice.'

'Monsieur le Duc has reason,' she smiled. 'I know every corner of those ruins – there are many places that are easy of defence, and there will be shelter for the little one.'

'Come then.' The Duke looked round quickly. 'Every scrap of food must go with us – also all the warm clothes that we can carry. Bring down the haversacks from the loft, Rex; also the arms and any ammunition you can find on those men. Let Simon sleep until the last moment. I will assist Mademoiselle.'

Marie Lou began at once to strip her bed, and spread out the blankets to make bundles. Unfortunately her food supply was very limited, but the iron rations in the haversacks remained practically untouched. She produced quite a number of furs and rugs.

Simon was lowered gently from the loft – the morphia had dulled his pain, but his face was deadly white – his eyes bloodshot and haggard. They laid him on the divan while they made their final arrangements.

'Now, Mademoiselle,' said De Richleau. 'If you are ready, we will start.'

She looked sadly round her little home, running her hand over the shelf of books. 'We cannot take anything that is not necessary, I am afraid,' added the Duke, gently.

She nodded, unhooking from the wall as she did so a large abacus, painted in many colours.

'Say, what's that thing?' asked Rex. 'Looks like the beads I used to count on when I was a kid.'

'It is for the same purpose, Monsieur.' Marie Lou held it up. A solid square frame with wires stretched across – on each wire a set of gaily coloured beads.

'Every Russian merchant uses one to do his sums,' supplemented the Duke. 'They use them as a kind of ready-reckoner. But, surely, Mademoiselle, it is not necessary to take it with us?'

'It belonged to my mother, Monsieur,' she said, simply, as she placed it in the bundle. 'She painted it for me.'

'As you wish, Mademoiselle,' agreed De Richleau, impatiently. 'But let us go.'

'One minute,' she said, as Rex was about to pick up Simon in his arms. 'Why should we not carry him on my bed – it is a framework of wire springs only.'

'Now that's certainly an idea. Let's take a look at that bed of yours.' Rex went into the inner room.

'It is not as the Russian beds,' Marie Lou added. 'It is part of the loot which came from the Château. See, the framework lifts off.'

'That's fine,' Rex nodded. 'Wait a minute, though. I'd forgotten the Duke's arm. He couldn't hump the other end with his shoulder all messed up.'

A muffled groan came from under the bed. 'Rakov,' she suggested quickly. 'He shall take the other end. He shall carry other things as well. We will shoot him if he tries to escape.'

'Keep him prisoner until we escape ourselves?'

'It is the only thing to do. He'll give information if we let him go before.'

'Sure thing, and his help in carrying that bed will be mighty useful. I've been scared stiff of this jaunt. If Simon loses any more blood he'll peg out.'

A few minutes later the little procession set out into the night, Marie Lou leading, the stretcher-bearers next, Rex at its head, and Rakov at the feet. Lastly De Richleau, automatic in hand, with which he occasionally prodded Rakov in the back. All were loaded down with heavy burdens; it was a slow and painful journey. Three times before they reached the gates of the gardens they had to rest. In spite of his magnificent physique Rex was almost dropping with exhaustion. His head was aching for want of sleep, and for all his care to avoid jolting Simon, he was so tired that his feet stumbled in the snow – he found his head sinking forward on his chest as he walked – black spots came and went before his eyes.

De Richleau was in a slightly better state, but he was weary and haggard. Centuries seemed to have passed since they had left their comfortable compartment on the Trans-Siberian. With grim humour he suddenly realised that the same train had only that afternoon steamed into Irkutsk. He was brought back to the present by seeing the stretcher-bearers set down their burden, and Rex stumble forward in a heap.

'If Mademoiselle will keep a watchful eye on our friend,' he suggested, indicating Rakov, 'I will attend to the boy.'

He shook Rex roughly by the shoulder. 'What the hell!' exclaimed Rex, crossly, as he hunched his back against a tree.

'Stand up, man!' said the Duke, sternly. 'You cannot sleep yet. Come, Rex,' he added, earnestly. 'Another half-hour, no more. I will make a reconnaissance, and if all is well we can bed down in some corner for the night. If you sleep now I shall never be able to wake you on my return, and you are too big to carry! Keep moving, my friend, I beg.'

Rex struggled to his feet. 'O.K.' he said, wearily. 'My head's aching fit to burst, but I'll be all right.'

After a short consultation with the girl, the Duke crept forward through the gates. He made a great circuit this time, approaching the house from the front; no sound came from the gaunt pile of masonry.

The moon had risen, but it was a night of scurrying clouds; the light was fitful and uncertain; big flakes of snow began to fall. De Richleau blessed their luck, for it would hide their tracks from the cottage. He lingered for a little in the trees, examining first one part of the Château, then another, as the light gave occasion. He could make out no sign of movement.

With the greatest caution he mounted the steps to the great roofless entrance hall; it was still and deserted. The room in which Leshkin had examined them must surely be the danger-spot if the place were still occupied. The Duke edged down the passage, holding his pistol ready. The door stood open and the room was empty. He re-crossed the hall to the big *salon;* here, too, the silent man who had stood waiting in the darkness had disappeared – the window to the terrace stood open just as he had left it.

The Duke breathed a heavy sigh of relief. He was a man of immense determination; in his chequered career he had faced many desperate situations. That he was in the depths of Siberia, fifteen hundred miles from the European frontier, that their enemies had wireless, aeroplanes, and machine-guns, did not matter. One thing, and one thing only, was essential – they must have rest.

Given the strength of Rex, rested and refreshed – given Simon, able to travel again and use his subtle brain – given his own experience and courage renewed after he had slept – they would get through. How he did not attempt to think – but *somehow.* Thank God the Château was unoccupied, and they could get that blessed rest.

Without hesitation he walked quickly down the terraces and rejoined the group by the gate.

'All's well,' he said. 'You know the Château, Mademoiselle. What part do you think would afford us the greatest security?'

'The foundry, Monsieur. It is at the far end, on the right. Monsieur le Prince carried out his lock-making there in the old days. The place is like a fort – with narrow windows and sheet-iron on the walls.'

'Lead on, then. Come, Rex – one last effort, then you shall sleep.'

They made their way up the terraces once more, and into the small building to which Marie Lou led them. There were windows on one side only, and one door which opened on a roofless corridor connecting the foundry with the main block.

The Duke flashed his torch round the place. In one corner was a rusty furnace with a great funnel chimney. Along one wall a tangled mass of wheels and piping, broken and rusted. For the rest, the place was empty.

Simon was set down in the corner farthest from the windows, blankets were piled on him, and he was given another dose of morphia. For a moment Rex toyed with the rusty machinery, thinking of the jewels, but fatigue overpowered him. The Duke had to lash the whining Rakov to the furnace and gag him. He took a last look round before switching out his torch. Simon and Rex were sleeping, Marie Lou sitting cross-legged on her coverings. He drew his blankets about him. 'We shall beat them yet, never fear,' he said, softly. 'We must do without a sentry tonight, but you shall take tea in Paris before a month is out!' Next moment he, too, was asleep.

The girl rose softly to her feet, and dragged her bedding to the doorway; she had her little pistol in her hand, the Duke's automatic lay heavy on her knees. Wide-eyed, alert, but motionless she sat, guarding the sleepers and weaving the fairy-story of the Princess Marie Lou, until the coming of the Siberian dawn.

Chapter XX

Sanctuary

For six days they lived in the foundry of the Château. In all that time they only saw one human being – a peasant walking with a load of firewood across the bottom of the garden.

The first day the three friends slept until the sun was high. It was difficult to wake Rex, even then, and almost immediately he went to sleep again. Simon's wound was re-dressed, and he was given a further dose of morphia.

The Duke watched during the afternoon while Marie Lou curled up like a kitten in her rugs, and slept well into the evening.

The second day they were in a better state; Rex completely revived, De Richleau's wound healing well, Simon able at least to talk cheerfully again, and Marie Lou flushed with health and excitement. Only Rakov was unhappy.

His ration consisted of a small piece of rye bread from Marie Lou's store, and as much water as he cared to swallow. During the first two days he was never free of his bonds and gag, except when he was feeding.

Their supplies were their principal anxiety; after the first two days their fears that the ruins might be searched were lessened; evidently they were believed to have taken to the woods, but their supplies would not hold out for ever.

The Duke was in favour of their remaining where they were as long as possible, in order to give Simon's wound a better chance to heal. Marie Lou offered to visit the farmers in the neighbourhood whom she could trust. The three friends all admired the courage she had shown on the night when they had sheltered in her cottage, but they would not allow her to take further risks. They would have kept from her, if they could, the fact that their supplies were so limited, but this was impossible, since she insisted on taking charge of that department herself.

They suffered considerably from the cold, which was intense; the second, third, and fourth day of their stay the snow fell unceasingly. Had it not been that De Richleau was well supplied with Meta fuel, they would never have survived the arctic weather.

On the second day Rakov began to have shivering fits, and, as they could not bring themselves to let the poor wretch die of cold, he was unleashed three times a day and made to skip, in order to restore his circulation. De Richleau would listen to no suggestion that he should remain permanently unbound – the loss of their previous prisoner, with the horses and sleigh, was too recent in his memory.

Rex spent much time among the broken machinery. When he woke, on the second day, his eyes were bright with excitement at the thought that, after all, fate had decreed that he should reach this room, which had held his imagination for so many months. He had no doubt that he would find the missing jewels; eagerly he set to work examining the rusty mass of struts and girders. Piece by piece, with infinite patience, he went over them. Marie Lou became his assistant, and the treasure was a constant joke between them. She would look at him with a humorous twinkle in her blue eyes each morning, on waking, and ask:

'Is it today that we shall find the jewels?'

'Sure,' he would cry, with enthusiasm. 'Today's the great day.'

Simon followed the search with interest from his corner.

'Try here – try there,' he would suggest.

Only the Duke remained uninterested in this perpetual treasure hunt; his thoughts were busy with more vital matters. When the food was exhausted they would have to make a move in some direction – but how? How, without horses, in a hostile area, were they to get away? In vain he racked his brains over this impossible problem, while he beat his chilled hands against his sides to restore some semblance of warmth.

The days passed, but the treasure seekers came no nearer to their goal; the fire had calcined all the ironwork, just as Prince Shulimoff had meant that it should. Fifteen successive winters had completed the work of locking the bolts and nuts into a rusty partnership that it was impossible to sever.

Rex wrenched and hammered, much to the annoyance of the Duke, who feared that the ringing clang of the iron might betray their hiding-place to some passing peasant. With his great strength, Rex levered whole sections apart, so that the rusty mass became more tortuous than before, but it seemed that the task was hopeless. None of the pipes or cylinders gave forth the tiniest brilliant or seed pearl.

Simon endeavoured to persuade Rex that someone had been before him, and that the treasure was no longer there, but he would not have it. He wished to remove the iron sheeting from the walls, piece by piece, and would have done so had not the Duke, on the fifth afternoon, called him into conference.

'My friends,' said De Richleau, as they sat on the floor by Simon's bedside. 'The time has come when we must once more make a plan; after tomorrow our provender will be exhausted. Simon's leg is far from well, but at least, with care, he will be able to travel without danger. Rex is rested, so, also, am I. Have you any suggestions to offer?'

'Rakov,' said Simon. 'If he values his skin he'll hand over his horses and sleigh. We could take him with us, part of the way – make certain that he doesn't let us down.'

De Richleau nodded. 'I had thought of that, but Marie Lou says the man has a family – we could hardly get his sleigh without their knowledge, and we cannot take them all!'

'Got to take a chance, someway,' said Rex. 'It's that or holding up some other farm – why not Rakov's?'

'We shall have Rakov as a hostage,' added Simon. 'Make him tell his wife that if the police chase us we'll – er – do him in!'

De Richleau smiled. 'An excellent plan, my dear Simon. Let us then take our chance tonight.'

'What's the hurry?' Rex wanted to know. 'We've eats enough for another day.'

'True, but you would not have us start empty-handed on our journey.'

'Not on your life. What's the matter with Rakov's place; we fed him five days – he can feed us ten. Let's fill up there.'

Simon tittered into the palm of his hand as his quick eyes took in the gaunt face of the peasant lashed to the furnace in the far corner. 'Think we need a slimming cure, eh?'

'Don't be a mutt, Simon,' Rex laughed. 'I didn't mean feed us as we've fed him, but honest, I want another day here.'

'You still persist in your idea that the jewels are hidden in this room?' asked the Duke.

'I certainly do. If I can't get 'em by tomorrow night, I'll throw my hand in. What's the harm in another day? Simon's going fine and dandy. Once we quit this place who know's where we'll land up; let's take the extra night while the going's good.'

Simon nodded, quickly. 'Um. Lots in what you say. Let's sit tight another day.'

'As you will,' the Duke agreed. 'Since you have solved the problem of supplies, I have nothing against it.' He stood up. 'I think perhaps it is time I gave friend Rakov a little exercise. His life has grown more precious in my eyes!'

Rex walked over to the window, and gazed thoughtfully into the garden. He idly fingered the round stumps of the iron bars that projected from the cement casement. They were the bars that Prince Shulimoff had sawn through on the night of his escape, fifteen years before. 'I think,' he said, 'I'll take a walk. I've got a hunch that a little exercise would do me good.'

'Surely, Rex, to show yourself is an unnecessary risk,' the Duke protested. 'If you must have exercise I would rather that you expended your energy on the old iron. There seem to be several quite nice pieces that remain unbroken.' He looked with distaste at the mass of rusted metal along the wall.

'Nope – this child's for the open-air today.' Rex picked up his automatic, and also an extra one that had been taken from the agent of the Ogpu. 'I'll be careful,' he added reassuringly. 'You bet I will. I know the risk all right, but I've had plenty practice hiding behind nothing, hunting old man grizzly in the Rockies, way back home.'

'Do you intend to be away for long?'

'I'll be back soon after sundown. That'll be what . . .? Round about a couple of hours.' He grinned at Simon and went out.

In the ruined corridor Marie Lou sat, making the most of the late afternoon sun, which streamed through a great rent in the wall.

'Have you come to tell me that you have found the treasure?' she asked, with a little smile.

He laughed, as he sat down beside her. 'Didn't you know?' he asked, in mock surprise. 'Tomorrow's the day I'm showing you where the goods are; all the tinkering so far has been just with the idea of getting you interested.'

'Of course.' She regarded him gravely with her big blue eyes. 'You knew where it was all the time, and to think that I did not guess? Poor Marie Lou!'

'Look here, fooling apart, I want to talk to you.' Rex spoke earnestly now, and for a few minutes they spoke together in low tones.

'O.K.' He got to his feet again. 'I'll be back half an hour after sundown, or an hour at the latest. Be a good kid and keep the Duke amused while I'm gone. He's that jumpy he can't keep still.' With a wave of his hand Rex disappeared into the ruins at the far end of the passage.

Marie Lou went back into the foundry. Rex was right about De Richleau. In the hour of action the Duke could be relied on to be utterly calm – his self-possession under fire had filled Simon with amazement. Even Rex, whose nerves had all the perfection of bodily fitness and youth, could not exercise the same calm judgment in a crisis. But these days of forced inactivity had played havoc with his accustomed serenity. He paced softly up and down – up and down – the centre of the room, like some powerful caged cat.

From morning to night he was revolving in his mind the problem as to how they could leave this dangerous forbidden territory with speed and secrecy – his brain was stale with it, and the more he thought the less likely it seemed that fresh ideas would come. He knew that, himself, yet he could think of nothing else, and that made him still more nervy and irritable.

Marie Lou drew him outside into the slanting sunlight. 'Come and talk to me,' she begged. 'You think too much – it is not good.'

He smiled, with something of his old charm. 'What would you have me talk about, Princess?'

'What you will. Tell me about Paris.'

'Ah, Paris . . .' He leant against the wall. 'Paris is a hundred cities. There is the Paris of Henry of Navarre, the Paris of the Grand Monarch, the Paris of the Revolution.'

'No, no, tell me of the Paris of today.'

He smiled again. 'There also, Mademoiselle – in the one there are many cities. Between the Paris of the old Catholic families and the Paris of the American tourists there is a great gulf fixed. Then there is the city of the artists, and the city of the night-life. There is the Russian colony, and the bicycle-racing world of the bourgeoisie. But I, myself, have not been to Paris for many years.'

'But why, Monsieur?' she exclaimed, in astonishment. 'Surely Paris is the one city in the world in which to live?'

'Perhaps – I am not sure of that – but like yourself, for many years I have lived in exile.'

'Tell me about this, Monsieur.'

'It was in '96, Princess; for us who preserve the loyalties of our birth, there is still a king of France. When I was a young man I was an ardent Royalist. In those days there was serious hope of restoring the monarchy – hopes which I fear are now for ever dead. I was deeply implicated in a conspiracy to bring about a *coup d'état*. I do not grumble at the penalty, it only makes me a little sad at times that I cannot return freely to the places which I love.'

'Freely, you say, Monsieur; you do then at times go back?'

'Yes, at long intervals – but it is a risk that I am not prepared to take so readily now that I am an older man. Besides, it is impossible for me to stay in the houses of my friends without bringing a certain risk on them too, and in the public places, where my world gathers, I should be recognised immediately.'

'That is sad, Monsieur. Where then do you live?'

'I have a villa in Italy, where I stay sometimes in the winter, and an old castle in Austria, but I do not care to go to Austria now. Since the War, all my friends there have lost their money. Oh, it is pathetic – all those dear, charming people, so hospitable. They never thought of money, and now they have none, they think of nothing else. Most of my life is spent in London now.'

'Tell me of London. Is it true that there is always fog?'

De Richleau laughed. 'By no means, Mademoiselle. On a May morning London can be as charming as any place in the world. We will take a walk down Bond Street one day, you and I!'

'Do you know the King of England and the Prince of Wales?'

'I have the honour to be known to His Majesty, also to the Prince.'

'Tell me about them, please.' She looked up at him with large grave eyes. He began to talk to her of Windsor and Balmoral – then Ascot and Goodwood – the yachting week at Cowes, days in the Leicestershire country, hunting with the Pytchley, summer nights on the gentle river that flows by Maidenhead – of the spires and courts of Oxford, and the beauty of the English country lanes in autumn, of all the many things he had come to love in the chosen country of his exile; and in the telling, for an hour, forgot the peril that beset them in the land of snows.

The shadows lengthened, the red ball of the sun dropped behind the trees, the bitter cold of the Siberian night chilled them once more.

Rex returned safely, a little less than an hour after dusk. He would say nothing of his excursion, but seemed strangely elated. They had their frugal meal, Simon's wound was dressed, and the miserable Rakov exercised; then they turned in for the night – perhaps their last night in shelter and security for many days.

In the morning Rex was up with the first streak of dawn, and systematically began to wrench and break the only pieces of rusted machinery that were not obviously solid; even the Duke, knowing that they were to move that night, and in a more settled frame of mind, lent him a hand. The furnace had been gutted long ago, and the slabs of stone prized up from the floor; every inch of the walls had been tapped for a hollow note, but each sheet of metal gave out the same dead sound. They worked without ceasing, except for a brief snack at midday, until four in the afternoon, and then at last Rex confessed himself defeated.

'It's no good,' he declared in disgust. 'Somebody's beat us to it, maybe years ago. Perhaps he's dead and buried with the stones still on him, but they're not here. If only the old bum had told me what place he really did put 'em before he died on me . . . Sorry, Marie Lou,' he added, hastily. 'I forgot the prince was your father!'

'No matter, Monsieur,' she smiled. 'We can only think of people as we knew them; to me, the Prince was nothing but a wicked old man – he was always malicious, often drunk and cruel, and I used to dread his visits here.'

De Richleau glanced through the window. 'In an hour,' he said, 'it will be dark; we should lose no time, but make immediately for Rakov's, that we may drive all night and put many miles between us and Romanovsk.'

'We'll put some miles between us and Romanovsk all right,' Rex laughed suddenly. 'Listen, children. I've been keeping something up my sleeve since last night. You know I took a walk?'

They all looked up at him, eagerly. 'Go on,' said Simon.

'Well, I had a hunch, and a darned fine hunch too; what do we want to monkey with a horse and sleigh for, when we've got a thousand aeroplanes sitting doing nothing within a mile?'

'You're not serious, Rex,' protested De Richleau.

'I certainly am. I went out yesterday to take a look-see. One batch of those four-seater fighters is parked a whole half-mile from the barracks, and there's only one sentry on every block of hangars. If we can nail him we'll get a 'plane and be away before the guard turns out.'

'What about the – er – electric fence?' asked Simon, dubiously.

'I've thought of that – it isn't higher than my chin. I'll pitch you over one by one.'

'But yourself?' asked Marie Lou.

'Don't worry about me. I wasn't the big boy in the pole-jumping game at Harvard for nix. I'd clear that fence with my hands tied.'

'It's a ghastly risk.' The Duke shook his head. 'To touch that fence is instant death. Besides, will there be petrol in the 'planes – enough to carry us any distance?'

'Now there you've got me. It's on the cards they empty all their tanks at night, in case of fire, but there's a pump to each row of hangars. If we take the end 'plane we should be able to fill up before we start. What d'you say?'

'I think the immediate risk is far greater; there is the fence – a sentry to overcome – the possibility that even if we succeed so far, we may be surprised by the officer on his rounds – and then the uncertainty about petrol. In our original plan we had only the Rakov family to deal with. Of course, if your plan was successful, its advantages are immense.'

'Sleigh won't take us far,' said Simon, 'and I'll tell you – I think Rakov's wife will go to the police, in any case, if she sees us tonight.'

'Are you certain that you can handle one of those 'planes, Rex?' asked the Duke.

'Sure, fundamentally they're not all that different to the ordinary types. The wing rake's to give them added speed, and the helicopter's to let 'em get up and down in a confined space – but if you can drive a Buick you can drive a Ford.'

'Mademoiselle.' De Richleau turned to Marie Lou. 'Your freedom and perhaps your life, also, depend on this decision. What is your view?'

'I think that Monsieur the American has had the great idea. In Rakov's sleigh we are almost certain to be overtaken. If we are caught it will be death for us all. Let us face death now, then. At least we have the wonderful prospect that we may get right away.'

'I agree with you entirely,' said the Duke. 'I did no more than state the dangers, that the position might be clear. It is decided then – we make our attempt by 'plane.'

There was a murmur of assent as he produced his map and spread it on the floor. 'Where do you propose to make for, Rex?'

'Due westward would bring us to Latvia or Estonia.'

'True.' De Richleau took a rough measure with his pencil. 'But that is nearly eighteen hundred miles. Surely we cannot cover so great a distance?'

'Not in one hop,' Rex agreed.

'I hardly think we can hope to land, find petrol, and proceed again. All air-parks are naturally barred to us.'

'That's a fact. Where's the nearest frontier?'

'Mongolia.' The Duke put his finger on a yellow patch. 'Just under a thousand miles.'

'I reckon I ought to be able to make that. I've done London to Cannes in one hop before now. That's over six hundred miles.'

'But Mongolia,' said the Duke, 'is a terrible place. We should land somewhere to the north of the great desert of Gobi, free from our enemies, perhaps, but faced with starvation and thirst in a barren land.'

'India,' suggested Simon. 'That's British.'

'Fifteen hundred miles, my friend; besides we could not fly the Himalayas, and even if we could we should probably be shot by the tribesmen on the other side.'

'What of Finland?' said Marie Lou. 'That looks to be nearer – thirteen hundred miles, perhaps?'

'Nope.' Rex shook his head quickly. 'Too far north – we'd sure run into blizzards this time of the year. Might get lost and forced down in the Arctic, and that'd be the end of the party.'

'Persia and Georgia are about equidistant – some sixteen hundred miles,' the Duke went on. 'But I do not fancy either. Perhaps it would be best to make for the Ukraine.'

'But that is Soviet,' Marie Lou objected.

'True, my child, nevertheless it is a separate country to Russia proper. If we were forced to land we might receive diplomatic protection there, and the frontier is only thirteen hundred miles. It has the added attraction that if the petrol does not give out, and Rex can make a superhuman effort, we might do the few hundred extra miles into Poland or Roumania, which would mean final safety.'

'I never knew Russia was so big before,' groaned Simon.

'I don't reckon the Ukrainians'll exactly ring the joybells,' said Rex. 'I've always thought they were pretty tied up with the rest of the Bolshevist bunch.'

'They preserve at least a measure of independence,' argued the Duke. 'Not much, but possibly enough to serve our purpose.'

'O.K. by me,' Rex agreed. 'What's the course?'

'Dead south-west.' The Duke folded up his map. 'It is dark already. Let us be going.'

'What'll we do with this bird?' Rex jerked his head at Rakov.

'He shall carry our knapsacks. Later we will tie him to a tree, and if he is lucky someone will find him in the morning.'

Their preparations were soon made; Rex was the last to leave the foundry which he had come so many thousand miles to search for the jewels of the Shulimoffs. It was with the greatest reluctance even now that he tore himself away.

In single file they crossed the garden; Simon put up a better performance than they had hoped with the rough crutches that they had made for him, but their progress was slow. It took them over an hour to reach the death-dealing fence.

They decided that it was better to allow the camp to settle down for the night before making their attempt. Simon lay stretched out on his furs in a little hollow they had found – the journey had tired him sorely. Rex spent a considerable time searching for a tall sapling that would bear his weight. At last he found one to his liking and made several practice jumps, sailing high into the air. They divided their last tin of sardines and a packet of stale biscuits. Rakov was tied securely to a tree, and at last they decided that it was time to start.

Rex took De Richleau in his strong arms, and lifted him clear above his head. With a great heave he pitched him feet-foremost over the deadly fence – four feet clear of the wire.

The Duke smothered a cry of pain as he landed partly on his bad shoulder, but he was soon standing ready on the other side; the rugs and knapsacks were then passed over.

Marie Lou was easy. To Rex she was like a baby, and he dropped her gently in De Richleau's arms.

Simon was lifted over with the greatest precautions – to throw him was to risk injuring his leg. De Richleau being so much shorter than Rex, the business was not accomplished without difficulty, and Simon passed some apprehensive moments while he was within a few inches of the wire – but they got him safely to the other side.

'Stand clear,' Rex warned them, and with a rush his big body hurtled through the air; he dropped his pole neatly as he sprang, and cleared the fence by a yard at least.

Together they crept forward the two hundred yards to the edge of the trees. A row of hangars stood, a dark bulk, no great distance away. They crouched in a small runnel while Rex gave his last instructions.

'I'll go forward on my lonesome,' he said. 'When you hear me whistle twice you'll know the sentry's got his bonus. Come over quick as you can, then this is the drill: we'll get Simon in the 'plane right away, the Duke gets the petrol hose and brings it to me in the shed, Marie Lou keeps her eyes skinned and her gun up outside. Is that all O.K.?'

There was a murmur of assent and he crept away; they watched his big form till it disappeared in the shadows, then they lay waiting with beating hearts and bated breath.

Chapter XXI

The Homing Pigeon

It seemed an eternity to them as they waited, crouching in the shadow of the last trees that fringed the open space of the giant aerodrome. Within a mile there must be several thousand men; on the left the glow from the hundreds of windows in the main blocks of barracks veiled the night sky and the stars. Sounds of wireless from many loud-speakers came faintly to them; in one of the nearer huts a group of men were singing a wild, plaintive song in a minor key.

Each second Marie Lou expected to hear the sharp challenge of a sentry, or a single rifle shot. Either would bring that singing to a sudden stop, men would come pouring out, running with lights and rifles. What would happen then? Retreat without Rex was impossible with that terrifying electric fence behind them – capture would be only a matter of moments.

Simon sat patiently, propped against a tree. He was thinking of the grey figure they had seen among the trees on the day they first saw the fence and met Marie Lou. It was to be hoped that the sentries became so slack after eventless days in lonely woods that they dozed on their rifles. There had been no sight or sound of one when they made their crossing, and Rex had reported that the nearest sentries were stationed a good half-mile apart. Nevertheless, Simon kept his eyes away from the hangars and towards the fence, clasping his automatic firmly, and watching with strained eyes for any movement in the darkness.

Two whistles, low but clear, came out of the night. All three silently left the narrow trench and wriggled forward across the open. The hangars loomed up before them, seeming preposterously tall from their position on the ground. Within a few yards of their goal De Richleau stood up, he helped Simon to his feet, and with Marie Lou on the other side, supported the wounded man round to the front.

The sliding door of the hangar stood a little open; they squeezed through. The only light was the reflection from Rex's torch – he was already busy in the cockpit examining the controls. No trace of a sentry was to be seen.

In the uncertain light the 'plane seemed a strange monster; Rex leaned out. 'There's a step-ladder by her tail. Get Simon in the back.' De Richleau found the ladder and propped it against the side.

'Go on,' said Simon. 'I can manage now, don't worry about me.' He hauled himself up by his hands and one sound leg; fortunately, his wound had not reopened owing to the care they had taken in getting him so far. The Duke disappeared to find the petrol pump, and Marie Lou to keep watch outside.

The pump was only a few yards away, and De Richleau struggled manfully with the heavy wirebound rubber hose. At last he got the nozzle to within a few feet of the 'plane – Rex climbed down and gave an extra heave – a moment later petrol was pouring into the empty tank.

'Do you think you can handle her?' De Richleau asked.

'Sure,' came back the cheerful answer. 'The helicopter's no essential part of the construction. I was scared it might be; we couldn't have sailed up through the roof! But it's all O.K. I reckon we can taxi out and take off in the open like any other 'plane.'

'Where is the sentry?'

Rex jerked his head towards the back of the hangar. 'Tucked up in a corner there, poor bum. I guess he never knew what hit him. Come on – now the reserve tank, then we'll get right out of here.'

They heaved again on the weighty hose; when the tank was full they threw it on the ground, and turned their attention to the hangar doors – great sheets of corrugated iron and steel on rollers.

Marie Lou was outside, a small silent shadow – standing motionless and intent, her eyes riveted in the direction of the wireless music – the singing had stopped.

Rex and De Richleau put their shoulders to the sliding doors. Luckily the runners were well oiled; before long they had the hangar wide open. They could see the 'plane better now, it was a big double-engined monoplane, the engines fixed centrally a few feet above the wide metal wings, with propellers fore and aft. Immediately beneath, in the body, was a small cabin, with open seats for the two pilots side by side in front. Before each was fixed a wicked-looking machine-gun. At the back of the cabin were twin seats for observers, each equally well armed. The roof of the cabin bulged up in a wide funnel to the engine so that a mechanic inside could attend to them in flight. A tall shaft rose from the centre of the engines bearing the wings of the helicopter.

The Duke touched Marie Lou on the arm. 'Quick, up into the back with Simon.'

He began to haul the nozzle of the petrol hose from under the 'plane. Rex had already clambered up into the pilot's seat. 'Don't waste time monkeying with that,' came his sharp whisper.

'One moment, my son,' De Richleau persisted, dragging the hose outside the hangar.

'The ladder! What shall I do with it?' came Marie Lou's voice.

'Shove it clear of the 'plane,' Rex called back softly.

From her seat beside Simon she gave the ladder a push. There was a loud clang as it struck the corrugated-iron side of the hangar. It shattered the silence like a blow on a giant gong.

'That's torn it,' said Rex, angrily. 'For God's sake come on.' De Richleau clambered hastily up beside him.

With straining ears they listened for the sound of running feet. It did not seem possible that such a sound should pass unnoticed, but nothing stirred.

'All set?' cried Rex, loudly. There was an answering cry from Simon and the girl in the back. 'Praises be she's the latest thing in 'planes with an electric starter,' he added to the Duke, but the latter part of his sentence was lost in the roar of the engine. In the corrugated-iron hangar the noise reverberated like thunder – the 'plane remained quite stationary.

'Can't you start her?' yelled the Duke, apprehensively, in Rex's ear.

'Sit tight!' Rex bawled back.

The roar of the engine drowned every other noise, but in the distance, on the right, squares of light showed where the hut doors were being thrown open, and against the light little figures could be seen hurrying forward.

Suddenly the dark shape of a man loomed up right in front of the hangar; he shouted something – but what, they could not hear. He did not carry a rifle, and in the faint glow his face expressed surprise.

De Richleau levelled his automatic – another second and he would have pulled the trigger. With a gasp he lowered his pistol and, stooping, yelled through the cabin to Simon: 'Don't shoot! For God's sake don't shoot!'

'Time to go home,' said Rex to himself, as he smiled in the darkness. He had not wasted the last few moments. Better to take the risk of a few shots as they left the ground, than chance a dead cold engine conking out fifty yards from the shed.

Slowly the big 'plane slid forward – the man ducked hurriedly under the right-hand wing – in a moment they were in the open and gathering speed.

As the 'plane left the shed the din of the engines lessened. A whole crowd of men surged out of the darkness, shouting and gesticulating. Somehow, to the occupants of the 'plane, they looked stupid and helpless – waving their arms and opening their mouths when not a word they said could be heard. One fell over backwards as he jumped aside to avoid the onrush of the metal wing. The speed increased – the cool night air rushed past – the 'plane began to bump gently in great leaps along the level ground; almost in an instant the running men were left behind, swallowed up in the shadows.

'We're off!' cried Simon, to Marie Lou, and for the first time the girl realised that they had left the ground. Another group of hangars rushed past them, twenty feet below – they both looked back. The crack of a rifle came to them faintly from the hangar. It was followed instantly by a great sheet of flame.

The Duke gave a chuckle of delight – he had come through the small cabin and joined them unnoticed.

'What – what happened?' gasped Simon.

'I left the petrol turned on in front of the sheds,' De Richleau smiled, grimly.

'That's why you called out to me not to fire?'

He nodded. 'I only just remembered in time myself. If I'd shot that man the flash from my pistol would have blown us up.'

'The hangars – they are on fire,' cried Marie Lou excitedly.

They were climbing swiftly now. Far below them, and to the rear, they could see the flames leaping upwards, and in the red glare little dots of men scurrying to and fro. The great arena of the camp was plainly discernible, and, encircling it, the darker ring of the illimitable forest.

A bright shaft of light shot up from one corner of the air-park, followed by another and another from different spots below. 'Searchlights,' said the Duke. 'They are trying to pick us up. I wonder if they have anti-aircraft guns?'

A blinding glare suddenly struck the rapidly climbing plane, making even the interior of the cabin as bright as day. Without warning the 'plane dropped like a stone into the black darkness below. Marie Lou felt a sudden sinking in the pit of her stomach; the blood drained from her face. De Richleau was pitched backwards off his feet.

'We're hit!' gasped Simon.

The Duke swore softly as he picked himself up off the floor of the cabin. 'It's all right,' he assured them. 'Rex is dodging the searchlights.'

As he spoke the 'plane shot forward again. Far above them the beams were now concentrated on a single spot – the place where they had been

only a few minutes before. Then they scattered and moved in grid formation across the sky in the same direction as the 'plane.

'Wonder if they've got sound detectors?' said Simon. 'They'll pick us
up if they have.'

De Richleau shrugged and pointed below. 'Rex has tricked them,' he
declared. 'Look, we are only two hundred feet above the tree tops. Even if
they knew our position they couldn't use their archies – we are below
their angle of fire at this distance.'

'Please?' said Marie Lou, suddenly.

'What is it?' asked Simon.

'Go – go away,' she stammered. 'I feel ill!'

'Will you be all right?' De Richleau spoke doubtfully.

She nodded angrily as he helped Simon into the small cabin. It
contained a fixed table with a settee at each side long enough for a man to
lie down at full length. At the front, through a mica screen, Rex's broad
back was visible.

De Richleau insisted that Simon should tuck up on one of the settees
and take what rest he could. Feeling that he could be of little use, Simon
did not need much pressing. He was terribly tired; it would be weeks
before he recovered from his loss of blood.

Marie Lou joined them, looking pale and miserable. The Duke settled
her, unprotesting, on the other settee, covering her warmly. Then he
joined Rex in the forward cockpit.

'How is she going?' he inquired.

'Fine,' Rex answered. 'She's a daisy – I picked this 'plane because I saw
a guy take her out yesterday; couldn't risk boning one that might have
been under repair.'

They were rising again rapidly, the searchlights had been left behind.
'How is our supply of petrol?' asked the Duke.

'Pretty good. I guess these 'planes are raiders meant to cover long
distances – fighting escorts for the big bombers – got to have juice to carry
'em the same distance, but much faster in manoeuvre. They stay behind to
keep the enemy 'planes down while the big boys quit for home when
they've dropped their eggs. We'll be good for a thousand miles, anyhow
– after that, may the Lord provide.'

'Sixteen hundred miles to the frontier,' the Duke bawled. 'If the petrol
lasts, do you think you can do it?'

'Be no ordinary performance if I do,' Rex grunted. 'We're flying
against the world spin, remember; that makes it darn near equivalent to
two thousand coming the other way. Still, it wouldn't be a record if we
made it, and I'll say this bus is one of the finest things I've ever been in

– I take my hat off to the Bolshie who designed it. What was the bonfire after we left?'

De Richleau explained about the petrol.

'Say,' Rex grinned, 'that was a great idea. Talk about singeing the King of Spain's beard! That fella Drake had nothing on you. Mighty dangerous, all the same – a back flash might have sent us all to heaven!'

Talking was a considerable strain, since to make themselves heard each had to yell in the ear of the other. For a long time they sat silent; the moon came up and lit the landscape of the endless forest stretching unbroken below.

After a long time, as it seemed, the moon passed behind a great bank of drifting clouds; a sprinkling of lights became visible directly in their course.

'Sverdlovsk,' called the Duke. 'Bear to the left, Rex; we must avoid flying over towns. They will hear our engine, and I expect the wireless at Romanovsk has been busy.'

Rex banked steeply, leaving the lights away to the north. 'How's time?' he asked.

'A little after one,' De Richleau replied, glancing at his watch. 'We have made splendid going.'

They were rising all the time now. The moon came out again and they could see that the ground ran sharply up in spurs and curves; the forest grew thinner, and for the next hour they were passing over the Urals. A gorgeous panorama was spread out below them. A world of white, made the more brilliant by the dark shadows of beetling crags with great rents and gashes in the glistening rock, seemingly fathomless pits of impenetrable blackness against the dazzling whiteness of the snow. A cold, hard, black and silver world, having something of unreality about it – the utter silence suggested death and desolation. Seen thus, the Urals might well have been the veritable mountains of the moon – a place where man had never been, could never go, where only evil lurked in the baleful, unrelenting light.

When they sank again to the foothills and forests on the other side De Richleau said: 'I think I shall try to sleep for a little now. Wake me at once if you need me.'

'I certainly will, but I don't figure I'll have to. She's going fine; the cold's the only thing that gets me.'

De Richleau buried his head in his big fur collar, and wriggled down into a more comfortable position. The even hum of the engines soothed him, and he soon dropped off. The 'plane sped on, ever westward.

The Duke was awake again before six and peering out into the half-light. By glancing at his watch he realised that they must have come many degrees to the south during the night for the dawn to be so early. At first he feared that they had swerved off their course. He turned to Rex.

Rex saw him move, and yawned sleepily. 'Thank God you've come to life. I've been terrified I'd drop off to sleep with no one to talk to.'

'Where are we? Do you know?'

'Haven't the faintest, but we've kept on the dotted line all right. I'm sick of the sight of this compass and nothing else to look at.' Rex yawned again.

De Richleau got out the map and began to search for landmarks by the aid of the increasing light. He had not long to wait before he found one about which there could be no possible mistake. Far below them lay a great broad river; it curved in an enormous horseshoe, extending over many miles, and on its southern bend straggled a dark patch of clustering houses. As they came nearer, it became clear that it was a city of some considerable size.

'Samara,' said the Duke, with conviction; 'and the river is the mighty Volga. Look at it well, my friend; who knows if you will ever see it again.'

'Thanks,' said Rex briefly. 'You can keep the Volga for me. I'd rather take a look at a plate of my favourite breakfast food.'

'Tomorrow, if our luck holds, you may!' De Richleau studied the map again. 'Do you know that we are already half-way – we have done over eight hundred miles!'

'That a fact?' Rex brightened. 'If so, we'll make it; we haven't used half the petrol yet.'

The Duke was overjoyed. He went into the cabin to tell the others the good news. The morning light had just awakened them.

Simon, who had slept well and was looking considerably better, was surprised that it was so early, but De Richleau explained that they were now far to the south of Moscow – somewhere about the latitude of Birmingham, perhaps – by noon they might be as far south as the Channel Islands.

Poor Marie Lou looked very woebegone; she was shockingly pale, with great dark circles under her eyes. During the earlier part of the night she had been terribly airsick. De Richleau insisted that she should sit out in the rear cockpit with Simon – she would feel better in the air. When he had installed them he returned to Rex and said:

'Would it not be possible for me to take over for a little? You seem to sit there doing nothing!'

'Just what I was thinking,' Rex nodded. 'A kid can fly an aeroplane these days once it's off the ground. I'll take her up another couple of thousand;

then, if you do slip a thousand there's no harm done.' He began to climb sharply.

The Duke settled himself comfortably at the second set of controls. 'I was watching you last night,' he said. 'I think I understand the principle of the thing.'

Rex laughed. 'I wouldn't have let you handle her over mountains; there's air-pockets and every kind of snag, due to the uneven ground – but you'll not get that here. Looks as though this plain goes on for ever – it should be dead easy.'

When they were well over five thousand feet Rex took his hand off the controls. 'All you've got to do,' he shouted, 'is to keep her steady, keep your eye on the indicator, and look at the compass needle now and again.'

For some minutes he sat watching the Duke's first efforts as a pilot. They bumped a little owing to De Richleau's eagerness to correct their altitude too quickly, but his long sensitive fingers soon found the right touch.

'You'll do,' said Rex, yawning again. 'If the ground gets broken, wake me; if anything goes wrong, you're not the sort of man I'd insult by telling not to panic – but for God's sake take your hands off the controls. Just give me one kick and drop 'em. Don't attempt to right her; leave that to me. I'll have her under control again long before we could crash at this height, even if she's in a falling spin.' Next moment he was asleep.

The distant plain stretched out interminably. With practice the Duke soon grew more proficient. He would have liked to have tried a few experiments, but would not allow himself to be tempted into taking any risks.

The morning wore on, the ground below changed to long rolling slopes of grassland, the seemingly endless steppes of Russia. At a little after eleven they passed another great river, which De Richleau thought to be the Don. He woke Rex in order to make certain.

Rex, still yawning, but much fresher, took over the controls again, and the Duke consulted his map. Yes, it was the Don – their progress had been wonderful. They were now about three hundred miles south of Moscow, another four hundred and fifty miles would bring them to the frontier of Roumania; it really seemed that they might get through in this one tremendous headlong flight. All of them, except Marie Lou, felt in urgent need of food – the lockers in the cabin had been searched and found to contain nothing edible.

Just after midday they left a city that the Duke declared to be Kursk on their right. Their hopes rose more strongly than ever, for far below them lay the frontier of the Ukraine; at least, they were out of Russia proper.

The 'plane bored on to the west through the sharp, crisp air. With perfect rhythm the engines droned on over their heads. Rex was enchanted with the machine. For some time he had been puzzling about the mechanism of the helicopter. It was unlike any that he had ever seen, having two blades only instead of four. At last he solved the problem to his satisfaction and turned to the Duke.

'Cute dodge, that helicopter. When it's not in action it forms another 'plane above our heads, both blades in alignment with the wings. They answer, too, at the same time to the controls. If you're going to use it on its own, the right-hand blade turns completely over, so that the thin edge of both spins in the same direction when it revolves. Guess I'll patent that when I get home!'

De Richleau looked up – it was true. Instead of four blades at an angle impeding the flying speed, and useless except for going up or coming down, the helicopter formed a small but perfect extra 'plane which helped to carry the weight of the machine. As he looked, the Duke's eyes narrowed, and his mouth set in a grim line. He had seen something in addition to the helicopter. Above, and to the right, hovered six 'planes flying in formation. He nudged Rex and pointed.

'Holy Mike,' Rex groaned. 'D'you reckon those birds are after us?'

'I fear so. Every air-park in the country must have been warned of our exploit at Romanovsk.'

Rex had already banked, and was heading away from the enemy flight towards the south when Simon touched him on the shoulder. He had crawled through the cabin. 'Not that way, man,' he shouted. 'Look below to the left – head north, Rex.'

Rex looked and swore – five hundred feet below him another flight were sailing. He tilted the 'plane sharply, to gain additional height, hoping to pass over them. That they were spotted was evident – the northern flight had wheeled swiftly and was climbing too.

'Hell's luck,' Rex exclaimed. 'Another couple of hundred miles and we'd have been safe home.'

'Do you think you can get through?' asked the Duke.

Rex shook his head. 'You bet we'll try, but there's not a scrap of cloud to get lost in. Aw, hell! There's another lot.'

Even as he spoke the Duke had seen them, too; a third formation, only specks in the distance, but in front, and flying high.

'They've been sent up on purpose to intercept us,' he shouted. 'We shall never get through this!'

Rat – tat – tat came the sudden warning note of a machine-gun in their rear.

Simon was at their side again. 'No ammunition in the guns behind,' he said. 'Got any in front?'

De Richleau shook his head. 'None – I looked just after we started – but it would be useless in any case, we could not hope to fight a dozen 'planes, and there are more ahead. Rex, we must come down before we are shot down,' he added, as there came another burst of machine-gun fire.

Rex nodded. 'Cursed luck; still, "while there's life". Let's get out of the way of the rude man with the squirt.' The machine dived suddenly, and it was none too soon; the quick stutter had started again, and the first three bullets pinged through the wing.

Marie Lou was sitting in the cabin where Simon had pulled her when he had first sighted the enemy 'planes. He spoke to her now, quickly, urgently: 'Look here, nobody knows you're with us – it's us they're after, not you. When we land you must run for it.'

'Where can I go?' she protested. 'It is terrible, this – that we should all be caught at last.'

'Anywhere's better than prison,' Simon insisted, 'and I want you to go to Moscow, as fast as you can that is, if you get away. Here, take this.' While he was talking he had unbuttoned his coat and torn the ikon that Valeria Petrovna had given him from his neck. He thrust it into her hand and struggled along to the front of the cabin again. 'Where shall we be near when we land?' he asked the Duke.

'Kiev,' said De Richleau, promptly. 'I can see the spires in the distance and the two great rivers.'

'Right – give me your money, quick.'

'Why?' asked the astonished Duke.

'Give it to me; they'd take it off us, anyhow.' As he spoke Simon peered out. The tiny squares of the fields below them were increasing in size every moment – the earth seemed to be rushing up to meet them. He shouted in Rex's ear: 'Land near that village to the right – near the trees, if you can.'

Rex shook his head. 'Bad landing; the fields'll suit us best.'

'Do as I say,' cried Simon sharply, taking the Duke's wallet. He handed both that and his own to Marie Lou. 'Here's money,' he said, breathlessly. 'Get to Moscow, if you can; see Valeria Petrovna Karkoff, she's the famous actress – anyone will tell you where she lives. Give her this locket and tell her we're prisoners in Kiev – understand?'

Marie Lou nodded. 'Valeria Petrovna,' she repeated. Yes.'

The 'plane began to wheel in great circles at a steep angle. Simon peered out again. He leant over Rex's shoulder.

'Think you can make the orchard?' he cried.

'I guess you're nuts,' said Rex, not understanding what was going on. 'There's a couple of police cars following us on the road – they're in touch with the 'planes by wireless, you bet – we haven't a hope in hell of running for it. Still, I'll do as you say.'

The roofs of the village seemed to be dashing towards them at a terrific speed. They skimmed the thatch of a big barn, and a moment later were bumping along a meadow at fifty miles an hour. With a sudden turn Rex ran the 'plane through a wooden paling, and they brought up with a mild crash against the first trees of an orchard.

'Splendid,' cried Simon, as the engine ceased to throb after its seventeen-hour journey. 'Couldn't have been better.' He was already helping Marie Lou to climb out at the back. 'Run,' he shouted, as she dropped to earth.

'My bundle,' she cried; 'throw me my bundle.'

'Never mind that,' yelled Simon. 'Run!'

She shook her head. 'Please – give it to me – I must have it.'

Angrily he spent a couple of precious minutes searching underneath the cabin table. At last he found it and flung it to her. 'Quick,' he cried; 'Valeria Petrovna; and if you ever get to London, go and see Richard Eaton – National Club – tell him what happened to us all.'

Rex had descended from the front. The Duke followed him more slowly. First he had secured a long flat tin from the cabin. It contained the last of the Hoyo de Monterreys. He lit one himself and offered the tin to Rex. 'Thanks,' said Rex, as he walked round the wing and called up: 'Simon, where are you?'

'Coming,' sang out Simon. He had just seen Marie Lou disappear among the trees.

Rex helped him down. De Richleau proffered him the last cigar. Simon took it with a grin. 'Didn't know you'd got any left,' he said, as he lit up.

'These are the last,' smiled the Duke. 'I kept them for an occasion!'

'Where's Marie Lou?' asked Rex, anxiously.

'She – er – stayed behind at Romanovsk,' said Simon. 'Didn't you know?' He drew the first puff from the long cigar. 'Magnificent stuff, these Hoyos.'

The aeroplanes droned and circled overhead. The siren of a high-powered car shrieked a warning, a moment later the men of the Ogpu, with levelled pistols, came running from the near-by road.

Chapter XXII

'He Who Fights and Runs Away – '

Valeria Petrovna was seated on the divan in her beautiful apartment, her hands were so tightly clasped that the knuckles showed white under the taut skin.

'And then?' she insisted, 'and then – '

'Madame, I do not know – how should I?' Marie Lou shook her head sadly.

'Ah,' Valeria Petrovna stood up with a quick gesture of annoyance, ' 'ow should you? You could 'ave stayed among the trees to watch. Now, 'ow do I know if 'e ees alive or dead?' She began to pace rapidly up and down, the draperies of her négligé swirling round her.

'But yes, Madame,' Marie Lou protested. 'I heard no shots. Surely they will be prisoners, and not dead?'

She was miserably unhappy; these last days had been a nightmare to her. Having spent all her life except her remote childhood in a sleepy Siberian town, with its stupid half-peasant population, shut off from the world by miles of forest and almost arctic snows, living a simple, monotonous existence and nearly always alone except when teaching children, she was amazed and terrified by her experiences in the big cities that she had so longed to see. And now this strange, beautiful woman, who scolded her because she had run away from the 'plane as quickly as she could, just as Simon had told her to.

' 'Ow long ago was this?' demanded Valeria Petrovna, suddenly.

'Three days, Madame.'

'Three days, child? Where 'ave you been all the time?' Tall and dark and lovely, Valeria Petrovna towered accusingly above the unfortunate Marie Lou. 'Why 'ave you not come to me at once?'

Marie Lou did not resent the manner in which the other woman addressed her, although actually there could not have been more than a couple of years difference in their ages. She tried patiently to explain.

'Madame, I hid for a long time in a cowshed, it would not have been safe for me to venture out. When night came I started to walk to Kiev; it was a long way – six, seven versts, perhaps; then in the town I did not know the way. I was afraid to ask. I thought every policeman would know about us. I wandered about looking for the railway station. Then there were some men; they were drunk, I think – it was terrible!' A shudder ran through her slight frame at the recollection.

Valeria Petrovna shrugged. 'Do you think that the 'ole police of Russia 'ave nothing to do but 'unt for you?'

'I didn't know, Madame. I was tired, you see, and half out of my mind with fear. Had it not been for the big sailor, I do not know what would have happened. He was kind; he got back my bundle and took me to the station. I slept on the floor of the waiting-room that night and the next night also.'

'Then you 'ave waste a 'ole day!' Valeria Petrovna waved her hands angrily again. 'Why 'ave you not come by the first train? You knew it was a matter of 'is life.'

Marie Lou shook her head. 'I had very little Russian money. All, nearly, that Monsieur Simon gave me was in foreign notes. I did not dare to change them; I had to wait for a place in the slow train. Last night I slept again upon the Moskawa station. All that I could do to reach you quickly, Madame, I have done.'

With a sudden change of mood, Valeria Petrovna sank down beside Marie Lou and took her hands. 'Forgive me, little one. I 'ave been rude, unkind, when I should thank you from the bottom of my 'eart; it is a terrible time that you 'ave 'ad, terrible; but I am upset – distraught – you see,' she ended, simply, 'I love 'im.'

Admiration struggled with fear in Marie Lou as she looked at the woman kneeling beside her; never, she thought, had she seen anything quite so beautiful. Valeria Petrovna, with her rich silks and laces, her faint delicious perfume, and exotic cultured loveliness, was like a creature from another world. Marie Lou had never seen anyone remotely resembling her before.

The weekly cinemas held in the dance hall of the inn at Romanovsk showed none of the productions of Hollywood or Elstree, only the propaganda films, in which the heroine was a strapping peasant wench or factory girl. Marie Lou could only compare her to those fantastic, unreal creatures that she had read of in her books.

Suddenly Valeria Petrovna burst into tears. 'What shall I do?' she sobbed. 'What shall I do?'

All Marie Lou's fear of this imperious beauty left her. She was, after all, but a woman like herself. 'Have courage, Madame,' she whispered. 'Never did I think to get away from Romanovsk. Never did I think to survive that terrible night in Kiev – but I have done so, I am here in Moskawa. Everything now depends on your courage to help those we love.'

Valeria Petrovna ceased weeping as suddenly as she had begun. 'Love?' she said, in her husky voice. 'Which of these men is it that you love?'

Marie Lou smiled. 'All of them, Madame. It may seem strange to you, but I am of the same world as they. For many years I have been isolated, shut off from life. Their coming was to me like being at home again after a long journey.'

' 'Ave you then known any of them before?' Valeria Petrovna frowned, puzzled.

'No – no. It is difficult to explain, but in the little time since they have come to Romanovsk we have all grown very close together. I know them better than any of the people who were my neighbours for many years. Those three have filled for me an empty world, they are all so kind, so brave, so splendid. Can you wonder that I love them? My freedom when I get out of Russia, instead of being a joy, will be a bitter thing if they are not also free.'

Valeria Petrovna drew away sharply. 'You would 'ave joy to leave Russia? To live with our enemies in the capitalist countries – 'ow can you say such things?'

'Madame, my mother, to whom I owe all that I am, was French – therefore France is my natural country – if I wish to leave Russia, it is no more than if you wished to leave France, had you spent much of your life there against your will.'

'It is yourself you accuse,' said Valeria Petrovna bitterly. 'Russia 'as fed and cloth' you, yet you would stab 'er in the back. You are a bourgeoise – in sympathy with the capitalists – a saboteure!'

Marie Lou shook her head. 'Please let us not talk of this. Can we not think of some way to help our friends?'

Valeria Petarovna's maid entered at that moment. She addressed her mistress: 'There is an Englishman outside, he wishes to see you.' As the woman spoke she looked askance at Marie Lou, an incongruous figure in that lovely room, travel-stained and dishevelled in her rough patched clothes.

'Some fool 'oo 'as seen me at the theatre,' exclaimed Valeria Petrovna. 'Send 'im away.'

'He is insistent,' said the maid, conscious of a twenty-rouble note tucked away in her stocking-top. She forced a visiting-card on her mistress.

'Send 'im away,' repeated Valeria Petrovna angrily. 'Richard Eaton,' she read from the card. 'I do not know 'im.'

'Madame, one moment,' said Marie Lou, quickly. 'Richard Eaton, did you say? That is a friend of Monsieur Simon.'

' 'Ow?' Valeria Petrovna turned sharply. 'A friend of Simon – 'ow you know this?'

'He told me himself. His last words to me were: "If ever you get to London, go and see Richard Eaton at the National Club; tell him what has happened to us."'

'Let 'im come in, then – 'e may 'ave news.'

The maid, who had been lingering by the door, smiled and beckoned to Richard, who was in the hall.

As he came in he looked at Valeria Petrovna with interest. He thought her more lovely in her *déshabillé* than when he had seen her in London. At the dusty figure of Marie Lou he hardly glanced, noticing only the intense blue of her eyes in her pale drawn face.

'I must apologise for troubling you like this,' he began, addressing Valeria Petrovna. 'I did meet you in London, but I don't suppose you'd remember that. I think you will remember a great friend of mine, though.'

'I 'ave remember' you, Mistaire Eaton,' she smiled, graciously. 'Not the name, but your face, at once – it is of Simon Aron that you speak, is it not?'

'Yes, and I don't know if you can help me, but Simon came over to Moscow just after you left England, and I thought – er – well, I thought that it was just on the cards that he might have come to see you when he got here.'

'You are right, Mistaire Eaton; your frien' came to me, not once, but many times.'

Richard gave a sigh of relief. 'Thank the Lord for that. I've been quite worried about him – you'll be able to tell me, then, where I can find him?'

'Please to sit down, Mistaire Eaton. I know, I think, where your frien' is, but 'e is in bad trouble – the poor Simon – 'ave you knowledge of what 'e came to Russia for?'

An anxious look came into Richard Eaton's eyes. 'Yes,' he said, slowly; 'yes, I know about Van Ryn.'

'It was I, then, 'oo obtain for 'im the information that 'is frien' is in the prison at Tobolsk – fool that I was! – after, 'e go there with 'is other frien', then there comes trouble – of all that this child can tell you better than I.' She waved her hand in the direction of Marie Lou.

For the first time Richard really looked at the younger of the two women. With a little shock he realised that she was one of the loveliest people that he had ever seen. Even the heavy boots, the woollen hose and the coarse garments could not conceal her small, perfectly proportioned limbs, nor could the stains of travel and the tousled hair disguise her flower-like face.

As Richard looked at her the ravages of sickness, sleeplessness and anxiety seemed to drop away. There remained the laughing blue eyes, the delicate skin, and the adorable little pointed chin.

She began to speak slowly in a musical voice, with just the faintest suspicion of a delicious accent; telling of her meeting with the three friends in the forest, of their adventures on the way to Romanovsk, as they had been told to her, then of the anxious days they had lived through since, and of their forced descent at Kiev.

'And you mean to say that you have come all the way from Kiev alone?' Richard asked her.

'Yes, Monsieur, not without difficulty; but to reach Madame Karkoff was the only hope of getting assistance for our friends.'

'I think you've been wonderful,' said Richard frankly. 'It must have been frightful for you not knowing Kiev or Moscow, and hunted by the police.'

Marie Lou felt a little glow of warmth run through her. Valeria Petrovna had almost made her wonder if she had not been cowardly in running away so quickly instead of waiting to see what happened when the agents of the Ogpu appeared on the scene.

Valeria Petrovna rose impatiently to her feet. 'I 'ad 'oped, Mistaire Eaton, that you would 'ave 'ad fresh news; 'ow long are you in Moskawa?'

'I only arrived this morning. I slept at Smolensk last night.'

She frowned. 'Slept at Smolensk? Why 'ave you done that?'

'I came in my own 'plane,' Richard explained. 'If I had arrived last night it would have been too late to do anything, so I preferred to take the last two hundred miles this morning.'

'So – and what plan 'ave you to 'elp your frien's?'

'I can go to the British Embassy,' he suggested, doubtfully. 'I set inquiries on foot in London before I came away.'

Valeria Petrovna waved the suggestion aside. 'Useless,' she exclaimed. 'Nevaire will the Kommissars admit that they 'ave them prisoners – they 'ave been in the forbidden territory – it will be said that they died there in the snows.'

She began walking rapidly up and down, smoking cigarette after cigarette in a long thin holder. Marie Lou was about to offer a suggestion, but Valeria Petrovna stopped her with an impatient gesture. 'Be silent – let me think.'

Her quick brain was working at top speed as she paced up and down; the Englishman was useless, she decided – a nice young man, but stupid – his presence would only increase her difficulties. As for the girl, she must be got rid of. 'Love them all indeed!' What woman could love three men at one time? She also was in love with the clever, attractive Simon, that was clear; good-looking little fool – did she think to deceive Valeria Petrovna by not admitting it? Did the minx fancy that she, Valeria Petrovna, would be willing to pick the chestnuts out of the fire for another woman? What a mistake to think that! She should be handed over to the police – was she not a bourgeoise? – but wait – what of the Englishman? He could not be got rid of so easily, and just the stupid sort of fool to create trouble about the girl. Look at him now, gazing at her like a moon-struck calf. No, it must be some other way – and what of Simon, in prison there at Kiev? She must see Stalin. Stalin should give him up to her – he had a sense of humour, that one! There would be conditions, but they might be turned to her advantage. If he refused, she would threaten never to act again; he had trouble enough to keep the people to the work he demanded of them – they would make more trouble if she left the stage because he refused to pardon her lover. A sudden idea came to her as to how to deal with Marie Lou. She stopped in her quick pacing and faced the girl. 'Leave us, little one, for a minute, I wish to 'ave a word with Mistaire Eaton.' She pointed to the doorway of an inner room.

Marie Lou obediently left them. As the door closed behind her Valeria Petrovna drew a chair close to Richard and sat down.

'Listen,' she said, quickly. 'I can save your frien'. Stalin, 'e will listen to what I 'ave to say; you can do nothing 'ere, also this girl. Now that she 'as brought my locket, she can do no more. You must leave Russia and take 'er with you in your airplane.'

'She may not want to go,' Richard protested. 'Besides, I would rather stay here and see this thing through myself.'

Valeria Petrovna smiled sweetly. 'I 'ave understanding, Mistaire Eaton. You are brave, but what good can you do? And this girl – she is in danger, she is 'unted by the police. Please to do as I say and take 'er out of Russia.'

'We'll ask her and see what she says?' Richard suggested.

'No.' Valeria Petrovna placed a hand on his arm. 'Mistaire Eaton, I will make to you a confession – I love your frien' Simon, and only I can save 'im. Give me a free 'and, then, and take the girl away.'

Richard Eaton was no fool. Valeria Petrovna had made it abundantly clear that whatever her reasons might be she wished to get rid of Marie Lou. He felt that in any case the sooner the girl was out of Russia the better. He dreaded to think what might happen to her if she was caught by the Ogpu after having concealed and assisted his friends. Personally he would much have preferred to go down to Kiev, but Valeria Petrovna said that she could secure the release of the prisoners, so she was obviously the person to be considered at the moment.

'All right,' he agreed. 'I'll clear out and take her with me – that is, if you're quite certain that you can get Stalin to give my friends their freedom?'

' 'Ave no fear.' She rose, smiling. 'That is settle', then. I will call 'er.'

The situation was explained to Marie Lou; Valeria Petrovna was now all solicitude for the girl. Richard himself urged upon her how little either of them could do, and how much wiser it would be for her to leave Russia at the earliest possible moment.

She looked from one to the other with her big serious eyes. She had no argument to oppose theirs, but somehow she did not trust this beautiful Madame Karkoff. It never occurred to her that she could be regarded as a rival. She did not understand in the least the passionate temperament that was responsible for these sudden changes from imperious anger to honeyed sweetness, and then to suspicious distrust. Had it not been for Richard she would have refused to go, but he was so obviously sincere that she accepted the decision, contenting herself with reminding them that there might be difficulties at the airport, as she had no permit to leave Russia.

'I will arrange,' declared Valeria Petrovna quickly. 'The commander of the airport, 'e is a frien' of mine. We shall say that you are my little cousin, Xenia Kirrolovna from Niji. You travel to your mother, 'oo is ill in Berlin. Your bag 'as been stolen – all your papers are gone – it is urgent, for the mother dies. The Englishman 'as offer' to take you in 'is 'plane. They will make no difficulty eef I come with you.'

Richard nodded. 'That sounds all right, if you can arrange it. When do we leave, tomorrow morning?'

'No, no, at once – this afternoon. You shall eat 'ere. In the meantime I get my clothes.' She clapped her hands loudly and the maid appeared.

'Quickly, Fenya,' she ordered. 'Bring food, and tell Vasily to bring the car to the door. After, come to me in my room.'

Marie Lou and Richard made a scratch lunch of ham, cheese and tea. By the time they had finished Valeria Petrovna joined them again, dressed in a smart travelling suit.

'Let us go,' she said at once. 'Mistaire Eaton, we will call on the way at the 'otel for your bags. You, little one, 'ave no luggage.'

As they stood at the door of the apartment she turned to the maid. 'I go to the airport, Fenya, after to the Kremlin, then I return 'ere in one 'our, perhaps two. Pack at once, that all may be ready – on my return we leave for Kiev immediately.'

At the aerodrome there was surprisingly little difficulty. Eaton's passport was all in order. A tall effeminate officer danced attendance on Madame Karkoff. He made no trouble about the little cousin who had lost her papers and was so anxious about her mother. He could not do enough for Valeria Petrovna – bowing, saluting, and twisting his little fair moustache. He even provided extra rugs, which Richard was to return on the Warsaw 'plane.

Marie Lou had been tucked into the passenger's seat, and Richard was about to climb into the cockpit. He turned to ask a last assurance from Valeria Petrovna.

'You are quite certain that you will succeed with Stalin?'

'Do not worry, Mistaire Eaton. I 'ave a way to make 'im do as I say.'

He nodded. 'Where shall I wait for Simon? Warsaw would be best, I think?'

She smiled above her furs. 'I would not do that, Mistaire Eaton. You would 'ave to wait a very long time.'

'Why?' Richard frowned.

'Simon cannot leave Russia – 'e 'as been to the forbidden territory – 'e knows perhaps too much. Stalin would not 'ave that.'

'But he can't stay here for ever!' Richard gasped. 'There's his business in London – all sorts of things!'

She shrugged her beautiful shoulders and smiled again. 'Why should 'e not? – 'is business is not everything. Many people 'ere in Russia 'ave learned to do without their businesses these last years.'

'But he'd be miserable,' Richard protested.

Valeria Petrovna laughed softly. 'You are not very complimentary, Mistaire Eaton – 'ave I not told you that I love 'im – also 'e loves me. All right, I shall register with 'im.'

'Register? What do you mean?'

'Marry 'im – as all things are, Stalin would nevaire release 'im – if 'e is to remain in Russia and become my 'usband, that is different – Stalin will not refuse.'

From comparative serenity Richard was thrown into a state of acute anxiety. How would Simon view this extraordinary plan? To give up his life entirely, everything to which he was attached, his active career, with its multitude of interests, and become the lapdog husband of this famous actress; to start life anew in this extraordinary country as a suspect, with principles utterly opposed to those of the State. Of course, Richard reflected, as he caught a glimpse of her beautiful smiling dark eyes, if he loved this woman enough, anything was possible. Besides, Simon was Jewish, and could make a home in any country; exile was never quite so terrible for them. Perhaps Simon would go native, become a Kommissar. With these thoughts whirling through his brain Richard looked once more at the tall dark woman by his side – the problem was too much for him! 'Well, you know best,' he said; 'but what about De Richleau and Van Ryn? You can't marry them as well!'

'What of them?' she shrugged again. 'They are saboteurs both – I 'ave no interest in what 'appens to them – it is for Simon only that I worry.'

'But you promised,' he protested, quickly.

'I promised nothing.' She gave him a sharp look. 'Only for Simon – 'e is your frien'. Why should you trouble for these others?'

'Look here,' said Richard firmly, 'they are all my friends. I don't know what you meant when you spoke about it in your flat, but I understood that you were going to get them all out of this. If you're not I won't go – I'll stay and do what I can myself.'

'So . . .' She raised her well-marked eyebrows. 'Think again, my frien' – I 'ave but to speak a word to the officer 'ere – to say I tell the untruth about my little cousin – 'e will 'ave 'er arrested quick – 'ow will that please you?'

Richard shot a sharp glance in the direction of Marie Lou. The girl was sitting in the 'plane, all unconscious of the subject of the conversation. He knew that he'd been tricked, and he was furious. Yet how could he stand by and see that poor girl hauled off to prison.

'It is time for you to go, Mistaire Eaton,' came the husky voice at his side, 'the officer 'e waits that you should depart, or shall I confess to 'im that I 'ave told a lie?' She laughed softly.

There was no alternative, but as Richard stepped towards the 'plane he turned and looked Valeria Petrovna squarely in the eyes. 'Perhaps you are right, Madame Karkoff,' he said, with a little smile, 'but I wonder if you have ever heard of the old English proverb: "He who fights and runs away, lives to fight another day".'

Chapter XXIII

A Passport Has Been Arranged

In a long graceful curve the 'plane left the Moscow airport. It was just before three o' clock, a lovely clear afternoon in early spring. The spires and domes of the ancient Muscovite city spread out below them, the winding river and the open spaces of the parks diminished in size; soon they were left far behind. For the time being Richard put anxiety for his friends out of his mind, and gave himself up to the joy of flight.

About half past seven they came down at Minsk to stretch their legs and eat a snack at the aerodrome buffet. Marie Lou had enjoyed the flight; it had been Rex's antics to avoid the searchlights at Romanovsk which had made her airsick on her first aeroplane journey. She also had ceased for the time being to worry about the prisoners at Kiev; after the strain of the last few days it was an enormous relief for her to be in comparative safety – she was content to leave all decisions to Richard Eaton.

Richard had taken the precaution to secure a note from Valeria Petrovna's effeminate friend for the airpark officials at Minsk, so no difficulty was made about their proceeding on their journey. From Minsk it was only some twenty odd miles to the Polish frontier. In the evening light they started on the long stretch over the plain of Grodno, arriving at Warsaw a little before midnight.

They were led at once to the passport office, and it was here that the trouble began. Richard's passport was all in order, but what of Marie Lou? They were taken before an official in a resplendent uniform with a plethora of gold lace. It seemed that had they come from anywhere but Russia the matter might have been arranged. The Poles, however, live in perpetual terror of their Soviet neighbours, and the strictest precautions are in force to prevent spies and agitators from entering the country. Richard told the story of the dying mother in Berlin, and the stolen baggage, but in vain. In no circumstances could Marie Lou be allowed to remain in Poland.

Richard asked the decorative gentleman where he thought they were going to sleep?

The man shrugged. 'You wish to go to Berlin? Very good, go to Berlin. It is three hundred miles only. You can rest here for an hour and then proceed.'

Richard did not in the least want to go to Berlin! 'Perhaps they will make the same sort of trouble there?' he suggested.

The official thought that undoubtedly they would. People could not go entering countries like this, just as they chose, without proper papers.

'But we can't just go on flying from place to place,' Richard protested. 'We must stop somewhere!'

'Undoubtedly,' the man agreed, stroking his carefully curled beard. 'One would get tired. The best plan is that you return to Minsk. They will give you there a proper passport for the lady. You can still be in Berlin by tomorrow. One thing is certain – the lady cannot remain here!' He began to gather his papers together.

Richard wished to return to Minsk even less than he wished to go on to Berlin.

'How far is it to Vienna?' he asked at length.

'Three hundred and fifty miles – about, but there, also, it is doubtful if they would let you enter.'

'I've got friends there,' Richard replied. 'Can I send a telegram or wireless?'

'Certainly, if you wish. Here are forms.'

'Thanks.' Richard addressed a brief wire to: The Honourable G. B. Bruce, Secretary, British Embassy, Vienna, in which he requested that gentleman most urgently to leave his comfortable bed and meet him at the Vienna air-park between four and five in the morning.

The wire was sent, they had some hot drinks and sandwiches at the buffet, and an hour later set off once more.

'It is a misfortune, this,' said Marie Lou. 'We shall not now be able to meet our friends when they arrive in Warsaw.'

'That's true,' Richard agreed, but he said no more. He had not told Marie Lou that there was no prospect of their meeting their friends anywhere in the immediate future.

Richard was dog tired. It was by far the longest flight he had ever made in one day, but his new 'plane was going splendidly. He thanked the Lord that he had run her in before he left England, and settled down gamely to the last lap. Marie Lou slept most of the way, and had to be awakened when they arrived at last at Vienna.

'Hullo, Dickybird? You're a fine fellow, keeping a lad from his hard-earned rest till this hour in the morning,' came a voice from the darkness as Richard was helping Marie Lou to alight.

'Hallo, Gerry.' Richard heaved a sigh of relief at finding that his friend was there to meet them. 'I'm glad they didn't pull you out of bed,' he added, as he noticed that Bruce was still in evening dress.

'No, I've been to a party, my ancient auk – didn't get your wire till I got in. What's the trouble?'

Richard explained as briefly as possible.

The tall, gaunt diplomat loomed over him in the darkness.

'My giddy aunt – you are a lad. Can't you find enough trouble among the young women in London without picking up bits in Bolsheville?'

'Shut up,' said Richard, in a savage whisper. 'She speaks English.'

'Sorry, Dicky,' the tall man apologised. 'Hope she didn't hear; introduce me to the lady, and I'll see if I can't work the oracle with Rupert of Hentzau, there.' Bruce nodded towards a slim-waisted officer who stood some distance away.

The introduction was made, Bruce took Richard's passport and held a short conversation with the so-called Rupert of Hentzau, there was much laughter between them, and the little officer gave an extra twist to his moustache as he looked at Marie Lou, then Bruce rejoined them.

'All serene,' he announced. 'He says you're a lucky fellow, Dickybird.'

'I – why?' Richard yawned, wearily.

'Well, I had to make up a bit of a story, so I said Madame, was your wife. In fact, I implied in a sort of way, that you were on your honeymoon – doing the round trip – Berlin, Warsaw, Vienna. Little chappie got quite excited about it. I thought it best not to mention Russia.'

'Idiot,' said Richard. He looked quickly away from Marie Lou and felt himself grow quite hot in the darkness.

' 'Fraid I can't offer to put you up,' Bruce went on as they climbed into a taxi. 'I occupy a palatial suite of two whole rooms and sleep in the bath most of the time myself.'

'That's all right, tell him to go to the Kurplatz,' said Richard, sleepily. 'Anywhere for a bed.'

'Righto, my Croesus – it's a guinea a minute, but as you're on your honeymoon, I suppose it's excusable.'

'If I were not so tired I'd knock your head off,' Richard yawned. 'As it is I'll poison you at lunch tomorrow, if you'll come, then we'll try and sort out this mess.'

'Does the poor but honest Briton, earning his living in a distant land, refuse the invitation of his rich compatriot? *No, Sir!* as our American cousins say. I'll be there, and tell 'em to get in an extra supply of caviare!'

At the Kurplatz Bruce left them. Richard threw off his clothes and tumbled into bed – within a minute he was fast asleep. But not so, Marie

Lou; the luxurious bedroom was a revelation to her, she drew her fingers softly down the thick silk curtains, examined the embossed writing-paper on the desk and the telephones beside the bed. Then she explored the tiled bath-room, she tried the taps, the water gushed into the low porcelain bath. Slowly she drew off her worn garments, and stepped into the clear water. She lay down, and steeped her tired limbs in its warm comfort, kicking her pink legs delightedly. Afterwards she wrapped herself in the big towel, and when she was dry, crept between the soft sheets with a little sigh of contentment. For a few moments before she switched out the light she lay, weaving a new chapter in the fairy story of the Princess Marie Lou. As the light went out the first rays of another day were creeping through the blinds, but Marie Lou was fast asleep.

It was after midday when she awoke to the shrilling of the telephone. She looked round her – bewildered – then she took off the receiver.

Richard's voice came to her over the wire. 'Hallo! How are you this morning?'

She snuggled down in the bed, the receiver held tightly to her ear. 'I am very well, and how is my husband?'

There was an embarrassed pause, while Marie Lou smiled wickedly to herself, then Richard's voice came again. 'I'm splendid, thanks. I only woke up ten minutes ago, but I've been busy since.'

'What have you been doing?'

'Listen.' He smiled into the mouthpiece of his telephone. 'Gerry Bruce will be here at half past one, and you can't very well lunch in the restaurant as you are.'

'Oh no, not as I am! That would never do!' she agreed, with an amused smile at her reflection in the mirror.

'Are you in bed?' he asked, suddenly.

'Of course – are you?'

'Yes – but I mean – er – you must have other clothes.' Richard smiled again. 'I've told the people in the hotel to send out to the shops and bring you some things to see. Just choose what you want. Shoes, stockings, and a frock, sort of thing – just for today, you'll have lots of time to get other things, later.'

'I think you are very kind, Mr Eaton.'

'Oh, not a bit – but I say, you might call me Richard, will you?'

Marie Lou smiled again. 'Well then, Richard, I think that you are one of the very nicest people that I have ever met!' She quickly hung up the receiver, and hopped out of bed.

When Richard called for her, a little after half past one, he was genuinely astonished at the transformation. She had chosen a simple blue frock and hat, but wore them with all the inherited chic that had made De Richleau hail her at once as a Parisienne born. She was admiring herself with childish delight in the long mirror, and swung round quickly as he came in.

'Do you like me?' she asked, gaily.

He smiled. 'You look perfectly lovely.' Then he shook his head with mock seriousness, and added: 'But I'm afraid you won't do like that!'

'I will not do?' she said, a little note of anxiety creeping into her voice.

'There's something missing,' he declared.

'But what?' She looked at herself in the mirror again.

'Why these.' Richard produced from behind his back a large bunch of Parma violets.

'Oh, but how lovely, Richard – give them to me quickly.' She took the violets and held them to her face, smiling at him over the tight mass; he thought her eyes were an even more lovely colour than the flowers over which they peeped.

'Come along,' he said, cheerfully, 'or Gerry will have drunk all the cocktails!'

'Cocktails?' she asked, puzzled. 'What is that?'

'Sort of drink we have in these nice old capitalist countries,' he laughed. 'Rex can tell you more about them than I can.' As they walked down the corridor he thought to himself what a lot of delightful things this child of the backwoods had yet to learn; he didn't suppose she'd ever been to a dance or play, or even seen a sea warm enough to bathe in. What fun it would be to show her all those things. The sight of Gerry Bruce's lean face, as he sat waiting for them in the lounge, reminded him sharply that there was some very urgent business to be done before he could show anybody anything!

'Well, Dickybird!' Bruce greeted him, cheerfully. 'Ordered in the caviare for your impecunious friend?'

'Lots of it,' said Richard. 'Brought half a dozen sturgeon with me in the 'plane last night!'

Marie Lou was introduced to the mystery of cocktails, and shortly after they were seated at a little round table in the restaurant, consuming an excellent lunch.

Richard began at once to tell the story of Rex, Simon, and the Duke; when he had finished Bruce looked very grave.

'Don't like it, Dicky, my boy. I don't want to be depressing, but those poor chappies have probably gone through the hoop by now.'

'I don't think so,' Richard disagreed. 'Valeria Petrovna will be in Kiev by now. She will have saved Simon's apple-cart, and he's not the man to forget his pals.'

For the first time Marie Lou heard Valeria Petrovna's views on Simon's future, and her intention of abandoning Rex and the Duke to their fate.

'What does the noble Richard intend to do now?' asked Bruce.

Richard smiled. 'Gerry, my boy, you don't seriously think that I asked you to lunch because of your good looks, do you? Only useful, practising diplomats are allowed to devour a pound's worth of caviare at a sitting. It's up to you!'

Bruce shook his head. 'Honestly, I don't know that there's much we can do. I'll have a few words with the old man when I get back to the Embassy. We can demand their release or public trial. Trouble is, ten to one the Bolshies will say they've never heard of them. I don't see what else we can do.'

'Well, I shall go to Kiev,' said Richard.

'My honourable and ancient auk, you're potty!' Bruce declared. 'What could you do?'

'Oh, punt round a bit. I suppose we've got a consulate there. I can stir them up. Have a return match with Valeria Petrovna perhaps, and if she's got Simon out I might be able to see him and hear the latest about the other two.'

'Much more likely to land your silly self in jug.'

'Not a bit of it', Richard protested. 'They've got nothing against me – probably don't even know of my existence, certainly not of my connection with the others. My passport's in order. I shall go with all the power and prestige of old England at my back. If *you* can't do anything but exchange polite notes with these rotten swine, I'm hanged if *I'm* going to sit twiddling my thumbs!'

'All right, my adventurous birdie, don't get wild about it – but as a matter of fact your passport is out of order. You'll need a new *visa* to enter the Soviet again.'

'How long will that take?'

'A fortnight, in the ordinary way, but if I go in and see the Soviet people myself I can get it for you in three or four days.'

'Right you are, Gerry. Be a good chap and see about it this afternoon, will you?' Richard pushed his passport across the table. 'And you might get your people at the Embassy to shoot off a letter tonight. With any luck they'll get a reply before we get the visa.'

'Thy will be done, O giver of good meals!' Bruce pocketed the passport.

'If you go back to Russia, I will go, too,' said Marie Lou, gently.

Richard laughed. 'My dear girl, you can't. I don't quite know what to do with you as it is. I had thought of entrusting you to Gerry, but he's not a fit companion for a nice girl like you!'

'Take me with you,' she begged, seriously.

He shook his head. 'It's sweet of you to want to come, but it's absolutely out of the question.'

'But why?' she argued. 'With me, also, no one in Kiev knows that I am the friend of your friends, even if my description has been sent out from Romanovsk. Who would recognise me in my new clothes?'

'That's true enough, all the same it just can't be done. The one bright spot in this whole ghastly mess is that you are out of danger.'

'You are wrong to refuse to take me,' she said, earnestly. 'What will you do in Kiev, all on your own, you cannot speak one word of Russian!'

'I know, that's the devil, isn't it?' Richard admitted. 'Means one can't make any inquiries at all, except through the Consulate. But, all the same, it would be frightfully dangerous for you to enter Russia again unless you are protected by a proper passport, so it's useless to talk about it.'

Gerry Bruce looked from one to the other with an amused smile. 'Pity you're not really married,' he said, with a twinkle. 'Nothing to stop a chappie taking his wife anywhere. She goes on the same passport.'

There was dead silence at the little table, the astute Gerry was thoroughly enjoying Richard's embarrassment. 'Wedding bells at the Embassy tomorrow morning, and there you are,' he continued, quickly. 'Always get an annulment afterwards if you don't – er – that is, if you feel you'd rather not keep it up.'

'Is that true, Monsieur?' asked Marie Lou.

'What nonsense!' exclaimed Richard. 'This isn't a French farce – besides, it might not be so easy to get an annulment afterwards as you think, and Marie Lou might not like the idea of being tied up to me all in a hurry like that!'

'I have not been asked,' said Marie Lou, with her wicked little smile.

'Now then, Dicky, my boy,' laughed Bruce. 'This is where chappies go down on their knees and put their hands on their hearts.'

'Oh, shut up,' said Richard. He had become very serious as he turned to Marie Lou. 'Look here. I know all this seems like the Mad Hatter's tea-party, but there's something in what this idiot says. Under English law a wife takes her husband's nationality. The Embassy is English soil – if we were married there, tomorrow you could be put on my passport, then there would be no difficulty about returning to Russia, and as my wife the police would never connect you with the girl at Romanovsk. I will admit, too, that there is very little I can do in Kiev without someone who I can trust that speaks Russian. Of course, I'd take all the necessary steps to give you your freedom directly we got back again.'

She regarded him gravely for a moment – then she nodded, slowly. 'Yes, I am sure I can trust you to do that. I know, also, that I shall be a help to you in Kiev. Let us then get married tomorrow.'

And so it was arranged – the following morning there was a marriage at the British Embassy. Immediately afterwards Bruce took the joint passport of the newly married pair to the Soviet Legation and pressed for a speedy visa. In the afternoon, on Richard's advice, Marie Lou visited the astonished Chaplain to the Embassy who had married them in the morning, and declared, vehemently, that she would never live with her husband, she had already discovered terrible things about him which she refused to disclose. In addition Richard moved to a different hotel. It was his idea that these precautions would materially assist them in securing an early annulment of their marriage on their return from Russia. Nevertheless, he dined with Marie Lou that night at one of the smaller restaurants, and thought it one of the most delightful evenings he had ever spent.

The following day he took his official wife shopping, having obtained fresh supplies of cash through Bruce, and never in his life had he experienced so much pleasure as in Marie Lou's delight at the lovely things he insisted on buying for her from the Vienna shops.

That night he took her to a musical show. In her new evening dress she was radiantly lovely – tiny but perfect – a real princess.

Many people turned to look at her and wonder who she was, but she had no eyes for anyone but Richard, that by no means silent Englishman, with his merry laugh, and his anxious, thoughtful care for her. Nobody who saw them doubted for a minute that they were lovers.

On the third day a reply was received from the authorities at Kiev – Moscow had been consulted; an American called Van Ryn had arrived in that city on December 4th, and left on the 11th for an unknown destination. Mr Simon Aron had arrived there on February 6th; he, also, had disappeared. Of the Duke de Richleau they had no knowledge. The suggestion that these three persons were being held prisoner in Kiev was quite unfounded.

'There you are, my dear old bird,' said Bruce, as he showed the reply to Richard. 'Just what I expected. Now, if you can *prove* that those chappies are in Kiev, we'll create diplomatic hell, but more we can't do.'

That afternoon Richard took Marie Lou out to Schoenbrunn; they walked in the gardens of the palace, rejoicing in the fresh green of the early spring. In the evening he took her to another show and afterwards to a cabaret – they had recovered completely from the fatigue of the long journey and did not go to their respective hotels until the early hours of the morning. Somehow, the more they saw of each other the more they had to say. There was an infinite variety of incidents in their past lives that they had to tell each other. Then there were all their plans and hopes for the future, into which, of course, the question of marriage – at least for some years, and even then only to some person vaguely reminiscent of each other – did not enter.

But Marie Lou came to have the fixed opinion that she would undoubtedly prefer an Englishman for a husband, because they were so kind and reliable; and Richard declared that he could never contemplate marrying an English girl because they were so dull!

The fourth day of their stay brought a different atmosphere. In the morning Richard had a long interview with Gerry Bruce and an elderly Polish Jew. It seemed that the latter knew Kiev as well as Richard knew the West End of London. He gave much interesting information, particularly about the Kievo-Pecher-Lavra, the ancient monastery that had been turned into a prison. Unfortunately his activities in the past had been such that he was no longer able to enter the Soviet, so he was unable to accept Richard's invitation to accompany them.

In the afternoon Richard's passport was returned, *visa*ed as good for a month's visit to the U.S.S.R. That evening he again took Marie Lou out to dinner, but their former gaiety had disappeared. Both were thinking of the morrow, and what was to come after. They were to make an early start in the morning, and so went early to bed.

Gerry Bruce drove them out to the air-park in the morning. He was more serious than usual, and as he shook hands with Richard he said:

'Go easy, old chap. I mean it. Don't do anything to get yourself into trouble. If you are tempted to' – he grinned, suddenly – 'well, think of the wife!'

The weather had turned grey and ugly; the going proved exceptionally bad. At Lemberg they landed for luncheon, and Marie Lou was pitifully white and shaken. It took all her courage to face the second half of the journey, but at last it was over. At six o' clock in the evening Mr and Mrs Richard Eaton stepped out of their 'plane at Kiev.

Chapter XXIV

Conferences in Kiev

Simon lay propped up on a chaise-longue near the window. It was over a fortnight since he had received the wound in his thigh, and thanks to Marie Lou's care, it had healed quickly. He was able to walk a little now with the aid of a stick, but he still had to keep his leg up most of the time.

The bedroom in the hotel at Kiev to which Valeria Petrovna had brought him after she secured his release, was a gloomy place. The heavy furnishings were of a date long preceding the revolution. Simon had seen similar rooms in old-fashioned provincial hotels in France, but this had the added dreariness that little attempt had been made to obliterate the traces of its generations of fleeting occupants.

A bottle of sweet Caucasian wine stood at Simon's elbow, and a French novel lay open on his knees, but he seemed to be deriving little pleasure from either – he was gazing vacantly out of the window at the busy street below. Kiev seemed to be a hive of activity, but much of it, he supposed, was to be attributed to the five day week.

He caught a slight sound at the door, and turned his head. 'Richard!' he exclaimed, in amazed surprise.

'Hullo, Simon.' Richard closed the door quickly behind him and locked it, then walked swiftly over to the other door, which led into an adjoining room, and locked that too.

'What on earth are you doing here?' Simon's wide smile showed his undoubted pleasure at seeing his friend.

Richard sat down on the edge of Simon's long chair. 'How's the leg?' he asked.

'Fine – how did you know about it – and – er – about me being in Kiev?'

'It's a long story, my boy. When will the lady be back?'

'Not for an hour, but why? *She's* been wonderful.'

'Splendid,' Richard nodded. 'All the same I'd rather not meet her again just yet. How about Rex and the Duke?'

'Out of it! She fixed up everything.'

'You're sure of that, Simon?'

'Um,' Simon nodded, quickly. 'They left Kiev yesterday.'

'I see. Don't mind my asking, do you – but why didn't you go too?'

'Well, I'll tell you,' said Simon, slowly. 'I'm – er – getting married.'

Richard smiled. 'Do I congratulate the happy man?'

Simon laughed. 'Well, I never thought I would get married, somehow, but I've changed my mind.'

'Splendid, old boy, you know how glad I am for you if everything's really all right. When are you bringing your bride back to England?'

'Well – er – as a matter of fact, I'm not coming back to England, you see it's this way – Valeria Petrovna takes the New Russia very seriously. She simply wouldn't hear of coming to England – talked about her art – that it belonged to the Russian people. Besides, she really believes that the Communists are going to make a better world for everybody, and that Russia's the one place to live. I'll tell you – I think there's a lot in what she says.'

'Simon, you're talking rot, and you know it. But seriously, are you really prepared to give up everything and live in a pigsty like this?'

Simon drew his thin hand over his long receding forehead. 'No,' he confessed, 'I hate it, but as she wouldn't come to England what else could I do?'

Richard stood up. 'Do you really love this woman very much, Simon?'

'Yes.' Simon nodded, gravely. 'I do, never thought I'd meet anyone like her.'

'Then I've got one of the most unpleasant jobs I've ever had in my life.' Richard began to pace uneasily up and down.

'How do you mean?'

'Why, to tell you the truth about Valeria Petrovna. I suppose she never told you about seeing me in Moscow a week ago?'

'Ner.' Simon looked puzzled. 'Didn't know you'd been there.'

'Well, I have; it's less than a week as a matter of fact, though it seems like a month in some ways. You remember you asked me to start digging round if I didn't hear from you in three weeks? That was at Miriam's party. Well, in the middle of February I began to get worried. I stirred up the Foreign Office, but I couldn't get any satisfaction, so by the end of the month I decided to come over myself. When I got to Moscow it occurred to me that you might have looked up Valeria Petrovna, so I went to see her. By an incredible slice of good luck that angel, Marie Lou, was there when I arrived.'

'I see.' Simon nodded. 'Of course, Valeria Petrovna told me that Marie Lou had turned up with the locket, and that she'd got her safely out of the country.'

'She did – I took her! But before we left your lady friend told me quite a lot about her plans for your future, and her views on Rex and the Duke.'

'Did she?'

'Yes.' Richard faced his friend. 'Now I'm not going to ask you, Simon, if you agreed to register with the lady, or whatever they call it here, solely because you do think it would be worth giving up the old life to be with her, or if she brought some pressure to bear about De Richleau and Rex, though I'm inclined to think it was the latter, but either way, you're not the man to sit here drinking that filthy wine unless she had promised to get your friends out of it, too!'

'Ner – of course she promised, and she has, too!'

'Don't you believe it, my boy, Rex and the Duke are still in prison, here, in Kiev, and thank God they are. I've been terrified that they'd have been shot by this time.'

Simon was sitting up now, his mouth wide open.

'It's not true, Richard. She fixed up everything. Got special permits for them to leave the country, from Stalin. It took a bit longer than in my case, But she told me, only yesterday, that they'd been taken under escort to the station, and were on their way home.'

'Then she told you a lie! She said, herself, to me, in Moscow, that the only way to get you out was to marry you and keep you here. You knew too much for them to let you leave the country. She couldn't marry Rex and the Duke as well, and they were enemies of Russia, anyway, so they could go to the devil as far as she was concerned. I should never have left Moscow, but she threatened to turn poor little Marie Lou over to the police – so I got out while the going was good.'

'That's days ago, Richard. About Marie Lou, it was different. She's jealous because Marie Lou looked after my leg. Got some silly idea that the girl's in love with me – you know what women are. She wouldn't have handed her over to the police really, but I dare say she was glad to get her out of the way. Rex and the Duke are different, she'd never deceive me about that.'

'I'm sorry, Simon.' Richard shook his head. 'I know you're in love with her, and it's rotten for me to have to tell you all this. I don't say that she wouldn't have got them out if she could, just to please you, but she's not powerful enough. Rex and De Richleau are still here, in Kiev. I know because one of our secret service people in Vienna put me on to a gaoler called Shubin at the Kievo-Pecher-Lavra. I saw him this morning, and they're only waiting for instructions from Moscow to have them both shot.'

'Good God! What the devil can we do?'

'I don't know. I'm worried out of my wits.'

Simon groaned. 'To think I've been sitting here doing nothing since Sunday. If only I'd known.'

'My dear old boy, you didn't know. It's no use fussing yourself about that. The thing is, what can we do?'

'What about your – er – gaoler friend?'

'No good, I tried him, he's one of the head men. Doesn't do ordinary duty himself. He'd be suspected at once if he attempted to tamper with any of the warders.'

'There's one chap who was decent to us,' said Simon, slowly. 'Used to be a peasant on the Plakoff estates, and remembers the Duke as a young man. Wonder if we could get hold of him?'

'What's his name?'

'Yakovkin – big strapping fellow with a beard and a scar over one eye.'

'They might be able to arrange something between them,' said Richard, meditatively. 'Anyhow, I'll try and see my man again this evening.'

'How about mun? I haven't got a bean.'

'I have, plenty; I got a supply from the Embassy in Vienna. But if I can arrange anything, how the devil can we get them away?'

'I'll get Valeria Petrovna's car.'

'Sorry, Simon, but I'm a bit nervous about bringing her into this.'

'I'll pinch it if necessary. We go for a drive in it every morning – the people in the hotel garage know me.'

'Good for you,' Richard smiled. 'But won't they stop you at the frontier?'

'Um – perhaps, still you know what Napoleon said about the Rubicon and the Vistula!'

Richard laughed. 'You're a bit mixed in your history, old chap; but I agree. If only we can get them out the Pecher-Lavra that's half the battle. Look here, I'd better leave you now, I don't want Valeria Petrovna to find me here, and don't let on to her for the moment that you know the truth about Rex and the Duke.'

Simon nodded, sadly. 'No, I won't do that yet. I want to think about what I'm going to do myself first. When shall I see you again?'

'When's the best time?'

'Tomorrow, about twelve. She's giving a special show at the theatre tomorrow night as she is in Kiev, and she's rehearsing in the morning. I shall be alone then.'

'Good. With any luck I'll be able to tell you then if I've succeeded in fixing anything. I'll be able to see Zakar Shubin again tonight and ask him about this Yakovkin, or rather, my beautiful wife will!'

'Your what?'

'Oh, of course I haven't told you.' Richard looked a little sheepish. 'I married Marie Lou. It was the only way for her to return here safely, and I couldn't have done much without her.'

'Good God!' Simon laughed into his hand. 'We are in a muddle – but I must say marriage seems to suit you!'

'I must go now,' said Richard, quickly. 'See you tomorrow.'

Marie Lou was in her bedroom. She had agreed with Richard that it was too dangerous to sit in the lounge. Every precaution must be taken to prevent Valeria Petrovna seeing them.

Richard joined her there and told her of his interview with Simon. They would not be able to see Zakar Shubin until he came off duty again in the evening, so Richard suggested that they had better go out as they were supposed to be ordinary tourists, and the hotel people might be suspicious if they stayed indoors all day. They collected the official guide who had been attached to them, and made their way through the beautiful old square of Saint Sophia, which joins the hotels to the cathedral.

'Mind how you go,' said Richard, taking Marie Lou's arm as they entered the gloom of the great building with its five long naves. The frescoes on the walls were quite wonderful; they were not religious subjects, but scenes of hunting and sport, dating back to the eleventh century. The guide told them that at one time a portion of the cathedral had been an ancient palace. Afterwards he took them to the Kievo-Pecher-Lavra. Before the Revolution it had been the greatest monastery in the Ukraine; now, a large part of it had been converted into a museum.

Richard was puzzled. It was here, somewhere in this vast labyrinth of buildings, that Rex and the Duke were held prisoners. He looked about eagerly for signs of warders or guards, while the guide reeled off facts and figures. Even in its decline the monastery had owned fifty thousand serfs. The monks had had a monopoly in trading in salt, and, until the Government took it over, in vodka. They had been bankers and merchants. The Metropolitan had had an income of eighty-seven thousand roubles a year. Thousands of pilgrims used to come annually from all over Russia to the Lower Lavra, or caves – great catacombs constructed in the dark ages, where the dead monks were buried; some property in the soil mummified the bodies – the guide laughed.

'The situation was such, that the ignorant people believed the papas who told them that it was their great holiness that prevented decay!'

Perhaps the prisoners were kept in the caves with the long-dead monks, thought Richard. How horrible, but he was disabused on this

point as they were walking under the great flying buttresses, in the courtyard of the printery. The guide jerked his thumb towards a forty-foot wall
in which the lower ends of the buttresses were set.

'Cells of the popes, then,' he said. 'Now it is prison – forbidden to go in
– but, no matter, nothing to see.'

They left the Lavra and the guide pointed to another vast building. 'See
– arsenal,' he explained. 'Stronghold for Revolution in 'seventeen, also
again in nineteen-eighteen – much fightings – see bullet marks on wall.'
After which he led them back to the hotel.

'My wife is tired,' Richard informed him, as he was leaving them at the
entrance. 'We shall not go out this evening.'

Nevertheless when the evening came they crossed the threshold once
more. In order to lessen the risk of running into Valeria Petrovna they
were not having meals in the restaurant of the hotel. Richard had asked
the hall-porter for the name of some restaurant in the old town, and
they found their way to the place he had suggested in the ancient street
of Andreyev, which leads from the palaces to the docks on the wide
Dneiper. After a far from satisfactory meal they went out into the
narrow, twisting streets of the quarter; the damp smell of the river came
to them from the near-by wharfs, mingled with a hundred other
unpleasant odours.

Marie Lou kept very close to Richard. Somewhere in these mean
streets lay the drinking shop into which she had been dragged on that
terrible night when she had been lost in Kiev and afraid to ask her way.

With some difficulty they found the ill-lit court they had visited in the
morning. Fortunately Shubin was at home.

Zackar Shubin was a bald man with cunning eyes set close together
in his head. He cursed roundly in Russian when he saw them. Did they
want to bring the Ogpu about his ears? Was not one visit from foreigners dressed as they were, enough? Two in one day was altogether too
much. They had the information which he had been paid to give them,
already.

Richard mollified him by placing a banknote of some value in his
pudgy hand at once, without argument.

Marie Lou spoke rapidly in Russian.

Yes, he knew Yakovkin – a true son of the Ukrainian soil. A *kazak* to
the backbone. Well, what of it?

Marie Lou questioned him about the prison organisation. They sat
round a bare wooden table, filthy with stains of oil and grease. A guttering
candle was the only light. Richard produced his wallet from his pocket.

For an hour they talked and argued. At last Shubin was persuaded to sound Yakovkin when he came off duty the following morning and see how far the man was prepared to go. If he were successful he would slip out of the Lavra himself for half an hour and meet them at a little café that he named near the Vladimirskaya Gorka. He did not seem to think that he was likely to meet with much success. Yakovkin would certainly have to face imprisonment himself if the prisoners escaped while he was on duty. It would have to be a big sum which would tempt him to do that.

As Richard saw Shubin's greedy eyes fixed on his pocket-book he wondered just how much of the promised reward was likely to find its way to the unfortunate Yakovkin if he accepted.

Having peered into the fœtid court to see that no one was about, Shubin thrust them out.

There was nothing they could do now but possess their souls in patience until the morning, so, as neither of them was tired, they secured seats for a cinema. The film, like all Russian films, had for its subject the eternal Five Year Plan. The photography was good, but the plot almost non-existent. Richard, however, did not care. 'In England,' he told Marie Lou, 'it is our custom to hold hands at the movies.' He took hers firmly in his own.

'Indeed,' she said, with a little smile; 'I should like to see you holding Simon's when you go together!' But she made no attempt to withdraw her own.

The following morning, having thrown off their guide, they were in good time at the café near the Gorka. It was with immense relief that Richard saw the fat figure of Shubin coming down the street. A tall bearded man was with him, who proved to be Yakovkin.

A hasty conference was held in low voices; it seemed that the matter could be arranged. Shubin raised certain difficulties, but Yakovkin, a shrewd, sensible man, quickly overcame them. Richard parted with half the sum agreed on as an earnest of good faith. It was a large amount, and he was loath to do so, but he had to take the risk. It was agreed that he should forward the balance from Vienna.

Immediately the details were settled Richard and Marie Lou hurried back to the hotel. 'I never thought that chap Shubin would fix it,' he confessed, 'but I believe he will, and I like the other fellow.'

'Yes,' Marie Lou agreed, 'he looked an honest man.'

'Now, if only Simon can get the car,' Richard went on, 'we'll go in the 'plane, of course.'

At the hotel Simon was impatiently awaiting him.

'Well?' he asked eagerly, as Richard slipped into his room.

'I've managed it,' said Richard, excitedly. 'Can you get the car tonight? That's the important thing.'

'Umm – no trouble about that,' Simon assured him. 'Tell me about it.'

'Splendid – now this is the drill. Shubin says that some prisoners escaped last year; they dug a tunnel down to the catacombs below. The flagstones were replaced, but the tunnel never filled in. Shubin's not supposed to know that officially, because he wasn't in Kiev at the time. He's going to find an excuse to transfer Rex and the Duke to that cell this evening. Yakovkin will be the warder on duty. He will smuggle in an implement for them to raise the flags and provide them with directions for finding their way through the catacombs. They will come out at an exit in the southernmost fort of the old Lisia Gora. Do you think you can find that?'

'Yes, I know where that is; we passed it yesterday in the car.'

'Good; then you'll be there with the car to meet them. The best place to try and cross the frontier is Mogilev, on the Roumanian border.'

'How far's that?'

'About a hundred and eighty miles – ought to do that in under six hours.'

'What time did you fix?'

'Zero hour is ten o'clock. Take them a little time to get through the catacombs, though.'

Simon nodded quickly. 'Good; Valeria Petrovna will be in the middle of her show. This is wonderful, Richard.'

'Yes, if only our luck holds. Now about the frontier. I'm going by 'plane. Look!' he produced a map from his pocket, 'here is Mogilev. I propose to land as near this cross-road as I can; it's about a mile and a half to the east of the town. Then I'll taxi you over one at a time; we all ought to be out of the country by morning. That is, unless you're staying behind?'

'Ner' – Simon shook his head – 'it's an awful wrench, but I've decided to cut it out – I'm going home.'

Richard smiled sympathetically. 'I know just how you must feel, old chap, but you'd hate it here after a bit, and I suppose it's mean to be glad about it, but I should miss you terribly.'

'I know,' Simon smiled sadly. 'What about Marie Lou, is she coming with us in the car?'

'Oh no, I can't risk having her mixed up in this. She's got a perfectly good English passport now, thank God, and she leaves the country in the proper way.'

'Look out,' whispered Simon, as the door handle rattled.

Like a flash Richard had crossed the room and opened the door leading into Valeria Petrovna's bedroom. 'Ten o' clock,' he whispered, as he disappeared. A minute later he stepped out into the passage through the other door of Madame Karkoff's room.

Chapter XXV

The Caves of Death

Rex sat on the floor of the cell with his long legs stretched out in front of him, his back propped against the wall.

'What o' clock d'you reckon it'd be?' he asked suddenly.

De Richleau was hunched on the bench, his elbows on his knees. He did not trouble to look at his watch, but answered listlessly: 'About six, I think.'

'Cocktail time again,' Rex yawned, 'and still no cocktails. Wouldn't it be just marvellous now to be in Paris hearing the ice tinkle in the Ritz bar.'

'I would prefer London,' said the Duke, seriously, 'and a decanter of the special sherry at the Mausoleum Club.'

'Aw, hell, what's the use – when d'you think they'll get busy with their rotten trial?'

'I have told you before, my friend, I do not think there will be any trial. One fine morning we shall be led out into the yard and put up against a brick wall – that is, unless Simon can arrange something. You may be sure he's doing everything he can.'

'Well, if he doesn't make it snappy I guess he'll miss the bus. We've been in this joint ten days now, and it's six since they handed him his cloak-room check.'

They lapsed into silence again. The strain had told on them heavily. The sound of footsteps in the corridor at any but the usual hours when they received their meagre ration might herald the approach of the end. Each night as they dropped into an uneasy sleep they marvelled that they had survived another day, and wondered miserably if, on the morrow, they would hear the sinister order 'Get your things together', which in a Bolshevik prison is the inevitable prelude to a firing-party.

During their first days of imprisonment they had investigated the possibilities of escape, but the prison at Kiev was run on very different lines to the one at Tobolsk. Here, the prisoners were visited at regular hours during the day. They never saw their fellow captives except during the short period when they were exercised each morning, and then a squad of Red Guards were always lounging near with loaded rifles.

Their cell was searched night and morning; instead of an ordinary door it had a strong iron grating, and as a warder was always stationed in the corridor he could see what they were doing as he walked up and down. They had soon decided that escape without outside help was impossible.

The presence of Yakovkin was the only thing that served to cheer their desperate situation. The man had been born on the Plakoff estates; as a youth he had been one of the old Prince's huntsmen. Many a time had he ridden behind the Duke, and once by his quickness and courage he had saved De Richleau from the tusks of an infuriated boar. Surreptitiously he showed them every kindness that he could, and managed to smuggle extra food to their cell.

The tramp of feet sounded on the stone flags of the passage. A sharp command, and a file of soldiers halted outside, the warder unlocked the barred gate of their cell, and the officer beckoned them to come out.

They obeyed quietly; there was nothing else to do. They were marched away, each with a Red Guard on either side, down the corridor, up a broad flight of stone stairs into an office on the upper floor. A few clerks were busy with files and papers. For some minutes they remained standing there, then they were taken into an inner room.

De Richleau smiled slightly as he recognised Leshkin seated behind a heavy table. The Kommissar looked more like a great red gorilla than ever. His low forehead, small eyes, and great protruding jowl sparsely covered with hair, all lent to the resemblance.

'You may go,' he ordered the guards sharply. He smiled slowly at the Duke.

'So we meet again, and for the last time, Mr Richwater.'

'That causes me no concern, since I set no value on your acquaintance,' the Duke murmured.

'Last time we met you alluded to an acquaintance that you did not possess – I refer to Stalin!'

'It pleased me to amuse myself by frightening you a little.'

'It is you who will be frightened tomorrow morning.' The big man nodded heavily.

'I trust not,' the Duke replied evenly.

'That we shall see – at least, the firing squad will do so – I shall be comfortably in bed. It was for that reason partly that I thought to have a last look at you tonight.'

'Well, if you've done looking, I guess we'll get back to our cell,' said Rex.

'Not yet.' Leshkin sat back and lighted a thick black cigar. 'To you, American, I wish to talk. You came to Russia for a purpose; with the aid of this man here and the little Jew you reached your destination. There is a possibility that I might save your life.'

'Now that's real kind,' Rex grinned.

'You have not the Shulimoff jewels upon you,' Leshkin went on. 'You have been searched; but you know the secret place of hiding. No man would take such risks as you have done if he did not. Perhaps you foresaw that you must be captured and left them in that place; perhaps you hid them a fresh time when you came to earth in the aeroplane. Where are these jewels?'

'What a hope you've got! D'you think I'd tell you if I knew?'

'Why not, young man? In prison you must remain – but that is better than the cold earth tomorrow.'

Rex shook his head. 'I guess you've got me all wrong. I wouldn't let on to you, not if you offered me the Woolworth Building.'

'Accept this proposal, Rex,' said the Duke, suddenly.

'Not on your life I don't. If we've having a party tomorrow we'll have it together and get done with it. This bird would do me in anyhow in a fortnight's time.'

'You're young, Rex,' urged the Duke; 'with myself it is different. Accept this offer.'

Rex smiled. 'No, there's nothin' doin'.'

'So you are obstinate, American?' Leshkin puffed out a cloud of smoke. 'Well, you have had your chance – that is all, I think.'

'I demand a trial,' said De Richleau sharply.

'Frightened a little after all?' Leshkin's small eyes came back to the Duke's face.

'You boast that Russia is a civilised country – to shoot us without a trial is murder. Let us be tried, and executed if we are found guilty.'

'There will be no trial, because you have no official existence, either of you. That ceased when you went outside the laws laid down for tourists in the Soviet.'

'Then I wish to be prepared for death by a priest of my own religion,' replied De Richleau. 'I ask for a postponement of execution till after Sunday in order that I may have time.'

'Time, eh?' Leshkin scowled. 'Time for the little Jew to help you to escape – that is what you wish, is it not? Let me tell you, then: do you think that I, Leshkin, would let him do what he has done to me, and do nothing? . . . Stalin did not know the truth when he listened to Madame Karkoff; he did not know that men . . . eight men of the Ogpu, had been killed. I had to go to Moskawa to arrange; had it not been for that you would have been dead a week ago. The decision regarding Aron is now reversed . . . he will be arrested tonight, and with you tomorrow when the time comes, and I . . .' he chuckled suddenly: 'I shall be in bed in the hotel!'

The Kommissar spoke with such quiet enjoyment that neither Rex nor the Duke doubted the truth of his statement. It was a terrible blow to them to know that their last hope of help was gone, and Simon, whom at least they had believed to be out of danger, was to be re-arrested. Nevertheless De Richleau was a great believer in the old proverb that 'while there is life there is hope', so he persisted.

'I am not ready to die – give me time.'

'So you still think God will help you when men will not?' sneered Leshkin. 'I am surprised that a man like you should believe these effete superstitions. What is death, after all, but a cessation of activity?' He leaned back and touched the bell.

'Remove the prisoners,' the Kommissar ordered when the guard appeared, and to the officer he added in a lower tone: 'The orders for tomorrow morning stand.'

They were marched down the broad staircase again, and this time across a yard into another block of buildings. Then they were locked into a bigger cell than the one they had previously occupied.

'This'll be the death house, I reckon,' said Rex, looking round at the bare stone walls. 'Sort of condemned cell.'

'Probably,' agreed the Duke. 'I fear that there is little hope for us now. I wish, though, that you had accepted his offer about the jewels.'

'Oh, nuts,' exclaimed Rex, irritably. 'Even if I'd been willing to quit I don't know where the damned things are.'

'If you'd insisted on being taken to Romanovsk, that would have meant another ten days of life at least – some opportunity of escape might have presented itself.'

'Don't you believe it. They know us too well by now to take any chances. They would have hooked a dynamite bomb on to my pants. D'you think he was giving us the straight talk about Simon?'

De Richleau nodded. 'I see no reason to doubt it. I was delighted when he was released, but I was surprised. After that night at Romanovsk I felt that, in spite of anything that Madame Karkoff might attempt, it would be certain death for all of us if we were caught. Personally I am glad that we are spared the mockery of a trial.'

'We certainly bumped off those bums at Romanovsk all right,' Rex agreed, 'but I'm damned sorry for little Simon.'

'Do not distress yourself too much about him. He is a philosopher, and for the first time he is really in love – the last week of his life has been spent with the woman of his desire. He will be arrested tonight and shot tomorrow at dawn . . . he will step from the pinnacle of happiness into darkness and will not suffer disillusion. If you must think tonight, think of all the pleasant things that have happened to you, and tomorrow morning try to recreate in your mind the pleasantest episode of all.'

At eight o' clock the evening inspection was carried out, and Yakovkin came on duty. They were pleased to see him, because they had feared that he would remain at the other cells. He brought them their frugal evening meal, a single bowl of greasy soup and a hunk of bread apiece. In addition he brought them on his own account a couple of handfuls of dried plums.

They ate the sorry mess in silence, and then sat talking for a long time in the darkness. Both looked up with surprise when the gleam of Yakovkin's lantern showed at the door of the cell.

'Quick,' whispered the gaoler, 'I have much to say.'

Rex and the Duke rose immediately to their feet, and Yakovkin spoke in a hoarse whisper: 'There are friends outside who arrange for your escape. Shubin tells me of this today . . . I would not believe him, thinking it a trap, but I have now spoken with them also – a woman and a man. Take this . . .' he thrust a marlinspike into De Richleau's hand. 'Shubin arranged for your transfer to this cell. Raise up the flagstones in the left corner there; beneath them is a tunnel leading to the sacred caves. Quickly to work, and I will be back.' He left them as silently as he had come.

'Give me that toothpick,' said Rex, with sudden animation.

'Thank God,' breathed the Duke, 'a woman and a man . . . Valeria Petrovna and Simon.'

Rex was already on his knees levering up the heavy slabs of stone. It was true – there was a tunnel hollowed out underneath. Ten minutes' frantic work and he had the opening clear.

Yakovkin rejoined them; he gave the Duke a big ball of twine and an electric torch. 'Take these,' he whispered, huskily; 'the caves run for many versts, twisting and turning, one upon another. If you are lost there it will be death . . . you would starve before you could get out.'

'Which way are we to go?' asked the Duke.

'To the left and to the left and to the left,' Yakovkin answered. 'That will bring you to a great hall with many passages. Take that which is second to the right of the altar; after, once to the left again. You will come out in the cellars of the old fort. Outside your friends wait for you with a car.'

'To the left three times . . . the second passage on the right of the altar . . . after that once to the left again,' De Richleau repeated.

'Tie the twine to a stone where the tunnel ends,' Yakovkin went on. 'Unroll it as you go – thus, if you lose your way, you can work back to the beginning and start again.'

'Good,' said the Duke. 'Yakovkin, how can I ever thank you for this help?'

'I would have done as much before, *Barin*,' said the man, simply, giving the Duke his old title, 'but without Shubin I could do nothing.'

'Will you not get into serious trouble?'

Yakovkin shrugged. 'A month or two in prison, perhaps, *Barin* – that is not much for one such as I . . . for the sake of our youth I would do that, but I must tell you also that I have been well paid.'

'I'm glad of that – if we get away I'll send you through the Consulate a token of my gratitude from London.'

'Do not delay, *Barin*, I beg – you have far to go before the dawn. Look, your comrade is already waiting.' Rex was half-buried in the tunnel.

De Richleau took Yakovkin's horny hand. 'I shall not forget,' he said.

The *kazak* withdrew his hand quickly and kissed the Duke in the old fashion on the left shoulder. 'The heart of Russia is ever the heart of Russia,' he murmured, cryptically, and De Richleau followed Rex feet foremost into the hole.

The tunnel was no more than six feet deep, and as it ended Rex dropped with a thud from the ceiling to the floor of the cave.

'Look out,' he called, and was just in time to save the Duke from an eight-foot fall.

De Richleau had the torch and Rex the ball of twine.

'Where'll we make this fast?' the latter asked.

'You have the marlinspike,' said the Duke, 'dig it firmly into the earth and tie the end to that.'

'No, that'll be handy for a weapon,' Rex objected. 'Here, this'll serve – show us a light.' An ancient stone coffin lid lay at their feet. Rex prised it up, got the twine underneath, and tied it firmly. 'O.K,' he announced.

The shaft of light from the Duke's torch pierced the thick, heavy darkness. The cave had the hot, dry atmosphere of an airless room when the central heating has been left on. They proceeded slowly along the passage, shining the torch to either side, fearful that they might miss the turning in the thick, hot gloom.

They found it easily, not more than twenty paces from the start. The passage opened into a wider, loftier cave.

'Holy Mike! What's here?' Rex exclaimed, as the beam of light played on the wall. It was a gruesome sight – a long row of silent figures stretched away into the blackness on both sides. Each wore the same grey gown corded at the waist . . . each face was bearded . . . and in each beard the gums drew back into a horrid grin, showing rows of yellow evil teeth.

'It is only the monks,' said the Duke, quietly, as he walked on. 'There are thousands of them buried here . . . I was brought to see them as a boy.'

'I guess you might have given me the wire,' Rex protested.

'I'm sorry; they are a terrifying sight, I suppose. Some property in the soil, together with the heat, mummifies the bodies.'

'Well, I'll say I'm glad I didn't make this trip alone – they'd make any feller's flesh creep. Why, they've got hair and skin and all.'

'Have you never been to that church in Bordeaux – St Michael, I think. In the crypt they have some bodies preserved in a similar manner, but only a small number.'

'No – only time I was in Bordeaux I was figuring how quick I could get to Biarritz to join a platinum blonde I knew. . . . Gosh, it's hot down here.' Rex drew his hand across his face, which was wet with perspiration.

'Yes, stifling. Never mind, it is the road to freedom. Here is our second turning.' De Richleau steadily advanced.

They entered another long gallery of the catacombs – more rows of grinning heads were ranged along the walls, casting weird shadows in the flickering light.

'How long have these guys been dead?' Rex asked.

'Two or three hundred years some of them, perhaps more.'

'Would you believe it? Well, it's the weirdest sight I've ever seen. You'd think they'd all crumple up and fall down.'

'No, they're propped against the wall, and they have little weight.' De Richleau stopped for a moment and tapped one on the chest. The parchment-like skin stretched tight across the bones gave out a hollow sound. 'They are little more than skeletons, only dust inside. The wire, too, that is stretched along the line helps to keep them in position; see, there is one that has toppled over.' He pointed to a grotesque bowing figure some distance away that hung suspended from the wire. The head had rolled off, and when De Richleau shone his torch on it, it showed a strange grinning mask, gaping through eternity in the darkness at the ceiling of the cave.

'To think that once they were all men,' said Rex, in an awed voice.

'They are as we should have been tomorrow,' the Duke replied. 'What are a few hundred years in all eternity – from dust we come – you know the rest!'

'Yes, that's about it. Just miles and miles of dust . . . I think it's pretty grim – say, isn't that the hall ahead?'

'I think so. I hope that more than half our journey is done; this heat is positively appalling.'

They emerged into a great open space. The ray from the torch failed to penetrate to the ceiling, nor could they see across to the other side, but other openings into it showed clearly on either hand.

'Puzzle, find the altar,' said Rex.

'Yes, let us try straight over on the other side.'

At that moment Rex trod on another skull. He stumbled against the Duke, who dropped the torch with a clatter. The light went out and the heavy darkness closed in upon them.

The blackness was so intense that they could almost imagine that they felt it pressing on their hands and faces.

'Sorry,' gasped Rex, 'I trod on some bird's brain-box.'

'Stay where you are,' ordered the Duke, sharply. 'Let me find the torch.' He groped on the floor, his fingers came in contact with the bearded head. He kicked it aside impatiently, and his fingers found the torch. As he stood up he pressed the button . . . no light appeared . . . he pressed it again. Still nothing but that inky darkness pressing round them.

For a moment he said nothing, as all the horror of the situation dawned on his mind. How was it possible to find their way in this impenetrable blackness without a ray of light? The atmosphere would sap their vitality and deaden their power of thought . . . in a few hours they would go mad. Shrieking through the hollow darkness, frantically trying turning after turning in these miles of caves. The horror of thirst would come upon them in this awful heat – already he found himself passing his tongue over his dry lips. Better even to go back, if they could find their way, and face the rifles of the Red Guards in the morning than the creeping certainty of insanity as well as death in this vast grave, to be found, perhaps years later, mummified like the rest, clawing the ground in an extremity of thirst and terror.

He turned to where he knew Rex to be standing. Monseigneur le Duc de Richleau had never yet lost his head, and he knew that now, if ever, his life depended upon his keeping it, so he spoke quietly.

'Have you the string, Rex?'

'Yes, but why don't you show a light?'

'It seems to be broken.'

'Pass it over, I'll see if I can fix it. I'm better acquainted with those things than you.'

De Richleau groped in the gloom till he found Rex's hand. 'Here,' he said, 'but whatever you do, don't let go of that string.'

Rex fumbled with the torch, unscrewing the battery and testing the bulb. 'That's about torn it,' he said. 'Bulb's gone.'

Not a gleam of light showed from any direction as they stood together;

the heat seemed to have grown more oppressive than ever in the heavy night-like stillness. An eerie feeling emanated from the knowledge of those rows of corpses standing on either hand.

'Have you no matches?' asked the Duke.

'No, those thieving Bolshies stripped me of every blame' thing I had. How in heck are we going to get out of here?'

'I wish I knew,' replied De Richleau, anxiously. 'Let us try groping our way round the big chamber – we may be able to find the altar by touch.'

'O.K. You go to the left, I'll go to the right.'

'No, no, once we are separated we should have endless trouble to come together again; you have no idea how deceptive voices are in a place like this. Here, take hold of my belt – and remember, our lives may hang on your keeping firm hold on that piece of string.'

'Just as you say,' Rex agreed.

They moved carefully to the left; De Richleau stretched out his hand and it came in contact with one of the monk's coarse robes; he knew that they must still be in the entrance to the passage – he moved on and then felt another – then bare wall. That must be the chamber. He followed the wall until it ended, touching another figure on the corner – that must be the entrance to the next passage. He stepped forward boldly, praying that there were no pits. His hand touched silky human hair – a beard. He withdrew it sharply, moving quickly to the right; once more the wall.

'Gosh, it's hot down here,' Rex gasped.

'Frightful, isn't it?' De Richleau was feeling up and down the wall for any trace of ledge that might mean an altar. There was nothing . . . he passed on. A few paces farther he encountered another mummy, and stepped out into the open again; this time he had judged the width of the passage more accurately and touched the wall again. Once more he searched for the altar, but failed to find it. He moved on – the wall seemed to continue ever so much farther this time.

'We've gone off the track,' said Rex, suddenly.

'No, we haven't passed another corner.'

'My sense of direction's pretty good; believe me, we've passed out of the big hall.'

The Duke was troubled, but he walked on. 'I think you're wrong, my friend. There are no mummies here, so we cannot be in a passage.'

'All right – go ahead, but I'll lay I'm right.'

They proceeded, the black gloom engulfing them on every side. Rex spoke again:

'Honest, you're going all wrong – air's closer here than ever, and the floor's sloping a bit on the down grade. What little I saw of that crypt place showed it flat.'

De Richleau swore softly in the darkness; he had to admit that Rex seemed to be right. 'We'd better go back to the last mummy,' he said, 'and start all over again.'

With Rex leading this time, they retraced their footsteps, winding in the twine as they went. From time to time he felt along the wall.

'Ugh,' he exclaimed, with a sudden shudder. There was a loud thud, and something moved in the darkness at their feet.

'This place gives me the creeps.'

'What was it?' asked the Duke.

'A man's head,' said Rex briefly.

'Never mind, we've found the last mummy that we passed. Let us start again from here – take my belt.'

The Duke stepped out in a different direction this time, walking slowly forward with arms outstretched like a blind man. They must have covered fifty yards when he came to a sudden halt.

'Found anything?' said Rex.

'We will try the other way,' the Duke suggested, quietly. In a few paces he had walked into a blank wall. 'I think we will rest for a little,' he said, wearily. 'I confess I haven't the faintest idea where we are.'

They sat down with their backs to the wall; despair was creeping over both of them.

Rex loosened his clothing at the neck. 'If only we could get a breath of air,' he sighed; 'we'll asphyxiate before we're done.'

His head was splitting. For a little time they sat in silence. Then he asked: 'How long d'you reckon we've been fumbling round since we lost the light?'

'Three-quarters of an hour; an hour, perhaps. It seems longer, but I don't think it can be more.'

'And there's Simon waiting with the car – he'll reckon the escape's proved a wash-out and clear off soon if we can't find a way out of this damn' place.'

'If he was ever there,' added the Duke. 'I have not counted on that car from the beginning; you will remember what Leshkin said – Simon has been under arrest for some hours, I fear.'

Rex got to his feet. 'Come on,' he said, 'let's take the first passage we come to and walk straight ahead – we must come some place some time.'

'No,' De Richleau protested, 'that would be madness; we should get hopelessly lost. We cannot be far from the central cave. You shall act as a pivot, holding the string, and I will walk in different directions from you, counting my paces each time as I go. That will at least give us the position and shape of the chamber.'

He took the end of the string and started off into the thick darkness once more. He reached the mummies and said: 'Six. Now I will try another way.' Suddenly his voice came in a sharp whisper.

'Rex – quickly, follow me along the string.'

Rex followed and saw at once what De Richleau had already seen: a faint blur of light showed clearly the entrance to a passage a few feet away. They were standing near the side of the great hall. Momentarily the light grew brighter – the sound of footsteps could be heard – the steady glow showed that whoever was approaching carried a torch and not a candle.

'Thank God,' breathed the Duke. 'Tackle him as he gets to the opening. You hit him on the head – I'll snatch the torch.'

Rex nodded; swiftly they moved to opposite sides of the archway, and stood peering round the corners. A bright light could be seen now advancing between two rows of mummies. Weird shadows flickered on the walls and ceiling – behind the light all was darkness.

As the man emerged from the passage they sprang upon him simultaneously. Rex delivered a swift blow with his marlinspike, De Richleau snatched the light – the man dropped in a heap without a sound.

The Duke gave a great sigh of relief. 'Light,' he exclaimed; 'golden, glorious, life-giving light!'

'What shall I do with this bird?' asked Rex, pushing the body with his foot.

'Leave him,' said De Richleau briefly. 'Poor devil, we cannot bother with him now.' Then, as the beam of the torch fell for a second upon the white bloodstained face of the crumpled figure at their feet, he stooped suddenly:

'Good God! It's Richard Eaton!'

Chapter XXVI

The Dash for the Frontier

Simon was walking slowly to and fro in the narrow space of his bedroom. He was too restless to sit still, and yet anxious not to tire his wounded leg.

It was past ten o' clock, but he knew that even if the prisoners had already left their cell the journey underground must take some little time, therefore he controlled his impatience to be off. He wished to be certain that they should reach the fort first; two waiting figures would be far less likely to attract attention than a stationary car, and in any case Richard would be there to meet them.

He had already been down to the garage and arranged for the car to be in immediate readiness. The man in charge, knowing him to be Valeria Petrovna's friend, had made no difficulties.

He opened the connecting door to Valeria Petrovna's room and looked about him sadly. Her silk garments were strewn on the bed, just as she had left them when she changed to go to the theatre, her favourite perfume hung in the air.

By his decision to leave with the others Simon was deliberately placing a unique experience in his life behind him. No other woman had ever meant so much to him – yet, when he had agreed to sacrifice his whole existence to her he had known in the bottom of his heart he could never be happy cut off from all other interests. Richard had been right in his surmise – Valeria Petrovna had asked a ransom for the return of Rex and the Duke, not in so many words, perhaps, but by definite implication.

Simon had been prepared to carry out his side of the bargain – she had not attempted to carry out hers. To him such failure was a breach of faith going to the very roots of life. He loved her, so if she had confessed her inability to help his friends, and given him the opportunity to do what he could on his own, things might have been different. As it was, she had tricked him, so he was determined to make the break.

He wondered how she would take his disappearance. After her deception he had not dared to confide in her again; there had been no good-byes. She had gone cheerfully to her gala performance full of vitality and happiness.

Simon gazed sadly at the little row of smart high-heeled shoes. 'Never again,' he thought, 'never again . . . what a blank she will leave in my life!' With a sigh he turned away, and switched out the light. He glanced at the clock in his own room once more; it was ten past ten – they should be there by twenty past – if he left now there should be no waiting on either side. He picked up the small parcel containing his belongings and left the room, locking his door behind him.

The car had been run out of the garage all ready for him; he stood beside it for a moment while he lit a cigarette, anxious not to show any sign of haste in front of the mechanic. As he did so he realised that he had struck his last match, so he sent the man for another box. Hardly had he done so when the half-hour chimed from a neighbouring clock. It was a good bit later than he had thought, and the knowledge made him impatient to be off. At last – after what seemed an age – the mechanic returned. Simon stuffed the matches in his pocket, nodded cheerfully to the man, and drove quickly out of the yard.

The neighbourhood of the old fort was dark and deserted; he drew the car in under the shadow of the wall, and peered round anxiously for the others, but no one came forward to meet him. After a moment he shut off the engine, switched out the lights, and stepped down into the road . . . Possibly they had thought it best to remain hidden round the corner . . . he whistled softly – there was no reply.

Simon began to feel worried; it must be nearly a quarter to eleven – he was terribly late – they should have been here for the last twenty minutes at least – and where was Richard? Had Shubin given them away? The escape been frustrated, and Richard arrested here a few minutes before his own arrival? He glanced apprehensively up and down the road. An occasional figure hastened by on the far side, only momentarily discernible in the dim pools of light cast by the infrequent street lamps. Nobody seemed interested in him or the car.

He limped round the corner and found the crumbling steps that led to the entrance of the fort. It showed – a pitch black rectangle in the faint glow that fell upon the pitted stonework of the walls; Simon climbed up to it, and stood for some minutes listening intently. An almost uncanny silence brooded over the close, musty darkness of the interior. 'Richard!' he called softly, and although his voice was hardly above a whisper it seemed to echo back at him from the hollow darkness as though he had shouted aloud. He waited, but there was no reply, so he stumbled down the steps again and round the corner to the car, really frightened now that something had gone definitely wrong. A quarter of an hour should have been ample for them to get through the catacombs – perhaps the escape had been delayed – but even then what could possibly have become of Richard?

He climbed back into the car and sat there in the dark, thinking furiously of all the possible hitches which might have occurred. Should he drive back to the hotel or wait there in the hope that they would turn up? He feared that at any moment a policeman might come on the scene and want to know what he was doing there; or worse, if Shubin had actually given them away, that some of Leshkin's people might arrive to arrest him!

By the time the sound of eleven striking was born faintly to him on the still night air, he was thoroughly jumpy, but he realised that if Rex and the Duke did make a belated appearance and he had already driven off, they would be stranded in a hopeless situation, so he determined to stick it out.

A moment later his quick ear caught the sound of footsteps near the corner of the wall, and a tall figure stepped up to the car, peering at him in the darkness.

Simon gave a sigh of relief. It could be no one but Rex, and that must be the Duke behind him.

'That you?' he whispered.

'Sure – Yakovkin told us there'd be a car to meet us – but we're almighty late; and we've had an accident.'

'Never mind – hurry! – where's Richard?'

'Hang on one moment.'

'For God's sake be quick,' urged Simon, as they left him without further explanation, 'the police may be on us at any moment!'

He waited impatiently . . . then shadows moved again in the darkness. Rex and the Duke were carrying what looked like a body between them – Simon's heart almost stopped – was that Richard? In another moment he knew that it was.

The others were propping him up in the back of the car. His head lolled helplessly; there was blood on his face.

'What's happened?' asked Simon anxiously, as he moved into the next seat. 'Rex, you'd better drive; my leg is still pretty dicky.'

'I coshed him,' Rex admitted, as he took the wheel. 'Didn't know who it was in that hellish place.'

'He . . . he isn't dead, is he?' Simon's voice quivered slightly.

'We don't know yet,' De Richleau answered from the back. 'I'll look after him – drive on now,' he added urgently, 'we'll talk later.'

Rex turned the car round away from the river, and soon they were out on the main highway heading for Birdichy and the frontier. It was a big, modern, powerful car, and the telegraph poles flashed past on either side as they roared through the darkness. They had over a hundred and eighty miles to go, so Rex was taking no chances, but settled down to a steady even pace.

As soon as they were free of the outskirts of Kiev the Duke pulled the flashlight from his pocket and began to examine Richard's head. Never in his life had Rex felt so wretched – he could not possibly have known who the man with the light was – had not even the least idea that Richard was in Russia. Now, perhaps, he had killed one of his best friends!

'Say, how is he?' he asked anxiously.

'He is alive,' came the Duke's quiet reassurance, 'we must be thankful that you only struck him with that small marlinspike. If it had been an iron bar his head would have cracked like an eggshell. How did he come to be in Russia, Simon?'

'He came over to look for us. I thought Valeria Petrovna had got you both safe out of it until he turned up in Kiev yesterday. He planned your escape. Is he badly hurt?'

'I can find no cut on his head – his hat saved him, I think – the blood is only from his nose.'

'How on earth did it happen?'

'It was in those darned caves,' Rex explained. 'They sure gave me the shivers – stuffed full of corpses propped up against the walls. Our light died on us – then it *was* hell! I'll tell the world – so hot we couldn't breathe, too. I figured we were there for keeps, but we spotted a guy coming down the corridor. I bumped him, and the Duke snatched his light.'

'He must have got worried when you didn't turn up and gone down to look for you.'

'It was fortunate for us that he did,' commented the Duke. 'If he had not we should have died for a certainty. I was afraid, too, that if we got out you would not be there. Leshkin has been to Moscow and seen Stalin; you were to have been arrested again tonight!'

Simon laughed jerkily.

'It's a fact,' added Rex; 'the old baby-killer told us that himself. There was going to be a shooting party for the bunch of us tomorrow!'

'Well, we're out of that muddle for the moment. I only hope he doesn't run into Marie Lou!'

'Marie Lou? Was she around as well?' exclaimed Rex. 'If that's so, why isn't she in on this party?'

'She was,' Simon informed him, 'but Richard didn't want her to be mixed up in this – '

'Say, not so fast! – you wait a minute.' Rex began to slow down the car. 'We can't leave her to get out alone.'

Simon shook his head. 'It's quite all right. Richard made special arrangements for her. She's got a British passport now; he married her the other day in Vienna.'

'Holy smoke! You don't mean that?'

'I do. He said that it was so that he could get her back into Russia to act as his interpreter, but if you ask me he's crazy about her!'

De Richleau leant forward. 'If that is so, surely it is all the more reason that he should have been careful for her safety. Are you certain that he meant her to travel alone?'

'Um,' Simon nodded. 'Told me so himself – said she was going to leave the country in the proper way.'

'Well – if you are sure of that – but I do not care to think of that child alone in Kiev.'

'She'll be on the train by now,' Simon assured him.

The car bore on into the night. They were beginning to climb now, up easy gradients, to higher ground. Richard began to groan loudly.

'He's coming round,' said the Duke. 'I doubt if he'll know what he's saying at first. I wish I had some morphia; sleep is the best thing for him at the moment.'

'Here – take these.' Simon delved into his pocket and produced a small bottle. 'They're sleeping-tablets that Valeria Petrovna got for me – there's medinol in them, I think.'

Richard swayed forward. He looked dazedly round, then sank back with a moan, shutting his eyes quickly.

'Take these,' said the Duke gently, spilling a couple of the tablets into his palm.

'Where . . . where are we?' muttered Richard.

Rex turned round to grin at him. 'Sorry, Richard – hadn't a notion it was you – 'fraid I nearly bumped you off!'

Richard moved his head painfully from side to side, groaned again, and tried to put his hand up to his head. It fell back helplessly. 'Where are we?' he asked again.

'We're in the car – you saved us all, Richard – we're making for the frontier,' said the Duke.

'No . . . no . . .' Richard struggled to sit up again. 'Stop the car – I'm going by 'plane.'

Rex laughed. 'I'd just hate to be a passenger in your 'plane tonight, Richard. You couldn't push a pram after the swipe I gave you!'

'I . . . don't mind leaving . . . the 'plane,' Richard muttered, 'if we . . . all get away . . . safely.'

'Don't you worry, Richard, we're all here. You take these and have a good sleep till we get to the frontier.' The Duke pushed the tablets into his mouth. He sank back on to the cushions of the car. 'Yes . . . the frontier . . . make the frontier . . .' his voice sank into indistinct mutterings – in a few moments he was fast asleep.

'D'you reckon they'll send out a warning about us?' Rex asked, after a long silence.

'Not about you and me,' the Duke replied. 'With Yakovkin on guard, it is unlikely that they will discover our escape till the morning – but I am afraid there will be trouble about Simon.'

'Certain to be if Leshkin meant to arrest me again tonight,' Simon agreed, pessimistically; 'they'll find the car missing, and try and trace us by that – probably try and hold us up on the road.'

'Have you got a gun?'

'Ner, but Richard may have.'

The Duke felt him over. 'No,' he said, 'he's unarmed.'

'That leaves me and the marlinspike,' said Rex, thoughtfully. 'Maybe there are a few spanners at the back. Guess we'll have to step on the gas if we've got to go through any towns, Simon.'

'Birdichy – that'll be difficult, biggish town – after that, there's nothing to worry us till we cross the Bug at Vinnitsa.'

'Better going on the highway,' Rex agreed. 'Got to take a chance about the towns.'

They had come into forest country now; the trees showed ghostly in the arc of the headlights. They gave the impression that the car was going at immense speed as they rushed to meet it and were swallowed up again in the darkness behind. Occasionally they passed through a deserted village street, but no attempt was made to stop their headlong progress.

Ten minutes later, the scattered houses became more frequent, the open road a street. De Richleau tapped Rex on the shoulder. 'Try to avoid the main street,' he suggested, 'take the first turning that you come to on either side.'

'We'll sure get lost,' protested Rex.

'No – no, do as I say.'

Rex switched the car sharply to the right. They ran slowly down a long hill.

'To the left, Rex, to the left!' came De Richleau's voice.

Rex obeyed. They ran along the turning for about a hundred and fifty yards, then had to pull up – the road ended in a gate leading into a field.

'Back her out, man – quick – if we're caught sitting we're done.' Simon peered behind as Rex backed the great car in a succession of curves and jerks on to the hill road. They took the next turn to the left and ran along it for nearly half a mile; the low houses became less frequent.

'We'll be out in the country again soon,' remarked Simon, anxiously.

'We have gone too far – there was a turning up the hill farther back – try that!' The Duke moved Richard's head a little on his shoulder as he tried to make out their position in the darkness.

Rex backed the car once more, and they took the turning up the hill.

'First to the right at the top, and then out of the town as fast as you can,' came the Duke's voice from the back.

He had judged rightly; a minute later they came out into the high street. As they turned a sudden shout went up from some men with lanterns fifty yards to the left, but their voices were lost on the night air as the great car went speeding out of the town.

'That was a picket, sure enough,' Rex grinned. 'Those guys wouldn't be standing in the street at half past two in the morning just for fun!'

'Yes, the hunt is up.' De Richleau sat back with a sigh. 'May we be as lucky at Vinnitsa.'

'Don't like Vinnitsa,' said Simon. 'We've got to cross the bridge there.'

'If we manage that, there is still the frontier,' De Richleau spoke gloomily. 'Have you got any plan about that?'

'I had,' Simon announced, 'but by knocking Richard on the head you've put paid to it. He was to have met us at the cross-roads about a mile to the west of Mogeliev – land his 'plane in the nearest field, and taxi us over one at a time. Lord knows how we shall manage now.'

They had entered wooded country once more, and the way was a succession of steep gradients alternating with sharp, down-hill bends. In the twisting and turning road it was difficult to see far ahead; the headlights on the trees were trying and deceptive, but Rex seemed to have a genius for judging the bends and twists. The low car roared through the tunnels formed by the overhanging trees. A dozen times it seemed that they must crash into some vast tree trunk looming up in front of them, but they always swerved in time, hunting down the miles that lay between them and Roumania.

They entered Vinnitsa at four o' clock. All three braced themselves, for they were certain that if a serious attempt was being made to stop them it would be here. It was useless to try side-roads this time, for there was only one bridge. The car flashed through the streets of the sleeping town, awakening thunderous echoes. A sharp slope led down to the narrow bridge; there were lights ahead, and little dark figures clustered at the bridge-head – their worst fears were realised.

Rex had to make a quick decision: should he stop, or risk charging through them? If he did the latter and chains had been drawn across the road, they would crash; even if there were no chains and he knocked down a man, the car passing over his body would be thrown out of control and might plunge into the river below. He decided to slow up.

The men were shouting and waving torches. The car moved towards them at a gentle pace; in the half-light Rex saw that they were armed. As the car drew level one of them sprang on the footboard – there were no chains – the car moved steadily on – the man shouted something in Russian – another jumped on the other side of the car.

'Ready, Simon?' asked Rex, quietly. 'I'm going to step on it.' As he spoke he slashed at the first soldier's face with the marlinspike, and the car leapt forward – the man fell with a loud cry.

'Duck!' Rex shouted, 'duck – they'll shoot!'

Simon had struck his man in the face, but the fellow still clung on – he struck him again, but his fist seemed to make no impression on the peasant's thick skull. There was a crack of rifles as the car tore over the bridge. With uncanny skill Rex zig-zagged from side to side – a bullet clanged into the metalwork behind – another crashed through the window at the back. The Duke was crouching on the floor, and had drawn Richard down beside him. Simon struck his man again, but the soldier would not let go; the rattle of another scattered volley sounded from the rear – Simon's antagonist straightened with a sudden jerk and dropped from view; the car rushed across the farther bridge-head and up the hill on the other side. A last bullet pinged on the mudguard, and they had crossed the Bug!

'When I last crossed that river it was stiff with corpses,' remarked the Duke, with a quiet chuckle. 'The fighting here was terrible during the War.'

'Reckon there's another corpse tonight,' Rex laughed; 'that chap on Simon's side got it in the neck all right.'

'I simply could not make him leave go,' muttered Simon angrily.

'If you had used one finger instead of your fist, and poked it in his eye,' suggested the Duke, mildly, 'he would have dropped off quick enough; these people have skulls like cannon-balls.'

'Must remember that,' said Simon, thoughtfully

Richard had slept through it all. The Duke had propped him up again, but beyond an occasional moan he showed no sign of life.

The car leapt forward; the going was easier now, long straight stretches of common land with scrub and occasional woods. Rex was getting every ounce out of the engine. The stars began to pale in the sky, and as the Duke glanced through the shattered rear window he saw the grey light that heralds the dawn. An hour and a half after crossing the Bug, they came to the outlying farms of Mogeliev; another few miles and they would be over the frontier into Roumania.

Rex was for pressing on, but De Richleau was against it.

'The wireless is certain to have been busy,' he said, 'and the frontier strongly guarded. To attempt to rush a second post in broad daylight would be madness – we should be shot to pieces.'

At Simon's suggestion they adhered to his original plan and took a by-road to the west at the entrance of the township. It was little better than a cart-track but it proved to be the same road that he had seen with Richard on the map, and a mile and a half farther on they found the cross-roads which had been decided on as the rendezvous. A solitary farmstead standing a little way back from the road occupied one corner. A few yards from the gate leading into the yard, Rex pulled up.

'What's the drill now?' he asked.

'Better wake Richard,' said Simon. 'Now we haven't got his 'plane to go over in we'll need all the ideas we can get.'

De Richleau shook the sleeper. Richard muttered angrily at first and refused to waken, but the Duke was persistent. At last he opened his eyes and groaned.

'Oh, God! my head!'

'Wake up, Richard – wake up!' said De Richleau loudly.

With heavy eyes Richard looked about him. 'What's happened?' he asked stupidly.

'I guess I nearly broke your poor old head,' Rex admitted.

'Gosh – it feels like it – still, you found the car – you'd better clear out.' Richard made an effort to get up.

'We're here,' said Simon. 'Mogeliev – Roumanian frontier.'

'What? What's that?' – Richard was awake now.

'The frontier,' Simon repeated. 'Want your ideas about getting across.'

'Where's Marie Lou?' gasped Richard, looking round wildly.

'She went by train, you know. You told me you'd made special arrangements for her.'

'You fool – you stupid fool,' cried Richard, angrily. 'I never said anything of the kind. She was coming with me by 'plane.'

Chapter XXVII

'There's Many a Slip . . .'

For a moment there was an appalling silence; then Richard said quickly: 'I'm going back.'

'Ner,' Simon shook his head. 'You're not up to it – I'll go. Richard, I can't tell you how sorry I am, but I could have sworn that you said you were sending her by train, so that she shouldn't be mixed up in this business.'

'I never said anything about trains, but it's not your fault, Simon. I ought to have made myself clear. Anyhow, I'm going back.'

'It's this child who's going back,' said Rex, 'neither of you boys is fit to travel.'

De Richleau had remained silent; he opened the door of the car and stepped out into the roadway. Then he smiled at the others, not unkindly.

'Now, my friends, if you have all done, I suggest that we should treat this misfortune like sensible people. It would be madness for any of us to dash back to Kiev in this quixotic manner. An hour either way can make no difference now, and we are all badly in need of rest. Let us breakfast first, and think about saving Marie Lou afterwards.'

Without waiting for a reply he walked over to the farm gate and held it open.

'That certainly is sense.' Rex put the car in gear, and ran her through into the yard.

'Hullo! What's that?' exclaimed Simon, as he got out stiffly. 'Sounds like a 'plane.'

'It is.' De Richleau was gazing up into the sky. 'Quick, Rex, run the car under that shed – it may be the frontier people looking for us.'

A moment later they saw her – a big grey air-liner, coming up from the direction of Mogeliev. With a dull booming of her powerful engines she sailed steadily over their heads, following the line of the frontier, the early morning sunlight glinting on her metalwork.

At the far end of the yard a tall, blond peasant had been harnessing a horse into one of the long, boat-shaped carts so common in the Ukraine. He left his work and walked slowly over to them; after De Richleau had spoken a few words to him he turned and led the way towards the house.

The aeroplane had disappeared towards the west.

As the small procession trooped into the clean, bright kitchen a portly, apple-cheeked woman looked up with some apprehension, but the farmer quieted her fears, and soon she was busy preparing a hearty breakfast for her unexpected guests.

The Duke went out again with the man into the yard, and when he returned he pointed through the kitchen window, which looked out on the back. The farmhouse stood upon a slight rise, an orchard lay to the right, but before them spread a gently sloping meadow – beyond it fields, and in the valley, not more than a mile away, the edge of a dark forest.

'You see those tree-tops, my friends? Their roots are in Roumanian soil. At last it seems that we have reached our journey's end.'

Simon let a little sigh escape him. It had been a terrible wrench to leave Valeria Petrovna, but over the border lay freedom – London . . . Paris . . . Deauville . . . Monte Carlo. The old world capitalist cities, with their life and laughter – their restaurants, the Opera, the print shops, and the excitement of big business deals; everything that he had always loved.

Rex laughed. 'My, won't we throw some party – when we get over there!'

Only Richard turned away disconsolate – not even for a single moment could he cease wondering what had happened to little Marie Lou.

Over breakfast they discussed the situation. De Richleau argued that there was no undue reason for alarm. When Richard failed to put in an appearance she had in all probability gone back to the hotel.

'But just think of her,' Richard explained, 'waiting for hours wondering what on earth had happened to us – thinking perhaps that the escape had failed and that we'd all been arrested!'

'Sure,' Rex agreed, 'or, like as not, that we were a rotten bunch of pikers, who'd taken her help and quit while the goin' was good.'

'Ner, she wouldn't think that,' said Simon. 'All I hope is that she hasn't worried herself into doing something silly – anyhow, I'm going back to get her.'

'No!' Richard looked up quickly. 'I am.'

'Well, in any case,' remarked the Duke, 'it would be madness for more than one of us to run his head into the noose.'

Simon nodded. 'That's true – and this is my muddle, so I'm going.'

'My dear fellow,' De Richleau protested, 'for you it is impossible. You forget your leg – you could never drive the car that distance.'

'Sure – that lets Simon out,' Rex declared, 'and since I'm the fittest of you all I guess it's my party.'

'No,' said the Duke, 'it is highly probable that there is another electric fence on the actual frontier, like that which we found at Romanovsk – whoever goes, *you* must stay to help the others over.'

Richard looked round with tired eyes. 'Please don't let's argue any more. The escape will have been discovered by this time, and all three of you are wanted by the police. I'm not – I'm in Russia with a proper passport – and what's more, she's *my* wife.'

His argument was incontrovertible, and ended the discussion. Breakfast was finished in thoughtful silence, then they strolled out into the meadow at the back of the farm to gaze upon the promised land.

The rhythmic throbbing of the big plane could be heard again, so they took cover in the orchard. This time it was beating back towards the east.

'She's a bomber,' said Rex, gazing skywards through the branches.

'Um – I bet she's carrying troops, though,' Simon laughed jerkily. 'A couple of pilots wouldn't be much good if they spotted us and landed!'

'When do we make the big get-away?' Rex inquired.

'Not till tonight,' said the Duke. 'That innocent-looking wood has probably got sentries posted in it at every fifty yards if I know anything about our friend Leshkin. We must lie low here today. I've had a talk with the farmer and I think he can be trusted – in any case I do not mean to let him out of my sight.'

Richard laughed for the first time that morning. 'If I make good going, and Marie Lou is still at the hotel, I could be back here in the 'plane before nightfall. I'm feeling much better now. I think I'll make a start.'

'Before you do that, Richard, I would like a word with you.' De Richleau took him gently by the arm, and led him farther into the orchard.

'Listen,' he went on, when they were out of earshot of the others. 'It is quite useless for you to try and take that car, Richard. You will not be able to move it from the shed.'

'Why?'

'Because, my friend, I removed the sparking-plugs before breakfast!'

'What the devil do you mean?'

'Simply that I will not allow any of you to venture your necks in this idiotic way.'

'Look here,' said Richard, angrily. 'I'm quite as anxious to get over the frontier as anybody, but you might remember that none of you would be here at all, if it were not for Marie Lou!'

'Thank you.' The Duke's voice had a trace of asperity. 'If you were not so young, Richard, and I was not so fond of you, I should resent intensely your imputation on my honour. As it is I merely ask you not to be a fool.'

'Well, I'm sorry. I didn't mean it that way.'

'No, I am certain that you did not – but surely you have the sense to see that you would not get farther than Vinnitsa. The car would be recognised. There is a bullet through the mudguard, and another through the rear window. They would have you in prison before midday.'

'Yes, I suppose that's true,' Richard agreed, reluctantly, 'but I can't leave Marie Lou in Kiev. God knows what will happen to her. I'll tell you the truth – I'm in love with her, and I'm half crazy with anxiety!'

De Richleau patted him on the arm. 'I understand, my friend. I have known love myself, but in this case you can do nothing. You must be a good fellow and cross the frontier with the others tonight.'

'No, I'm damned if I will.'

'Yes, Richard – I wish it. Hasten to Bucharest and get in touch with the British Consul at Kiev as soon as you can. She is a British subject now, and that will stand her in good stead if she is in trouble.'

'But that will take days. Anything may happen to her in the meantime. She must be frantic with anxiety.'

'Don't worry, my son, I am going back to Kiev to look after her.'

'You!'

'Yes, and I am the only one of you all who can do this thing success-fully. I know the language, the people, the country. I shall buy clothes from this peasant – drive the car as far as the outskirts of Vinnitsa tonight, and then abandon it – walk into the town, and take a fourth-class ticket on the train like any *kulak*; tomorrow morning I shall be in Kiev. If Marie Lou is still at the hotel I will place her under the protection of the British Consul immediately – if not, I will find her for you.'

For a moment Richard was silent – then he turned and faced the Duke. 'I say – that's splendid of you, but I just can't leave Russia without Marie Lou; let me come, too?'

De Richleau shook his head. 'No, Richard. I would rather go alone.'

'Please – ? Hullo – what's that?'

'Only the big 'plane again.'

'No, it's not!' Richard was peering up through the trees. 'It's a different one – quite different.'

'Well, what of it?'

'But it's extraordinary. It's got a note just like my own 'plane. Look! There she is!' Richard pointed excitedly. 'By Jove – it is!'

They ran back through the orchard to the meadow where the others were standing.

'Are you sure?' asked the Duke.

'Certain. She's got the same markings. Look! She's coming down!'

Above them in the clear blue of the early morning sky the little 'plane was slowly circling towards the earth.

'Say – who'll this be?' asked Rex, anxiously.

'Marie Lou,' said the Duke.

'Ner . . .' Simon shook his head. 'She can't fly a 'plane.'

'It must be . . .' Richard laughed excitedly. 'No one but Marie Lou knew about my 'plane and where to meet us.'

The machine was down to five hundred feet now; in a long sweep it curved into the wind and 'planed down towards them.

'Two people in her,' murmured De Richleau.

'Clever kid,' grinned Rex. 'She's squared a pilot to bring her along.'

They began to run across the meadow to the place where the 'plane would stop. 'Best be careful,' panted Simon. 'We'll be in a muddle if it's not her.'

'It is,' shouted Richard. 'I can see her in the back.'

In another minute they were crowding round the 'plane and Marie Lou, her cheeks flushed and her eyes bright from the swift flight through the early morning air, had jumped to the ground.

Richard could see that despite the colour in her cheeks, her face was drawn, and her eyes swollen by crying. She gave him a long searching look as she said, quickly:

'Richard – what happened? Why did you leave me behind?'

He seized her hands and for a moment could hardly speak, it was such an enormous relief to see her safe and sound. 'Marie Lou . . .' he stammered, 'Marie Lou . . . Simon bungled things, he thought you were going by train . . . and I was hit on the head, so they brought me with them, unconscious, in the car. . . . I've been through agonies this morning!'

'Oh, Richard,' she gave a little sob. 'I thought I should go mad last night. I waited in the aerodrome till three this morning. I was *terrified*. I thought you had been killed or captured – and then when I heard that you had all been seen on the road in the car . . . I thought . . . oh, I do not know . . . it was awful!'

'You heard that – but how?'

'When it seemed that there was no more chance that you should come I went back to the hotel – the lounge was almost in darkness and I ran straight into Valeria Petrovna – she had been walking up and down all night waiting for news.'

'Good God! I wonder she didn't give you up to the police.' As Richard spoke he followed Marie Lou's glance, and realised that the tall pilot in breeches and field boots, standing near Simon, was Valeria Petrovna.

Marie Lou nodded. 'She was nearly off her head because Simon had left her. One moment she was threatening to have me arrested, and the next pleading with me to let her know where Simon would cross the frontier, that she might see him again. At last we make a bargain – I agree to tell her the place, but she should take me with her.'

'You clever child.'

'No – it was an awful risk – because she might have betrayed you, but I have my little revolver still, and I said that I would shoot her dead if she should try to trick me.'

'What luck that she could fly a 'plane.'

'Yes, her friend taught her – you remember, the tall officer at the air-park in Moscow. But tell me about your hurt – my poor Richard, you look so ill and haggard!'

Richard laughed light-heartedly. 'Oh, I'll be all right now you're safe. It's only worry that got me down. We were just fixing up about going back to get you.'

'Oh, Richard!' Marie Lou's eyes were full of smiles again, then, almost at once, her face grew grave. 'But we are not safe – not yet. Leshkin has had all the guards along the frontier trebled, and last night he left Kiev in an aeroplane. He is determined to stop us getting across.'

'Good Lord! I wonder if he's in the big bomber that's been sailing up and down. If so, he's bound to spot my 'plane. We can't possibly hide it.' Richard turned to Rex.

'Look here, there's not a moment to lose. We must get out before the Bolshie 'plane comes over again. I'm going to take Marie Lou across right away. I'll be back for another of you as soon as I can.'

'O.K.' Rex nodded. 'Make it snappy, or they'll get us yet!'

Valeria Petrovna had flung herself into Simon's arms the moment she reached the ground. He looked at her with mingled love and amazement. She was still dressed in the riding kit she had worn for her part at the theatre. Her make-up had not been properly removed, and little furrows down her cheeks showed that she had been weeping bitterly.

'Simon – dear one – this is terrible, that I 'ave to lose you,' she sobbed, breaking into fresh tears. 'An' last night . . . oh, it was 'orrible. Did you know that Leshkin meant to arrest you again? But no, you could not. 'E come to my dressing-room after the secon' act – 'e say that 'e 'as been to Moscawa. Oh, why did you not tell me of those men?'

'What men?' asked Simon, puzzled.

'The men you kill. Eight men of the Ogpu! Oh, you are a lion, my Simon, but Stalin, 'e was furious. Nevaire would 'e forgive that – an' 'e 'as take back your pardon that 'e give me.'

'It was in self-defence!'

'No matter – you 'ave kill them, that is what Leshkin say; 'e is so 'appy that 'e do not know 'ow to contain 'imself. That is why 'e tell me. Then I leave the theatre – to warn you, just as I am – but when I arrive at the 'otel you are no longer there!' Valeria Petrovna struck her breast passionately with her clenched fists.

'Oh, my dear.' Simon slipped his arm round her shaking shoulders. 'That was splendid of you.'

'I was distraught. I do not know what I do. Then, when I 'ave left the theatre, the manager 'e make announcement in the middle of the third act; 'e say that I am ill all suddenly, but Leshkin suspect at once and come rushing to the 'otel like a mad bull. 'Ow I laugh at 'im when 'e find that you 'ave gone already – but 'e find that my car is gone, also, and 'e go mad with rage because 'e think that it was me that 'elp you to escape – but I, myself, do not know what to think.'

Valeria Petrovna burst into a fresh fit of sobbing, then, when she had recovered a little, she went on: 'Leshkin question all the police on the telephone from the 'otel – they 'ave seen my car on the road to Birdichy, but you are not alone – there are others, also! Then 'e speak to the prison, an' 'e find that your frien's have escape through a tunnel in the ground . . . 'e is furious – livid – 'e order troops to 'old the bridge at Vinnitsa, then 'e rush off to follow you by 'plane, shaking 'is great fist in my face, and 'e swear that 'e would put his foot in the face of that damn' Jew yet!'

'I'm so sorry – so dreadfully sorry. You must have had an awful time,' Simon tried to comfort her. Out of the corner of his eye he saw Rex helping Marie Lou back into the 'plane, and, realising the immediate danger now that he knew Leshkin was somewhere on the scene, he looked apprehensively at the sky-line for signs of the big troop-carrier.

'The suspense! It was 'orrible,' Valeria Petrovna cried. ' 'Ow I live through the night I do not know. I wait . . . wait . . . wait in the lounge of the 'otel, praying for news. Then, at last, when I am worn out, the little one arrive! But why did you not tell me that you mean to leave me?'

'You didn't tell me that you left my friends in prison to be shot – did you?'

' 'Ow you know that?'

'Doesn't matter much now, does it?'

'Oh, Simon, I 'ave been wrong about that. I know it! But what would you 'ave me do? I could not save you all!'

He frowned. 'If only you had told me.'

'My brave one. You would 'ave run into awful danger to try an' save your frien's. It is you I love. I try to save you from yourself!'

'Well, let's not say any more about it.'

'But, Simon, 'ow could you leave me without one word?'

'Seems I've got to leave you in any case – unless you'll come with me?'

'Oh, Simon – Simon – ' She wrung her hands. ' 'Ow can I? Russia is my country. I love 'er, even as I love you.'

Rex stood by the Duke watching Richard wheel above them to gain altitude. The little white 'plane banked sharply and then, straightening out, headed for the Roumanian frontier. It had hardly disappeared above the tree-tops to the south when his quick ear caught the note of another engine. 'Look out!' he yelled. 'Plane over!'

Simon gripped Valeria Petrovna by the arm. 'Quick! We must run for it – the farmhouse!'

The dull booming of the big bomber could be clearly heard now. They had hardly crowded into the doorway of the farm when Rex spotted her. 'Look!' he cried. 'There she is!'

'It is Leshkin,' exclaimed Valeria Petrovna.

Rex nodded. 'If he spots Richard I guess our number's up.'

At that moment Richard was flying low over patches of wood and growing crops on the Roumanian side. He noticed a broad meadow and 'planed down into it, making an easy landing.

'Jump out, Marie Lou,' he called. 'I'll be back in five minutes with one of the others.'

She climbed out, laughing – her blue eyes brilliant in the sunshine. 'Be back soon,' she cried. 'I will be waiting.'

Richard took off again, and in a few minutes had all the altitude he needed for this short flight. He could see the roof-tops of the tiny township to the east, how the streets twisted in and out among the houses. The orchards and fields spread out before him like a patchwork quilt; he could see the farmhouse again now.

De Richleau saw him first. 'But they will see him for a certainty,' he cried, anxiously.

The others had their eyes glued to the giant 'plane sailing serenely, high up among the little white clouds that flecked the empyrean blue. Suddenly it swerved from its course!

'He's spotted!' cried Rex. 'Look! The big boy's circling!'

'We'll never do it,' said Simon, nervously. 'Richard's 'plane can't take us all. What about the car?'

'Useless,' the Duke replied, curtly. 'The frontier guards would get us. It's Richard – or capture!'

Valeria Petrovna was right. Leshkin himself was in the big 'plane; since the first light of dawn he had been patrolling the frontier, scouring the roads for her car, determined that the fugitives should not escape. The sight of the small 'plane coming in from Roumania had roused his suspicions immediately; he knew that his enemies had powerful friends outside Russia.

'Higher,' he shouted to his pilot, 'higher!' He did not want Richard to suspect their presence until he had actually landed.

Two thousand feet under the big bomber Richard's 'plane showed like a cardboard toy against the flattened landscape. As it circled, and its wings gave free vision, Leshkin could see the tiny group of figures huddled in the farmhouse doorway through his binoculars. Sharply he gave the order to descend.

Richard had landed; he waved a greeting to his friends as they ran towards the 'plane. He was a little surprised at the excitement they displayed, gesticulating as they ran. The roar of his own engine drowned the noise of the other; he had taken out his cigarette-case and was just about to light up when Rex reached him.

'Great stuff, Richard,' he shouted. 'But it'll be a mighty near thing. Can you take us all?'

'Don't be silly – one at a time.'

'Holy Mike, man, don't you see the Bolshies are on your tail?' Rex pointed upwards.

Richard looked up, and saw, for the first time, the air-liner slowly descending in great sweeps above his head.

'Good God! I had no idea. Look here – the 'plane's only built for two – she'll never carry five!'

'She's just got to! If one of us stays behind he'll be bumped off for sure!'

'I do not come with you,' said Valeria Petrovna.

'But you must,' exclaimed Simon, seizing her arm.

The Soviet machine was at less than five hundred feet now.

'All right, with four we'll chance it,' shouted Richard. 'Take the seat, Rex, you're heaviest. The Duke must manage, somehow, on your knees.'

'Please – please,' Simon was urging Valeria Petrovna.

'No . . . no . . . that I cannot do.'

'Why not?'

'I would 'ate it in your capitalist country.'

'Come on, Simon,' cried the Duke.

He took no notice. 'Have you ever thought how I might hate it here?'

'That is different. I do not belong to myself. My art belong to the 'ole Russian people; after they 'ave 'seen me act they 'ave new strength for the work they 'ave to do.'

'Simon!' pleaded De Richleau.

Still he took no notice. 'Work!' he said, angrily. 'Destroying all free-dom, you mean, and preventing anybody having a chance to get on in the world.'

'No!' she cried, her eyes lit with a fierce enthusiasm. 'For the greedy and selfish we 'ave no place, but we give life and 'appiness to all the thou-sands that toil in the factory and the mine. We free the women from the children that they should not be forced to bear, we save them from the drudgery of the 'ome. In a hundred years we will 'ave destroyed for ever that any 'uman being should suffer from 'unger and disease. Christ 'imself taught the brother'ood of all men, and that will He realise here, in Russia, two thousand years after 'e is dead.'

It was the supreme declaration of the Bolshevist ideal, and Simon was almost stunned by her outburst. Long afterwards he wondered how she reconciled her theories with the fact that she lived in the same state of luxury as the daughter of a capitalist multi-millionaire; but at that moment De Richleau seized him from behind and flung him bodily on to the fuse-lage of the 'plane.

'Hang on to the back of the seat, and lie flat, with your feet to the tail,' he cried.

With one pull of his strong arms Rex had hoisted the Duke up beside him. 'All set,' he shouted. 'Let her go.'

They ran forward slowly, bumping on the uneven ground. The 'plane lifted slightly, then bumped again, then rose once more, but only a few feet from the earth. Richard was nervous now that he would not be able to clear the bars at the end of the field. He was frightened, too, that with the extra weight on the tail they might stall at any moment. Quite suddenly the 'plane rose sharply – they were over the barns, sailing freely – rising every moment higher in the air.

Rex looked round to see if the enemy was following; he caught his breath – Simon was no longer there! He hit Richard on the back. 'Simon,' he bawled. 'We've dropped him.'

Richard banked steeply; they peered anxiously downwards, fearing to see a little crumpled heap in one of the fields below. The Soviet 'plane was circling slowly over the farmstead, apparently uncertain whether to land or give chase.

Leshkin scowled from his seat beside the pilot. In his anxiety that Richard should not see him before landing, he had misjudged the time it would take him to descend. His pilot obstinately refused to be hurried; the Kommissar cursed furiously as he saw Richard take off and glide, hesitatingly, towards the barn. Then he saw Simon fall.

'Descend!' he cried. 'Make your landing at once.' But the pilot had already begun to follow the other 'plane, now he banked steeply away from the field.

'Descend!' yelled Leshkin again, his small eyes black with anger.

'Have patience, Comrade,' the man answered, sullenly. 'I must circle now, to come again into the wind. I have no wish to break *my* neck.'

Valeria Petrovna had seen Simon slip off. In a second she was beside him, helping him to his feet. 'Run, Simon – run,' she urged. 'Your frien' will come back and it will be less far for 'im to come.'

'Say, there he is!' cried Rex, suddenly, pointing from the other 'plane. 'Good old Simon – run, boysie – run!' Almost at the same moment Richard and the Duke saw him too, a small dark figure running hard in their direction – a field away already from the meadow, with Valeria Petrovna urging him on some hundred yards behind.

'What bravery!' exclaimed the Duke. 'He must have dropped off purposely when it seemed that we should crash into the barn.'

Richard wheeled again, and headed for the frontier, his mouth set tight. It was useless now to try and land again to pick Simon up. He must unload the others first.

A rifle cracked below them, then another. It was the frontier guards. They had realised that something must be amiss; they fired again, the flash of their rifles could be seen distinctly, but the bullets went wide.

Richard did not attempt to reach the field where he had left Marie Lou, he came down in the first he could find on the Roumanian side – that was a decent distance from the frontier guards. His landing was sheltered from their view by a small wood.

'Out you get,' he said, sharply. 'Marie Lou's in a field about half a mile away over there.' He pointed as he spoke. 'I'll join you, if I can.'

'O.K.,' Rex sang out, 'all the luck,' but Richard was already mounting into the air again.

The big troop-carrier bumped and bounded over the uneven ground of the meadow. The pilot brought it to rest with a jerk, only thirty feet from the barn that had so nearly proved the end of Richard. Leshkin sprang out – a sharp order and his men followed.

Valeria Petrovna turned her head and saw them coming round the corner of the barn as she ran through the farther field. She could see Simon, too, a field ahead of her. Her heart ached for him; how could little Simon, with his recent wound, hope to out-distance those hardbitten soldiers. They would hunt him like a hare, and remorselessly shoot him down in some ditch or coppice. Dashing the tears from her eyes, she stumbled on.

Simon jumped a ditch; he groaned from the pain as a sharp stab went through his leg like a red-hot needle. Panting and breathless he ran on, looking from time to time over his shoulder. He could no longer see the Soviet 'plane – they must have landed now. Richard had disappeared from view. If only he could get back in time after landing the others. Good job he had dropped off or they would never have cleared that barn. He must be half-way to the wood by now ... if only he could stick it ... but the frontier guards might open fire on him at any moment. God, how his leg hurt! His head was dizzy and his chest bursting.

Simon stumbled and fell; he picked himself up again, white and shaken. His hands were torn and bleeding from the hedges he had forced his way through. He cursed his folly in having taken the straight line across a ploughed field. His boots were heavy as lead with the soil that clung to them. If only he had gone round he would have reached the opposite side in half the time. A shot rang out. He glanced over his shoulder and saw that Valeria Petrovna was stumbling along about two hundred yards behind him. His pursuers had crossed the last hedge and were streaming across the field in open order with Leshkin waving them on. Another shot sounded sharply on the still morning air – the bullet sent up a little spurt of earth some way to his right. A sharp order came – there was no more firing; Leshkin did not want to kill Valeria Petrovna! Simon reached the farther hedge; he burst his way through it regardless of fresh tears and pain, and stumbled into a meadow on the far side ... there – glorious sight – was Richard in his 'plane, waving encouragement, and steadily coming down.

Three frontier guards had come out of the wood and were blazing away at Richard, but they ceased firing as he landed, fearful of hitting Leshkin's men. Simon thought his head would burst as he made a last desperate effort to reach the 'plane. The soldiers had crossed the plough now – they were shouting as they struggled through the hedge. Richard stood up in the 'plane and yelled wildly.

'Run, Simon ... run!' He saw the soldiers were rapidly gaining ground, and climbed out of the 'plane to go to Simon's assistance.

Leshkin was through the hedge and bellowing like a bull – his face purple with the unaccustomed exercise. The foremost soldier was running level with Valeria Petrovna. Suddenly she struck out with her crop – a fierce back-hander, that caught the man in the face; he stumbled and stopped with a yelp of pain. Simon had reached the 'plane, white, exhausted, almost fainting. Richard had him by the arm and leg, half-lifting him towards the passenger seat. He grabbed at the rim and hoisted himself over the edge. Valeria Petrovna had stopped and turned – facing the soldiers. With all her remaining force she was lashing at them with her whip, driving off the nearest with her fierce, cutting lash. Richard was in the cockpit again – the 'plane ran forward – one of the men made a futile grab at the wing, and was flung to the earth.

'Shoot!' roared Leshkin, 'shoot!' But the soldiers were panting and breathless. By the time they had fumbled with their rifles and taken unsteady aim, the 'plane was sailing high into the air.

Simon looked down into the green field below. A bullet whizzed past his head – another hit the tail with a loud 'phut'. The soldiers stood in a little group mopping their perspiring faces; Valeria Petrovna was standing a little apart with Leshkin – she waved her crop in farewell. Simon waved backhand then he saw a curious thing.

She turned suddenly and struck Leshkin with her whip; the lash took him full in the face. For a moment he was blinded by the pain; he sprang back, holding up his hand to protect his head; the swift lash came down again.

'You fool,' Valeria Petrovna was shrieking, 'you fool. I 'ave trick you. I pay you now for what you make me suffer – that you 'ave been to Stalin and make me lose 'im I love.' She struck again and again with her swift, cutting lash, until Leshkin's face was a mass of blood; at last she was hauled off by the soldiers.

The 'plane had vanished into the distance, when he was once more able to see her out of feverish, bloodshot eyes. 'It is you who are a fool,' he said, harshly. 'You have forgotten that these men have done murder – and that there is a law of extradition.'

Chapter XXVIII

The Last Round

I

Marie Lou gave a little wriggle of her shoulders and her new dress settled gracefully round her slender figure. She looked at herself gravely in the long mirror. It was a pretty frock – in fact the prettiest frock that Marie Lou had ever seen. She wondered if Richard would like it as much as she did.

Tonight there was to be a party. It was just forty-eight hours since their arrival in Vienna, and so they were to celebrate their freedom.

On the morning after their escape out of Russia the Duke had taken the train to Bucharest. He went to secure, through the Embassy, a temporary legalisation of their position for the satisfaction of the Roumanian police, and also to get passports for them to travel to Vienna.

With a humorous look De Richleau had suggested, before his departure, that Richard should proceed to Vienna alone. Someone must make the necessary arrangements for their arrival, and send off telegrams for clothes to be sent to them by air from London. Richard had not seemed pleased at the idea; Simon's wound had been badly inflamed by his race for life, and Marie Lou must stay and nurse him. Richard thought he ought to stay too. 'Just in case,' he explained, with a vague wave of his hand. No one was indiscreet enough to press for an explanation of this hypothetical emergency, and he seemed quite ready for Rex to take his 'plane and do the job, so it was arranged thus. They had had to stay three nights in the little Roumanian village near the frontier. By that time Simon was recovered, and the Duke returned. They reached Vienna the following evening.

There was a knock on the bedroom door; Marie Lou knew that knock by now. 'Come in,' she called, gaily.

'You are comfy here?' Richard remarked, looking round the well-equipped room.

'Why, yes,' she replied, as she thought how terribly attractive he looked in his evening clothes. 'It is so lovely that I almost regret to leave it for the restaurant or the shops. But are you not comfortable at your hotel?'

'Oh, I'm all right, but something's gone wrong with the central heating since the afternoon. It was as cold as Siberia when I changed just now.' He held out a spray of catlias with a smile.

'Richard – how lovely.' She took the orchids. 'You spoil me terribly. Look at all the lovely flowers you sent me this morning.' She waved her hand towards the roses and lilies that stood about making the room a perfect bower.

'I'm so glad you like them,' he said, softly.

She felt herself blushing under his gaze, and moving quickly over to the dressing-table, pinned on the orchids.

'I am so sorry you are miserable at your hotel,' she said, not looking at him.

'They'll put it right,' he remarked, casually. 'It'll be on again by the time I get back tonight.'

'Richard,' she said, after a moment. 'Would you mind if I came down to you in the lounge? I have one little matter that I would like to see to.'

'Of course,' he agreed. 'I'll be waiting for you.'

When he had gone Marie Lou picked up the house telephone; all their party, with the exception of Richard, were staying at the same hotel; she tried De Richleau's room, but could get no reply, then she tried Rex – he was still dressing.

A wicked little smile lurked round the corners of her mouth while she was talking to him – his laughter came clearly over the line. 'Sure,' he said, chuckling. 'Sure, I'll fix it!'

'And you won't tell?' she begged.

'Not on your life. You leave it all to me.'

Marie Lou's little face was grave as she hung up the receiver.

2

The Duke was in his dressing-gown, the brilliantly coloured robe of honour of a Chinese mandarin. The house telephone tinkled, and he picked it up. He thought that he had heard it ring a few moments before, when he was in his bath.

'Yes,' he answered. 'This is the Duke de Richleau ... who? Herr Murenberg? ... I don't think that I ... what? ... he says that I shall remember him as Fritz of the Baumgarten? ... ah, yes, of course, let him come up.'

A few minutes later an official in a handsome uniform was shown into the Duke's room.

De Richleau extended his hand. 'My dear Fritz, this is an unexpected pleasure.'

Herr Murenberg took the Duke's hand with marked deference, he clicked his heels and bowed low over it. 'For me also, Altesse.'

'How many years is it since I have last seen you? Fifteen – no, twenty it must be – dear me, but you have prospered, my dear Fritz.' De Richleau patted the Austrian on the shoulder. 'What a fine uniform you have got, to be sure.'

Herr Murenberg bowed and smiled again. 'I hope, Altesse, you will be kind enough to forget the little restaurant where you so often gave me your patronage in the old days, many things are changed since then, although I remember your kindness with much gratitude.'

'That would be impossible, my dear fellow; many of my most cherished memories have an association with the dear old Baumgarten which you used to run so well. Nevertheless I am delighted to think that the upheaval of the War has brought good fortune to one of my friends at least. What splendid position has Fate decreed for you?'

'I am deputy chief of the police, Altesse; that I knew many languages has stood me in good stead.'

'Dear me,' the Duke made a grimace. 'I – er – trust that this is not an official visit?'

'I fear, yes, Altesse,' he bowed again. 'It is a serious matter that I come upon.'

'Sit down, my friend. Let us hear how I have broken the laws of your delightful city.'

The Chief of Police sat gingerly on the extreme edge of an armchair. 'Unfortunately, Altesse, it is not here that you have offended – if that were so . . .' he spread out his hands, 'it would be my pleasure to put the matter right; it seems that you have come from Russia?'

De Richleau's eyes narrowed. 'Yes,' he admitted, 'that is so.'

Murenberg was obviously troubled. 'Altesse, in the old days you were a gentleman who liked his amusements; the cabmen of Vienna, they knew you well – and if you smashed up their cabs with reckless driving after a party – what matter. If you broke a few heads even – you paid handsomely in the morning, and all was well, but now it seems that you have taken to killing men for your amusement – Bolsheviks, it is true, but even so it is a serious thing.'

'Hardly for amusement, my dear Fritz,' the Duke smiled, grimly. 'It happened that I was called on to defend myself. I did so to the best of my ability.'

The Chief of Police shook his head sadly, he raised one arched eyebrow, and scratched the back of his neck; he was evidently much troubled. 'An order has been applied for – for the extradition of yourself and others, Excellency. What am I to do?'

De Richleau was thinking quickly. 'What is the procedure in such cases?' he asked.

'It is my duty to issue a warrant for the arrest of you and your friends.'

'You have not done it yet?'

'No, Altesse, when I saw your name on the paper the memory of the old days came to me, I thought to myself, "Tomorrow will do for this – tonight I will go informally to pay my respects to my old patron".'

'That was very good of you, Fritz; tell me, what happens when this warrant is executed?'

'There is a man from Russia here. He will identify you; we shall supply an escort to the frontier, and with him you will go back to Moscow to be tried.'

'Do you know the name of the man they have sent?'

'Yes, Altesse. It is an important man, a Kommissar Leshkin. He stays in this hotel.'

De Richleau nodded. 'Now if we leave Austria tonight, this man will follow us, will he not, and apply for our extradition in any country in which he finds us?'

'I fear that is so, Altesse, but the world is wide; there are many very comfortable trains which leave Vienna this evening. If you travel it will mean delay – important witnesses against you may disappear – time is on your side in this affair.'

'If there were no one to prove our identity, however, they could not apply for our extradition, I imagine,' the Duke said, softly.

'No, that is true.' Herr Murenberg stood up. 'But this man is here, Excellency. For the sake of the old days I trust that I may not have to make this arrest tomorrow morning.'

De Richleau took his hand. 'I am more grateful to you, my dear Fritz, than I can say, you may rely on me to spare you that painful duty.'

3

The dinner table was adorned with flowers, the string band was worthy of the Viennese traditions, the champagne sparkled in the glasses. To Marie Lou it was like fairyland.

Richard sat on her right, Simon on her left. Across the table were Rex and De Richleau, between them the long, humorous face of Gerry Bruce.

Dinner was over, the Duke was handing round cigars, the first of a new box of the famous Hoyos, that had arrived with his clothes that afternoon from London. Marie Lou had just finished a peach, the first that she had ever seen in her life, the flavour lingered, exquisite, on her tongue – she was in Heaven. She looked across at Rex. 'Have you arranged everything?' she asked.

He grinned. 'Sure thing. There won't be any fool – '

'Hush!' she exclaimed, quickly.

'Sorry,' he apologised. 'I nearly spilled the beans that time, but it's all O.K., you can take it from me.'

'Thank you. It is a little surprise that Rex and I have arranged for you,' she explained to the others, who were looking completely mystified. 'He has got me a nice strong file; I spent a busy hour this morning.'

Rex began to look mystified, too; he had got no file for her, and it was only while dressing for dinner that she had asked for his co-operation in a little secret.

She produced a flat square parcel from under her chair, and laid it on the table. They had all wondered what it could be when she had brought it in to dinner with her.

Richard and Simon cleared away the plates and glasses to make room; Rex was looking more and more puzzled.

A waiter paused beside De Richleau's chair and laid a heavy triangular parcel on the table beside him: 'The manager's compliments, sir, and he hopes that will do.'

'Thank you.' The Duke nodded, and gave the man a coin, then he felt the package carefully and transferred it to the pocket of his tail coat; the others were far too interested in Marie Lou's big parcel to pay any attention.

She smiled at Rex as she undid the wrapping. 'For a long time,' she said, 'he has been telling us that it will be tomorrow that he will find the jewels – I have decided that it shall be today!'

She removed the last sheet of paper from her parcel. Rex and the Duke recognised at once the gaily painted abacus that she had insisted on taking from her cottage at Romanovsk when they fled to the Château. It lay there, incongruous enough – a childish toy, the solid square frame and the cross wires with the gaily painted beads, upon which every Russian learns to calculate.

'As I have told you,' she said slowly, 'my mother always said that if I ever left Russia, I must take this with me; and it was not because she feared that I should forget how to count. I knew that she had taken it from the walls of the foundry after the fire – it was she who cleaned and painted it after that. This morning I filed through the iron tubing which makes the frame – see, now, what it contains.' As she finished speaking she divided one piece of the framework from the other where she had filed it through. She swept some wafers from a dish in front of her and poured out the contents of the hollow pipe.

With a little rattle they fell on the china dish – a heap of diamonds, rubies, emeralds, sapphires, a glistening pile of precious stones sparkling and flashing in the electric light. She took the second and third and fourth sides of the abacus and added their contents to the shining heap. The men sat round, speechless, gazing in wonder at the heap of stones sparkling with hidden fire from their many facets.

'There are the pearls still,' she cried, delighted with the success of her surprise; 'each bead is a great pearl from the famous necklace of the Princess Tzan, dipped in some substance which protected it from the fire.' She drew them off the wires, putting them beside the glittering stones already in the dish. One she retained and began to scrape it with her knife; the covering flaked away, leaving a great rosy pearl.

'Princess, you may not know it, but you have a fortune here,' said the Duke. 'Even I have never seen such rubies; they are of the true pigeon's blood, worth a king's ransom.'

'It is said, Monsieur, that a Prince Shulimoff who lived in Catherine the Second's time was granted rights over all the Russian lands that lie adjacent to Persia. It is believed that he got these during his Khanship there.'

The Duke nodded. 'I do not doubt it; the Shah himself has no better stones than these.' His long, elegant fingers played with the pile. Red, green, and blue, the stones glittered under the big electrolier – a dazzling sight which held them fascinated.

'And now,' said Marie Lou, 'I wish that you all should choose such stones as you may like to be keepsakes of our days in Russia.'

They drew away shyly. Marie Lou's mouth drooped with disappointment.

'Princess,' said De Richleau, voicing all their thoughts, 'this is your fortune; on it we trust that you may live in happiness for many years. We could not rob you of your inheritance.'

'Oh, please,' she begged, 'it will spoil it all for me if you do not – had it not been for you I should still be at Romanovsk.'

She looked so disappointed that Richard bent forward and picked up a square diamond from the pile.

'I will keep it for you in trust, Marie Lou,' he said, smiling. 'I shall treasure it always because it comes from you, but if you ever need it, it is yours.' She squeezed his hand gratefully, and his pulse raced at the pressure of her tiny hand in his. The others each picked a jewel in turn, with the same reservation.

'Say,' Rex grunted, 'this packet's going in the hotel safe tonight; we've had all the trouble we're needing for a while.'

A waiter stood beside De Richleau. 'The gentleman you were inquiring for has just gone into the grill, sir.'

'Thank you.' The Duke carefully placed the beautiful ruby he had chosen in his waistcoat pocket. 'Be good enough to inform me when he goes up to his room.'

Rex took Marie Lou's hand. 'Come on,' he said, 'let's hit the floor again.'

He was teaching her the gentle art of modern dancing. Like most Americans, he had such a perfect sense of rhythm that it was impossible not to follow him. Richard sat watching and wished that he could dance as well. Marie Lou seemed to be picking it up easily and quickly, but he knew that it was too soon for him to attempt to dance with her yet, and he was too wise to try – let her learn with Rex. When they returned to the table Gerry Bruce took up his glass. 'Well, fellers,' he declared, 'as I'm the one and only guest, it's up to me to give a bit of a toast.'

'Hear, hear!' Simon filled up the glasses with champagne.

Gerry lifted his glass. 'May you all live to give your old friend Gerry Bruce many another good dinner in the years to come. How's that?'

They drank it with enthusiasm. A little later Marie Lou turned to Richard. 'Would you mind very much if I went to bed?'

'But it's early,' he protested.

'I'm tired,' she said.

He shrugged his shoulders. 'Well, just as you like.'

She rose from the table and he followed her out into the hall. 'I've hardly seen you alone all day,' he said reproachfully, as she was about to enter the lift.

'I'm sorry,' she smiled sweetly at him, 'but I'm tired; I want to go to bed.'

'What about tomorrow?' he asked. 'I thought we might get a car and go for a drive. You'd like that, wouldn't you?'

She shook her head. 'No, tomorrow I mean to have a long morning in bed.'

'Right-o, if that's how you feel,' he said, a little sulkily. 'What about lunch?'

'I will lunch in my room, I think.'

'Dear me,' he raised his eyebrows; 'well, if you change your mind, let me know. Good night,' he turned away abruptly.

The Duke and Rex were with the manager. They had tied up the jewels in a napkin, and were now transferring them into three stout envelopes, to be sealed with wax before being deposited in the hotel safe.

Gerry Bruce bade them good night and left. The four friends remained standing in the hall. Simon limped to the hall porter's desk and asked for his key; the man gave it to him, and with it a letter.

'Hullo,' he said, 'wonder who this is from – no one but my office knows where I am.'

There was a second envelope inside the first. 'Letter addressed to Miriam's house,' he remarked to Richard. 'Can't think who can have written to me there; she sent it on to the office.'

'It's got a Russian stamp,' said the Duke with interest.

'Valeria Petrovna!' exclaimed Simon, looking at the large sheets covered with a round, childish hand. 'This is awkward; she warns us that Leshkin is applying for extradition papers.'

'I have reason to know that they will not be executed,' remarked De Richleau, with a little smile.

'Say, are you sure of that?' asked Rex.

'Quite certain,' the Duke answered firmly. 'I am taking steps to ensure that we shall not be troubled with any unpleasantness of that kind.'

'Great business,' grinned Rex. 'Well, I'm for hitting the hay; I've had quite enough hectic business to last me for some little time.' He yawned loudly as he turned towards the lift.

'I will go with you,' said the Duke.

'Hope the thought of those pretty toys of Marie Lou's don't keep you from your sleep,' said Rex.

De Richleau had just exchanged a few words in a low tone with the hall porter. He smiled. 'I think I shall read for a while; I have found a most interesting book on the subject of murder, the theory of the game as opposed to the practice causes me considerable amusement.'

Simon had just finished reading his letter. He held it in one hand, stooping a little as he smiled at Richard, who was getting into his coat preparatory to leaving the hotel.

'She wants me to meet her in Berlin next month – that is, if we don't get extradited!' He laughed his jerky little laugh.

'Shall you go?' asked Richard, curiously.

Simon nodded his clever, narrow head up and down. 'Got to – Valeria's in a muddle with her contracts – have to see what I can do.'

4

Richard was disturbed and unhappy as he made his way slowly to his hotel. Could Marie Lou be getting spoilt, he wondered. Why must she go rushing off to bed like that, having danced half the evening with Rex – he had hardly had a word with her all day. And then this absurd business of stopping in bed all the next morning; there were so many things in Vienna he wanted to show her. Lunching in bed, too! It really was the limit. . . . Could it be the jewels that had made the difference? . . . She was independent of him now. Tomorrow he supposed she would be asking him to see about the annulment of their marriage – of course he'd have to set her free – he couldn't hold her to it. But how he wished that he could.

When he got to his hotel he went up in the lift and down the corridor to his room. It was innocent of all signs of occupation. 'Hullo – wrong room,' he muttered, switching off the light again; 'I must be on the next floor.' He looked at the number on the door: '218'. Surely that was right? What an extraordinary thing; perhaps they had shifted him because of the central heating. Still, they ought to have let him know.

He went down to the bureau in the hall. 'What have you done with my things?' he said.

The night clerk looked surprised. 'We sent them over on your instructions, sir.'

'My instructions? What do you mean?'

'The American gentleman, Mr Van Ryn, who took the room for you, came here just before eight o' clock. He said you wished to transfer to the Regina, where your friends were staying. We were to pack for you and send over your things at once. He paid your bill. I hope we have done right, sir?'

Richard frowned. What in the world had bitten Rex? Still, there it was – he'd better go and find out. Absently he walked out into the street again.

At the Regina he was told that Mr Van Ryn had booked a room for him, No. 447 – the night porter gave him the key.

What the devil had Rex been up to? thought Richard, as he walked over to the lift. If this was supposed to be a joke, it was in damned bad taste – 447 was next to Marie Lou. Richard walked angrily down the corridor. He supposed he'd better have his things moved again to another room.

He opened the door – yes, there were all his belongings, unpacked, too – what a fool Rex was. This sort of thing wasn't like him, either.

The communicating-door to No. 448 stood a little open. Richard was tempted; here was an opportunity for a word with Marie Lou – he could explain that he was moving.

He looked into the bedroom. There she was, the darling, lying in bed. She made no movement; perhaps she was asleep? Only the light by the bed was still on. The orchids that he had given her that evening stood near it in a glass.

He tiptoed over to the side of the bed. Yes, she was asleep – how divinely pretty she looked with her long dark lashes lying on her cheeks.

One lovely arm thrown back over her curly head; she lay quite still, breathing gently.

His heart began to thump as he looked at her – he simply *must* steal just one kiss – he bent over and very gently touched her forehead with his lips.

He turned reluctantly and began to tiptoe back to the other room.

'Richard,' said a soft voice from the bed.

He swung round, the picture of guilt. 'Hullo,' he said, in a voice that he tried to make as casual as possible, 'I thought you were asleep.'

She shook her head. 'Do you like your new room?' she asked slyly.

'So you knew about that, eh?' He was quite at his ease and smiling at her now.

'Of course; I asked Rex to manage it – it is a wife's duty to look after her husband,' she added, virtuously. 'I couldn't have you sleeping in that cold hotel.'

He sat down on the side of the bed. 'Look here,' he said, with an effort, 'if we do this sort of thing we shan't be able to get the annulment, you know.'

She sat up quickly, clasping her hands round her knees, a tiny perfect figure, Dresden china flushed with rosy life.

'Richard,' she said gravely, 'do you want that annulment very, very badly?'

He drew a sharp breath. 'There's nothing in the world I want less!'

She laughed. 'And you won't be sulky if we don't go out tomorrow morning – or if we lunch in bed?'

'Marie Lou! You angel!' He leant over her. Her soft arms were round his neck; she whispered in his ear: 'Richard, my darling, this is the perfect ending to the fairy story of the Princess Marie Lou.'

5

The Duke de Richleau put down his interesting book on murder and picked up the shrilling telephone at his side.

'Thank you,' he said, 'I am much obliged.' He replaced the receiver and took up his book again, reading quietly till the end of the chapter. He carefully inserted a marker, and laid the book beside the bed. Then he examined the automatic which the waiter had brought him in the restaurant, also a small bottle, taken from among those on his washstand. He put the bottle and the weapon in his pocket, and lighting a fresh cigar, he left the room. As he came out into the corridor he glanced swiftly to right and left; it was in semi-darkness, and no sound disturbed the silence.

Outside the door to the left of his room a neat pair of black shoes reposed – Simon's. Opposite lay a pair of large brogues, Rex's. Outside Marie Lou's door were a tiny pair of buckled court shoes, and beside them – 'Strange,' thought the observant Duke – a pair of man's patent evening shoes.

'Very strange,' the Duke thought again; then a gurgle of delighted laughter came faintly from beyond the door. De Richleau raised one slanting eyebrow meditatively. Sly dog, that Richard; what a thing it was to be young and in Vienna, city of dreams. How fond he was of them all, and how fortunate he was – that, at his age, all these young people seemed to take such pleasure in his company. Life was a pleasant thing indeed. He drew thoughtfully on his cigar, and quietly strolled down the corridor.

His walk had all the assurance that marked his every movement with distinction; nevertheless, his footsteps were almost noiseless. He came to a baize door, and passed through it to the service staircase beyond. He mounted slowly in the darkness, his bright eyes gleaming like those of some great cat. From a long acquaintance with continental hotels he knew that spare pass-keys were always to be found in the floor-waiter's pantry. Two floors above his own he found the room he sought, with its nails and brushes. The light was on, a tired chambermaid was sleeping in a chair, a paper-covered novel on her knees. With infinite precaution De Richleau took the key he needed from its hook above her head. He was easier in his mind now – the possession of that key was the one thing that troubled him. Soft-footed he walked down the passage, seeking Leshkin's room. He found it and inserted the key in the lock. He turned it gently and the door opened without a sound. He slipped inside.

Kommissar Leshkin was late in going to bed. He stood in his stockinged feet and shirt-sleeves, removing his tie and collar. He had some little difficulty, as his fat fingers still bore the angry weals where Valeria Petrovna's whip had caught them. He took a pot of ointment from the dressing-table and was just about to apply it to the cuts on his face; in the looking-glass he caught the reflection of a white shirt-front. He dropped the pot and spun round.

It was the Duke, grey-haired, immaculate in evening dress. In his right hand he held an automatic, in his left a long, evenly burning cigar. For a moment the Kommissar did not recognise him; he looked so different from the ragged prisoner of the Pecher-Lavra Prison.

'So we meet once more, and for the last time, Kommissar Leshkin,' the Duke said softly.

Leshkin backed quickly towards the bedside.

'Stay where you are,' De Richleau spoke, sharply now; 'put your hands above your head.'

For a moment it seemed as if the Kommissar was going to charge him; his great head was lowered and his bull neck swelled above the collar of his shirt – but he thought better of it and slowly raised his hands above his head.

De Richleau nodded. 'That is better,' he said, evenly. 'Now we will talk a little; but first I will relieve you of the temptation to secure the weapon by your bed.'

He put his cigar in the ashtray on the table and moved swiftly to the bedside, keeping his eyes fixed on the Kommissar's face.

Having secured Leshkin's weapon, he slipped his own pistol in his pocket and again picked up his cigar.

'I understand,' he addressed Leshkin evenly, 'that your presence in Vienna is due to an application for the extradition of myself and my friends?'

Leshkin's uneven teeth showed in an ugly grin. 'That is so, Mr Richwater, and if you think to steal my papers, it will do you little good. Duplicates can be forwarded from Moscow, and I shall follow you to England, if necessary.'

'I fear you misunderstand the purpose of my visit. I do not come to steal anything. I come to place it beyond your power to enforce the extradition once and for all.'

'You mean to murder me?' Leshkin gave him a quick look. 'If you shoot you will rouse the hotel. The police here know already the purpose for which I have come – you will be arrested immediately.'

De Richleau smiled. 'Yes, I have already thought of that.' He moved softly to the big French windows and opened them wide. 'It is a lovely night, is it not?' he murmured. 'These rooms in summer must be quite charming, the view is superb.'

Leshkin shivered slightly as the March air penetrated the warm room. 'What do you mean to do?' he asked.

'You are not interested in the sleeping city?' De Richleau moved away from the window. 'But of course one would not expect that from you, who seek to destroy all the beauty of life – you have your eyes so much on the gutters that you have forgotten the existence of the stars.'

'What do you mean to do?' repeated Leshkin thickly. There was something terrifying about this quiet, sinister man with his slow measured movements.

'I will tell you.' De Richleau put down his cigar again and picked up a toothglass from the washstand. He took the small bottle from his pocket, uncorked it carefully, and poured the contents into the glass.

'Ha! You mean to poison me,' Leshkin exclaimed. 'I will not drink – I refuse.'

The Duke shook his head. 'You wrong me, my dear Leshkin – that is not my idea. It seems that in this question of extradition it is necessary to prove identity. You are the only person who can identify Mr Simon Aron, Mr Rex Van Ryn, and myself as the men concerned in the shooting that night at Romanovsk.' He carefully picked up the tumbler in his left hand. 'If you were to become blind, Leshkin, you could not identify us, could you?'

'What are you going to do?' Fear had come into the Kommissar's eyes.

De Richleau held up the glass once more. 'This,' he said, softly, 'is vitriol. I purpose to throw it in your face. You will be blinded beyond any hope of recovery. After that you may go back to Russia if you will.'

'No – no – ' Leshkin cringed away, an awful horror dawned on his coarse features.

The Duke stepped round the little table, fixing the Kommissar with his brilliant eyes. Leshkin backed again quickly towards the window; he held his hands in terror before his face. 'No, no, I will go back – I will destroy the extradition – '

'I fear it is too late.' De Richleau took another step forward; Leshkin made a sudden movement, as if to rush him, but as the glass was raised he gave back quickly. Now he was standing between the open windows.

'Are you ready?'

A grim smile played round the corners of the Duke's firm mouth.

'Shoot me,' said Leshkin. 'Shoot me!'

De Richleau waved the Kommissar's automatic gently up and down. 'You would prefer to die?' he asked evenly.

'No . . . no . . . I am not ready to die . . . give me time.'

'So – ' the Duke mocked him. 'You still think that God will help you when man will not? I am surprised that a man like you should believe in these effete superstitions. What is death, after all, but a cessation of activity?'

Leshkin was out on the balcony now, his hands behind him on the low stone coping, sweat was pouring down his brutal face.

'I prefer that you should be blinded. To shoot you might inconvenience myself.' With a sudden gesture the Duke raised the tumbler.

Leshkin shuddered and gave back once more. He shrieked as the contents of the glass hit him full between the eyes. For a second he swayed, wildly endeavouring to regain his balance, clutching with desperate fingers at the empty air – then, with a little moan, he disappeared into the depths below.

De Richleau smiled as he carelessly slipped the little bottle into his pocket, he replaced the Kommissar's pistol beside the bed – the innocent borrowed weapon, for which he had no bullets, went into his pocket too. He laughed softly at his own handsome reflection in the mirror as he straightened his white tie. Then, picking up his cigar, he left the room as quietly as he had come.

As Leshkin hurtled towards the pavement a hundred feet below he was conscious only of one swift thought – his enemy had tricked him – it was nothing but cold water trickling down behind his ears.